GLASSMAN

Steve Oskie
Published by Open Books

Published by Open Books

Copyright © 2023 by Steve Oskie

Interior Design by Siva Ram Maganti

Cover image © by rangizzz shutterstock.com/g/rangizzz

"Up On Cripple Creek"
Written by Robbie Robertson
Published by Canaan Music, Inc. (ASCAP)
Licensed Courtesy of Iconoclast

For Rosemary:

Her love led me out of the darkness, her patience made everything possible, and her beauty amazes me still.

THE TROUBLE STARTED WHEN I was nineteen, after I made the willful decision to give my mother a hard time.

"Mom," I said, "does Harry really expect me to work as a busboy?"

"Why wouldn't he? He already talked to Mitch."

Mitch Frankel owned the coffee shop in the lobby of 2601, our apartment building on the Benjamin Franklin Parkway. He owed Harry a favor, but he had no idea how big a favor it would be if he actually offered me a job. I was a slacker before the word was invented.

"What right did he have to talk to Mitch? I never agreed to that!"

My poor mother. She was a hapless, handwringing go-between in my interactions with my stepfather, which meant that she had to do the talking whenever Harry refused to take up a topic with me directly. As a result, there was a worn path in the shag carpet between their bedroom and mine, where I typically blasted "Monkey Man" by the Rolling Stones or some other sonic assault on middle-aged ears.

"You're nineteen years old," she said. "You'll have to work eventually."

"You know what? Maybe I'll join the army and get shot up in Vietnam. Is that what he would prefer?"

"Where did *that* come from?"

"I'm serious. If they ship me home in a flag-draped casket, Harry would have some explaining to do."

My mother paused for a moment, staring at my blood-shot eyes. "Were you up on the roof again?"

This was her euphemism for smoking pot. A day after we moved in to 2601, I discovered a fire exit that led to an unlocked door on the roof, where I could fire up a joint, look out over the city, and dream my dreams of a permanent vacation.

"I mighta been—why?"

"Because you say things that you wouldn't dream of saying if you hadn't been up there."

"It must be the altitude. It goes right to my head."

"All right. We'll finish this discussion another time. I've gotta get my brisket in the oven."

Obviously, she was just as relieved as I was that we had an excuse to change the subject.

"Are you making farfel?" I asked.

"Yes, I'm making farfel!"

"Do we have apple sauce?"

"Yes, we have apple sauce!"

Her nostrils tended to flare when she was dealing with the teenage version of me—especially when I was getting to her. Whenever her nostrils did that, it was a beautiful thing to behold.

"Musselman's or that cheap kind you buy in the commissary?"

"Oh, for God's sakes! Musselman's!"

"I'm just asking. I like to drag the brisket through the apple-sauce every few bites."

"I'm well aware of that. I made you a spice cake also."

"I appreciate it, but the spice cake has no bearing on whether or not I get a job."

"You won't work in the coffee shop? Is that final?"

"Probably not."

Her frightened expression was priceless—especially for a pervert like me.

"What should I tell Harry?"

"Tell him I have an idea."

Now that we were on the verge of a breakthrough, my mother restrained herself, not wanting to jinx her possible good fortune.

"Really?" she followed, deliberately removing any trace of optimism. "You'll get a job?"

"I know you want me to become a doctor, a lawyer, or an

accountant, but this is the wrong way to go about it."

"I thought you had an idea."

"I do. Now please, get that brisket in the oven. I want to finish eating by seven. The Phillies are playing the Pirates."

———————

Despite the fact that the Phillies were a poor excuse for a baseball team, I followed them religiously. So when I encountered an employment ad to sell Cokes at Veterans Stadium, I actually considered working. Unfortunately, my hopes were dashed when I went to the stadium to apply. When a representative of the Nilon Brothers conveyed the specifications of the job, I learned that the vendors were required to purchase the trays of soda before they began to sell them, a policy that made it impossible to realize a profit until later in the game. And so the original brilliance of my idea was foiled and I found that I couldn't work for an inning or two in order to get my mother off my back and then settle down in the farthest reaches of the upper deck to enjoy the rest of the game.

By doing the math on the C bus, I realized that I would have to carry the heavy trays up and down the concrete steps of the stadium for at least seven innings before the job became worthwhile, and because the task fell into the general category of physical labor, I rejected it as firmly as I had rejected the idea of working at the coffee shop. And so the only benefit I derived from the misadventure was the I.D. photo they had taken when I completed the application, a likeness in which my outrageous "Isro" haircut was revealed in all of its offensive glory.

It would have made complete sense if the Nilon Brothers were a mob-connected vending company that had strong-armed some poor schmuck of a purchasing agent into granting them the concessions at the stadium, but they had actually worked their way up the hard way with no mob connections at all, selling hot coffee on freezing cold days at construction sites in order to establish themselves. Eventually, their breakthrough occurred when they scored a contract to serve food at an Army-Navy game through a military connection of the owner. Because they did a good job that day—and the game was attended by 120,000 fans at JFK Stadium—word got around, additional doors opened for them, and they went on to earn the first of their many millions. Whatever their origins, I held onto the I.D. card for years, despite the fact that I never worked for the Nilon Brothers, not even for a day. At the time, however, that was me: "Mark Glassman, Vendor #227654."

When I got back to the apartment, my mother was wiping off the electric mixer with a damp paper towel. The spice cake had given it a vigorous workout, and a wooden spoon was still present in the mixing bowl. "Do you want to lick the spoon?" she asked.

"Does a bear shit in the woods?"

"Mark, please!"

She handed me the spoon, and I proceeded to lick it clean.

"You'll be glad to know that I made a good faith effort to get a job today."

"You're kidding? That's great!"

"How do you know? You haven't asked me what kind of job it was."

"It doesn't matter!"

"OK. What if I told you I'm going to be the personal assistant of a child pornographer?"

"Then you're right. It would matter."

"Hey, I'm just making a point. Actually, I went to the ballpark to see if they needed any vendors."

"Did they?"

"Yeah, but I turned it down. I would miss too much of the game."

Her nostrils flared again. "So what if you miss the game!"

"The Phillies have pulled to within thirteen games of first place. They actually have a chance."

"Thirteen games? Isn't that a lot?"

"Not if they sweep the next seven doubleheaders between the two teams."

"Has that ever happened?"

"No, but there's a first time for everything."

"Except for you getting a job."

"Good one, Mom. I'm proud of yuh."

"Are you finished with that spoon?"

"Yeah, you can put it away. It's clean as far as I'm concerned."

"No, I think I'll put it in the dishwasher."

Still not willing to give in to the pudgy little matriarch of our exceedingly dysfunctional family, I answered a second ad that called for office clerks at the Keystone Insurance Company. The job sounded dreadful, but it had the virtue of being situated at 20th and Market, which meant that I could take the elevator to the lobby, hop on the "house bus," and get off in front of their office building without breaking a sweat. They needed warm bodies, and as long as you swore an oath to the soul-killing tedium of folding hundreds of letters a day, inserting them into their pre-addressed envelopes, and sealing the envelopes with a sponge and a bowl of water, the job was yours. After that, you placed the envelopes into a wire basket that was wheeled around the office on a cart by a developmentally disabled forty-year-old named Charlie Marto-rano—the only person lower on the totem pole than I was. But at least Charlie got to stretch his legs once in a while and gawk at the women in the secretarial pool.

As it turned out, the sponge worked just fine once I determined that the company frowned upon the kind of glue that could be sniffed effectively, but it carried with it the unforeseen challenge of having to fight the urge to urinate after dipping the sponge in the water eight or ten times an hour. Was that the reason that I only worked there for a week or was the frequent urination merely a coincidence? I can't really say, but I quit the job after earning a single paycheck shortly after a letter arrived from Florida, my brother Carl concluding the missive with the following observation: "Stuffing envelopes? Not bad, dummy. Prep school education. College. And stuffing envelopes. Hoo boy, that is rich. Another maladjusted Glassman bellyflops into the world."

———

Stanback was a headache product that my mother used on a regular basis. Elaine Kessler had recommended it to her the year before. Elaine was a similarly afflicted parent with a teenager of her own.

"Are you going to the drug store?" my mother asked. "I can use some more Stanback."

"How many boxes? One or two?"

"Just one. Here's some money."

She reached into her pocketbook and removed a twenty-dollar-bill, but when I went to take it from her she held onto it. "Bring me the change."

I tugged a little harder until she released the money. "Would it be so terrible if you bought me a copy of the *Sporting News?* It's only two dollars."

"Your father gives you an allowance. Why don't you buy it with that?"

Coincidentally, my allowance was twenty dollars also—the going rate for an ounce of pot. My father mailed me a check once a week from Harrisburg, Pennsylvania.

"Because—I use that money for something else."

"That's not my problem. Take it up with him."

"You think I should ask for a job when I'm at the drug store? Maybe they're looking for a pharmacist."

"Very funny. You know perfectly well that you need a college degree to become a pharmacist."

"I'm already into drugs. Wouldn't that count as commensurate experience?"

"Just get me the Stanback, OK?"

There was a little pharmacy in the lobby of our building, squeezed between the coffee shop and a beauty parlor. Once you stepped off the elevator on the ground floor, you made a right turn, walked up a set of steps, and there it was. At the end of the hall, there was a barber shop, which I had managed to avoid for the better part of a year.

When I entered the pharmacy, Mitch Frankel was buying a pack of cigarettes. I froze in my tracks and strongly considered walking out the door.

"It's too late," Mitch said. "I saw you. You're Miriam's kid, aren't you?"

"Who? Me?"

"No, the fat guy standing next to you."

"That's a good line. Do you mind if I steal it?"

"Be my guest. You've been avoiding me for weeks. I forgot what you looked like."

I walked over to the aspirin aisle, grabbed a box of Stanback, and joined him at the cash register. A sign taped to the counter said "Delivery Boy Wanted." Could I use this as leverage in negotiating my salary with Mitch if God forbid I accepted the position?

"Listen," he said, "I gotta get back to the coffee shop. I can't dick around with you. Do you want the job or don't yuh?"

"Not really, no."

"Let me level with you. Harry had a heart attack when he was thirty-eight years old. He's grossly overweight. Stress is not his friend. And your poor mother is addicted to that shit you're holding in your hand." I looked down at the box of Stanback while Mitch moved in for the kill. "She also hits the bottle every afternoon. Why don't you give 'em a break and take the fucking job? It's one day a week on Saturday mornings."

"Do you actually believe it would increase Harry's life expectancy?"

Mitch shook his head. "I'll tell you what. If you were my kid, I'd give you such a zetz you'd be on your back for a month."

"I'm sorry. I couldn't resist."

"It wasn't funny, Mark. I'm leaving."

"Saturday's your busiest day. It's packed in there! Maybe I should start off a little slower."

"I don't need you on the slow days, genius."

Mitch started for the door, tearing the cellophane off his pack of Marlboro's.

"Hold on," I said. "I want to ask you something. How do you know so much about my mom and Harry?"

"Do you see that beauty parlor over there? Goldie compares notes with your mother every Friday morning. They have a standing appointment to sit next to each other at the blow dryers."

"I'd like to be a fly in the wall for that."

"There's no mystery to it. They complain about their husbands."

Goldie worked the cash register at the coffee shop, so I'd be seeing a lot of her also. She was a nice Jewish lady who reminded me of my Aunt Shirley. They both had towering hairstyles and played mah-jongg on Tuesday nights.

I glanced at the sign for a delivery boy. "How much would you pay me if I accept the job? I may have another offer."

"Sure you do. I pay $5.25 an hour and all the cheeseburgers you can eat."

"What about tips?"

"You share the tips with Lawrence. He's my dishwasher."

I knew Lawrence. He was a tall, skinny kid who walked around with an Afro-pick in his hair. He attended Simon Gratz High School and once got his name in the paper for catching a seventy-two-yard touchdown pass against Bok Technical Institute. I had seen him loitering near the kitchen door one day and asked if he got high.

"Don't worry about the Saturdays," Mitch said. "We get a rush from 11 to 1 and then we coast until it's time to go home."

"No breakfast crowd? I thought I saw one."

Mitch made a face. "Hardly any. Bagels and cream cheese. That's about it."

I had a sinking feeling that I had already accepted the job, but there was nothing I could do about it.

"If you say so," I said.

"Don't look so excited. Show up at 7. You'll be fine."

"Seven? On a Saturday morning? You gotta be kidding!"

"When I said morning, what did you think I meant? Three in the afternoon?"

I was blushing now. "It's a little early, that's all."

"What—you gotta watch cartoons?"

"You might not realize it, but you just had a lapse in your sur-veillance of my family. I watch 'The Three Stooges' on Saturday mornings, not cartoons."

"Same difference. How old are you now?"

"I'm nineteen, but you're wrong about the stooges. A law firm called Dewey, Cheatum, and Howe? That's classic comedy in my book."

"You wouldn't know a classic if it bit you on the ass."

"You may be right, but if something bites me on the ass, I doubt it'll be a classic."

Just then, Goldie walked up to the door of the pharmacy and gestured at Mitch wildly, tapping her wristwatch for emphasis. Her voice was muffled through the glass, but we were able to hear her. "Yo, Mitch, what the fuck?"

"I'm conducting an interview," Mitch said. "I'll be back in a minute."

Goldie squinted through the glass to see who Mitch was talking to. "Is that you, Mark? Tell your mother I said hello." Before I could answer, she made her way back to the coffee shop.

"So I'll see you on Saturday morning?" Mitch asked.

"I don't know. Can I start next week instead?"

"There is no fuckin' way—none. You start this Saturday or I give the job to somebody else."

"OK, I'll work this Saturday and see if I like it."

"Let's set our sights a little lower. I'll settle for you tolerating it."

"Your point is well taken. I have one more question."

"I can't wait. What is it?"

"Who's that hot blond that works for you on Saturdays?"

Mitch glared at me. "That's my niece. Don't even think about it."

"I'm a teenage boy. I can't promise that I won't think about it."

"What's the protocol here?"

"What do you mean?"

"Is it kosher for me to fire you before you start the job?"

9

———————

My mother had conventional views on the subject of employment, while I preferred the more radical approach of avoiding employment entirely. And yet, I didn't hate the job. Lawrence and I got along well; Mitch's niece wore low-cut tops; and Goldie kept things interesting by cursing like a longshoreman whenever the pressure got to her. In fact, the differences between Goldie and my Aunt Shirley were becoming more pronounced by the minute. No matter what I did, I couldn't picture my aunt uttering a profanity, but Goldie swore enough for both of them.

More importantly, now that I was working, some of the tension went out of my relationship with my mother—though not all, of course. She was still the person who had caused my parents' divorce in my warped, grossly oversimplified view of things; and though it had been years since my mother had initiated an affair with Harry when she and my dad were still married—and I had shifted all of my sympathy to my sweet, unsuspecting father—a few pleasant weeks lusting after Mitch's niece weren't going to change that.

Needless to say, my mother noticed the difference in my behavior early on.

"Why are you being so nice to me?"

"What are you talking about?"

"Never mind—I shouldn't have said anything."

———————

On my first day on the job, I told Lawrence to meet me in the supply room at the end of our shift. Once he arrived, I started down the hall toward the freight elevator.

"Where we goin'?" Lawrence asked.

"To the roof. Where do yuh think?"

Lawrence stopped in his tracks. "Man, I ain't goin' to the roof."

"How come?"

"I'm afraid o' heights."

I cracked up laughing.

"What's so funny?"

"A big strong guy like you? I thought *I* was neurotic."

"You prob'ly *are* if I catch your drift."

"OK, we won't go to the roof. Did you bring the pot?"

Lawrence glared at me. "I thought *you* brung it."

"I'm just fucking with you. My brother sent me some in the mail."

For a period of several weeks, Carl worked at a candle factory in Florida. It was a shitty job, but he learned a valuable lesson about smuggling. By hollowing out the bottom of a candle, inserting his drug of choice, and replacing most but not all of the wax so that the secret compartment was invisible, he was able to evade the authorities. This was during his younger days, of course, before he met my sister-in-law.

"For real?" Lawrence asked.

"Yeah. He put a chunk of hash in there, too, but I don't have a pipe."

"Man, why didn't you say so? I got a pipe right here."

Lawrence removed a hash pipe from his pants pocket.

"You carry that thing around with you?"

"Yeah, you never know."

"I was wondering what that bulge in your pants was, but for obvious reasons I didn't want to ask."

"What do you think of Marcy?" he followed.

He said it as though it was the most natural follow-up question in the world, and maybe it was.

"Mitch's niece? I lust after her every minute of the day."

"You gonna do somethin' about it?"

"What planet do you live on? She'd laugh in my face."

"Suit yourself. Me personally? I don't have that concern."

On the following Saturday, I went looking for Lawrence in the supply room, but he wasn't there. When I found him ten minutes later, standing on a street corner, he and Marcy Braverman were dry-humping with Marcy's tongue in Lawrence's mouth. Mitch would not have been pleased. I immediately came to a halt, turned around as discreetly as I could, and smoked the joint myself.

When I returned to the coffee shop, Marcy was counting her tips, Lawrence was mopping the kitchen floor, and Mitch was bickering with Goldie. Later, before he hopped on the 48 bus to return to his "crib" in North Philadelphia—this was Lawrence's word for the house he shared with his grandmother—he took me aside and said, "You best not say nothin' 'bout me and Marcy. I'd hafta hurt you."

I smiled at him. "I don't know what you're talking about."

"Good. Keep it that way."

"If you guys get married, can I at least be the best man?"

"Man, don't be talkin' foolishness. Ain't nobody gettin' married."

"Why not? You should be so lucky. Marcy's drop dead gorgeous."

"I told yuh—I ain't marryin' her. The girl's way too bossy. It muss run in the family."

"That reminds me of a Joe Tex song."

"Oh yeah, how's that?"

"It was called 'If You Wanna Be Happy,' and it made a strong case for avoiding girls like Marcy Braverman."

"That wasn't Joe Tex—that was somebody else. Jimmy Soul or some shit like that. Joe Tex did 'Skinny Legs.'"

"You knew that? I'm impressed."

"You think you the only clever person around here? That's jus' your ego talkin'. But I'll let it go for now."

One Saturday morning, a little old lady stopped chewing on her bagel and made a face as though she had swallowed a worm. Goldie immediately abandoned the cash register—which would normally have been unthinkable for her—and hurried over to the woman.

"Is something wrong?"

"That's him!" she cried, pointing at me from across the room. I was standing at the soda dispenser with Lawrence.

"Who?" Goldie asked. "Our dishwasher?"

"No—the other one!"

"Uh, oh," I said.

Lawrence looked at me. "What's the problem?"

"We have a situation. She saw me drunk the other night. I was passed out near the elevator."

The old lady had a single gray hair protruding from her chin. She could have easily snipped it, so if this was any indication of her eyesight, there was a chance I could discredit her testimony. At the same time, though, she had the truth on her side. After Dan Hiller's college professor parents left for an economics conference in Rhode Island, Dan had an impromptu party that ended with me totally bombed in their basement on St. Mark's Square, drinking from a bottle of vodka while balanced precariously on the spindle of their washing machine.

Jeff Cohen had dropped me off in front of the building, but he had miscalculated my ability to traverse the lobby, locate the elevator, and identify the button for the tenth floor. This miscalculation enabled me to miss a step or two in the process, so that I found the elevator but pressed the button for the ground floor instead. At that point the door of the elevator opened and deposited me onto the very spot that I had staggered past a moment before, causing me to take my usual right turn and find not the long hallway that led to apartment 1012 but to the set of steps that led to the drug store. Thoroughly confused by my surroundings, I had apparently lain down on the steps and gone to sleep, only to have my snoring cause the little old lady to investigate.

But the incident wasn't over until the woman shook me awake and alerted Teddy the doorman to the fact that there was an inebriated teenager passed out in her lobby. Teddy meant well, but he made the same mistake that Jeff Cohen had in assuming that I could complete the journey myself. After escorting me to the apartment and letting me in with a master key, he assumed incorrectly that I could find my way to my bedroom, and instead of sleeping in my bed I fell asleep on the shag carpet just inside the front door, which is exactly where my mother and Harry found me the next morning when they returned with their suntans from

San Juan, where the accounting firm of Rosenthal and Glickstein had sent Harry to conduct an internal audit.

Now the old lady blew the whistle on me for the second time in a week, and urged Goldie to call me over to her table.

"Man, she's trippin'!" Lawrence said. "You got this?"

"Yeah, I'll cop to it and see what happens."

"Well, they ain't gonna fire you. You a good busboy."

"Really? Thanks for the compliment."

"Mark," Goldie said, "our customer has something to say. Be nice."

"I will."

"Can I trust you? I've gotta get back to the register."

"Yeah, you can trust me."

Goldie looked at me long and hard, her maternal instincts warring with her grim experience of the world. Ultimately, she decided to cast her fate to the wind and return to the cash register as planned.

"Young man?" the old lady began. "Do you remember me?"

"I'm not sure. Are you a friend of my grandmother?"

"I don't know your grandmother. I'm the person who found you in a deplorable condition in our lobby."

"I know—I was bombed."

"Do your parents know that you drink like that?"

Before answering, I glanced over at Goldie. Four or five customers were waiting for her to ring them up, and she was no longer paying attention to me. I had an opening a mile wide, but I decided to hold my tongue.

"No, ma'am, they don't. It'll never happen again."

"I certainly hope not."

Later that day, the barber from up the hall walked into the coffee shop.

"How many?" Goldie asked, handing him a menu. "One?"

"None—I'm not eating."

"OK, enlighten me. What do you want?"

"Is your busboy around?"

"He better be. He's still on the clock."

Goldie entered the kitchen and found me eating a French fry. "Was that yours or a customer's?"

"It was a customer's. He said he was through with 'em."

"You actually asked him for the rest of his French fries?"

"Of course not! How long have you known me, Goldie?"

"Never mind. You have a visitor. Make it quick."

The barber's name was Nick Romano. I had never actually spoken with him.

"I meant to ask yuh'," he said. "You go to college, right?"

"Off and on. Why?"

"I gotta write a paper, and I can't write for shit."

"Where do you go to school?"

"St. Peter's in Jersey City. I'm takin' a night class."

"What's the paper about?"

"'Eleanor Rigby' by the Beatles. I'll give yuh a free haircut if you help me."

"That was the wrong thing to say, but I'll still help you."

"You will?"

"Sure—why not? What's the essay question?"

"I got it right here."

He pulled a mimeographed sheet from his pocket and read it to me. "What are the major themes of 'Eleanor Rigby' and how did Lennon and McCartney incorporate them into one of the greatest songs ever written, paying particular attention to their use of imagery?"

"First of all, tell your professor that's a run-on sentence. I'm fond of them myself, but he oughta know better."

Goldie caught my eye and tapped on her wristwatch like she did with Mitch.

"I'll tell yuh what. Lemme finish my shift. I'll meet you in the lobby at three."

Nick was waiting for me when I clocked out.

"When's your paper due?" I asked.

"Toos-dee."

"Whoa. That doesn't give us much time. How many words is it supposed to be?"

"Five hundred. Not counting the title."

"No, we won't count the title, I promise."

I ended up writing an excellent essay for Nick, but the professor disagreed.

"Nick, what's the matter?" I asked, when I saw him a few days later. He looked like he wanted to strangle me.

"I got a fuckin' 'C'. I needed at least a 'B' on that essay."

"How come?"

"I had a 'D' average goin' in."

"So what you're saying is, I improved your average but not enough."

"That's not the point. I thought for sure you'd get me an 'A.'"

"Hey, don't blame me for your poor study habits. What did the professor say?"

"I got it right here."

Nick reached into his pocket and pulled out our essay. I read the comments slowly. Thirty seconds in, my mouth dropped open in disbelief.

"This guy's nuts!" I said.

"That's what he said about you."

"One of the major themes is loneliness. That's indisputable!"

"I'm just tellin' you what he said."

"I can see what he said. I'm reading it!"

I looked down at the professor's comments and continued. "What the fuck? Does he even know the lyrics to that song?"

"Don't sing. Please."

"I'm not singing—I'm quoting the lyrics! They spell it out, for Christ's sakes!"

"Turn it over. Read what he said on the back."

I turned it over as instructed and read the rest of the comments. "Nick, your writing has improved since the beginning of the semester. But this is a Catholic university. The idea of Eleanor Rigby and Father McKenzie hooking up to ease their loneliness is beyond the pale. In good conscience, I couldn't possibly give you anything higher than a 'C'."

"Hooking up? I never said that! It was merely implied!"

"What does he mean 'beyond the pale'?"

"How should I know? It's not good, I'll tell yuh that."

"I shoulda asked my son to write the fuckin' thing, but he's only in the seventh grade."

"Yeah, maybe you should have. That's the last time I'll do *you* a favor."

"Oh, yeah? We finally agree on somethin'."

"Nick, I'm sorry. I thought it was a perfectly good essay."

"Maybe *you* shoulda gone back to school, heh? Instead o' takin' the semester off."

"You're probably right."

"If you do, I'll give you some free advice. Don't take no writing courses."

I handed the essay back to Nick. He tore it up, threw it in my face, and walked away.

Other than those brief hiccups, things went swimmingly at the coffee shop until Mitch started to slip in barely perceptible ways. On one memorable occasion, he plugged a space heater into the wall of a walk-in freezer; and on another he made an inappropriate remark to Marcy. But eventually his behavior became more flagrant, with Mitch openly insulting the customers, addressing Lawrence with a racial slur, and smacking Goldie across the face during a particularly violent quarrel. None of that was like him, and the mystery went unsolved until a neurosurgeon discovered a brain tumor in Mitch's frontal lobe that turned out to be inoperable. Goldie tried her best to run the coffee shop herself—and even brought in their daughter Debbie to help out, but Debbie enjoyed the concept of employment even less than I did. Before long, they came to the conclusion that the business was unsustainable without Mitch, and they were forced to sell it for less than market value.

After the sale, my mother and I had one more discussion about it. She had failed to acknowledge the fact that I had worked for Goldie until the bitter end, when the new owners closed the place to complete their renovations. Nor had she recognized the modest strides I had made with my work ethic.

"I think I was a pretty good sport about it. After all, I tore myself away from the air-conditioned comfort of our penthouse apartment to slave away in a sweatshop. I think that speaks volumes about my character."

"It's not a penthouse," she replied. "There's another floor above us. And the restaurant in the lobby hardly qualifies as a sweat shop."

"It doesn't? Ask Lawrence. He'll tell you."

———————

Every summer, my grandmother would visit us for a month at 2601. She and Harry were like oil and water, and I have no doubt that it was Harry's least favorite time of the year. But the real fireworks occurred between the two women. The only time I turned down the music in my bedroom was to listen to my mother and grandmother go at it. Afraid to fly since her deceased husband had instilled an irrational fear in her decades before, my grandmother would take the train up from Florida, and my mother and Harry would meet her at 30th Street Station.

Adoring one moment and hateful the next, my mother and grandmother played out the same scenes repeatedly, with slight variations on the theme, and those subtle distinctions provided the only reassurance that they weren't caught in a time warp that would have them clashing for all of eternity. Still, on a bad day, it seemed like hell on earth.

"Will you have a drink with me?" my grandmother asked.

"No, mother—go ahead."

"Why not?"

"Harry doesn't like it when I drink."

"Who is he to tell you what to do?"

"He's my husband! Besides, it's too early for me."

"I shouldn't drink in the afternoon?"

"I didn't say that."

"What's the difference if I have a little drink? Where am I going?"

"All right—I'll have a drink."

"Did I say anything?" my grandmother followed innocently.

"Of course not—you're an angel."

"You know what? You're fresh. I'm still your mother."

"I know you are. How could I forget?"

"I didn't ask to come here—you invited me."

"I want you here!"

"But Harry doesn't. To tell you the truth, I'd be happier at home. I'm all alone there. If I want a drink, who's gonna stop me?"

"I'm not stopping you. I don't want to join you, that's all."

"You said you'd have one!"

"Would it be so terrible if I had a Fresca?"

"What about *my* drinking? What does Harry say about that?"

"You said it yourself—it's harmless."

"But what does he say?"

"He doesn't say anything."

"Don't lie to me, Mir'. I drink more than you do."

"No, you don't!"

"Why doesn't he leave you alone?"

"I don't know. Why don't you ask him?"

Clearly, this startled my grandmother. "I would *never* interfere."

"Let's have our drink."

"Maybe I should wait. What time is it?"

"It's twenty after three."

"I'll have it after my story. Do you mind if I watch the television?"

My grandmother watched *The Edge of Night* every afternoon at three-thirty.

"Do you have to ask? You know you can!"

"I'm afraid to open my mouth around here."

"Obviously, you're not."

When I was leaving for work one day, my mother and grandmother were sitting in the living room together. My grandmother had a romance novel on her knee. It had a lurid photograph on the cover depicting an illicit couple caught in a steamy embrace. At least that's what the cover was trying to convey. There was a glass of Old Grand-Dad on the coffee table in front of my grandmother with a single ice cube melting in the light brown liquid. My mother was attempting to read *Better Homes and Gardens*, but my grandmother was interrupting her every five minutes. The younger of the two women was drinking a Fresca.

"Did I tell you?" my grandmother asked. "Ruth's going on a trip with her daughter."

"No, you didn't."

"Freda's taking her on a cruise. I guess you and I will never do that."

That was just what my mother needed—to be confined to a cabin with my grandmother with no way to escape for days at a time.

"That would be difficult for me. Where are they going?"

"I get the names mixed up."

"Bermuda?"

"I don't think so."

"The Bahamas?"

"No—somewhere else."

"I don't know then."

"Bermuda, I think."

"I said Bermuda!"

"No, you didn't. You said the Bahamas."

"First I said Bermuda!"

"I didn't hear you."

"Yes, you did. You answered me!"

"What's the difference? You'll never take me on a cruise. You can't stand to be with me."

"Don't say that!"

"It's true!"

"Please, Mother. We can't get along for five minutes. How would we do on a cruise?"

"We'd be on our best behavior, and you wouldn't talk fresh to me."

"I can't leave Harry for two weeks. You know that. He isn't well."

"And I am? I have emphysema and shortness of breath!"

"If you'd quit smoking you wouldn't have shortness of breath."

"You should talk. I've seen those cigarettes in your pocketbook."

"What are you doing in my pocketbook? Never mind—I don't wanna know."

For my part, I adored my grandmother—and not only because she bought me coconut custard pies at Hanscom's bakery; or because she covered her mouth whenever I saw her dentures in a little plastic container on her bedside table; or because she rooted for George McGovern with me to win the 1972 presidential election while referring to Richard Nixon as "a louse." No. She and my brother were the only members of my family that I loved without bitterness or resentment.

After I had visited my father and stepmother many times, I knew exactly what my brother meant when he referred to them as "self-abusers." Initially, as a junior in high school, I had taken the Greyhound bus from 17th and Market in Philadelphia to the dingy little bus station in Harrisburg, where my father would pace the sidewalk, smoke a cigarette, and crush it out on the cement when I disembarked. Later, when I was old enough to drive, I sometimes arrived at their apartment before my father did, when my stepmother was there alone. Either way, I bore witness to their singular lifestyle.

Pat's shift at the Hershey Medical Center ended at three, and by the time she got behind the wheel of her Volkswagen Beetle, drove a quarter of a mile to the Briarcrest Gardens Apartments, and entered their unit at 205 Hallmark North, her afternoon routine would be under way. Without taking off her coat, she would turn on the television, pour herself a scotch, and walk over to the birdcage, where her fourth consecutive parakeet would await her arrival. An otherwise formidable woman, my childless stepmother would communicate with the bird in a grossly exaggerated way, descending into idiocy without an ounce of self-consciousness.

"How yew doing, Scott? Yeh! Mama fix your water."

While removing the plastic water dish from the side of the cage, Pat continued the conversation with Scott, who I was almost inclined to think of as a half-brother.

"You like Mike Douglas—no? Mama turn it up for you."

On her way back from the kitchen with a refill of the water dish, she took a brief detour to the television to turn up the volume as promised.

"You like it when he sings," she continued, while I watched from the sofa bed that I slept on whenever I stayed over. "He's not singing now—he's talking to Charo."

Sure enough, Xavier Cougat's talentless wife was making her 57th appearance on the *Mike Douglas Show* when the bird began to respond. Emitting a tentative little chirp at first and then a full-fledged squawk, he conveyed the fact that Pat had his full intention, which encouraged her even more.

"How yew doing? Yeh! Do go-go's! Give mama kiss!"

The parakeet fell silent now, while Pat pressed her lips to the cage.

"No kisses?" she asked, while the parakeet cocked his head and looked at her. Only then did she remove her coat and toss it onto a nearby chair, revealing her X-ray technician uniform.

I can't say I blamed the parakeet at that point, as Pat had issued contradictory commands. "Go Go's" were one thing, but kisses were another, and the bird exhibited the wisdom to let a few seconds pass and allow Pat to make up her mind. "Go-go's"—to the uninitiated—signified my stepmother nodding her head up and down in quick succession and the parakeet following suit. The bird might have thought that Pat was nuts, but if he did, he kept the observation to himself and refrained from biting the hand that fed him—or perhaps I should say the mouth that fed him because every breakfast with my father and step-mother included at least one instance of the bird sitting on Pat's shoulder, Pat extending her tongue, and offering a speck or two of scrambled egg, at which point she would swallow whichever specks the bird had left behind after pecking at them for a few seconds.

Foregoing kisses for the moment, she began to nod her head up and down, her motions growing frantic until the bird obliged, dipping his own head up and down, squawking wildly, and gripping the perch more firmly with his tiny little claws, the parakeet version of talons.

While she was in the kitchen filling up the water dish—and before swinging by the television to turn up the volume—she had slipped a few saltine crackers into the pocket of her starched white uniform. Now she chewed on one and moved the dough to the tip of her tongue, offering it through the bars of the cage. But before the bird could say "yea" or "nay" with his response, the telephone rang a few feet away.

The voice on the other end of the line was garbled from where I sat, but I could hear Pat clearly. When the caller identified herself, Pat greeted her without enthusiasm.

"We're fine," she said. "How are *you*?" But then she glanced at the birdcage. "He's fine. He's in his cage."

I had to hand it to whoever was on the other end of the line. Asking about the bird made all the difference in the world.

"Ril nice," Pat enthused. "How was yours? Saturdee night we went to a bar-bee-cue at Gator's. Mm-mm-mm—Gator was waffled!"

Pat had dark circles under her eyes, and now she raised a hand to the side of her head and scratched one of them with her pinkie while the bird commenced "Go-go's" without her.

"I got the *shmika* toy," she continued, employing another one of the words she had invented, which often had a Jewish flavor to them, after she had converted to Judaism so that she and my father could be married by a rabbi in 1966. "Thank you very much. Howard said you got it at Doctor's Pet Center. Rilly? Thank you very much, love-child-bird." Suddenly, she took on a darker tone. "Not any more," she concluded, apparently referring to the toy and whether or not it was still in use. "Howard stepped on it after the bar-bee-cue."

Just then, my dad walked through the front door of the apartment. He was carrying a memorial candle, a deli tray, and a stuffed animal, which Pat and I immediately recognized as a replica of the Phillie Phanatic, the mascot of the Phillies baseball team. Children, teenagers, and adults couldn't get enough of the Phanatic on television and in person at the games, but I had been holding a grudge ever since 1978 when he blocked my view of a Mike Schmidt home run in order to overturn a box of popcorn onto the head of the fan in front of me.

"It's Carol," Pat said, addressing my father and gesturing toward the phone.

"Lemme talk to her."

"Will you *wait?*"

"I'm gonna get loose," he replied, carrying the items into the hall.

"Howard just came in. He's going mental, as usual. Can I call you back? Thank you very much."

"Who's Carol?" I asked, after Pat hung up the phone.

"The Colonel's sister. She's a doll."

A few minutes later, my father returned in a pair of "shortie" pajamas. Pat turned to greet him. "Hi, Cakes." This was short for "babycakes," one of his many pet names. My father bent to kiss her, employing a similar pecking motion to Scott's with the scrambled eggs. Pat responded by pinching his thigh. "Those legs, Cakey!"

"How are you, little one?"

Before she could answer, he started away.

"C'mere!" she cried, in a tone that was truly aggrieved.

"What?"

"I want kisses!"

"You just had one."

"I want another!"

My father trudged over to her, enabling Pat to wrap her arms around his neck and kiss him elaborately. "Awright, awright!" he said. He straightened up, but Pat didn't release him. She caught my eye and laughed, her shoulders heaving up and down. My father started away.

"I want keeses!" she repeated, pronouncing it differently this time.

"You had enough already. Look what Billy gave us."

He retrieved the deli tray from the kitchen.

"Billy Nettles?"

"Yeah."

"Heh?"

"Yeah! How many Billy's do we know?"

"We know Billy Nettles and Billy DeAngelis. That's two right there."

"Whatever."

They sat down with me on the sofa while my father removed the Saran Wrap from the deli tray. Pat hovered over it like a bird of prey, removing a green pepper and biting into it, despite the fact that it would repeat on her in the middle of the night. "Mm-mm-mm!" she said, while my father rose from the sofa suddenly. He had been sitting for all of fifteen seconds. "No, Cakey, sit with me!"

"I'm gonna light the candle."

"You never sit with me," she said glumly.

"Oh, bullshit."

She turned to me. "Your father can't sit still. Didja ever notice that?"

"I notice it all the time."

My dad returned with the stuffed animal and handed it to Pat to keep her quiet. "Here," he said. "Hold this for a minute."

Off duty now, the parakeet fell asleep standing on one leg, while Pat rose from the sofa with the deli tray. "What am I gonna do?

I don't have room for it in my refrigerator."

"Don't worry. You'll think o' somethin'.'"

He repositioned himself to let her pass, brushing up against her in the process. Pat reacted to the near collision in her customary way, which she usually employed when they were in my father's car. "Watch your fenders, Cakey."

My father sat down on the sofa again. His weight caused the cushion to shift slightly and the Phillie Phanatic fell to the floor. Ignoring the Phanatic, he pulled out a folded copy of the *Daily Racing Form* from his pocket and continued to study it while Pat rearranged her refrigerator to accommodate the deli tray. The second she returned to the living room, she noticed the stuffed animal on the floor.

"You dropped him!" she cried, picking up the stuffed animal, carrying it to the birdcage, and waking up the parakeet from a sound sleep.

"See? It's the Phanatic! Yeh! C'mere, Cakey—show him the Phanatic!

"You're showing him.

"He wants you to play."

"How do *you* know?"

"Play with him, Cakes."

My father had a thing for parakeets, too, but it was nothing like hers. He trudged over to the birdcage. "Hey, zoo-woo. Yeh!" Hoping that this was sufficient, he returned to the sofa.

"Is that all?" Pat asked.

"That's it.

"He wants you!"

"Leave him alone—he's eating his seeds."

The parakeet was doing nothing of the sort. Instead, he was preening himself at the far end of his perch, as though he wanted to be left alone. But Pat was having none of it.

"You never play with him anymore. Daddy's tired, Scott. He'll play with you later. Yeh!"

My father glanced down at the *Racing Form* again, doing his best to change the subject. "I saw the Colonel today. He gave me a tip."

"Where'd yuh see him?" she asked suspiciously.

"At the Swamp."

"I thought you weren't gonna drink for a month."

"I'm not, but I haven't started yet."

"Wrong."

"I'm not!"

"Challenge."

"Do yuh want the tip or don't yuh?"

"Didja eat?"

"I ate with the Colonel."

"Whadja have?"

"I had a hamburger and French fries."

"Didja share the fries or didja have your own?"

"I had my own."

"What'd the Colonel have?"

"Nancy made him a Chef's Salad."

"Did she?"

"It looked super."

"Did it? Mm-mm-mm!"

My father lit *Yahrtzeit* candles for his parents every year, after purchasing them in the gift shop of Temple Beth El, where my brother and I had been bar mitzvahed three-and-a-half years apart. My own ceremony had been punctuated by the scene that Aunt Pearl made in Sisterhood Hall, when she went out of her way to snub my mother in retaliation for her harsh treatment of her brother. And now my father leaned forward and shifted one of the memorial candles onto a copy of the *TV Guide* that sat on the coffee table in front of him.

"Not on my *TV Guide!*" Pat exclaimed, flipping him a coaster. A step ahead of him as usual, she removed a book of matches from the pocket of her uniform while my father positioned the coaster. She waited for him to ask for matches, which he did a second later.

"Can you get me a match, love-child?"

My stepmother burst out laughing. She handed him the

matches. "Do I know you or do I know you? Zi-vay many gee."

Pronouncing the last word with a hard "g," she completed another one of the phrases that she had invented. It would be impossible to untangle it in its entirety, but "Zi-vay" had descended from "oy vey" and Manny was the name of her second parakeet, which had met its fate seven or eight years before.

My father lit the memorial candle, ignoring her last remark. "I have to go to the cemetery one of these days."

"Can I come with yuh?"

"If you behave."

"Yeah, yeah," she sneered. "Can we do my mother, too?"

"Uh huh."

"Who do yuh wanna do first?"

"We'll do Maggie first and get a bite to eat at Ponzio's."

"Rilly? D'yuh wanna get a bite to eat?"

"Yeah."

"Heh?"

"Yeah, I said!"

Turnabout was fair play, and now Pat ignored my father. "Can we stop at the Italian Market?"

"If we have time."

"We'll have time after we do Rosie. I'll get my cannoli. Mm-mm-mm!"

My paternal grandmother was an introspective Holocaust survivor named Rose. She was "Bubbie" to me and my brother—part of the "Bubby" and "Zaydie" tandem—but our stepmother referred to her as "Rosie," which had a cheerful ring to it.

"We'll stop at DiBruno's," my father replied.

"D'yuh want cheese, Cakey?"

"We may as well if we're right there."

"Mm-mm-mm! Lemme get my book."

Pat emptied her pocketbook onto the coffee table—a pack of Kents, a wad of Kleenex, and a bottle of Tums.

"Gimme a Tum," my father said.

"Will you *wait?*"

After a moment or two, she found her datebook, opened it, and handed my father a Tum, which he swallowed without the aid of a liquid. While Pat made the notation about DiBruno Brothers and the trip to the two cemeteries, my father noticed that her glass of scotch was empty.

"Want a 'nother'?" he asked.

I'm not sure which of them made this one up, but "nother" rhymed with "bother."

"Yeah—easy on the water."

My father disappeared into the kitchen and returned with two drinks.

"Are you havin' a beverage?" Pat asked, when it was perfectly obvious that he was.

"Yep."

"Wanna get waffled?"

"Wrong."

"C'mere," she replied suggestively.

"What are we doin' on Saturday?" he asked, evading the suggestion entirely.

Pat flipped through her datebook. "We're playin' poker."

"What about the week after?"

"We have a party to go to," she sneered.

If I didn't know better, I would have thought that she was belittling him for his failed attempt at scheduling.

"That's right. What about the week after that?"

"We're goin' to Liberace with the Kellers. I told yuh—August is shot!"

"I've gotta check my mother's grave!"

"So do I!"

"We'll go the first week in September."

The telephone rang. My father crossed the room to answer it.

"My man! What's happenin'?"

He took on a puzzled expression, shuffling through the magazines on the coffee table. In addition to the *TV Guide*, there were copies of *Gourmet*, the *Jewish Exponent*, and the *Sporting News*, a publication that he had introduced me to when I was twelve.

"What are yuh lookin' for?" Pat asked.

"The football pool."

Pat sneered again, producing the football pool from under my father's nose. My father took it from her and resumed the conversation with the caller.

"I didn't fill it out yet," he said.

"Who's Dee-troit playing?" Pat interjected.

My father held his hand over the phone. "Will you *wait?*"

"Be nice to me," she pouted, forcing my father to answer.

"They're playing Baldy-more."

"Who's favored?"

Unwilling to delay the telephone conversation any further, he ignored the question. "Nothing. I was talking to Pat. OK, mah man—I'll get back to yuh at halftime."

"You took the Raiders, I hope."

"I took the Broncos."

"The Raiders are undefeated!"

"I took the Broncos and seven points."

"Wrong."

"They're playing in Denver."

"Challenge. Can I get in on it?"

"Certainly you can get in on it. I'll call him back." He dialed the phone and waited for the bookie to answer. "Gator, what's happenin'? Pat likes the Raiders." He turned back to Pat. "Here, talk to him."

"I don't wanna talk to him!"

My father handed her the phone anyway. "I have to use the Little Boys' Room," he said, disappearing into the hall.

"Hello, love-child. I'll take the Raiders." She waited for Gator to respond, then narrowed her eyes. "Eight? Howard said seven. How could the line change?" She held her hand over the phone. "Howard, get in here!"

"I'm in the bathroom!" he said, his voice muffled by the door.

"The line changed!"

We heard the toilet flushing, and then my father returned. He took the phone from Pat. "What do you mean the line changed? Aren't *you* somethin'." He waited for Gator to explain himself, then glanced at his wife. "Don't listen to him—he's teasing."

Pat grabbed the phone. "You were teasing? Were you rilly? You're a scream!"

"I told yuh the line was seven," my father followed irritably.

"How much did Howard bet?"

My father frowned as soon as he heard the question. My step-mother turned back to him a second later. "You bet fifty bucks?"

"I like the Broncos," he said firmly.

"Put me down for fifty. That'll cancel his out."

"Oh, bullshit," my father replied, while Pat hung up the phone.

"If I win, I want it t'morrah."

"Awright, awright!"

"Thank you very much," she said coolly.

"Now can I go to the bathroom?"

"You already did!"

"I wasn't finished!"

Pat's jet-black hair towered above her head, and their second-to-last ritual of the day was to cover it with Kleenex. This was a two-person operation that required a teasing comb, a can of hairspray, and a roll of Scotch tape, with the two of them sitting next to each other on the sofa. Not known for his patience—or for sitting still for any length of time—my father taped the pieces of Kleenex together lovingly, over a period of several minutes, until my stepmother's hair was completely obscured. Why they did this was purely a matter of conjecture. I never asked them and they never volunteered the information. Did they do it to protect their pillowcases from Pat's hairspray, or was there a more obscure reason? And why did she use hairspray before she went to bed anyway? It was another minor mystery that never got solved.

Just before they turned in for the night, Pat would cover the birdcage, using one of the pillowcases that had outlived its original purpose, but not before she said a proper goodnight to the bird.

"Mama will cover you. You need to be covered. Yeh!"

"Awright, awright!" my father protested.

"I'm saying goodnight to my bird. Can't I say goodnight to my bird?"

"Hurry up."

"Thank you very much," she said coolly, before turning back to the birdcage in open defiance of my father's wishes. "Now you are covered. See? Tomorrow mama will clean your cage. No more seeds and feathers. Yeh!"

"And no more shit," my father said. "Let's go!"

On that particular visit, my father got the bad news that the Denver Broncos had lost by more than seven points. In fact, they had lost by more than thirty in what is commonly known as a "blowout." That meant that he was forced to listen to Pat's "I told you so's" as I made my exit.

Despite his misgivings about them, I often called my brother after visiting the folks. I'm not sure why I did this, unless it was to keep him in the loop.

"I saw them yesterday."

"How are they?"

"The same."

"Meaning?"

"They're happy in their little bubble, and who are we to burst it?"

"You're right. I'm sure we look strange to them, too."

"I keep telling myself that, but you have to admit: Pat could be involuntarily committed on the basis of her parakeet alone."

———

David Rosner rescued me from another round of job hunting after my sophomore year at the University of Pittsburgh. He had gone to Penn after we graduated from high school, and because his semester ended two months later than mine, his family invited me to work at their bookstore until David became available. The idea of getting paid to read books sounded good and it wasn't long before we worked out a schedule in which David's mother managed the store in the daytime and I replaced her at night.

Although his folks helped him with start-up capital, the concept of the store was David's. He purchased used books from a company called Brodart and sold them for a profit. These books were called "remainders" because Brodart supplied multiple copies of them to libraries throughout the United States at the height of the books' popularity and then bought all but one of the copies back when the demand for them diminished. Operating out of a tiny little space with room for only two or three customers might have worked for the tailor shop that preceded us, but it wasn't going to cut it now that the store was gaining traction.

I usually showed up at four in the afternoon and worked until midnight, with foot traffic slowing down within an hour of Sylvia's departure. This freed me up to read whichever "remainder" interested me and to ring up the occasional sale on a second-hand cash register that Sylvia had purchased from the old Jewish guys at Trenton China. The septuagenarian shop owners had attempted their usual double talk, but they had more than met their match with Sylvia. Not only were they unable to gouge her as they intended, but they ended up selling the cash register to her for less than they had asked originally. If I had found out later that the encounter had caused the shop owners to retire, it wouldn't have surprised me. Sylvia had that effect on people, although she was exceedingly nice to me.

One afternoon at a quarter to five, Sylvia walked back into the store with a brown paper bag and a can of cream soda. I was reading *Music Is My Mistress: The Duke Ellington Story*.

"You're back," I said. "What's the occasion?"

"I brought you something,"

She handed me the bag and placed the soda on the counter. "Will you eat a Reubin sandwich? It's from the Latimer Deli."

"Of course. Thank you!"

"What are you reading?"

I showed her the book.

"Is it any good?"

"I like it. Duke's an interesting guy."

"It must be an intimate portrait of him if you're on a first name basis."

I was rarely surprised by my own witticisms, but when someone else came out with one, it was a healthy reminder that I wasn't the only person who could formulate an intelligent thought.

"Don't get any cole slaw on that," she said. "We still have to sell it."

Something was off in that situation, but I didn't know what it was until David showed up unexpectedly also. "Feel like goin' for a walk?" he asked. "My mom can watch the store."

"Sure—where are we going?"

"Don't worry about it. You'll see."

David led me to a storefront a few blocks away, and asked me what I thought.

"What? We're movin'?"

"Mark," he said, "we need a bigger space!"

David told me later that I looked terrified, and that I sounded just like the "Yiddishe mouse" that Saul Bellow wrote about in *Humboldt's Gift*, another one of the "remainders."

For a good thirty seconds, I peered through the window at 1334 Walnut Street, realizing that it was ten times larger than the space we currently occupied.

"How much is the rent?"

"It's a lot," David replied.

I thought it over for a few more seconds, then came out with my pronouncement. "Don't do it, Dave—it's too much of a risk."

David nodded in an inscrutable way. "Ok. Let's go back."

"You're not mad, are yuh?"

"No, I asked for your opinion."

In my own personal history, my response has assumed legendary proportions. Not only did I fail to realize that I sounded like my mother, but it never dawned on me that David might have asked the question for his own amusement. Certainly he realized that I had nothing of value to offer, and that he would learn nothing from the likes of me, particularly when it came to operating a business. But even more significantly, I took to recounting the incident years later after David realized his destiny as a multi-millionaire by locating a vendor for best sellers and coffee table books that had never been touched, a development that broke things wide open for him by expanding his sphere of influence beyond the thrift shop crowd and into the realm of the more privileged shoppers with far more disposable income. They were the sort of people who found used books distasteful for reasons they didn't care to explore.

On the other hand, I was free to explore them, and I came to suspect that David had tapped into a population that recoiled in horror at the motley collection of stains that beset nearly all of the "remainders"—the fingerprints, the ketchup, the blood, and God knows what other bodily fluids. When David made that essential discovery about human nature, he was able to solve the riddle of limited sales and hook up with a New York Sharpie named Phil Klein who kept the coffee table books coming, multi-colored volumes that enabled David to revolutionize the concept of book-selling in this country, open more than fifty stores throughout the East Coast, and become independently wealthy by selling the business to a national drug store chain in the late 1980s. The entire breathless phenomenon persuaded me to share the incident in a humorous, self-deprecating way whenever David's name came up in the decades that followed.

———————

During my senior year in high school, I was diagnosed with scoliosis and confined to a bed for three months recovering from a spinal fusion. My reality included a body cast, a bedpan, and a plastic urinal; but my mother and grandmother worked together to pamper me outrageously and transform the experience into something I could endure.

After a week or so, my brother sent me a package that included copies of *Winesburg, Ohio*; *A Passage to India*; and *The Universal Baseball Association* by Robert Coover. To that point, I had read very few books that hadn't been required of me in school; and the few that I did read were sports-related. So, Carl's recommendation of the Coover novel was particularly inspired.

The reading list helped me survive my summer in bed, urged me in a better direction, and started me on my way to loving books almost as much as my brother did, which was another reason that the job at the bookstore was so pleasurable.

The other benefit of working for David—besides the books and the corned beef sandwiches—was the presence of Heather Freeman, another classmate who had accepted an offer to work there. I had a history with Heather that dated back to a card she sent me on my seventeenth birthday. The card urged me to "stop drinking, clowning around all the time, and wishing you were six-foot-two." Not only did the message hit home, but it represented the first time that a girl had taken a genuine interest in me, other than laughing at my jokes.

Now, two years later, Heather was sleeping with David, and she and I would sit together and remove the plastic book covers that had the word "Brodart" printed on them. That was the year that a Lenny Bruce movie came out with Valerie Perrine and Dustin Hoffman, and we took to recreating the scene in which Lenny tormented his elderly aunt by bucking his hips in a lascivious way and approaching her seat at the table. Lenny's obscene body language caused his aunt to shriek at him in mock-horror, exclaiming "Feh, Lenny, feh!" an exclamation that encouraged Lenny to liken her to "a Jewish seagull." Since the kind of physical contact that I craved with women had still not become possible for me, few things in my world were sexier than Heather's willingness to engage in the play-acting with her dead-on mimicry of the aunt. I did my best to pick my spots and refrain from clowning around desperately, but there were specific instances in which Heather doubled over with laughter, grabbed my arm, and rewarded me with an embrace.

Shortly after we moved the store from 13th and Pine to Walnut Street, a man leaped to his death from a fleabag hotel two or three doors away. An ambulance crew had arrived too late to save him, and he was lying face-down on the sidewalk. Surprisingly, there was very little blood, but his head had come to rest at a grotesque angle. This was the first time that I had seen a dead body anywhere other than a funeral; and it served as a stark reminder that the Rosners weren't the only ones who meant business. Life meant business, too, and if you weren't careful—if you couldn't find your way to some kind of happiness or acceptance—the consequences could be severe.

Nothing changed when I saw the dead man on the sidewalk. It should have, but it didn't. As Heather realized, I was in no real hurry to accept the reality of my behavior.

"Do you remember the card you gave me?"

"Of course I do."

We were sitting at the back of the store, putting price stickers on *Working* by Studs Terkel. The Rosners were selling it for 10% off.

"You had to grow up, Mark. You still do."

I winced. "Wow. I was going to ask if you had seen any improvement."

"I've seen some, but not a lot."

"That's not gonna happen any time soon—growing up, I mean. I might as well enjoy myself until it does."

I would have given anything for that beautiful young woman to love me, but I had thrown away whatever miniscule chance I had—all because the need to be sarcastic overwhelmed everything else.

"If you say so," Heather said sadly. "Hand me that book. I'll put it in the window."

The next day, my mother attacked me on similar grounds.

"Do you think you might want to manage the store some day?"

"Manage it? Absolutely not! That's not what I'm in it for."

"What *are* you in it for? I'm trying to understand."

"Can't I just pass the time?" I said. "Millions of people do it every day, and they don't have to justify it to *their* mothers."

"You're not millions of people. You're my son."

Before I moved out of my mother's apartment, I worked for several months in the coffee shop at the Benjamin Franklin Hotel, getting up at five in the morning, venturing a block or two into the working class neighborhood behind 2601, and taking Lawrence's 48 bus downtown. I had applied for a job as a cook but had lost out to a more experienced person, settling for the position of "food checker" instead.

Ever since I had attended the University of Pittsburgh, I had romanticized short order cooking as the kind of thing I would like to do in renouncing my privileged background and making a statement to my mother once and for all. In retrospect, I can trace the romanticism to my late-night visits to the Old Original, a greasy spoon restaurant a block from my dormitory. Since the university's dining plan required its participants to eat dinner at five o'clock in the afternoon—and since I was usually stoned by ten or eleven and craving something to eat—I often staggered down Forbes Avenue and took my place in the take-out line, where I would stare in fascination at the pot-bellied, hairy-armed cook as he masterfully worked his grill, sweating profusely, mopping his brow, and wiping his hands on a badly stained apron that barely made it around his circumference.

For minutes at a time, the cook held my attention by flipping the hamburgers, poking the hot dogs, and striking his spatula on the grill, the only method he had of dislodging the grease, commanding his kingdom so thoroughly that he was undaunted by the fact that fifteen or twenty orders were flapping on the line above him. These innocent slips of paper demanded that he produce chili dogs, Texas Tommies, bacon cheeseburgers, and cheese fries at an impossible pace, while all the time meeting the challenge of the occasional oddball order when some greenhorn would enter the establishment for the first time and make the mistake of requesting a New England fish sandwich, forcing the cook to venture into the walk-in freezer and emerge with a cod fillet that had made its way not from New England but from a soon-to-be-closed processing plant in Donora, Pennsylvania, a town made famous by the baseball player Stan Musial.

Once I overcame my disappointment at not landing the cooking job and following in the footsteps of the fat little man from "the O," I was able to console myself by dividing my time between a little glass enclosure that had been strategically placed in the kitchen of the coffee shop and the cash register out front. Fortunately, there was enough downtime at each of these outposts for me to reflect upon my role model from Pittsburgh and the habit I developed of imagining his entire history while I waited in the take-out line, where I assigned him a marginal existence in the home of his aging mother, whose only requirement was that he bring her two hot dogs and an orange soda every Friday night, which was my own order whenever I visited the restaurant.

As a food checker, my job was to rat on my co-workers if they attempted to remove an item that had not been recorded on the check, while my principal responsibility as a cashier was to ring up sales on a cash register that was even older than the one at the bookstore before the Rosners computerized that function. The cash register at the hotel contained a component that sent the customer's change tumbling down a little chute until it gathered in a receptacle at the bottom, a mechanical mystery I was unable to penetrate until a Puerto Rican dishwasher explained it to me in broken English.

It was there, in the depths of that kitchen, that I experienced the reality of hard labor for the first time since Goldie Frankel sold the coffee shop at 2601, slumming, consorting with the great unwashed, and loving every minute of it as I rubbed my mother's nose in my refusal to pursue a degree. This enabled me to enjoy my proximity to the tired old waitresses and commit their patter to memory, the kind of waitress speak that I've heard in every diner I've ever been to, phrases like "Watch yer back" and "Hot behind, hun'" and "I need a number eight with a side o' bacon" until one of the cooks barked at them in a surly way—"I told yuh—eighty-six the bacon!"

There, too, I imagined the lives of those around me, ascribing to them something hopelessly depressing, sparing no one as I doled out the cancer, the brutish husbands, the unspeakable loneliness, and any other harsh fate I could dredge up from the bleakness of my world view, until my imagination was utterly captured by the waitress Peg, a pale, wasted–looking woman with bad feet, gnarled hands, and a heartbreaking amount of makeup on her wrinkled face, an appearance that caused me to make a series of wild assumptions in which she struggled up the steps to a fourth floor apartment and passed through a hallway that was redolent with the odor of rotten cabbage. This hallway was populated by emaciated, mangy-looking cats and dogs that meowed and whimpered at her plaintively, only to have her take out her anger by kicking them as violently as she could, uttering a profanity that she had learned from a dead lover whose name she forgot, and disappearing into her cramped, dimly lit unit where she would nurse a bottle of cheap scotch, chain smoke, and fall asleep to old episodes of *The Honeymooners, Ozzie and Harriet,* and *What's My Line,* never able to guess the occupations on that show and vicariously win a prize. Dragging herself to her bathroom at four in the morning to remove the caked-on makeup from the day before, she would apply another coat of rouge, mascara, and eye liner until she looked like an old whore. Years later, my brother and I would run into her on the street and she would smile at me vaguely, as though she remembered me from somewhere, and Carl would comment that she had "a face like a thousand blow jobs."

A month into my stay, two hundred science fiction writers descended on the hotel for their annual convention, and I recognized a few of them from their book covers at the Rosners' store. As I rang up a tuna on rye for Arthur C. Clarke, I greeted him by name, and as prominent as he was, I actually think the quasi-famous author of *2001: A Space Odyssey* enjoyed being recognized. However, because there were no other sightings of near celebrities—and there was nowhere else to go in my mimicry of the waitresses for the amusement of my friends—I quit the Ben Franklin Hotel job shortly after that.

———————

In the summer of 1976, Frank Meltzer needed someone to share the rent with him in West Philadelphia. He was subletting from Martha Cade, a professor of his from Villanova. Martha had gone off to Italy with her exotic Jamaican boyfriend, whose half-naked photographs enlivened her sprawling home on Osage Avenue. She lived a block or two from the houses that were incinerated several years later in a blundering attempt to overpower the MOVE people by mayor Wilson Goode, police commissioner Gregore Sambor, and fire commissioner William Richmond. I had always suspected Richmond of being a latent homosexual who lived in fear of the barrel-chested Sambor, despite the fact that I had no evidence whatsoever to support my position, a point of view that—like so many of my others—arose almost entirely from the problems I had with my own sexuality.

It was on Osage Avenue that I battled on a regular basis with Meltzer's legendary frugality and his stubborn insistence on playing "Don't Stop" by Fleetwood Mac four or five times a day (since he was too frugal to buy another album), until I finally confronted him with the fact that he was taking Christine McVie too literally when it came to listening to her record. The highly intelligent Meltzer began to sputter in the same red-faced way that I recalled from our school cafeteria when he and Dan Hiller would argue about something trivial and cause whatever beverages they were consuming to be expelled from their noses, their arguments lasting until one or the other of them came dangerously close to choking.

But now, living with another human being who was just as neurotic as I was represented another lesson in humility and made a strong case for making money in this world and giving myself some options. Unless I wanted to return to my mother's apartment with my tail between my legs, I had to find another job quickly.

The only highlight of that six-week period while Martha Cade toured the Coliseum and walked the beaches of the Mediterranean with her boyfriend was that I had the entire house to myself and could listen to music and read to my heart's content while Meltzer clerked in a Center City law firm. It wasn't until he returned in the late afternoon that we battled over buying the groceries, preparing the evening meal, and washing the dishes. Things got so bad that I started eating before Frank even came home and disappearing into my bedroom while Meltzer charged around the kitchen, grumbling to himself while the Fleetwood Mac record went around on the turntable.

This precarious situation continued until we were shamed into an uneasy truce by the presence of Laurie Rosenberg, Dan Hiller's girlfriend from college, who needed a place to stay while waitressing at the Moshulu, a vastly overrated establishment in which diners ate and drank on an old converted schooner until it too eventually burned down. And now, in the two weeks that preceded her return to Bryn Mawr, Laurie exerted a civilizing influence, causing her hosts to work cooperatively in the kitchen, prepare meals that were touchingly inept, and lock horns over the right to serve them. In the end, though we pampered her absurdly, Laurie was too bright, sensitive, and tactful to betray her amusement. (Because she was Dan's girlfriend, I had never paid attention to Laurie until the day she paused in her sunbathing in the back yard, entered my room in a bathing suit, and delivered the latest letter from my brother, a moment of indiscretion that caused my mouth to fall open at the staggering voluptuousness of her body, and that caused our eyes to meet in an awkward way when Laurie realized that she had made a mistake.)

Until I actually lived with him, I had never believed the accounts of Meltzer's penny-pinching that Mike Magnelli and John Cardone brought back with them from Europe after having the misfortune of traveling with Meltzer for two weeks while I lay in bed in my body cast. Cardone was the six-foot-two classmate that Heather Freeman had accused me of envying in the birthday card four years earlier, but I couldn't hold that against him; and his point about Meltzer's incorrigible nature was brought home whenever we went to the store and Frank waited until we got to the check-out line to announce that he was "short of cash," making it sound like a temporary condition that could easily be remedied once we stopped at a bank or got back to the house. Meltzer presented it as an annoyance that was unlikely to reoccur, but it had a way of happening whenever we went anywhere, as though Frank had not yet mastered the fact that his parents were no longer paying for him and that he had to have money in his pocket or people were going to wash their hands of him forever. When Meltzer compounded the offense by helping himself to my orange juice one day—and leaving less than an inch of it in the bottle—it was clear that his behavior was unlikely to improve.

Hastened to some extent by Frank's overreliance on the funds I was compelled to provide, I soon ran out of money myself and was forced to accept a job as a mail clerk at the Fidelity Bond and Mortgage Company downtown, ending the latest period of unemployment that I had treated myself to over the objections of all concerned.

In addition to delivering mail to the various departments of the company, the mail clerk position called for me to serve as a lackey whenever one of the higher-ups required me to pick up his dry cleaning, take one of his huge, gas-guzzling vehicles to the carwash, or stand in the interminably long lines at Charlie's Water Wheel restaurant for a cheesesteak. The portly, middle-aged owner insisted on hand-slicing the best steak he could find, displaying an over-sized array of condiments, and dropping miniature candy bars into brown paper bags on his customers' way out the door.

From 11 am until 2 pm every weekday, Charlie had customers lined up outside of his door and onto the sidewalk outside, impeding foot traffic and alienating his neighbors on either side, including Oscar's Tavern and Sherman Brothers Shoes. Charlie kibitzed with his customers and barked orders in broken English with a thick Italian accent, another immigrant living the American Dream until a food court drove him out of business a year or two later.

Although I began my employment as a combination mail clerk and gofer, Bill Moore, the head of the auditing department, saw something in me and offered me a promotion. The idea of "moving up" was distasteful, as it suggested that I had bought into the idea of having a career, but because it carried with it a raise in salary, even I wasn't foolish enough to turn it down.

What I didn't suspect, however, was that the promotion would require me to rat on my co-workers again. This time, instead of inspecting trays of food that the waitresses were removing from the kitchen at the Benjamin Franklin Hotel, I was auditing the loan documents that were prepared in the underwriting department, making certain that all of the I's were dotted and the T's were crossed in the paperwork, and verifying that the titles, home inspection reports, and agreements of sale were present in their folders as required. When they weren't, I had to drag myself in embarrassment to the desk of the offending employee, apologize profusely for their mistake, and check a day or two later to make sure they had rectified the error, any failure to do so requiring me to escalate the matter further up the chain of command and increase my embarrassment exponentially, potentially taking money out of the pockets of my co-workers or threatening their livelihoods if the offense was egregious enough. You would have thought that I had committed the oversight or intentional misdeed myself, or that I was the lowest form of life imaginable to make trouble for my co-workers. The only comparison I can make to my misplaced mortification was the way that Dan Hiller apologized profusely for scoring a goal on me in the table hockey game that we played in my bedroom at 2601. I was fantastic at that game but Dan was even better, and our classic, high-scoring matches nearly always concluded with scores like 17-16 before the bell rang on the timer from my mother's kitchen. (I had originally bought the game as a Christmas gift for John Cardone's little brother, but in the process of inspecting it and making sure that all of its components were present—my excuse for opening the box—the game looked like too much fun to give away and I ended up keeping it myself, with the only improvement that the game required being the substitution of a marble for the little plastic puck that came with the original package. The marble speeded up the game so that it was played at a breakneck pace with Dan always besting me by a goal or two in the end. If my memory serves me correctly, I never did replace the gift and buy Scottie Cardone something else. I just pretended that I hadn't intended it for him in the first place.)

Bill Moore was a kindly, conservative, and exceedingly over-worked man who desperately needed an assistant to flag the occasional irregularity in the company's mortgage applications; and I was in no position to quit the nine-to-five job, particularly when the assignment promised to balance out the additional exposure to Meltzer with the unforeseen benefit of working in close proximity to a typing pool made up almost exclusively of sweet-natured, gum-cracking girls from South Philadelphia.

Now that my brother had urged me to "get shit on and lonely and loved up and crazy" in one of his letters, I began to take a greater interest in the girls from the mortgage company. Despite an overnight visit by Russel Durst, however—a friend from Pitts-burgh who commented on my hairy chest and informed me that "girls like that"—I was still under the impression that I would never get anywhere with women simply by being myself, taking a genuine interest in them, and becoming a good person. In fact, I was still several years away from the realization that I could be attractive to them even if I turned down the volume on my sarcasm, provided that I compelled them in a more straightforward way by virtue of the other qualities that I possessed.

If I attracted these young women at all, it was simply because they liked me, as Regina D'Imperio explained one night when a group of us went to see *Saturday Night Fever* at a multiplex in Cherry Hill, tried out our dance moves at the Emerald City night club across the street, and ate breakfast at the Diamond Diner at 3 in the morning. As Bill Moore's secretary, Regina had watched me interact with the women in my early days with the company. While sipping a Diet Coke in a ladylike way at the night club, she patted my hand and said, "You're sweet, Mark—don't try so hard." Regina towered over me by several inches, so there was never any chance of my mistaking her remark for an invitation to pursue her romantically, even when she gave me a copy of *The Four Seasons Greatest Hits* at the office Christmas party. It was just another good turn that a woman did for me along the way of my eventually growing up.

As it happened, the mortgage company had more than its share of desirable women and provided a perfect environment for me to flirt openly for the first time, since so many of them were receptive to it. Kathy Quigley, an Irish girl from the rough and tumble Port Richmond section of the city, proved to be one of only three or four exceptions when it came to the surnames and ethnic backgrounds of the women in the typing pool. In addition to Regina D'Imperio, the South Philadelphia contingent included Maria Stolfo, Natalie LaPaglia, and Celeste Spaddacini.

Since my early flirtations went well—and were not rebuked with the sort of cutting remark that I had dreaded from the time that females became desirable to me as a prepubescent teen—I became progressively more emboldened until the day that Alicia

Fleming returned from lunch in a new dress that she had bought at Knit Wit on Chestnut Street. Before I knew what I was doing, I demanded that Alicia turn around so that I could look at her from every angle. Shockingly, I had done it in such an authoritative way that it must not have occurred to her to refuse; she just smiled and did as I asked. Despite the slight improvement in my prospects, however, I found out that another one had gotten away, as Alicia had recently become engaged to a junior underwriter.

Alicia and some of the others were strikingly attractive, but for some unaccountable reason, the Italian girls intrigued me the most; and to this day, I can't drive down Broad Street without looking up at the Stolfo Funeral Home and remembering my days at the mortgage company.

A few weeks later—after Martha Cade returned from Italy— Frank Meltzer and I ran screaming from one another at last, and I took up residence in a house at 40th and Pine, where I joined a group of medical students, a molecular biologist, and a Ph.D. candidate in twentieth century fiction. From the beginning, it was obvious that my housemates possessed a great deal of brain power and that they were serious about their studies, and I quickly established myself as the only member of the group who wasn't enrolled in a degree program. When I look back on it, I can only shake my head at the pleasure I took in setting myself apart from the others, as though I were covering myself in glory with the fact that I wasn't studying around the clock and driving myself toward an admirable goal. Instead, I caused the telephone to ring eight or ten times a night, forcing my housemates to look up from their textbooks as I communicated with my growing network of friends, and as I created a life in which I returned from the mortgage company at five in the afternoon, ate dinner with whichever of the students was available in the antiquated dining room, and lazily read for an hour before going to bed.

Just to have a group of young people encouraging my sense of humor proved to be enough for the longest time; and I soon became the unofficial social chairman of the dwelling, urging them away from their studies with the mood I created at the dining room table, feeding off the intellectual energy of my housemates to conjure up a pervasive sense of hilarity, and becoming "a champion of humor," as my brother put it a year or two later. It was my way to listen carefully when I found myself in a group of people, pick my spots, and move in and out of the conversation with my rather pronounced cynicism, my anecdotes from barhopping and high school, and my impressions of the mortgage company.

These impressions invariably featured copious descriptions of Henry Grubman, a homely, obese, and deeply disturbed individual who worked in the mailroom, talked to himself incessantly, and developed something of a following after I conveyed the particulars of his homosexuality to Steve Levin, Rich Greenberg, and Ira Orloff, a trio of highly intelligent medical students who went on to imitate Grubman in a pitch perfect manner, Greenberg leering salaciously and intoning "Get the grease, Bernice!", Orloff assuming a highly effeminate tone in order to capture the subtle nuances of "Tommy Tucker's a fairy!", and Levin walking down the long hallway on the first floor of the house, shaking his right arm in an exaggerated way, and exclaiming "Let go, Robert!" in precisely the same manner that Grubman did while delivering the inter-office mail, despite the fact that Grubman was utterly alone at the time. I gave Grubman credit for originality until a few years later when I learned that he had borrowed his mannerisms from the Mart Crawley play *The Boys in the Band.*

When the three medical students fell silent, I did my best to top them with something even more perverse from Henry's repertoire or with a caustic impersonation of Milt Most, a wiry, stoop-shouldered man who deliberately ignored Henry's sexual orientation, referred to Henry as "Hank," and clipped disaster headlines from the *Philadelphia Daily News.* His exact motive remained a mystery until one of the clerks discovered a scrapbook behind the Pitney Bowes machine and it became apparent that Milt hoarded the disasters in order to reinforce his contempt for the rest of the world, his disgust with the people around him, and his conviction that the pessimism he felt was entirely justified.

When I finally mastered Milt's Brooklyn accent, his sad sack demeanor, and his perpetual scowl, I had my housemates in the palm of my hand, and could cause the entire table to explode with laughter, a development that enabled me to ignore my male housemates in favor of the young women, seek the women out one at a time, and gaze into their eyes as I concluded my performance, hoping upon hope that there might be some form of romantic encouragement there, fueled by their radiance until three of four of them grew fond of me in a limited way.

Now that I was enjoying the presence of women instead of shrinking away from them, the pleasure I took in being fully recovered from the scoliosis intensified and the others responded to it, until I injected a certain liveliness into the proceedings and made their long hours of studying more palatable. As it turned out, we had some good times as we began to interact, and as we became acquainted with the quirks that marked each of our behavior. Because we were thrown together from different backgrounds, our commingling fashioned a series of recollections that have remained with me to this day: Sally Briggs traveling to Houston for a six-week clinical rotation and returning with an absurdly exaggerated Texas accent; Rich Greenberg playing rather roughly with Reg, a little black kitten that Allen Rothenberg had named after the hockey player, Reggie Leach; and Ira Orloff bonding with his own cat, a hopelessly obese feline that Greenberg nicknamed "Fats" after witnessing Orloff's ritual of sharing his French fries with the animal while studying at the dining room table, Fats swallowing the French fries one at a time as Orloff proffered them, the two of them alternating methodically while Orloff buried himself in a cardiology textbook, raised an index finger, and traced little patterns in the hair on the side of his head, never once looking up until the percentages caught up with him and he realized that Fats had eaten the last of his food.

On nearly every occasion the cat would blink up at Ira calmly until Greenberg began to anthropomorphize, attributing an attitude of scornful defiance to the cat that could not have possibly existed. Through it all, Ira withstood Greenberg's teasing calmly, blinking up at him in much the same manner as the cat, as though he accepted his fate as the one person in the group that we most liked to tease good-naturedly, his sweet nature encouraging us to do that.

Within several weeks of my moving in, I realized that the house would be perfect for a party and that the dining room could easily be converted into a dance floor; and so I began to push hard for a commitment from the others, overcoming their initial reluctance through the sheer force of my will, which by then was relentlessly frivolous, and causing them to succumb to the infectious enthusiasm I felt for being twenty-three years old and perfectly healthy. And so, on a Saturday afternoon at the end of September, I sat down with Rich Greenberg and Susan McCormick and we pooled our record collections and created a dance tape that was talked about for months, building to a climax with "Money" by Pink Floyd, "Born to Run" by Bruce Springsteen, and "Saturday Night's All Right for Fighting" by Elton John, the finishing touch I applied in a moment of pure inspiration for the sole purpose of leaving a horde of young people drenched with sweat and savoring their vitality, collapsing into each other's arms, and exchanging phone numbers as I created a strobe-like effect by flipping the light switch on and off in quick succession while imitating Fergus, the gruff, oversized bouncer from J.C. Dobbs, who brought the festivities to a close every night with a vaguely threatening command ("Drink up, motherfuckers—we're closin'."), having acquired his manners from a motorcycle gang in Delaware County, with whom he had raised hell for the past twenty years. And when I pulled it off perfectly, down to the final imitation of Fergus, Susan blew me a kiss from across the room, shook her head, and told me I was too much, drawing out the "too" in her lilting Scottish accent, the strikingly handsome Greenberg having swept her off her feet the summer before while completing a semester abroad at the University of Edinburgh.

When it was all over and our guests had vacated the premises, Ira Orloff was alone in the dining room, shaking his head, chuckling to himself, and demonstrating my technique of dancing with my hands behind my back. That particular absurdity remained in Ira's memory for another twenty years and caused me no small embarrassment whenever he mentioned it to the woman who eventually became my wife.

It was prior to the same party that Lucy Williams gave Kate Ford a makeover, the two of them disappearing into Lucy's room for an entire afternoon while Levin, Greenberg, and I speculated openly about the results. Before long, we arrived at a cruel consensus in which we found it difficult to believe that Lucy would be able to work any real magic on Kate, only to have the young woman emerge timidly from Lucy's room with enough mascara on her eyelashes, padding in her bra, and fishnet in her stocking to elicit a flash of lust in each of us. This caused us to stare at Kate like a group of chimpanzees and fall into a stunned, slack-jawed silence before offering a round of applause, a development that compelled Lucy to laugh out loud at the sight of us while Kate hurried off to her room with a mixture of delight and embarrassment, immersing herself in quantum mechanics until our first few guests arrived.

Sure enough, Kate managed to attract an exceedingly polite little man from Israel who took to calling on her in a courtly way, showing up in a yarmulke as soon as the Sabbath ended on the next three Saturday nights and escorting Kate to a kosher restaurant and a movie that was rated PG, their brief relationship ending under mysterious circumstances a month or so later. Not to be graphic about it, but my bleak worldview, my negative imagination, and my sexual confusion concocted a horrific scenario in which Kate lost her nerve at the last possible instant before intercourse with Moshe was achieved, locked her knees together, and caused the over-eager young man to climax prematurely, covering Kate's legs with his semen. The fact that I not only envisioned all of this in excruciating detail but communicated it to the others strikes me now as an obvious indication of the unhealthiness of my inner life, although Levin and Greenberg seemed to appreciate my grisly speculation at the time. (Later, though, Lucy revealed the more mundane particulars of the breakup, informing us that Moshe had lost the battle he was waging to rationalize Kate's Christianity at approximately the same time that Kate had grown weary of altering her physical appearance in order to go on a date. Ultimately, they came to an understanding that they would study together chastely and allow the sexual excitement to dissipate, and when they made their feelings known, whatever physical sensations that passed between them disappeared with a dry little handshake and were replaced by the celibacy that preceded it.)

Within weeks, though, the sexual urges returned to Kate and she made one last attempt at a makeover and began to flirt with me in a halting, uncertain fashion; but the modesty that existed at the center of her being prevented her from devising a single remark that would even remotely approach sexual innuendo or double meaning, let alone give me a signal that was blatant enough to penetrate the thick fog of my ignorance. As it turned out, the flirting would have gone completely over my head if Rich Greenberg's instincts hadn't been keener than mine, and if Rich hadn't pulled me into the kitchen one day to tell me that Kate liked me. But once again my fundamental distrust of myself as a sexual creature prevented me from believing it. Even when Susan McCormick reduced it to its simplest terms by insisting that Kate would welcome my making a pass at her, the only reaction I exhibited was to blush reflexively, cover my face with my hands, and peer at them through my fingers, an unguarded moment that enabled them to see through my false bravado once and for all and confirm my suspected virginity.

———————

My initial sexual experience occurred a month later, after I had gone on a few dates with Amy Kirkpatrick, a friend of one of my housemates. Given the life-long anger that I harbored toward my mother—and my generalized resentment of women—was it any wonder that I had a difficult time with the sex act, or that my initial encounter was shocking in its brevity, unrewarding for my partner, and humiliating for me? And can I really be surprised that the evening ended with my virginity intact but my pride nearly shattered? In retrospect, it all makes sense that my final date with Amy concluded that way, and that it would be a long time before I would attempt that form of intimacy again, unless, of course, I consumed a vast amount of alcohol beforehand.

Martina had no intention of ordering the veal, despite the fact that it was the most popular item on the menu; but she was a good sport about it.

That was a positive development, and once I determined that her vegetarian tendencies were not of the militant variety—and that she would be happy enough with an order of gnocchi in a red sauce—I realized that it would be safe for me to order the veal scallopine. She would be watching, of course, and I would have to exhibit better table manners than the ones I employed when I tore into a cube steak at home, talking with my mouth full and dripping ketchup into my lap. Martina worked in the admissions office of Bryn Mawr College, and I had to control myself if I wanted to enjoy even a platonic relationship with her.

Our attachment had no staying power, but I believe that I intrigued Martina and that her curiosity worked in my favor. As a result, I got a taste of what I had been looking for in refusing to become a Nice Jewish Boy in the first place. If I had given in to the intense maternal pressure to become utterly conventional, I doubt that Martina would have spent the time with me that she did.

Although Martina's icy demeanor combined with my recent

sexual failure to prevent an attempt to kiss her, I made my intentions clear by bringing her a bag of oranges, a bottle of Cognac, and a copy of *Cosmopolitan* on the day she complained of a cold. If nothing else, this indicated that I had seen through her rather pronounced feminism to the teenaged girl within, tacitly encouraging her to indulge that component of her personality if only for the duration of her illness. Martina accepted these gifts with a knowing smile and absolutely no romantic encouragement whatsoever, but she gave me points for the items I selected.

Whether Martina found me attractive or not, it was clear that I was immature, and that I was fortunate to amuse her to the extent that I did. And though we never became close, I found it encouraging to realize that she had granted me four or five dates, something that I never would have imagined when Dan Hiller introduced me to her at a party.

Toward the end, I threw a Hail Mary, revealing the crush I had on Barbara Feldon, the actress who played Agent 99 on *Get Smart*; but Martina was unmoved by her resemblance to her, and there was no point in my saying any more about the television shows of an earlier era. Instead of mentioning the Elly May Clampett character on *The Beverly Hillbillies*, Audra on *The Big Valley*, or Mary Ann on *Gilligan's Island*, I kept quiet and was glad that I did. The sexpot Ginger terrified me, and my preference for Mary Ann wasn't as innocent as it seemed.

All of this occurred before I ran out of options, and before I admitted Martina into my personal pantheon of unrequited love, a structure that suffered from overcrowding.

———

A year or two later—when I was finally ready to try again—I had the good fortune of meeting Karen Marcus, a kind-hearted divorcee who married a colleague of Todd Millstein. After I eventually slept with her, my friends thought I was making it up when I told them that Karen worked as a layout artist for the *Jewish*

Exponent, the same publication that my father had on his coffee table in Hershey, but that was an actual job title in those days.

As it happened, Karen got a kick out of me when Todd introduced us at Chaucer's, and because I had mentioned the chicken salad scene in *Five Easy Pieces,* I was the first person she thought of when she won free tickets to the Ritz Five movie theater in a *Jewish Exponent* raffle. Not only did an orphanage in Tel Aviv benefit from this charitable endeavor, but my sex life finally got on track when Karen removed my inhibitions with a pitcher of piña coladas after the movie, climbed onto my lap, and executed a startlingly effective French kiss. In that way, I was able to enjoy a sexual experience without having to agonize over it in the moments that immediately preceded it. Once Karen did that, the fear that usually visited me had no place to go and there was no time for me to collapse into a state of complete and utter incompetence in which doubts about my fitness, the required physical attributes, and my sexual performance would remove so much of the pleasure.

Now that she had banished my feelings of inadequacy by plying me with alcohol, mounting me, and eliminating the paralyzing need for me to initiate the encounter, she was able to climb off my lap and lead me to her bedroom, where she removed all of her clothing. Although I didn't realize it at the time, the pain of her divorce must have melted away when she saw the unmistakable appreciation that lit my face from within.

Seconds later, Karen undressed me, exerted a gentle pressure on each of my shoulders, and urged me to the bed, covering me with her body, placing my glasses on a bedside table, and rendering her entire bedroom a blur. And while I gazed up at the unfocused image of her breasts, she did the one thing that Amy Kirkpatrick had neglected to do all along, the thing that seemed so pure in its simplicity, realizing all at once that I had no idea how to get inside her.

Although Karen made it easy for me by doing what needed to be done, I proved my immaturity all over again by silently congratulating myself for losing my virginity. But at least one of us knew what we were doing, and in that moment of pure physical sensation my mind wasn't working at all, and I finally began to participate before I experienced an orgasm. It was only then that I was visited by the question of whether or not the intercourse had lasted a long enough time, the issue of whether or not Karen had experienced an orgasm, and the possibility that I had embarrassed myself sexually. But from the way that she squeezed me with her arms and legs and buried her face in my neck, it seemed obvious that I had nothing to fear and could give myself over to the kind of post-coital contentment that Hollywood lies about so easily, duping one generation after another into believing that sex is easy for everyone.

But of course I understood none of it, and the next day I apologized to Karen over the phone and expressed regret over the fact that I had "let her down." Fortunately, however, Karen adopted the same tone of backslapping camaraderie that she had employed in urging me to continue drinking the night before, saying "Sorry, you had your chance" in such a humorous way that I was able to feel good about my sexuality for the first time. It turned out, though, that my sense of relief began to diminish after we hung up the phone, and as soon as her words began to fade, I realized that my sexual performance had improved only slightly and still had a long way to go. Despite the fact that these feelings persisted, Karen was able to remove nearly all of the anxiety that remained when she led me to her bedroom that evening, explaining that she rarely experienced an orgasm, informing me that she simply enjoyed being held, and stating that the pleasure she had given me had meant as much to her as anything else.

It wasn't until several weeks later that I began to consider the possibility that Karen had fabricated the assurance in order to put me at ease, and though it was a long time before I learned her actual intent, I harbored that suspicion in the most grateful way in the weeks that immediately followed her departure for California, Karen having made me aware on our first date that she had wearied of Philadelphia and intended to relocate. But the realization that Karen might have made me the beneficiary of a remarkable act of perception didn't occur until I had already declined her offer of accompanying her when she started a new life.

Before Karen packed her bags, I persuaded myself that she might "fall in love" with me if we continued the relationship, and I decided to "let her down easily" before she suffered "a broken heart," employing all of the stock phrases that young men call upon when their sense of right and wrong can no longer permit them to use a woman sexually. But that was only part of it. The truth is, my judgment was clouded by the subconscious belief that the sexual experience had been too good to be true, the deeply held conviction that I would be humiliated eventually, and the cowardly impulse to quit while I was ahead.

———————

Initially, I couldn't find any pop culture comparisons for Teresa, since she occupied a territory of her own. But more than a few of them occurred to me later.

"I like what you're wearin'," she said.

"You do?" Mike replied.

This was Mike Magnelli, my classmate from high school.

"Well, yeah," Teresa said, "it's cute!"

Earlier that day, I had taken Mike to a thrift shop, where they offered a dubious selection of clothing.

"Tell her where you got it," I followed, and Mike shot me a dirty look.

"That won't be necessary."

"Come on," she said. "You can tell me."

"No, that's OK."

Getting down to business wasn't a priority for her, despite the presence of her boss a few feet away. He went by the name of "Rickie," since his Chinese name was difficult to pronounce; but he was just another authority figure to her.

"What a hammerhead," she muttered.

"What was that?"

"Nothin'." But instead of picking up the pace and encouraging us to look at the menu, she continued to gaze at Mike in the same flirtatious manner as before. "What's that?" she said finally, gesturing toward a package that sat next to him on the seat.

"It's a poster," he replied, spreading it out on the table.

Whether it was instinct, calculation, or purely a spontaneous act, she rose to his level of excitement. "Whoa! David Johansen!"

"What—you like him?"

"Are you kiddin'? He's great!"

Johansen was the lead singer of the New York Dolls, and Mike had several of his cassettes, a fact that enabled him to remove a cassette from his pocket, insert it into his boombox, and play "Bohemian Love Pad" at the highest possible volume. Right on cue, Rickie returned to our table at the precise instant that his waitress gave Mike a high-five.

"Is there a problem?" Rickie demanded, while Mike ejected the tape.

"Heck no, Rick, we're fine!"

"Did you get their order?"

"Of course not," Teresa replied, employing an infuriating logic that Mike and I would come to know. "They haven't even looked at their menus!"

In fact, I had looked at the menu. Rather than dwell on the mysterious substance that was splattered across the cover, I ordered a cheeseburger with lettuce and tomato.

"What about you?" Rickie asked wearily, turning back to Mike. By then, he had abandoned all hope that Teresa would actually do her job.

"I'll have a pepper and egg sandwich."

Looking back on it, Mike and Rickie had something in common: they were both questioning their careers. Mike had invested two years of his life in law school, only to realize that he had no desire to practice law, while Rickie had purchased a restaurant that forced him to deal with the likes of us. He glared at Mike now.

"What do you want to drink?"

"What kind of beer do you have?" Mike asked, meeting Teresa's gaze to let her know he was kidding. He knew perfectly well that they didn't have a liquor license.

"We don't serve beer, wise guy."

"If that's the case, I'll have a black and white milkshake."

"I thought you were through with milkshakes," I said. Teresa looked confused—until I explained. "He broke his jaw in high school."

"You poor guy. Did they have your jaw wired shut?"

Normally, Mike would have responded with sarcasm, but Teresa had tamed him immediately.

"Yeah, they did," he answered.

"I'll have an orange juice," I said. It was sometimes possible—after ten or fifteen screwdrivers—to drink orange juice without missing the vodka.

Teresa turned back to Rickie. "Do you want me to write this down?"

"Don't bother," he sneered, making his way to the kitchen as Teresa resumed the flirtation with Mike.

"He's comin', you know."

"Who is?"

"David Johansen."

"You're kiddin'!"

"Nope. He's comin' to the Tower."

Mike frowned, realizing that I would start in on him to ask her out. "I didn't know that," he said glumly.

"On the twenty-eighth," Teresa replied. "Wanna go?"

Mike's mouth fell open. Teresa looked down at him and smiled.

"Sure!"

"Great!" Teresa said. "What's your name?"

After an initial period of intense excitement, he was shocked to learn that her behavior was completely erratic; but just when he was sure that he would expel her from his life, she would reel him back in with a joke, a gesture, or an uncanny remark that surprised him with its intelligence.

Her speech was working class Italian, with the occasional profanity mixed in, and though it was an exaggeration to say that she was drawn to the criminal element, he came to realize that her enthusiasm for the relationship would increase if he had a little outlaw in him. And so he tended to put people down in her presence, and to become a little crude when he was showing off. The fact is, she encouraged him to feel that way, and that was part of her charm.

Of course, there were other factors as well. She had a habit of focusing her attention and leaning into him as she spoke, as though they were the only two people in the world; and when she combined her ability to do that with her manner of dress and the obvious fact of her appearance, the effect was impressive. She was a pretty girl rather than a classic beauty, and that proved to be advantageous by providing her with an accessibility that classic beauties lacked. Later, she made herself even more accessible by hanging all over him in a shameless way, running her hands over his arms, and touching his cheek whenever she had the chance, whether she considered him her boyfriend or not. Finally, as if that particular set of characteristics weren't enough for him to remember her forever, she possessed the most irresistible trait of all: she was perfect to party with and had the ability to drink with him all night and listen to whatever he had to say—however undisciplined or boastful—provided that he was sufficiently attentive, his demeanor had a certain masculinity, and he took his place without complaint alongside the other men who were receiving the same set of favors.

In the beginning, they saw each other every night, careening through the early stages of their relationship until they ran out of things to say. Drinking from Teresa's flask, doing the occasional line of crank, and tooling around town in a pickup truck from the Colonial Dredging Company (the civil engineering firm operated by Mike's father), they found what they were looking for in their shared need to escape.

Within days, they began to arrive at my door, showing up in different outfits every time, bursting into the living room, and imploring me to go out with them. On those occasions, Mike looked happier than I had ever seen him, and I watched as he poured me a drink from the flask, played me a song on the boombox, and described their plans for the evening. While he did that, Teresa occupied herself at the kitchen table, reaching into her pocketbook, removing a plastic bag, and systematically rolling two or three joints to take with us. Invariably, the joints were perfect, as though a fastidious schoolgirl had prepared them for art class: tight, compact little missiles without the telltale signs of twisting that characterized my own creations, the only method I had discovered in all my years of carelessness that prevented the precious narcotic from leaking from the ends of the cigarette. Then there was the quality of the marijuana itself, Teresa having received it as a gift or obtained it for next to nothing from one of her many male admirers.

Later, when they completed their preparations, we piled into the truck, smoked the first of the joints, and headed downtown with the boombox blaring. Before we knew it, she introduced us to a set of nightclubs that broadened our horizons from South Street. These included the London Victory Club, Teresa's personal favorite, which had been converted from a funeral home to provide four or five separate bars, huge speakers, and a set of acoustics that were perfect for Billy Idol. Teresa's enthusiasm for the place—and the fact that the disc jockey knew what he was doing—made it possible to stare in fascination as Teresa brought her own individual style to "White Wedding," "Rebel Yell," and "Dancing with Myself," which she had no hesitation in doing after proceeding to wear each of us out, first Mike and then me, until she was in the middle of the dance floor without a partner for the four or five minutes it took Mike to recover. (Now, however, the London Victory Club is deader than their relationship, boarded up and covered with posters for performances that have come and gone.)

In one of the more painful flaws in her character—from the male perspective—Teresa slept with Mike on their second or third date only to reverse herself the rest of the week, behaving as though she weren't that kind of girl until Mike was utterly confused, not quite realizing that it had very little to do with him. A multitude of factors had caused this, not the least of which was the Catholicism that she outwardly disavowed. But just when Mike began to question his own adequacy as a lover (another reason that we got along as well as we did), Teresa returned to her previous attitude, behaving once again as though she couldn't keep her hands off him. As a result, they established a pattern in which their contentment depended almost entirely upon Teresa's mood swings, since they were the only outward sign of the turbulence that existed below the surface. Needless to say, she promptly deflected any attempt to examine these factors and insisted that you accept her on her own terms, despite the petulance, irrationality, and psychedelic logic that characterized her daily life. Then, if it came to an ultimatum, she was able to deliver it with the supreme confidence of knowing that still another young man was crazy about her.

Eventually, the pain of being involved with Teresa began to counterbalance the pleasure, ushering in an intermediate stage in which they continued to see one another despite serious misgivings on Mike's part. The more he discussed their relationship with me, the more fascinated I became, as Mike's own fascination wore off, until Teresa came to replace my housemate Sarah Sloane as the latest young woman I was studying, doing so from the safest possible vantage point of not being involved with Teresa myself. By that time, I had already fallen for Sarah—a cold and lifeless person if ever there was one—and Teresa was a welcome distraction.

Just as it did my heart good to see that Mike was having a good time with Teresa, it gratified him to see that she was making me happy as well. But once he reported that they had run out of things to say, my presence was harder to justify, and I began to feel awkward about it. When that happened, I even declined one or two of his invitations—something that I never would have done before we met her—and they were left to the true chemistry of their relationship.

Ultimately, Mike made a pointed attempt to do something different with Teresa, so that they could have a quiet time together; but his decision to take her to a museum was an utter failure and they ended up getting as drunk as they usually did, sitting in on one of the acoustic sets that Kenn Kweder played on Sunday afternoons at Dobbs. (Kweder was a local hero, and he worked in the rich musical tradition of performing while intoxicated, a tendency that created a symbiotic relationship with his audience. While the energy passed back and forth between them, it was easy to see why South Street had become a mecca for the impaired.)

After Mike and Teresa had been seeing one another for less than two weeks, Mike began to report that they were struggling to converse, and that Teresa had seemed distracted when he attempted to discuss their future, saying all of the right things but giving the distinct impression that she was incapable of backing them up, now that she had given herself entirely to a present tense existence. Mike had every intention of stepping gingerly around the subject of their future, but despite the wisdom of that strategy, his hand was forced by the fact that he had agreed to work for his father.

Staying local would have been one thing, but Mike was headed to the Gulf of Mexico, where his dad's dredging project was already under way. Predictably enough, his relationship with Teresa suffered.

We were at J.C. Dobbs when he told her, with Robert Hazard and the Heroes blasting rock and roll from the stage. I was a few feet away at the time, ordering a drink for each of us, when I heard Mike shouting to be heard.

"I have to tell you something," he said.

"What?" Teresa followed.

"I have to tell you something!"

"Oh, yeah? What's that?"

"I have to go to New Orleans."

"New Orleans? For how long?"

"I don't know."

Teresa glared at him. "I thought I meant somethin' to yuh."

"You do! You know I'm workin' for my father!"

"Gee, Mike, that's a shame. I was really enjoyin' your company."

"What are you talking about? I'm enjoying yours, too!"

"Who's more important—me or him?"

"Are you serious?"

"Do I sound like I'm kidding?"

"No, but—"

"But what?"

"Do I mean somethin' to *you*?"

"I wouldn't be sleepin' with yuh if yuh didn't."

Mike hesitated. "Come to New Orleans with me."

"What do you mean—to live with you?"

"Yeah, why not?"

"Whoa. Hold on now."

"What's stopping you? You hate your job."

"My job has nothing to do with it."

The bartender had already poured our drinks, but I stayed where I was, staring straight ahead to give them some privacy. At the time, I doubt they would have noticed.

"Forget it," Mike said, "it was a bad idea."

"Don't get depressed. I'm not ready to live with yuh, that's all."

Teresa had a kiss for every occasion, and the one she gave him took away the pain. "OK," he said. "Don't worry about it."

"When are yuh leavin'?"

"I don't know. Next week sometime."

"Are yuh drivin'?"

"I have to. I need the truck."

"D'yuh want some company on the way down?"

"Yeah!"

"I could drive down with yuh. We'd have a great time."

A week later, we found ourselves at Koffmeyer's bakery, where I devoured a series of chocolate chip cookies in a clear case of sublimation. Teresa sat on Mike's lap at one of their tables, Mike lifting her chin and kissing her again and again, as though he were absolutely mesmerized by how pretty she was and had no desire for the minutes to turn into hours and the hours to turn into days.

"Come on," I said, "give her a break!" And Teresa smiled at me from the exact center of her loveliness. "That's O.K., Mark, I don't mind."

Within minutes, Mike fell asleep with his head on Teresa's breast, and she and I began to talk while Mike snored lightly, his head rising and falling with every breath she took.

"Your dad's a pipefitter?" I asked.

"Yeah, he works at the Navy yard."

"How long's he been workin' there?"

"Christ, Mark, all his life."

"How's his health?"

"Fine, as far as I know. Why do you ask?"

"I just read something in the paper. There's a lot of asbestos at the Navy yard. Some of the men are getting sick."

"What happens to 'em?"

I realized that I was upsetting her, but it was too late.

"I forget how it affects them."

"No, you don't."

"I'm not even sure it's the Navy yard."

"You're not gonna leave me hangin'. I won't let yuh."

"OK. It fucks up their lungs."

Teresa winced. "What's the matter?" I asked.

"My dad coughs a lot. I've been worryin' about him."

"Does he smoke?"

"He used to, but he's been pretty good about it lately."

"I don't know. Maybe he should see a doctor."

Teresa considered this for a moment. "That was pretty cool

of yuh, Mark. Thanks a lot."

"No problem. I hope it works out."

"I hope so, too."

For a second or two, she held my gaze to convey the possibilities between us, and I was the first to look away.

When it was time to go, Teresa lowered her head and kissed Mike with tenderness and precision, and we walked back to the Toyota pickup with Mike's boombox blaring. A moment later, Mike tossed Teresa's suitcase onto the bed of the truck and covered it with a tarp.

After Mike and I shook hands, Teresa asked if she could call me when she returned from New Orleans, causing me to glance uncertainly at my friend.

"Come on!" he said sharply. "Of course she can!"

Just as Mike could only enjoy the partying when he ignored the larger issue of his career, he could only appreciate the relationship with Teresa when he kept it in the here and now; and so his future with that incredible young woman was just as unsettled as the plans he was making for the rest of his adult life. The truth is, he was unable to come up with a plan, and the more he struggled the more painful it became, until he regarded the trip to New Orleans as the last thing he could look forward to with pleasure. Judging by the postcard he sent prior to their arrival, his future was entirely up in the air, and their trip to New Orleans took on some of the desperation that I had come to know so well.

"Crankin' our way to New Orleans on I-65," he began, slipping a subversive reference to methamphetamines past the United States Postal Service in the process. "Passed your regards to Thomas Wolfe in Asheville. Teresa located a great collection of sunglasses and when she wears them she looks like a star. Only one more day off scheduled. Love, Mike"

Before leaving, of course, Teresa had failed to mention the trip to Rickie, and in so doing was fired in absentia from her job at the restaurant, with Mike and Teresa laughing about it over a barbecue beef sandwich in Gulfport, Mississippi.

For some reason, I could really talk to Teresa, and I came to discover a kind of street smarts in her that I hadn't expected. Taken together with the powerful physical attraction that was fueled by her constant need to touch the man she was with—and my fascination with her as a case study—it wasn't long before I began to romanticize Teresa out of all proportion. I seemed particularly fascinated with the observation that she could surprise you with her intelligence, a charitable conclusion that lent a certain mystery to her high school education; but it seems to me that it went further than that, and that Teresa possessed the ability to understand the young men of her acquaintance, identify a specific thought process, and allude to it in a remarkable way, creating an inside joke that only the two of you could share. Once she got to know you well enough to do that, every conversation became an adventure.

By then, I had developed feelings for my housemate Sarah Sloane, but Sarah insisted on keeping her distance from me. As a result, something changed in my tendency to study women as I became involved with them. Teresa's need for male attention led her to not only accept my attraction to her but encourage it, until I began to recognize something healthier in my feelings, something sturdier and less conflicted than anything that I had felt before. I was studying Teresa, but she was banishing some of my caution. Within days of my becoming aware of that development, however, I was tormented by my loyalty to Mike and found myself feeling conflicted all over again.

This was particularly true after a conversation that Teresa and I had at Dobbs. She had been back from New Orleans for a week, and somehow we got on the subject of her boyfriends. My recollection is that Teresa initiated the discussion, but I wouldn't swear to it, given my level of interest. At any rate, she went on to mention a number of the men that she had seen in the past and others who were pursuing her currently. The sheer volume of the men made it difficult to keep up. Although she started the timeline in high school—and eliminated whatever dalliances she may have had before that—a dizzying number of names came spilling out of her mouth, until it no longer mattered who was who. Finally, I had heard enough.

"Where's Mike in all of this?"

"What do you mean? I love the guy—I really do."

For a moment, I studied her expression. There was something different this time, and it took a moment for me to realize it. Unless I was wrong, she actually meant what she had said. That wasn't always the case with her, and as she described her feelings for Mike, a commitment to him seemed possible.

"I'm glad," I said. "He'll be a good influence on you."

Although she had every reason to resent this, she took it in stride.

"He already is," she said. "Did he tell you? He wants me to lay off the crank."

"I'm not surprised. Crank's not his thing. He only did it because you wanted him to."

She thought about it for a moment, and her expression changed. "In other words, I'm not a good influence on *him*."

"I didn't say that."

"He's going through a rough time, isn't he?"

"Things are up in the air for him, but he'll figure it out."

"I just want him to be happy," she said.

"Yeah," I replied, "me, too."

I wasn't in love with her yet, so I was pleased to hear her talk that way.

In the earliest days of their relationship, Mike had suspected that he was just another one of Teresa's boyfriends, but things began to change prior to their trip to New Orleans. He couldn't dismiss the possibility that she would forget about him when he was away, or that she would go on with her life as she had before; but now he wasn't so sure. There were positive signs when they were together, and Mike had every reason to be hopeful.

Despite the love that she professed for Mike, it would have been unrealistic to think that she would never mention other men again, or that she would refrain from spending time with them while Mike was away. From what I could tell, she had very few female friends, and the other men weren't going to fade into the background any time soon. Unfortunately, they were too big a part of her social life for that to happen.

Although I refused to listen to any criticism of Mike—just as she refused to discuss her irrationality—I was too weak to deflect Teresa's interest in other men, and I would get angry when she brought them up. The truth is, I was too attracted to her myself, too fascinated with her as a type, and too dependent on her for the inflation of my ego, an area of true mastery for Teresa at the beginning of her relationships.

A few days later—after I had already replaced Mike in seeing her every night—Fergus approached our table at Dobbs. Fergus had been a bouncer there for years, and he was on a first-name basis with Teresa, which meant that he had already paid his respects by waiving the cover charge and letting us in for nothing.

"Some guy was lookin' for yuh," he said.

"Oh, yeah?" Teresa replied. "Who?"

"I don't know. He was wearin' a uniform."

"Army or Navy?" Teresa followed.

"Navy," Fergus answered, turning to me in a sadistic manner, as though he were measuring my discomfort. This was a payback, of course, for all of the times that I had smoked pot in the second floor men's room, locking the door and preventing him from emptying his bladder.

"Ed," Teresa frowned, without explaining herself any further, and my voice rose with alarm.

"Who's Ed?" I cried, drawing the attention of a couple at another table.

"Ah, some guy," Teresa sneered, waving her hand dismissively.

"I realize that. That's exactly what Fergus said."

Teresa smiled slightly, recognizing the jealousy for what it was. "Take it easy, Mark. It's not worth talkin' about."

"All right, fine. It's just that I'm in a funny position here."

"What do you mean?"

"What do you think I mean? I thought you were goin' out with my friend!"

"Well, yeah, I was."

"Is that in the past tense?" I asked.

"I don't know, Mark. I guess that's up to him."

"Can we change the subject? This is making me uncomfortable."

"Sure. Suit yourself."

"Tell me about Ed," I frowned, as hooked on her as any of the others were, but with the complicating presence of a best friend.

"I went out with him for a while. It was no big deal."

"Was it a big deal for him?"

"I guess so," Teresa shrugged. "He calls whenever he's on leave."

"Were you expecting him tonight?"

"Of course not!" she exclaimed. "I was gettin' together with you!"

It was clear that she was offended, but I had a more immediate concern.

"Fergus, don't you have somewhere to be? This is a private conversation."

Fergus, of course, could have torn me limb from limb, but his job as a bouncer was to prevent physical confrontations, not cause them.

"Sure, fella, I can do that."

Winking at Teresa, he returned to the front door.

"Mark, that was so cool!" Teresa declared.

"I was in mortal danger. I'm glad you enjoyed it."

"Yeah, I did enjoy that," she followed thoughtfully, as though a flicker of self-realization had surfaced. Before she could do anything with it, however, it disappeared back into the muck. "When he was home, all he wanted to do was kiss me," she continued, and it was a second or two before I realized that she was talking about Ed. "I felt like sayin', 'All right, let's get this over with so we can get down to havin' some fun.'"

Suddenly, I looked away, thinking back to the uncertainty that she had put Mike through by refusing to sleep with him after she already had. For three or four days, she had evaded the issue, but eventually she drifted back to her previous attitude, a rather startling mood swing that she never bothered to explain. She probably knew that Mike would be grateful that they were sleeping together again, and that he was unlikely to question her about it. And so, for the first time, it occurred to me that she was somewhat indifferent toward sex, that she could take it or leave it, and that she was more interested in other things.

"Did you hear me, Mark? I was talkin'!"

"Sure I heard you. I was thinkin' about what you said."

"Yeah? I didn't think it was that memorable."

But it was obvious that she was pleased.

During their trip to New Orleans, Mike mentioned that I worked in a restaurant, and Teresa asked me about it the next time I saw her.

"You don't seem like the type," she said.

"That's because you don't know my mother."

I surprised myself with that, but Teresa had looked at me in a certain way, as though she were genuinely interested in probing that area of my life. It felt like a form of intimacy, and before I knew it, I was opening myself up to her about Mitch Frankel, Bill Moore, and the other authority figures who had insisted on my growing up. The lone exception was Sheldon Greenblatt, who accepted me for who I was.

———————

"It's hard work," Sheldon warned. His forehead was damp with perspiration, and his glasses were sliding down the bridge of his nose.

"I'm not afraid of that. When do I start?"

"How 'bout right now?"

"Right now? I'm not really dressed."

He had me cornered, and he knew it.

"Come on, I'll introduce you to Morris."

"Who's Morris?" I asked in the same uneasy tone as before.

"My cook," Sheldon replied, cocking his head toward the kitchen, where one of his employees was using a pumice stone to clean the grill, his muscular arms emerging from a sleeveless shirt. "You'll be working with him."

"Is that him?" I followed warily, employing the conspiratorial tone that I had often detected in my mother. It was clear that I was appealing to him on ethnic grounds alone, despite the fact that we were strangers.

"Don't worry about it," Sheldon smiled, "he's a pussycat."

"OK, if you say so."

"Morris!" Sheldon bellowed. "Come out here!"

Morris paused, scowling at Sheldon with obvious resentment. "Man, you know I ain't through!"

"Come out here anyway."

Morris tossed the cleaning device onto the grill, wiped his hands on his apron, and made his way to the front of the restaurant, taking his sweet time and muttering his signature phrase, which can only be conveyed with a dialect: "I can't uh-*sept* that."

"Yes, you can. Sit down."

Morris took a seat, eying me warily and turning to Sheldon with a belligerent stare. "Now who would that be?"

"Who do yuh think?"

"Man, I done tol' you to git me some help!"

"What are you talking about? He's an experienced cook!"

"That little bitty thing?" Morris flared, pinching my biceps. "Look at this here!"

"Let go of his arm!"

Morris rose to his feet, waving at Sheldon in disgust. "I'm warnin' you, man. I'm gonna walk outa here."

"Nobody's stopping you," Sheldon said easily, without an ounce of concern, introducing us now and forcing Morris to shake my hand. "This is Mark Glassman. He's gonna work with you at night."

"How you dawn?" Morris drawled, smiling in a friendly way.

"I'm doin' all right."

"Thass good. You say you an esperienced cook?"

I turned back to Sheldon. "I thought *you* were interviewing me."

"Yeah, I was."

"I'm an experienced *busboy*," I said.

That wasn't the answer that Morris was looking for, but Sheldon was unconcerned.

"See that, Sheldon? I be doin' your job. He ain't esperienced."

"What are you talking about? I hired *you*, didn't I?"

Morris shook his head. "For real, Sheldon—you don't give me no respect."

"Give it a few days, OK? We'll see how it goes."

"You gonna break my back in here!"

"I doubt it."

"Who's gonna pay mah hospital bill? You?"

"Absolutely. If I break your back, I'll pay your hospital bill."

"You watch," he said. "I'll still be doin' the nigger work."

I winced, shocked that he had used "the N word." But Sheldon had heard it from him before.

"He'll do everything you do—believe me."

"Yeah, we'll see about that."

"Do me a favor—tell him what he needs to know."

"Yeah, I'll tell him all right."

I glanced uncertainly at Sheldon.

"I told yuh," Sheldon smiled. "He's a pussycat!"

"Oh, yeah? Is zat what I am?"

"You better be if you're goin' to bible school," Sheldon answered mysteriously, as I blinked at them in confusion.

"Don't you concern yourself with that," Morris replied, glaring at Sheldon again.

"You're going to bible school?" I asked.

"Yeah," Morris beamed. "I'm gonna be ordained as a minister."

"That's great," I followed. "Congratulations."

Morris chuckled. "Man, you a trip!" He took on an innocent expression, as though he hadn't insulted me at all. "I'm gonna have mah own congregation one day."

"I believe you. You're serious about it."

"Man, I'm serious as a heart attack!" he said.

Once again, I glanced at Sheldon.

"Just ignore him when he gets like that."

"Ignore him?"

"Yeah, he's just playing with you."

Morris tapped me on the shoulder. "Come on, p'fessuh. Get you a apron."

———————

For some reason, Morris took a crazy kind of pride in his own stereotypical behavior. For instance, when we were getting to know each other, he went out of his way to tell me that he had been fired from his previous job, a personnel action that he provoked by falling asleep at the control panel of a state-of-art security system. Instead of sleeping fitfully and waking every few minutes—which might have preserved his employment at The Tasty Baking Company on Hunting Park Avenue—my co-worker slept from the beginning of the graveyard shift to the end, while the computer system responded to the transitory occurrences of the night: a parking lot gate clanging against its post, a trespasser cutting across company property, a homeless person curled up on the loading dock. Each of these caused the computer system to come alive, its color-coded lights blinking frantically to alert the attendant to a possible emergency. The entire setup was dependent upon the wakefulness of the attendant, a prerequisite that carried with it the expectation of sentience. Since my co-worker fell asleep on each of his first three days on the job, he was unable to respond to the alarm system until the police arrived to investigate, an arrival that set off a chain of events in which Morris's boss was interrupted in the middle of a sound sleep in his modest little home in Cinnaminson, New Jersey, a fully authorized stupor that he had earned by patrolling the grounds from 7 a.m. to 3 p.m. the day before. And so, when Morris failed to stay awake after his final warning, his boss had little choice but to relieve him of his duties, making the announcement by pinning a termination slip to Morris's shirt collar, though that too failed to rouse him. Eventually, Morris's boss shook him violently by the shoulders, and Morris awoke to the knowledge that he was out of a job, rubbing his eyes as he unfastened the safety pin, removed the termination slip, and squinted at the unequivocal message that the boss had left behind: "You're fired, Braxton. Turn in your keys." (At first, I mistakenly believed that the stereotypes defined Morris, but when it came right down to it, he blew the stereotypes away by taking me under his wing, looking out for me, and letting the kids in the neighborhood know that he had my back if they got too boisterous.)

To hear Morris tell it, he wasn't lazy at all, but was simply overburdened by the demands of fatherhood, his work at Mr. Martin's, and his bible study at The Third Pentecostal Church of Our Lord Jesus Christ, where he was pursuing an unaccredited degree in theology. But this sense of righteousness didn't prevent him from juggling two girlfriends and a wife, each of the women blissfully unaware of one another until Morris began to call them by the wrong names during intercourse, a series of sexual encounters that he described to me in excruciating detail. When I questioned him, he explained the adultery with a rather unusual claim, saying "I got me a problem: mah wife can't take me duh whole way."

"What do you mean?" I asked innocently, lowering a mop into a bucket of filthy water.

Morris shook his head. "What you think I mean, P'fessuh?"

"You tell me," I answered defiantly, getting a little tired of the "professor" routine.

Spelling it out with explicit language—and leaving nothing to the imagination—Morris explained that he was well-endowed and that sex was painful for his wife.

"Be careful what you wish for," I followed, turning away from him to hide the fact that I was blushing.

"Say what?"

"I mean—that would be a pleasant problem to have."

Clearly, I had answered without thinking it through. It might have been pleasant for Morris, but it would have been just the opposite for his wife; and instead of considering it any further, I began to mop furiously, avoiding my co-worker's gaze.

Morris stared at me in amazement. "Do it like this here," he said finally, removing the mop from my hand and demonstrating his technique, and I stood there looking at him while he moved the mop back and forth across the floor, stunned that I had revealed as much as I had and that Morris had responded so gently. As it turned out, we never spoke of our genitalia again, though Morris's remark bothered me for longer than I cared to admit.

_____

After much discussion, Sheldon and I decided that I would work a split shift, helping out at the grill at lunchtime, making deliveries, and closing the place at night. In addition to my quality time with Morris, this arrangement enabled me to enjoy the entire Mr. Martin's experience, and to make the acquaintance of Ann Marie McCafferty, an exceedingly attractive woman with flawless skin, perfect features, and the rather suggestive nickname of Bunny. At the time, there was a widely held assumption that she and Sheldon were sleeping together, but if that was the case, their relationship did nothing to disturb Sheldon's marriage to an up-and-coming executive of a local mortgage company. Nor did the adultery that Sheldon and Bunny were allegedly committing prevent a wild stampede for Bunny's affections. This amusing spectacle had all of the virtues of a soap opera and none of the commercial interruptions, and featured a cast of characters that sniffed around Bunny at all hours of the day. Taken together, Bunny's admirers represented a cross-section of humanity that encompassed the unemployed drunks from Fairmount, the depressed, lower-middle-class neighborhood that surrounded the little sandwich shop; the yuppies who had begun to gentrify the area by moving into newly constructed townhouses three or four blocks to the north; and the motley collection of employees, customers, delivery men, and other individuals whose daily commerce brought them into the vicinity.

One of these individuals was Frank Boyko, a Philadelphia cop who double-parked his squad car outrageously and ate two meals per shift while standing at our counter for the privilege of scoping Bunny out as she bent down and reached into the refrigerator case for ice cream, her shapely breasts shifting enticingly inside her clingy Ann Taylor top. Whenever she did this, Boyko's dark, hooded eyes tightened at the sight of her, longing and lust making a sniveling thing of him, although he bore up manfully and projected a cheerful image, even answering the phones for us in a pinch when he was on the clock with the city and should have been fighting crime. Much to his dismay, however, Boyko learned that he wasn't the only gentleman caller that Bunny received.

Within days of accepting a position as a grocery manager at Stein's supermarket across the street, Charlie Perna was snared by Bunny's ever-widening net, making his way over to the hoagie shop, ordering a cheesesteak, and discovering Bunny's many charms. Once he made the discovery, he took his place next to Boyko as still another candidate for Bunny's affections, whiling away every one of his coffee breaks by bemoaning his fate at the supermarket. Whenever he got on the subject, he complained bitterly about being blocked in his ambition by the presence of Albert Stein's two sons, describing the solid, conservative, older son, Bart, and the mustachioed playboy, Barry, who showed his mettle one day by giving the bum's rush to a rather intimidating shoplifter who towered over him and outweighed him by thirty pounds, Barry shoving the man so forcefully that he staggered backward for a good fifteen feet before falling to the ground.

By working in the daytime—when everyone but Morris was present—I was able to consort with the entire staff, including the little white-haired cook Andy, who had been slaving away in kitchens for the better part of fifty years. In that time, he had developed a set of idiosyncratic expressions that caused me to give free reign to my mimicry, and I was able to delight Bunny and the others by borrowing freely from Morris, Andy, and Billy McDevitt, a neighborhood youth who had been dishonorably discharged from the Navy once it became apparent that he was a hopeless alcoholic at the age of eighteen. Although he tried desperately to keep up the pretense that the expulsion had occurred after he had bludgeoned a man to death in a jousting exercise, that particular version of the events was nothing more than a violent fantasy, and his pals from the neighborhood arrived at a rather sensible way of handling the situation, scoffing at it in private but indulging it in Billy's presence, as though it were a harmless concession to his essential innocence and good nature.

By running my mouth ceaselessly and clowning from morning till night, I was able to take our minds off the fact that we were working incredibly hard, and that we were making a furious attempt to stay a step ahead of the children who streamed out of the St. Francis Xavier Elementary School to devour our chocolate chip cookies. We generally succeeded in keeping our heads above water until their recess ended, but we were pressed to our limits by the pimply-faced teenagers who made their way over from Roman Catholic High School at lunchtime, an unruly mob that ordered slices of pizza with unspeakably bad manners in purple and gold windbreakers from the football team. And so, in my first few weeks at Mr. Martin's, I came to feel that I had it all (with the possible exception of sex), and that my life was perfectly aligned, basking in the laughter I engendered in Bunny and the others; relishing the modest wad of bills that overflowed from the pockets of my blue jeans; and reading one book after another as though I were actually in school.

Although Morris insisted that he was in class at the Third Pentecostal Church of Our Lord Jesus Christ in the daytime—and couldn't help us if we became shorthanded—my suspicion that he was shacking up with one of his mistresses was confirmed in my second week on the job. It was then that Sheldon asked me to call Morris at eleven in the morning after Andy requested a day off. This directive set a domestic farce into motion, and before it was over Morris's wife mistook me for Sheldon on the phone, launched into a diatribe in which she protested Morris's low wages, and complained bitterly that she hadn't seen Morris for days. Before she hung up, she warned me that she wouldn't hesitate to visit the restaurant in person if I failed to locate Morris on her behalf, a noxious threat that caused me to flip through the Yellow Pages in a terrified manner, only to learn that the Third Pentecostal Church of Our Lord Jesus Christ existed only in Morris's imagination.

Shortly thereafter, Andy followed Morris's fabrication with the claim that he had needed the day off in order to celebrate his anniversary. Punctuating the explanation with a leer, he informed us that he had shown "the wife" a good time, and though his advanced age caused me to doubt his ability to do that, the fact that I was blushing furiously prevented me from disputing it with any vigor. At that very moment, Bunny entered the kitchen for an ice cream scoop of cottage cheese, caught the tail end of our conversation, and glanced at each of us with an identical look of pity, putting two and two together the second she realized that my face was bright red and Andy's dentures were gleaming.

In addition to canned peaches and a generous amount of lettuce, the cottage cheese represented still another element in the rather rigid diet that enabled Bunny to maintain her figure and fuel the fires of Frank Boyko, Charlie Perna, and the endless stream of customers that increased their visits to two or three times a week simply to flirt with her while their tuna hoagies, pizza cheese steaks, and BLTs were being prepared. Needless to say, Bunny's nutritional regimen created a set of fortuitous circumstances for Sheldon, enabling him to make money hand over fist, pay Bunny an outrageously high wage for functioning essentially as a cashier, and keep her in expensive perfume. In turn, Bunny was encouraged to show up for work every day in a little Mazda sports car, completely overdressed for a job in a hoagie shop. At the same time, I was convinced that the routine they worked out afforded Sheldon the added benefit of enjoying Bunny's sexual favors without really trying since Bunny was unwilling to remain celibate while looking for Mr. Right. For my entire stay, life at the restaurant seemed to revolve around Bunny's sexuality and the strange mating ritual that she inspired, as the men in her circle of acquaintance vied for her attention, either to sleep with her or make her laugh, which of course had become my sad little substitute. Whatever my limitations, however, I seemed to experience a good deal more success with Bunny than most of the others—at least in terms of the objective that I had allowed myself—now that I had withdrawn from the contest of getting into Bunny's pants. From the moment that she swung her legs over the running board of the Mazda, removed her sunglasses, and shook her long, reddish-brown hair, I kept at her with my mimicry, rasping out the phrase "Nice cookin'!" which I had shamelessly stolen from Andy, crying out "Bunny baby!" at odd intervals in the manner of Billy McDevitt, and warning Sheldon to "Get off my back!" as Morris had done on numerous occasions.

When I exhausted the mannerisms of my co-workers, I took to imitating the customers, winning a cherished smile from Bunny in my mimicry of a bearded guard from the art museum, a rotund individual who stammered his order into the phone. "G-g-g-g-gimme a roas' beef hoggie," he would say, "and drag it f-f-f-f-frew duh garden," by which he meant that we should insert every condiment known to man. This tendency enabled us to enjoy an inside joke until the day that I constructed his sandwich with mustard, ketchup, relish, pickles, onions, sweet peppers, hot peppers, oregano, provolone cheese, and absolutely no roast beef at all, having been lured into a false sense of security by the thickness of the sandwich and befuddled by the mind-numbing possibilities offered by the little plastic containers that sunk so snugly into the refrigerated case on the other side of the cutting board. In completing his order, I overlooked the main ingredient, an unfortunate turn of events that compelled the fat little security guard to come striding through the door with a broad smile, wave the greasy brown bag in my face, and intone good-naturedly: "You done forgot somethin'—mah roas' b-b-b-b-beef!" With everyone sending their gaze into the kitchen, I didn't collapse into self-consciousness as I would have in the past but rode the crest of their laughter in a supremely confident way, rasping out the phrase "Nice cookin'!" and adding the missing ingredient, gazing into Bunny's baby blue eyes as I did so.

As the weeks passed, a stream of new customers entered the restaurant, transient at first but showing up repeatedly once they got a look at Bunny and a whiff of her perfume, as their siren continued to ignore the fact that she was completely overdressed for a job that required her to operate a soda dispenser, scribble orders on a little pad, ring up sales on a cash register, and flip the occasional burger when the other workers were overburdened. Even Andy got into the act by rasping out a flirtatious greeting when Bunny came strolling into the restaurant every day, making her entrance two or three minutes before all hell broke loose at lunch time, despite the fact that Billy and I had been slaving away for hours in order to prepare. The success of the restaurant required us to dice onions, slice tomatoes, bake pizzas, and replenish the little plastic containers that housed the meats, vegetables, and condiments that represented any self-respecting hoagie shop's stock in trade; but Bunny had her own schedule and couldn't be bothered with ours.

By mid-morning, Andy would join us in order to complete the preparations, arriving in plenty of time to undress Bunny with his eyes, rasp out "Hiya, baby!" as she made her way through the door, and show off with the one hole card he had—his cooking prowess—just as I had attempted to impress Bunny with my wit, the two of us equally pathetic in the conceits we brought into the world. For a period of several weeks, Andy would punctuate the lunch rush with cries of "Nice cookin', Markie!" and make a big show of his grill work by cracking his spatula on the counter, frying the onions, and breaking apart the chip steak with as much flair as possible. Despite the fact that he was twenty years past his prime—and his face was alarmingly red—he seemed to enjoy himself immensely while Sheldon and Bunny worked the front counter and I climbed in and out of my car to make deliveries and Billy manned the pizza oven, baking pies and reheating slices while the phones rang off the hook.

Despite his flirting, however, Andy went out of his way to wrap a care package for his wife at the end of his day's work, lovingly preparing it and slicing it in half and telling us who it was for, the innocuous charade continuing until his landlord became a customer, threw his hat into the ring with Bunny, and startled us one day by saying, "Wife? What wife? He lives alone in a basement apartment." This indiscretion on the part of the landlord put us in a position where we had to smile with false encouragement whenever Andy patted his hair into place when he was ready to leave, threw on a splash of cheap cologne, and told us that he had to look good for "the little woman." Finally, Sheldon took him aside, draped his huge hand over Andy's bony little shoulder, and told him what the landlord had said; but instead of the kindness that Sheldon intended, Andy regarded it as the final humiliation, failing to show up the next day and quitting the day after that. Later, when Sheldon tried to change his mind, Andy said "That's

OK, Shelly, I'm gettin' too old for it anyway."

Despite a growing number of men who were drooling over Bunny, she and Sheldon were free to disappear every day between two and five in the afternoon; and if their activities were as spirited as the rumors, innuendos, and circumstantial evidence indicated, they were enjoying themselves a lot more than Billy and I were in operating the restaurant in their absence. Without fail, however, they left just enough time for Bunny to get a pedicure at a downtown salon while Sheldon picked up a piece of restaurant equipment at Trenton China, the same supplier that Sylvia Rosner had bested in their negotiation over a cash register. When it came to earning a living, Sheldon was more carefree than Sylvia, and he ended up kibitzing with the shop owners as they grossly overcharged him for a display case, a bug-zapper, or some other superfluous item. For my part, of course, I was free to picture Sheldon and Bunny's trysts in my fertile, sex-starved imagination, and to usher in pornographic images of them as they made their way through an illustrated copy of the *Kama Sutra*.

Although it remained uncertain as to whether or not Frank Boyko or Charlie Perna ever hit paydirt with the presumably promiscuous Bunny, it came to be known that Billy McDevitt received a single mercy fuck after hounding her for six consecutive weeks. But things did not go well to judge by their stony silence the next day, and my co-worker remained uncharacteristically glum when we exchanged our usual greeting, not answering "Markie, baby!" at all but getting right to work on the six pizzas he had to produce by 11 a.m. Instead of engaging in the teasing, insults, and trash-talking that characterized our relationship, he lifted the pizza dough from its little round containers, kneaded it, stretched it, and tossed it into the air until it was flat enough to apply the sauce, cheese, and toppings, avoiding Bunny's gaze until the entire scene had the unmistakable feel of a sexual failure. At that point, I turned off the slicer and allowed the eighteen-inch pepperoni stick to droop limply in my hand so that I could ask if something was wrong, enabling Billy to hold forth on a miserable evening in which he totaled his girlfriend's car for the second time in two weeks after she had just gotten it back from the body shop. In describing his girlfriend's response—and her rather sudden decision to throw him out of the house—he scrupulously avoided the subject that I wanted to discuss, ignored the fact that he had pleaded with Bunny beforehand, and pretended that he hadn't begged Bunny as though his life depended on it. Now that he had engaged in an evasive maneuver (as though he had actually learned something in the military prior to his expulsion), I realized that tough love was my only option, but even when I teased him unmercifully he refused to cooperate. In the final analysis, his silence on the subject left me completely in the dark about their ill-fated coupling and gave me nothing more to go on than Bunny's glaring demeanor, an obvious expression of displeasure that she wore for an entire day. But as difficult as it must have been for them, the situation wasn't particularly healthy for me either, since it did nothing to dissuade me from the firmly entrenched point of view that sexuality was fraught with peril.

Despite the decrepit condition of my Chevrolet Vega, I was only too happy to accept Sheldon's suggestion that I make deliveries whenever I was present, since it enabled me to pocket an extra twenty dollars a day in gratuities and escape the nerve-racking mayhem of telephones ringing off the hook, customers complaining bitterly, and orders flapping on the line above the grill. But now all of the others were doing the hardest work while I came and went as I pleased, gathering up the orders as soon as Bunny rang them up on the new-fangled cash register that Sheldon had yet to master, and as soon as she placed all of the items into their brown bags with her tiny little hands and perfectly manicured nails, which she tended with an emery board between phone calls. Although we obtained new customers all the time, most of the calls came from MAB Paints; the Reliance Standard Insurance Company; a tavern called 99 West; the Pennsylvania School of Ballet with its gorgeous, anorexic ballet dancers and their intriguingly flat chests; and the aforementioned yuppies on streets like

Meredith, Taney, Aspen, Brown, Wallace, and Corinthian, creating a rich variety of deliveries that enabled me to tool around in the Vega and get to know the neighborhood like a cab driver, another occupation that I insisted on romanticizing.

Although Sheldon had performed an eminently competent tune-up during my first week of employment—and had only charged me for the spark plugs—it was obvious that the Vega had less than a year to live; and so I availed myself of my father precisely as I had in the past, requesting that he put "Curly" Goodrich on notice that I was in the market for a car. Within days, the crusty old mechanic made some phone calls from his ramshackle garage in Hummelstown, and he and my father came through for me once again. Fully cognizant of the fact that I didn't have a pot to piss in, they presented me with a choice of vehicles in the $100 to $300 range, although I went on to ignore their recommendations for a period of several weeks, purchasing a huge, oversized convertible from an otolaryngologist at Abington Hospital. This enterprising physician charged me $75 for the privilege of owning the car for the month of March, after which it promptly failed the state inspection. Because he was exceedingly fond of my father, Curly broke it to me as gently as he was able, saying "Mark, you don't want me to inspect this car, you really don't." But there was no getting around the fact that the vehicle needed $2,700 worth of repairs. Reacting promptly to Curly's warning, I acquired an inspection sticker for $25 from Joe McBride, put the top down on the car, and drove to the Jersey shore on a cold day in April, my fingers turning numb against the steering wheel in the forty degree temperatures for the sole purpose of saying that I had done it, the kind of adolescent stunt that you never quite regret.

This was the same Joe McBride who sold lilies at Easter, fir trees at Christmas, and marijuana in between, mixing in the occasional assortment of marginally fresh vegetables that he hawked from a beat-up Chevy truck. As it turned out, this vehicle had problems of its own now that its ball joints had collapsed, a mechanical failure that left it with a comical lopsided appearance when viewed from the front or the rear, although it was exceedingly unsafe to linger in close proximity to the vehicle for very long owing to the presence of McBride's foul-looking German shepherd, a broken-toothed old mutt whose sour expression suggested the possibility of a canine ulcer. For all of Joe's girth, however, his porcine features, and his legendary temper (for it was said that he routinely took on three or four men whenever a brawl broke out at 99 West), Joe was an exceptionally friendly individual who had been outside of the Philadelphia city limits on only one or two occasions, so content was he with the life that he had built in Fairmount. This sense of contentment revealed itself in McBride's easy interaction with the old ladies who gathered for the vegetables, the young married couples who bought the Christmas trees, and the motley assortment of neighborhood pot smokers who acquired ounces of harsh-tasting weed from him year-round. In that way, the days ran together smoothly until one of the neighborhood yuppies made the mistake of walking his golden retriever within a few feet of Joe, causing Joe's dog to go berserk inside the truck, growling, baring his rotten teeth, and salivating in the pure, unadulterated desire to mangle the golden retriever, the canine equivalent of the dumb blond, a gentle house pet that had mirrored her master's folly by prancing along the sidewalk in a particularly infuriating manner.

In the end, however, I lacked the courage to drive around town with a fake inspection sticker and placed an ad in the Sunday paper instead, selling the convertible to an antique car collector for $150, congratulating myself for having the moxie to double my initial investment, and traveling to Hummelstown to evaluate the three or four vehicles that my father and his mechanic had made available. Although the decision was difficult, I finally settled on an olive green Chevrolet Impala that was neither more nor less sound than any of the others, but that distinguished itself by eliciting a pang of sick and twisted nostalgia for my parents' divorce. When considered in the proper light—and with favorable atmospheric conditions—its color closely resembled the fondly remembered pigmentation of my mother's Pontiac Tempest, a vehicle that she purchased once the divorce was finalized. Looking back on it, of course, I realize that my reckless disregard for the health and wellbeing of the Vega—and the sheer willingness I exhibited to run the car into the ground—primarily arose from the live-for-today attitude that I had developed as a dropout.

Despite the fact that I hastened the necessity of shelling out a couple hundred dollars for another used car, I was simply having too much fun to inject a measure of self-discipline, precisely as I had carried on at the University of Pittsburgh, skipping classes shamelessly, smoking ounces of pot, and consuming hot dogs at "the O." A reasonable person might conclude that my theory about my work history is too simplistic—and that it's impossible to believe that I would take a series of embarrassing jobs to spite my mother—but when you factor in the amount of fun I was having, it changes the equation. Putting the embarrassment aside for long periods of time—which I developed an uncanny ability to do—enabled me to enjoy myself a great deal. I had a ball in those days, and as foolish as it seems in retrospect, I wouldn't have traded my misspent youth for anything else in the world.

Now that I think about it, the only bumps in the road occurred when Sheldon's inattentiveness surfaced more powerfully than it usually did, and when the minor incidents that we were used to seeing became more significant. On those occasions—when his preoccupation with other interests crossed the line in severity—it was impossible for us to prevent the inevitable misfortune. For instance, Sheldon tied up the phones for over an hour one day in order to schedule a flying lesson; and on another occasion he forgot to defrost the back-up bag of hoagie rolls when my car was out of commission. Because the oversight occurred on a Friday, our busiest night of the week, Bunny was forced to lend me the Mazda for an emergency trip to Amoroso's Bakery, and for over an hour I felt like a million bucks during the round trip, experiencing the immense difference between a beat-up car that struggles for every mile and a sleek, fine-tuned machine that is unburdened by an endless repair record. Because the Mazda effortlessly devoured the road and made no noise while doing it, it enabled me to blare my Elvis Costello tape, fire up a joint, and declare "I could get used to this!" as the basic foundation of my impoverished lifestyle suffered the slightest tremor, like a fault line that caves in years later.

Although he erred with some regularity, Sheldon's most memorable lapse occurred when he sat down with his accountant, the two of them conferring while the high school kids played video games a few feet away. As the scene unfolded, the accountant spread his paperwork out on a table and forced our happy-go-lucky proprietor to confront the fact that he had been losing seven cents every time he sold an Italian hoagie, having failed to perform the cost analysis that the accountant had recommended in their previous meeting. It seemed that Sheldon was struggling mightily with the fact that the price of provolone cheese had gone through the roof and that he had picked a bad time to upgrade the capicola. Of course, if Bunny had been less interested in her fingernails, she might have helped Sheldon identify the problem before it got out of hand, but she too failed to discern the mistake he had made with the basic ingredients of our most popular item.

While Sheldon and the accountant were talking, Eddie Gallagher ordered the last Italian hoagie that we ever sold for $3.99, and I recognized him as the neighborhood kid who had delivered groceries to our apartment at 2601 seven or eight years before, Eddie having worked for a concentration camp survivor named Leon Levitt who ran the commissary in our building. While I lined the bread with provolone—one of two offending ingredients that had made a fool of my employer—I recalled the guilt-ridden way that I had retreated into my bedroom whenever Eddie rang the doorbell, deeply ashamed of the arbitrariness of my social status, my mother having married a wealthy accountant, brought me with her from Florida, and placed me in the lap of luxury. This series of statistical quirks resulted in Eddie Gallagher acquiring the status of a poor delivery boy while I evolved into a pampered teenager whose mother didn't even have to take the elevator downstairs in order to do her shopping, but who could pick up a telephone and order the buttermilk, raisins, and Gold Medal flour that she needed to bake her son a cake. As I wrapped Eddie's sandwich, I felt an exaggerated sense of pride at having rejected my mother's values and become a working class stiff like Eddie, although it was obvious after Eddie spread the word about me that the guys in the neighborhood placed me in another category entirely. For the next six months, Eddie behaved as though he had gained a newfound respect for me, and I began to savor that development in the privacy of my thoughts and scrupulously ignore the mounting evidence that the men in the neighborhood had me pegged as someone who was simply playing at being poor and who could reject the poverty at any time.

As it turned out, this was particularly true of a neighborhood drunk named Tom Harlow who persisted in borrowing money from me whenever I ran into him at Grendel's Lair, calculating the precise amount of cash that he would need in order to hang around until last call. At that point, he would miraculously show up in the general vicinity of whichever beat-up car I was driving and bum a ride home, taking advantage of the fact that I admired him for venturing away from 99 West (something that his friends from the neighborhood rarely did, having succumbed to Joe McBride syndrome, an epidemic that caused them to drop anchor in their comfort zone). But if I had any illusions about Harlow, they were dispelled when he bragged to the others about the amount of money he had borrowed from me. In the end, however, the slight was easy to ignore once I realized that these same young men were capable of open racism to Blacks. "There's Blacks and there's niggers," Harlow remarked one night, gazing serenely from the window of my car. "Them are niggers."

"What can I say, Harlow? Thanks for clearing that up."

Not only had Karen Marcus invited me to accompany her to California, but she offered to support me; and though it was an extraordinary offer, my unfortunate decision to decline it left me without a lover for another six months, until Todd Millstein introduced me to his sister.

Resembling the British actress Helena Bonham Carter, Jane discussed books and records with me, turned me on to Pat Metheny, and fell asleep with her head on my shoulder at a bar in New York, where a local band covered "And the Healing Has Begun" by Van Morrison. And if spending an entire day with her wasn't enough for me to develop feelings for Jane, a postcard arrived at Mr. Martin's shortly after we returned. At first, I didn't recognize the handwriting, but its obvious femininity caused Bunny to experience a moment of confusion, as though she were regarding me as a possibility for the first time. But in another instant her expression changed and she looked right through me as she had in the past, handing me the postcard in a disinterested way.

For my part, I experienced a moment of triumph, no longer needing to elicit the hard-won smile from Bunny now that I had Jane in my life. Although I ignored the pastoral scene on the front of the postcard and turned immediately to the message on the back—reading the message repeatedly in a neurotic attempt to recreate the original feeling—I was forced to examine the front of the card more closely when I read the postscript, Jane mysteriously encouraging me to "Note mammals in LR corner." Though it took me several seconds to determine that LR corner meant the left rear section of the card and not the lower right, my confusion about the rolling farmland, herd of cattle, and farm workers eventually abated, and I was startled by the image of two of the bovine creatures in what appeared to be a compromising position. Because the exact perspective of the artist caused the cows in the foreground to be rendered in much sharper detail, there was a certain ambiguity about the actual intent of the postscript and about the two farm animals that Jane had specifically mentioned. Consequently, I was forced to purchase a magnifying glass from Pete's Variety Store on Meredith Street and examine the postcard more closely. In the end, it was impossible to determine with any certainty that the cows were in fact copulating, but the examination I conducted while a pepperoni pizza grew cold in the back seat of my car could not have yielded any other explanation for the fact that Jane had called my attention to those two cows in particular, so indistinguishable did they seem from all of the others when considered from the perspective that they weren't copulating. With that in mind, I felt reasonably certain that they were, or at least that Jane *thought* they were and had gone out of her way to admit them into our relationship. Despite the fact that the thought was somewhat terrifying, I made a conscious decision to *believe* that the cows were copulating and that Jane was attracted to me physically; and whenever I wavered in that regard, I reminded myself that she had sent the postcard to Mr. Martin's and not to my house, a decision that made the arrival of the postcard more enticing. But absurdly enough, after admiring the sure-handedness of the gesture (and believing it to be the female equivalent of a man sending flowers to a woman's office so that she can bask in the glow of envy), I was somewhat intimidated as well, as though the gesture had risen to the level of calculation, which meant, of course, that Jane was experienced in matters of the heart and that she was able to walk the fine line between flirtation and courtship with more balance, coordination, and confidence than I could.

Lugging dirty dishes around the coffee shop at 2601 added muscle to my scrawny arms, and working for Sheldon continued the transformation; and now, some of the women were responding to me differently. But Jane's encouragement lay in perfect balance with the terror I felt at the thought of having sex. In the end, the scales weren't tipped one way or the other until she stopped me in my tracks at a little ice cream parlor at the corner of 23rd and Spruce. While consuming a dish of pistachio ice cream, she mentioned a young man that she had been seeing until a month or two before. He had broken off relations with her without an explanation.

"Why did he do that?" I asked.

"I don't know why I'm telling you this," she said.

"That's OK. Was it sexual?"

"It was," she said. "How can I put it delicately? He was unable to control himself with me."

It was a second or two before I could answer. "I'm familiar with the concept," I said, without specifying whether I had experienced it personally.

"He got really upset, and he wouldn't talk to me about it. I tried to tell him that there were other ways to please me."

Here, she looked me in the eye to determine if I understood.

"I'm familiar with that concept, too."

Jane smiled, then she got serious again. "Is it OK that I'm telling you this?"

"Yeah, I feel bad for the guy, that's all."

Jane had no way of knowing what an outrageous crock of shit that was—but now she would never know. Rather than subject her to the cruel possibility that she would become involved with two young men who suffered from the same malady—and subject myself to another round of humiliation—I had already made up my mind to assume an advisory role in Jane's life.

"I'm probably telling you something you already know," I said, "but the issue could be physical, psychological, or some combination of both. Has he seen a doctor about it?"

"I have no idea. He won't return my calls."

"Yeah, I'd be the same way."

"He was a nice guy—I would help him if I could. But it's not like I'm pining away for him."

"No, I get it," I said. But before I concluded this thoroughly mendacious display, I had one more tip for Jane in case the issue arose in the future. "Apparently there's a set of exercises a guy can do, and there are books on the subject. I have no idea if they would help."

"You're sweet. Thanks for talking with me about it."

"Don't worry—it's OK."

"I guess I needed a guy's point of view."

"That's understandable. But couldn't you have talked to Todd?"

"Are you kidding?" she said, "He's my brother!" And she burst out laughing.

"Yeah, I guess that was a bad idea."

At the time, it seemed a good deal wiser to retreat from Jane's life voluntarily rather than risk the more debilitating form of withdrawal that I had experienced with Amy Kirkpatrick. If nothing else, my decision to do that enabled me to go quietly from the possibility of sleeping with Jane, come to rest at a safer place, and concoct an elaborate rationalization in which our courtship would almost certainly have resulted in our sleeping together if not for the sexual problems of the young man that Jane had been dating. In so doing, I was able to perform an act of gallantry, let myself off the hook for the paralyzing fear that I would not measure up, and preserve the possibility in Jane's mind that I would have been as spectacular a lover as any she had ever had, judging by the quality of my advice.

———————

Just as I came to know the entire cast of characters at my job as a short order cook, I made the acquaintance of nearly all of the men that Teresa was seeing or stringing along, her need for male attention combining with a natural curiosity, a desire for experience, and an openness that was endearing one minute and terrifying the next. It was as though the next hitchhiker that she picked up—or the next stray human being that she brought home to appall her mother—would be the one to do her in. It wasn't long before I realized that this formidable young woman—all five foot three of her—had come to know men from every walk of life. When I examined the list of male acquaintances (and believe me I did, with a masochistic intensity), I realized that she was making her way steadily through a breathtaking array of humanity, and that this was literally the case from garbage men to college professors. The truth is, she wasn't overly impressed with any of them, and she granted them an equal chance to succeed.

Some of these relationships were more problematic than others and more disturbing to witness if you had designs on Teresa also. This was painfully clear now that I was looking out for both Mike and myself, laboring as I was with feelings that were obviously personal. For the first few minutes of every one of our meetings, I tried to keep up the pretext of hearing about her relationship with Mike, but it lasted about as long as it took to look at her.

One evening, she left our table at Dobbs to speak to someone she knew. In and of itself, there was nothing alarming about it, as I had already gotten used to her tendency to do that, and to the set of feelings that invariably arose when she left you sitting there alone: the glow she left you with when she first walked away; the intermediate stage in which you wondered where she was; the full-blown panic in which you questioned whether or not she would return; and finally the stage in which you began to seethe with anger, no longer smiling falsely, bobbing your head to the music, and pretending that nothing was wrong. Instead, you glanced anxiously in the general direction of the exit, suffering the final indignity of the pitying glances of the people at the other tables (people who had obviously not been taken in by your histrionics), until she shocked you by coming up to you from behind, putting her hands over your eyes, and saying "Guess who?", as though you hadn't already committed to memory the combined fragrance of her various soaps and lotions and the indescribable softness of her skin. But on that particular evening, she lowered my spirits by bringing someone back to the table with her.

"Mark, this is Romeo," she said. "He works for Rickie."

Romeo sat with us for half a drink, he and Teresa doing most of the talking, and I was content to watch them together, focusing for some reason on the suntan that she had obtained in New Orleans. While they conversed—with Romeo addressing Teresa in a courtly, old world manner—my gaze lingered for a moment over the exact spot where the suntan stopped on her thigh, disappeared into her skirt, and gave way to the pale skin that had covered her prior to the trip. The contrast enabled me to realize that Teresa led a nocturnal existence, and that the suntan would fade in a matter of days.

Before long, however, I was incited by Romeo's Middle Eastern accent, and I became preoccupied with his curly black hair, sharp nose, and thin moustache, until my racist tendencies surfaced once again. By the time Teresa and I were alone, I had reduced him to a cultural stereotype, drawing a sharp rebuke by stating that he was unsavory. "Mark," Teresa said, "you have mean thoughts." And my only defense was to remind her that she liked that about me.

This was the signal for Teresa to describe the problems that Romeo was experiencing with the Iranian government, an untenable concoction that featured the rather melodramatic possibility that Romeo was in danger of being deported and placed before a firing squad if he failed to obtain his American citizenship. As Teresa explained it, this sobering requirement was entirely dependent upon his finding an American wife.

Needless to say, I listened to this with all the stability of a pinball, changing directions every time Teresa made the leap from Point A to Point C in her logic. The difficulty in keeping up didn't prevent me from being way ahead of her when it came to the idea of marriage, however, and I interrupted her five or ten seconds before she introduced the possibility of marrying Romeo herself.

"Teresa, don't tell me you'd consider it," I winced, imagining her in full Muslim regalia, a scarf and a headpiece obscuring her face in such a way that Romeo would be the only man to ever see it again. And I began to scoff at her answer before it even left her mouth.

"Gee, Mark, I don't know. Firing squads are pretty heavy duty." And she sat there with the most remarkable expression on her face, a picture of little girl concern.

"That's probably an understatement."

"Do you think he's telling the truth?"

"Absolutely not. He's looking for sympathy."

"I hope you're right," she replied coldly, as though she were fully prepared to abandon Romeo now that I had told her how to feel.

"I hope so, too," I frowned, with just the slightest doubt creeping in.

Teresa stared at me for a few seconds, studying my expression. Then she placed her hand on my arm.

"A firing squad...that's a sin."

"It's not your problem, Teresa. It really isn't."

"I guess not," she said. "Can we at least give him a ride home?"

———————

Frank Tattaglia was the garbage man in question, and though a severe case of acne had left him with a pockmarked face, he did very little to help himself with the other aspects of his appearance. Looking at him, it seemed as though he rarely washed his hair or visited a dentist. Nor did he make an effort to cover the needle marks on his arm or the unsightly tattoo on his biceps, that particular marking having faded to the lurid, bluish green color that prison tattoos always seem to degenerate into with the passing of the years. If he had even had the sense to wear long-sleeved shirts, he could have indulged in his current addiction in private, but with the track marks as visible as they were it was apparent that he was shooting either heroin or speed. In the end, though, he never failed to clear up whatever mystery remained about his narcotic of choice. He did this by proffering a line of crank at every opportunity, whether you were driving in a car or sitting in someone's living room, his mind so addled that the lines he set before you were of an unprecedented length, so that you had to cut them in half with a razor blade in order to live to see the next day. Even when we sat with him at J.C. Dobbs, Frank took my brazenness a step further by doing lines of crank in the men's room, jumping up two or three times every hour to add more of the crank to his bloodstream.

But as repulsive as some of his physical characteristics were,

I returned repeatedly to his acrid, sickeningly sweet cologne, a scent that was more off-putting than any ill-conceived Christmas gift had ever been, and a selection that could only be explained by a combination of financial difficulties and bad taste. This problem was so pronounced that Teresa remarked on it the night she introduced Frank to me, waiting for him to make his first trip to the men's room to say "What's that smell?" Her question caused me to lapse into the worst of my Pygmalion tendencies and add a layer of mean-spiritedness to my reply: "Garbage and cheap cologne."

Unlike my remark about Romeo, Teresa seemed to appreciate the characterization, now that Frank had crossed the line into something slavish and was no longer behaving in the manly way she required. On the night that Frank and I met, in fact, he had made the mistake of bringing her a drink whenever he returned from the men's room, failing to notice that the drinks were lining up in front of her and that she couldn't possibly have consumed them in a reasonable amount of time. Instead, he had his hands full with the rupturing of the blood vessels in his nose, as well as the powdery remnants of the last line of crank that he had sent into his nostril. When the blood finally trickled down from the nostril, all he could do was employ one of the little cocktail napkins that had come with each of the shots of Old Grand-Dad that he had delivered in a muddled fashion.

In addition to the drinks lined up in front of her, Teresa reached a state of high annoyance over the fact that Frank proposed marriage to her the last time they were alone. When she reported their conversation to me, it was as though it had no real connection to her and was merely a fact of life.

"Hey, Frank, what did we talk about last night?"

"What do you mean, what did we talk about?"

"We didn't talk about getting married, did we?"

"I don't know—I was pretty wasted."

"So was I. When I woke up this morning, I felt like I had talked about getting married. But I couldn't remember who I talked to!

I'm a real burnout sometimes."

"You were afraid we got engaged?"

"Well, yeah—I wasn't sure. I can remember bein' real serious at the time."

"But you couldn't remember who you were with."

"I was with all of yuh at one time or another." And apparently, she looked him in the eye. "I could never marry you. You know that, right?"

"You let me walk out on my father for nothin'?"

"What are you talking about? I've been telling you all along!"

"I said I'd give it up for you. Did you think I was kidding?"

"Give what up?"

"Bein' a garbage—bein' in waste removal!"

"What does that have to do with me?"

"Everything! You touched me on the cheek, remember? You touched me right here!"

I could picture him raising his hand to his cheek.

"I told yuh right to your face—I can't see myself with a gar-bage man!"

"That was before!"

"OK, I'm tellin' yuh now, once and for all. We're just friends! We're not gettin' married!" And then she described the look on Frank's face, and how he was holding back the tears. "Are you all right?"

"I don't think I can go on seein' you," he replied softly.

She concluded the discussion with the remark she had used on my friend, having forgotten that I had heard it before. "Gee, Frank, that's a shame. I was really enjoyin' your company."

———

By then, Mike had already filled Teresa in on my love for Sarah Sloane.

When I look back on the depth of my emotion for Sarah—and the uninvited feelings that I encouraged myself to sustain—it is impossible for me to forget the surprise of my friends. Certainly my housemate was unimpressive in her appearance, lacking in warmth, and fearful of getting too close; but she had a certain quality that got to me early on, and that activated a protective instinct that I had no idea I possessed. Once that happened, the more lighthearted feelings that I experienced initially crossed the line into something improper, and I had my heart set on rescuing Sarah as a human being, an impossible objective if ever there was one.

Now that I had experienced the palpability of Sarah's gloom—and had been touched by her circumstances—it no longer mattered that I hadn't been attracted to her at the outset, and I began to look at her differently. I had no right to be proud of a breakthrough of that nature, but the physical characteristics that had repelled me at the beginning of our relationship had begun to attract me instead, although it was several months before I realized the unhealthiness of the attraction and how dependent it was on the belief that she was helpless.

Night after night, she would wrap herself in a sweater and brood, occupying a couch in our living room. Despite the fact that it was a shabby piece of furniture, Sarah claimed it as her own, sitting cross-legged, painting her toenails, and holding her head at a painful angle in order to press a telephone to her ear. Even though she applied the wildest nail polish she could find, it never relieved her gloom or prevented the lethargy from returning; and once the listlessness recurred, the color of her toenails became incongruous, as though it was far too lively for a person such as herself. While she sat there, she would chain-smoke and leaf through fashion magazines with the materials for her master's thesis in front of her, neglecting the project for the second consecutive year. As the weeks passed, the possibility that she would complete the thesis became more and more remote, until the degree eluded her entirely.

Within a month of my arrival, I obtained an abandoned wooden spool from the phone company and converted it into a living room table. With that in mind, I persuaded Joe McBride to leave his foul-smelling mutt at home and drive me over to the old Bell Telephone lot across from the 30th Street train station. Proceeding carefully—and looking up and down the tracks for oncoming locomotives—McBride and I heaved one of the spools onto the bed of his truck, a process in which I faked my way through the act of hoisting and allowed Joe to do most of the work. Once Joe completed the task, I repaid him by making free cheesesteaks for his friends (never bothering to put any money in the cash register at Mr. Martin's), and Sarah took to spreading her thesis materials out on the table. Not only did the latest addition to our living room fit right in with our sorry-looking sofa—which had recently lost still another section of upholstery and several cubic feet of foam—but it provided Sarah with another flat surface to work with. Despite the fact that she promptly covered the table with issues of *Mademoiselle*, she never failed to open one of her textbooks to the same chapter as the night before and dutifully underline its most significant passages, employing a series of highlighter colors that were every bit as garish as her nail polish.

Sarah was helpless in the face of my attention and so afraid of the world that she had to let me help her, despite the fact that my assistance weakened her all the more. Although she never fell in love or encouraged a sexual relationship, the experience of living with her approximated the domestic harmony that I had lost in my parents' divorce. As satisfying as that was, however, I continued to pay a heavy price for the experience by agreeing to be her husband until bedtime, an act of emasculation that I was unable to resist. The masochistic pleasure of loving her would always be substantial—and would enable me to fool myself into thinking that I was involved with someone when I wasn't—but I realized that the relationship was deficient. In the end, its protracted nature might have been the most powerful inducement of all, since it enabled me to go for months without putting myself on the line sexually.

As it turned out, my time in Sarah's house was also characterized by the strange ritual of hopping from one section of the hardwood floor to another while removing my work clothes. This was a pathetic attempt to protect the shag carpet from the rank odors of the restaurant. Ever since I had salvaged the carpet from my mother's apartment, I had exhibited the dubious behavior pattern of dragging it with me from one living arrangement to another in an effort to preserve at least a shred of the luxury that I had enjoyed in high school; and now that I had lugged it to a total of three houses before laboriously dragging it up the steps on 22nd Street, the cherished but shrinking remnant had become progressively more stained and threadbare. Despite my best efforts to preserve it, the last vestige of luxury had left the carpet long ago, even though I had developed the habit of removing my sneakers and hopping from one uncarpeted section of the room to another while tearing off my pants. Once my olfactory nerves adequately processed the secondary odors of onions, peppers, stale pizza sauce, and canned tuna, it became obvious that the ragged pair of blue jeans bore the unmistakable scent of raw garbage. At the time, however, I was operating on the belief that my strange little dance would enable me to avoid the carpet, and that I would be able to wipe down the floor and remove the telltale odors. As far as I was concerned, it was absolutely essential that I prevented the odors from getting into the carpet, because the minute they did there was nothing I could do, since my preliminary inquiries into renting a carpet cleaner from the Shop n' Bag on Girard Avenue made it clear that the cost was prohibitive. If I had been the least bit flexible on this issue, the carpet might have been in better shape, but I was unwilling to dip into my screwdriver money and alter a routine in which I spent all of my gratuities on bar-hopping until the last three days of each month, when I curbed my spending in order scrape together my $100 share of the rent.

After working all night at the hoagie shop, I wasn't always

successful in avoiding the carpet entirely and some of the scents were inevitably transferred from my sweaty feet to the beloved shag carpet from my mother's apartment, and the strange little dance didn't end until I removed all of the malodorous clothing and balled it up in an uncarpeted corner. Once I accomplished that, I could wrap a towel around my waist and walk down the steps to the only bathroom in the house, hoping upon hope that my hairy chest would finally get to Sarah.

In addition to my refusal to rent a carpet cleaner, the ingrained frugality of my father found its way into the schedule I devised for going to the neighborhood laundromat. This schedule was constructed upon the necessity of making my four or five hand-me-down towels last as long as my two bed sheets. All too often, this required me to dry myself with towels that hadn't been clean for a week and sleep in bed linens that had been soiled for twice as long. And though the strategy may have saved me a few dollars over the course of my adhering to it, I hadn't counted on the nasty case of impetigo that I came down with in its second or third month. At that point, I had to do a mad juggling act with my budget, avail myself of the laundromat more frequently, and consult the Physician's Referral Service at Jefferson Hospital. As soon as I described my complaint, the service representative informed me that Dr. Patrick Mullin maintained a small office two or three doors down from the Pennsylvania School of Ballet, and Dr. Mullin immediately recognized the nasty looking rash for what it was and prescribed an antibiotic cream for me to smear across the afflicted area on the bridge of my nose. Not only did the antibiotic clear up my rash, but it ended the brief, two-day period in which Sheldon Greenblatt cut into my income even more by refusing to allow me to prepare the food and limiting my role to deliveries. Later, after the hilarity of my relationship with Billy McDevitt caused me to lose my concentration at the meat slicer one day, I was forced to run dripping to Dr. Mullin once again and the kindly physician stanched the blood, stitched me up, and sent me on my way.

It was during the same period of time that I began to torture my hair with a blow dryer, straightening out the kinks as best I could and using a brush and comb to arrange the bangs just so. For some unaccountable reason, I believed that I looked better when my eyebrows were raised and my forehead was less pronounced. Once I realized the physical impossibility of contorting my face, stretching my skin, and walking around with raised eyebrows, the bangs represented the next best option. Almost immediately, this realization led to a routine in which I would come home from Mr. Martin's at 10:30 on a Friday night, hop around my room to avoid the shag carpet, remove the work clothes, and walk past Sarah's room with one of the towels wrapped around my waist, taking my shower, blaring Elvis Costello, blow-drying my hair, and combining a white shirt with blue jeans.

Although I succeeded in turning that particular combination into a fashion statement, it must be said that it proved to be wholly unoriginal after I stole it from Tom Goffman, whose father Erving had published a scholarly work with the no-nonsense title of *Deviance*. Looking back on it, I had forgotten that Tom's ability to impress others was entirely dependent on the fact that he was strikingly handsome and blessed with one of the more silken varieties of blond hair, a physical attribute that did not require excessive primping in front of a mirror. At that time, I didn't realize that even without the blue jeans and white shirt, Goffman possessed an animal magnetism that I never could have aspired to.

At any rate, this routine of blaring Elvis Costello led to a night in which Sarah had to knock on my door as vigorously as she was able, the only means by which she could inform me that someone was asking for me on the phone. In the process of doing that, Sarah bruised her hand and elicited a sharp pang of protectiveness in me as I stood there with my hair in disarray, the patches sticking out from my head at odd angles, not yet plastered down by my regimen of strategically arranging them. But instead of mocking me or laughing aloud, my housemate stood there in perfect self-possession, glancing at my hair for only a second before lowering her gaze politely, smiling just a little as she rubbed her hand, and delivering the message while the tenderness I had felt a moment before gave way to a slight erection under the towel that was still wrapped around my waist. In the end, I was able to thank her and close the door at the same time before the erection gathered steam and caused the towel to fall to the floor, by which time Sarah was safely down the stairs and well on her way to her room, where she consulted her medical encyclopedia to determine if anything catastrophic could occur in a human hand after strenuously knocking on a door.

By approximately 11:30, I would consume three or four screwdrivers in less than thirty minutes at Chaucer's, look up and down the bar for unattached females, and visit for a period of time with Derrick Moore if I failed to identify a woman that I had the courage to approach. For years, I had marveled at Derrick's tendency to occupy the first table, eye the young women as they entered, and fearlessly address them when he found them sufficiently attractive. Somehow, he injected enough charm into the brazen remark that he had established as his signature phrase—"Where do you think you're going? You have to report in."—that he was able to win them over, with a high percentage of them lagging behind their girlfriends, pausing at his table, and flirting for a moment before making their way up the aisle.

In turn, Derrick converted a high percentage of these flirtations into an opportunity to invite the women to sit down, causing them to forsake their girlfriends entirely until the girlfriends declared their intention of leaving. At that point, the young women would interrupt the backrub that Derrick had also charmed them into providing for the five or ten seconds it took them to tell their friends that they intended to stay, risking their disapproval not only because Derrick was handsome but because he was a well-adjusted individual who was sincerely interested in other people's lives. In reversing their original impression of him as a vulgar pick-up artist, it didn't hurt that his twenty years as a social worker with violent, court-adjudicated young men had enabled him to develop the listening skills, counseling ability, and unflappable nature that made a conversation with him memorable.

A guy named Michael Greenburg witnessed more than his share of Derrick's barroom encounters, as the two of them often sat together. Michael called Derrick "Deke" when no one else did and won me over by uttering a classic witticism. "I'm half-Jewish and half-Italian," he said. "If I can't steal it, I can get it for you wholesale." I had actually introduced myself to Michael before I realized that he and Derrick were friends, when he let out an infectious laugh from the front of the bar and I just had to introduce myself to whoever was responsible.

After several more screwdrivers, I would walk out of the bar and head down Lombard Street until I found a garage door open on one of the little row houses. There, I would smoke the poorly rolled joint that I had stashed in my pocket for that purpose, returning to Chaucer's for one or two more drinks before making the nightly decision of whether I had laid enough groundwork with any of the women to justify my foregoing J.C. Dobbs for the evening. If I hadn't made the necessary progress, I would drive the fifteen or twenty blocks to Dobbs, where the decibel level was higher and conversation was more difficult and the women were a little rougher than the girl-next-door types that represented the best that Chaucer's had to offer. Many of the women at Dobbs were loosely connected to the same motorcycle gang that had produced the bouncer Fergus, although on Saturday nights you would occasionally find a group of coeds from St. Joseph's, Cabrini, or Immaculata College slumming there, drawn to the place by the quality of the live entertainment.

As it turned out, the groundwork that I laid with the young women at Chaucer's would have to be particularly promising for me to forego J.C. Dobbs for even a single evening. Not only did the music generate a certain amount of excitement, but Dobbs offered the additional inducement of being a loosely run establishment. Only a half-hearted effort was made, for example, to prevent a person from firing up a joint in the men's room; and even then, the only real danger arose when Fergus bellowed through the locked door. Although his urgency arose more from a need to relieve himself than from any real fear of Dobbs being shut down, he never failed to give you a dirty look if he detected the unmistakable scent of cannabis as he moved to unzip his pants.

Because of Fergus's obesity, laziness, and seeming unconcern for narcotics regulations, he rarely forced himself to vacate the stool that he occupied just inside the front door, faithfully manning his post until he felt a need to empty his bladder. His main responsibility, of course, was to "card" people when they entered; but he found the responsibility distasteful. Not only did it require him to read hundreds of driver's licenses with a flashlight—which left him with a severe case of eye strain the next day—but he was also expected to turn people away at the door, something that he couldn't bring himself to do in the case of an attractive woman. Not surprisingly, the cover charge was a problem as well. Although he recognized the fact that it was a matter of some significance to the owner, he tended to enforce it in an arbitrary manner, collecting differing amounts on a case-by-case basis. Depending on the gender of the individual, the amount of sleep he had gotten the night before, and the somewhat quixotic moods of his girlfriend, the cover charge was liable to vary by as much as five dollars; but if you wanted to get in, you were forced to hand over the money.

There was an even greater laxity higher up in the chain of command, and Fergus may only have been following orders. Immediately above him was a man named John Tyler, a pretty boy with a suntan, the droopy handlebar moustache of a porn star, and a rather alarming taste for cocaine and under-aged girls. Any even-handed examination of Fergus's performance would have to take these predilections into account. Although she may have had an axe to grind, Tyler's ex-girlfriend contended that he had gotten away with his casual management style for more than a year before the coke habit overtook him and before the musicians no longer found it acceptable to be paid off in groupies rather than in currency that could be spent elsewhere. In fairness, however, Tyler was always kind enough to me, having committed my favorite drink to memory after my second or third visit and taken it upon himself to be overly generous with the amount of vodka he mixed with the orange juice.

Due to the loose atmosphere of the establishment, the amount of money I spent there, and my apparent success at contributing to their reputation, it soon became possible for me to turn the men's room it into my own private club, ducking into it for minutes at a time in order to get high with an odd assortment of characters that I had met along the way. This continued until I developed a friendship with a freeloader named Harold McTeer, a tall, goateed individual who never failed to be delighted whenever I bought him a Courvoisier at the upstairs bar and turned him on to some of Joe McBride's pot. And though I got him drunk and stoned many times (the two best things straight men could do for each other in a bar-hopping culture), Harold never really hit pay dirt until I drove him past the Arco refinery, directed him to hold his nose as we approached a sewage treatment plant, and conveyed him to the end of the Schuylkill Expressway, where I led him to the greasy front counter of the Dog Cart, schooled him in the complexities of the menu, and invited him to order anything he wanted. This rare sign of largesse enabled him to consume two hot dogs with everything at three in the morning, and before I knew it Harold was dripping ketchup, mustard, relish, onions, and chili sauce onto the already compromised front seat of my car, hunching up his shoulders as bits of food fell from the overflow in his mouth (as though the hunching motion would somehow prevent the food from falling or enable him to miraculously catch the food particles in mid-air) and emitting a guttural sound that was unlike anything I had ever heard. This sound turned out to be a phonetic impossibility when I attempted to reproduce it for the amusement of others.

"Damn, these suckers are good!" Harold pronounced finally, holding the last two inches of a hot dog at arm's length and regarding it in a studious manner, a pink sliver of meat peeking out from the bite marks on the bun. Once he finished eating, he removed a preposterously expensive handkerchief from the pocket of his tattered sports jacket and dabbed away at a fleck of relish that was clinging stubbornly to his lower lip, passing judgment with pure epicurean delight. "What did you say that was—the Dog Cart? They got some righteous hot dogs!"

By then, of course, I was frequenting chop suey joints, dive bars, and other holes in the wall, and the Dog Cart was one of them.

Despite the fact that I was falling in love with Teresa, I never did anything about it, save for the occasional breadcrumb that I left for her to follow. The first of these occurred when we were saying goodnight to one another at the house I shared with Sarah. I was reclining on our couch when Teresa reached for her pocketbook.

"Don't leave me," I said. "I'm lonely."

This may have surprised her, but she recovered quickly enough.

"D'yuh want me to lay down with yuh?" she asked, and my only option was to force a smile.

"No, that's OK. I'll see yuh t'morrah."

Until I answered, she had no idea that I was terrified of her sexually.

"All right, Mark, if that's the way you want it."

Teresa's pride prevented her from offering herself a second time, but she found different ways to deliver the same message, like the time she called me at Mr. Martin's to ask for my advice about Frank.

"I don't know, Teresa, it's been so long since I've been involved with someone, I can't really comment on that."

"You're involved with *me*," she said quickly, and I felt an immediate surge of electricity, a jolt of excitement that eclipsed everything else. "Mark, are you there?"

"I'm here," I said.

"Did I say something wrong?"

"No, you didn't."

"I'm glad. I'll see yuh later."

———————

Now that she had scrambled all of my thinking—and I was incapable of rational thought—I accepted an invitation to spend Easter Sunday with her. I realized that a family gathering would be instructive, and that it would enable me to understand her to a greater degree, but I had no idea that I would lose a little more of myself in the emotion she engendered. Without my even realizing it, she had drawn us forward, well past the partying, until we came to share minor events such as these and I began to succumb to the magic of doing things as a couple.

When I arrived at her parents' home in Barrington—a dingy little town on the South Jersey side of the Walt Whitman Bridge— her father roused himself from the television, padded to the front door in his slippers, and greeted me with the wrongheaded confidence of a man who was out of his depth in nearly every situation, provided the circumstances did not involve the mind-numbing repetition of pipefitting.

"You must be Mike!" he cried, committing the gaffe with an almost heartbreaking gregariousness before his daughter could intercept him, save him from himself, and spare me the shock of remembering that I still had a friend in New Orleans, a fact that I had somehow forgotten over the past several weeks. While Teresa applied the finishing touches to an outfit that took me apart and put me back together again—in this case a delicate pearl necklace that drew attention to the perfect femininity of her clavicle—I was forced to express the precise spot that I occupied in the growing constellation of young men that she had mentioned or brought around.

"No, actually, I'm Mark. Mike's a friend of mine."

Ralph paused now, still a second or two away from realizing that he had blown it, although his suspicions had certainly been aroused. "I don't think she told me about you. Maybe she told her mother."

Before I could apply myself to the problem that his remark created, Teresa descended the steps from the second floor. "I was savin' the best for last," she said, smiling radiantly and with absolutely no idea that she had slighted my friend. "Mark, howya doin'?"

"I'm doin' fine," I said softly, as Teresa kissed me in an ambiguous manner. It wasn't sexual, but it wasn't platonic either, and it carried with it the possibility that she had restrained herself out of respect for her father. But at that moment, as I lowered my gaze to her cleavage (a part of her anatomy that boldly defied the religious holiday), I experienced the sort of erection that typically occurred on specific occasions with Sarah, when a remark, a gesture, or a facial expression made Sarah seem vulnerable. With Teresa, of course, I was the vulnerable one, and there was nothing of the damsel-in-distress dynamic that I experienced with the other woman I loved.

When Teresa disappeared into the kitchen with her parents—keeping me quiet with the decidedly inferior sports section of the *Camden Courier Post*—it became obvious that her father still hadn't given up on the idea that I was Mike. Despite vigorous attempts to set him straight by the women with whom he was living, Ralph persisted in defending his own recollection in a conversation that was distinctly audible from the living room, although there were one or two instances in which I had to strain to hear their discussion over the sound of a Japanese horror movie.

"I know just who he is!" Ralph declared, contradicting his earlier statement that Teresa had failed to mention me.

"Come on—you have no clue!" Teresa followed, at which point her mother joined the fray. Somehow, she managed to defend her husband and insult her daughter at the same time.

"How could he? There's a million of 'em!"

Cringing at this calculation of her boyfriends, I nevertheless searched for the remote control, so that I could turn down the volume on Godzilla and make myself miserable with further developments in the kitchen.

"He has a friend in the Air Force," Ralph continued, confusing Mike with Ed and erring on Ed's military affiliation.

"No, Dads."

"No? Not in the Air Force?"

"'fraid not," Teresa replied. "The friend's workin' for his father."

"Whereabouts?"

"In New Orleans."

"That's right! I told yuh I remembered!"

The next voice was Lorraine's, as only an unhappy spouse could achieve such a mocking tone. "No, you didn't. You got it all wrong, Ralph."

"I don't see you rememberin' nothin'."

"Why bother?"

Once she emerged from the kitchen, Lorraine addressed me directly. "Mark, I'm so embarrassed. I made a ham!"

"That's OK. Don't worry about it."

"But you don't *eat* ham!" Lorraine said sadly, thrusting out her lower lip. All at once, I realized that Teresa's pouty, little girl expression had descended directly from her mother.

"I'm sure I'll find something to eat."

Now that I had defused the situation with his wife, Ralph rewarded me with a slap on the back. "What are yuh drinkin'?"

"Whaddayuh got?"

"Terry said you like screwdrivers," Ralph followed, and the two women in his life startled me by gazing at him fondly. There was hell to pay on the frequent occasions on which he fucked up, but apparently things could be lovey-dovey again in a heartbeat.

"That would be correct," I replied modestly.

"Can I fix yuh one?"

"You better fix him two," Teresa frowned, not without a certain pragmatism.

"Teresa, help me with my puh-tay-tuhs," Lorraine said suddenly.

"Aw, Mom, you know I hate to cook!"

"Come on, it'll only take a second."

Instead of interrogating me on my intentions toward his daughter, Ralph mixed the screwdriver, handed it to me, and waited for me to taste it.

"How's that drink?" he asked.

"It's great."

"Did I put enough vodka in there?"

"I don't know. It's too early to tell."

With that, Ralph stretched out on the floor, turned his back to me, and balanced on his side to look up at the television. As he rested his head on his hand, he looked like a child in the unabashed simplicity of his soul. Although he lacked the streetwise intelligence of his daughter and the bitter cunning of his wife, it was easier to respect him as a gentle and straightforward human being, though I had to admit that I was distracted by his proximity to the television. This would have been a real problem had he been watching a ballgame instead of the mindlessly fake destruction of a badly rendered Japanese city, a completely unbelievable annihilation by an oversized, web-footed monster that owed its very existence to crude 1960s special effects and a viewing audience that had never grown up.

Left to my own devices, I began to ruminate on the whole crazy dynamic of the Devlin family, which seemed to begin and end with the irresistible force of nature that Teresa's mother seemed to be. Although she was an undersized little thing, I had gathered enough anecdotal evidence to suggest that I shouldn't be taken in by the fact that Lorraine had been nothing but nice to me so far. On our many nights together, Teresa had recounted the entire sordid affair, and even when I factored in Teresa's bitter subjectivity I felt confident that her description was accurate. By then, a picture had already emerged in which Lorraine had been irrevocably altered by the medical problems of her son, Teresa's brother Vince having undergone a number of surgeries for a cleft lip before the age of five. Apparently, the intense sympathy that developed between Lorraine and her first child became difficult for her subsequent children to penetrate, with the result that Teresa and her older sister Donna had been forced to share whatever of Lorraine's infrequent kindness remained. By the time I grasped the full extent of the Devlin family bitterness—and formed even a tentative sense of their pecking order—I developed certain suspicions where my love interest was concerned, and these suspicions were followed by the hypothesis that Lorraine's love for Teresa was a dotted line and that men like me were given the task of filling in the blanks. Of course, at that point I was still in the early stages of my relationship with Teresa and the task was a happy one, and Teresa was drawing me along toward the darkness of what was really waiting for me, as she had with my friend Mike and all the other young men who preceded us.

In addition to the multiple surgeries that had been inflicted upon Vince, Lorraine was only slightly more at peace with her economic lot in life, the house she lived in, and the address she called home. In the past several years, she had worked her way up from a waitress job only to find that she was still married to a stooge, and despite the fact that she had left her girlfriends and their sore feet behind to accept a position in the home furnishings department at Sears and Roebuck in the Moorestown Mall, the dignified effect of her moving up in the world was obliterated by her almost comical kewpie doll voice. Although the position at Sears enabled her to entertain pretensions of being a lady, she emitted a high-pitched sound whenever she attempted to speak, and for that reason it was hard to take her seriously. Short of radical surgery on her larynx—which no respectable physician would have performed—she had realized a long time ago that there was nothing she could do about the fact that she sounded like Betty Boop on helium; but that didn't prevent her from working away relentlessly at the things she could attempt to control, like the near idiocy of her husband, the flagrant behavior of her daughter, and the financial ceiling that she faced in her work at Sears. In fact, for the past several months she had been taking a real estate course in the hope of obtaining a license and had been shooting off her mouth during particularly malevolent family quarrels about the possibility of leaving her husband and moving to Myrtle Beach, South Carolina, a modest destination that for some reason represented the height of glamour to Lorraine. With it all, however, her preoccupation with the course could not adequately explain the shared failure of Lorraine and her daughter to have so much as a cup of coffee together in the six months that Lorraine had been working at Sears, even though the Western Union switchboard that Teresa operated five nights a week was less than a mile away.

"You'll meet my son later on," Lorraine stated, when she and Teresa emerged from potato duty in the kitchen.

"That'll be nice. I've heard a lot about him," I said, scrupulously withholding the fact that Teresa had denigrated Vince every chance she got.

Despite the fact that observing her with her family was a sobering experience, I felt a rush of warmth toward Teresa when Lorraine finally greeted Vince. This greeting was so effusive—and the disparity between that particular emotion and the one that she had offered Teresa was so great—that I felt a little dazed, particularly when I watched Teresa as she peered across the room. More than anything else, she looked like a sad little girl, although there was nothing childish about her lush red lip, which she began to bite as Lorraine and Vince embraced, completely unaware of my presence and seeming less than tough-minded for the first time. Then, as if to drive home the point that she adored Vince and found Teresa wanting, Lorraine crossed the room to embrace Brenda, Vince's wife. It was perfectly obvious that Brenda had never been a source of displeasure to Lorraine, and that Brenda had surpassed Teresa in Lorraine's estimation.

"Vince, this is Mark," Lorraine said happily. "He's a friend of Teresa's."

Vince shook my hand with a crushing grip; then he greeted his sister.

"Hi, Ter'. How's it goin'?"

"Good, Vince, how's it goin' for you?" But there was no emotion in it for either of them.

A moment later, they introduced me to Brenda, a young woman so sweet, soft spoken, and self-possessed that you couldn't help but like her, traits that caused me to adjust my view of her husband. There must have been a whole other side to Vince, a side in which the hard-ass met the humanizing influence of a woman's love.

When it came to Brenda, however, I had obviously miscalculated. All of my logic told me that Teresa would behave poorly toward her by way of Brenda's close association with Vince, but nothing could have been further from the truth. Before they even greeted one another, Teresa's gaze fell on Brenda's earrings and she rushed over to her and took one of the earrings in her hand. She did this in a supremely gentle fashion, drawing her shoulders together ever so slightly, leaning forward, and lifting Brenda's earlobe with three of her fingers. "Bren'," she said, "they're so cute!"

Just as Teresa inherited the pouty expression from her mother, her ability to know what a man was thinking may also have been passed along, for at that moment Lorraine suggested that Ralph replace the horror movie with a ballgame. "You're a big sports fan, aren't you, Mark?"

"Oh, yeah. I used to hide a transistor radio under my pillow."

"When you were a kid?" Lorraine followed.

"No, Moms—when he was on his honeymoon."

Lorraine glared at Teresa while Vince burst out laughing.

"You were married, Mark?"

Lorraine was concerned now. Vince touched her elbow lightly. "They were kidding."

Lorraine glanced from Teresa to me, exploding into nervous laughter. "Oh, my God! How stupid can I be?"

"Do you really want to know?" Teresa sneered, falling silent as Vince and I joined forces to shoot her a dirty look.

As it happened, Brenda's presence in the kitchen shamed Teresa into helping out as well, while Vince and his father joined me in front of the television. There was very little conversation between them, but it was obvious that they were comfortable with each other, sipping their beers, passing a basket of pretzels around, and offering the occasional prediction on what may or may not transpire in the game. Unfortunately, most sports fans reveal their ignorance in making these predictions, and there always seems to be someone a row or two behind you who gets it all wrong at the stadium, calling for a bunt with the cleanup hitter at the plate, pleading for a double play when there are already two outs, or botching an explanation of the infield fly rule to an impressionable child.

During their first few years together—when they were as happy as Teresa and I were that day—Lorraine had gotten Ralph involved with their local parish, and had provided him with a set of minor responsibilities that made him feel more important than he was. But as Lorraine became more ashamed of him, she withdrew from the church incrementally, leaving Ralph in charge of the softball game at picnics, calling out the numbers at bingo, and safeguarding the collection plate at morning Mass. Teresa and I dropped something off to him at bingo one night, and I'll never forget how proud he looked to be calling out the numbers, settling disputes, and feeling like a big-shot.

For the past several years, Lorraine had skipped most of these functions entirely, going to church only on Christmas and Easter, hedging her bet in the same way that many Jewish people do by attending only on the High Holidays. And when that particular course of action was too scandalous—like the day of a wedding or a funeral—she would hide in a corner so that she could neither see nor hear her husband, and would fight down the embarrassment she felt. Despite her pretensions of being a lady, however, her self-image accommodated a rather voracious appetite for real estate, and by the time she enrolled in the course she had already purchased one dumpy little seaside property and was saving money for another.

Teresa's sister had married her husband ten years before, but after all that time, they couldn't keep their hands off each other, and the physical nature of their relationship took some getting used to. At one point, Keith picked Donna up and swung her around, kissing her as he returned her to the floor. The whole thing was so natural, so spontaneous, and such a picture of healthy sexuality that I was forced to look away. Even Teresa, as physical as she was, had trouble with their demonstrativeness as well, although her reasons were different than mine. The love she felt for her sister was genuine, but her eyes clouded with jealousy and resentment. I realize now that she felt as though she was just as attractive as Donna and couldn't understand why her own life was less successful, conveniently forgetting that Donna was more stable than she was.

For their part, the McCormicks saw me as one of Teresa's strays, though one of the more promising ones she had brought around. In evaluating me as a possible mate—just as Teresa had done when she was still going out with Mike—they looked at the situation more cynically than Lorraine, whose fondest wish would have been for Teresa and me to enjoy a lasting relationship. At the same time that Lorraine experienced a temporary lapse in her negativity in favor of an unaccountable maternal optimism, Keith and Donna doubted that Teresa could pull it off, leaving Ralph as the non-factor he was and Vince a disinterested observer.

In the void created by a weak husband—who failed to offer resistance—Lorraine had placed all of her hopes in Vince, and with that came certain privileges. It was a great setup for a son who could do no wrong, until he considered his sisters, a pair of formidable young women who obviously knew the score. Because they were the only thing that stood between Vince and a free ride emotionally, the presence of his sisters made him exceedingly self-conscious, and he was nearly as bitter as they were. By banking the currency of his many surgical procedures, Vince behaved as though Lorraine's favoritism was well deserved, and he had been behaving that way for almost thirty years. Any late attempts to present interference, correct his behavior, or persuade him to abandon a point of view in which he had it coming to him were met with an unmistakable resentment. And so, their pecking order became apparent early on: Vince was the most highly treasured, followed by Donna (who at least had a husband), with Teresa bringing up the rear, a young woman whose star quality was obvious to all of them but who had given them nothing but grief for years. To assess their bitterness, one simply reversed the order. The entire family dynamic, of course, was presided over by Lorraine, who was locked into an orientation toward her son.

Once we gathered at the table, the Devlins walked a fine line between curiosity and anti-Semitism, although they held that last thing in check with true gentile civility. The greater problem occurred, however, when I let a beautiful piece of ham go to waste, a decision that caused their best intentions to fall apart. When that happened, they began to stare at me until Vince spoke for all of them, talking with his mouth full and pointing with his fork: "You're not gonna eat that?"

"No, he isn't," Teresa followed testily, "and you're gonna hafta deal with it."

Vince's eyes bulged slightly and he waited for himself to swallow. "I am dealin' with it. I don't give a shit."

"And he doesn't give a shit what you're eatin'," Teresa said, regressing to childhood before my very eyes, until her older sister calmed her down.

"Let it go, Teresa. What's the difference?"

"You're right, Don'. Pass the ham."

———

Recollections of my parents' divorce came pouring out of me that night, as well they should have in considering Teresa's remark. My honeymoon, indeed.

In a very real way, my sexual history began when my parents fell apart, and my response to that event went a long way toward making me the warped young man that I was. I am referring, of course, to my fundamental distrust of women.

———————

In 1962—when I was eight years old—our parents called us into their bedroom.

"Boys," our father began, "we have something to tell you." And like the gullible child that I was, the hopeless little rube, my eyes lit up with excitement. But at that moment, I happened to turn to my brother Carl. Even then, he was more worldly, and as he glanced at our parents, I realized that something awful was about to happen.

When I think of that day, all I have are fragments—the shards that I haven't blocked out—and even those are purely subjective. The cigarettes, the headache powder, the possibility that the discussion took place in the bedroom—they are entirely plausible if in fact I dreamed them up; but in the end, there is no official version of these events, and I am left with an extrapolation that rings true for me emotionally, whether or not it is accurate.

At this point, I can't even be certain that our mother remained silent for the longest time, and that she allowed our father to do the dirty work; but that is precisely how I remember it. In the part of me that will always remain a child, it was our father who told us about the divorce, while the person who "caused" it said nothing until the worst was over. In the version that I live with—whether or not is it largely an invention—our mother waited until the breakup of our family was revealed before she attempted to speak; and though I concede the fact that she said all of the right things, that particular fragment is missing, and I am left with the rather dubious recollection that she forced our father to do the talking, and that my father and I gravitated toward one another because we were weaker than the other two, because we felt sorry for ourselves, and because a certain empathy had passed back and forth between us.

The rest of that day is a blur, but even without embellishment, I know that in one of their last acts as a married couple, they conveyed the more practical details of the divorce, and that they revealed the arrangements they had been making for weeks, and that the revelations of the day set a chain of events into motion, a devastating sequence in which the house on Rumson Drive was sold; my mother, my brother, and I moved into a cramped little apartment uptown; and our father was banished to a bachelor pad he wanted no part of, a one-bedroom unit at the Towne House Apartments, a couple of blocks from the Family Stamp redemption center on 6th Street. The plan was for our father to swallow his pride and continue to operate the redemption center for Jack and Lena Feldman, the crude, upwardly mobile, and decidedly pretentious cousins of our mother; and he went on to furnish the apartment with items from the Family Stamp catalog, cheering himself up with a subscription to *Playboy*, which he made no attempt to hide, eliciting the salacious interest of my older brother, who tried in vain to distract me with the gorgeous centerfolds and the racy Annie Fannie cartoons, failing in this noble effort when I buried my nose even deeper into the box scores in the *Harrisburg Patriot News*, clinging desperately to my boyhood whenever my brother attempted to unburden me of my adulation of our father, and whenever he tormented me with the truth about our father's late night visits to Sheila DeMarco, a voluptuous but pockmarked divorcee who lived on one of the lower floors of the building, whose household appliances always seemed to require our father's attention when he was tucking us into bed, despite the fact that he had never been the least bit handy when we lived together. At such times, I never failed to infuriate my brother by maintaining a posture of hangdog loyalty to our father and by taking at face value our father's innocuous description of Sheila, leaving my brother without an ally in the mind-blowing trauma of the divorce, frustrating his attempt to exact some measure of revenge from a family dynamic in which my father and I had little league baseball and hockey games at the Hershey Park Sports Arena; my mother had a piece of Harry Pomerantz, our flashy, free-spending neighbor; and my brother had nothing, save for his loneliness, his insecurity, and his glue-sniffing a few years later, until he showed up at the apartment one night in frighteningly bad shape, having been mugged at a Wilson Pickett concert and falsely accused of rape by a classmate in a desperate attempt to conceal an inter-racial romance from her father, who pounded on our door at three in the morning before realizing that my brother was too wasted to get out of bed let alone attack his daughter sexually.

When our mother fell out of love with our complacent, oblivious, and financially conservative father (so oblivious that he taught our parakeet to say "Call the cops!" and "Stand back—I'm an eagle!"), our father was blown away by the shock of her treachery and condemned to a life of backwoods travel to service his accounts and replenish his redemption centers and pore over the books in places like Shamokin, Lewistown, and Salisbury, Maryland, and when I began to comprehend the sadness of his existence (with its "army omelettes" at the Towne House and its solitary meals on the road), I bonded with him to an even greater degree than before, our relationship intensified by our shared victimhood at the hands of my mother. But it was years before I realized that my brother had it just as hard as I did and maybe even harder, since he was forced to experience adolescence without a father to talk to, given the fact that our father had already begun his slow withdrawal from our lives, a steady progression that had been precipitated by the pain of our parents' divorce, a pain that could only be assuaged by distancing himself from his children, since they were such a stark reminder of the woman who had rejected him. But he had started the withdrawal one son at a time, and I was the beneficiary of our father's unconscious need to withdraw from our lives incrementally, since I was still giving him pleasure with my batting average and my fielding prowess and my half-assed commitment to Judaism, activities that my brother had never bought into, preferring to read voraciously whenever the tension at home drove him to a quieter place.

All of this came down in such a way that my brother and I were on our own little islands when our father wasn't around and when I wasn't soaking up our father's love, so that Carl and

I reached out to each other just long enough to engage in hateful, venomous, and nearly apoplectic exchanges in which we teased each other unmercifully, discovered every variation of "fatso" and "big ears," and synthesized all of the pain into a red-faced nuclear war that invariably ended with my hurling a solid object at my brother at the precise moment that he disappeared behind the bathroom door, locking the door behind him, bringing himself to safety, and relishing the sound of the last two or three objects as they bounced harmlessly off the door until my tantrum subsided. The lone exception was that deliciously satisfying occasion on which my brother's timing was slightly off and I was able to hurl a triangular ashtray into the flesh of his right knee, the aerodynamic qualities of that object leaving a three-inch scar that my brother still bears to this day.

This incident and others like it occurred while my mother was being chased around her desk by her employer, an internationally known inventor of soft contact lenses, and while she was pining away for our future stepfather as he attempted to disengage himself from Elaine, his hideously vindictive wife who went on to tie up their divorce in legal proceedings for the next seven years. And it was the same hangdog loyalty that caused me to hold out on my mother when she attempted to move us to Florida in order to be closer to her parents and rendezvous with Harry whenever he audited the Diplomat Hotel, forcing me to choose between my parents in a decision that really wasn't a decision at all, but that nevertheless caused me to become conflicted in a swirling vortex of guilt and resentment. It was clear that I was subjecting my mother to the continued abuse of the Jewish community in Harrisburg, which regarded her as a homewrecker, whispered about her behind her back, and stared at her whenever we entered the R&L Deli in the Uptown Shopping Center. But in the end, the idea of tearing myself away from my father was too much for me to bear, and for several years I held out stubbornly so that I could continue to enjoy a relationship whose lost sweetness had once contained the fact that his hands smelled like talcum powder when they covered mine during the benediction, the fact that we used to travel the back roads together in the summertime, and the fact that I used to stare out the window at the rows of corn, fascinated with the parallelism.

It wasn't until 1968 that I was ready to give up the vindictive pleasure (if that's what it was) of keeping our mother from her parents and from her sporadic interludes with Harry, and of keeping my brother from the promise of a better life (since it couldn't have been any worse for him than it was in Harrisburg). I probably would have maintained that same stubborn posture if our father hadn't married Patricia Huber in 1966 (the year that Richie Allen hit forty home runs), and if he hadn't drifted away from us even more and landed in the arms of a woman whose pent-up sexuality terrified me, whose Catholicism appalled our Bubbie and Zaydie, and whose obvious disapproval caused me to behave cautiously around the only source of filial warmth I could enjoy without constant bickering, with the result that I capitulated to my mother's request and agreed to move to Florida, ending a period in which our mother checked every impulse to assert her authority and overrule the scrawny little boy who held such power over her.

Our mother quit her job as Dr. Kauffman's secretary and we packed up her olive green Pontiac Tempest in June of 1968 (in the middle of Don Drysdale's epic streak of 58 shutout innings), and though our mother was relatively steady in the face of my opposition for the first hundred miles, my pouting finally got to her and she drifted into the lane of a tractor-trailer whose horn blared a second before impact, a collision that sent us spinning out of control on the Baltimore-Washington Beltway, and that left our mother in tears on the side of the road, facing the wrong way in her Tempest, the guilt from the divorce combining with the guilt from the move to Florida, expressing itself all at once, and ushering in the precise moment in our family history in which my brother turned the corner on his adolescence and took a giant step toward becoming a man, comforting my mother, taking over behind the wheel, staring me down in the rear-view mirror, and doing all of the driving the rest of the way, past the Stuckey's restaurants, the racist billboards for South of the Border, and the anticlimactic little tourist trap itself, until we reached the palm trees, the blazing heat of Florida, and the final stretch of highway that would carry us to the spotless, sweet-smelling apartment of our grandparents, with its incomparable breezes and the mustachioed visage of our grandfather, who would go on to replace my father as a source of paternal affection and remove some of the sting of the divorce by teaching me how to fish from the dock of the Twin Towers Apartments, a rather grandiosely named complex consisting of two modest structures with a swimming pool in the middle, an investment masterminded by Jack Feldman. And now, instead of seeing my father on the weekend and occasionally during the week, I was able to enjoy our grandfather every day, walking with him to Eddie's newsstand, where he would buy me copies of the *Sporting News*, and accompanying him to the Polly Davis Cafeteria, where we would wait for my mother and grandmother under a weather-beaten awning, so that antebellum looking black men could serve us hand-carved roast beef and flawlessly smooth mashed potatoes, and where you could help yourself to as much of the sickeningly sweet fruit punch as you wanted, simply by removing a hot, squeaky clean glass from its plastic tray and holding it up to the triggering mechanism on the dispenser without the aid of an adult, the entire rapturous experience topped off with a glass of chocolate milk and a piece of lemon meringue pie, the perfect ending for a fourteen-year-old who was stuck at the age of eight emotionally, and who was suffering the absence of still another man in his life now that his brother had taken a job at Karlin's drug store, discovered diet pills, and become handsome enough to be seduced by Emily Segal, the gorgeous daughter of one of Mr. Karlin's customers, a free-thinking 1960s psychotherapist who encouraged her daughter to express herself sexually, the kind of parental guidance that she was only too happy to oblige, and that enabled my brother to lose his virginity a month or two into his senior year at Miami Beach High School, where he fell in with a group of teenagers who accepted him for who he was, introduced him to marijuana, and persuaded him to dabble in heroin, turning my brother into a stranger who cleaned pounds of pot in our bedroom, sat-cross-legged with a junkie named Bill Farley, and woke me up by poking at me with an album cover, so that my first visual image of the day was a horrific photograph of the albino rock star Edgar Winter, sending me off to Nautilus Junior High School, where jaded teenagers gaped at my wing-tipped shoes, dry-humped in the halls, and tore around Biscayne Bay on $200,000 speed boats.

Within a year, though, Carl would meet Catherine at the University of Florida, and Catherine would insist that he pay attention to his studies, a stipulation that returned my brother to me and banished the stranger that he had become. When Carl emerged, he was in love and full of heart and excelling in English literature; and by the time our grandfather died at the end of Carl's freshman year, Carl had curbed his reckless tendencies, developed a healthier perspective on the divorce, and gained a better understanding of the effect he had on my well-being. The turning point may have been an incident in 1969 when I walked in on Carl and Catherine in the bedroom that we previously shared, interrupted their love-making, and became alarmingly upset. Piecing it together now, I must have realized that Carl had left me behind, and that I would never be as important to him as he was to me; and there is little doubt that I harbored the irrational belief that I had another Sheila Demarco on my hands, an additional example of funny business between a man that I loved and a woman. But the most startling aspect of the situation as Carl relayed it to me years later is that I had buried the incident so completely. Although Carl laughed about it and found it endearing, I immediately recognized it for the revealing thing that it was, and for the sense it made in my sex life. Apparently, I had subjected Catherine to the sort of tantrum that I indulged in up north, but without the aid of an ash tray; and Catherine became upset and felt guilty about the incident for years. And yet when Carl described it to me, I had no recollection of the incident at all.

When it was all said and done, the turbulence that I experienced in my parents' divorce sent me spinning toward a decade of drunkenness, a period in which I obscured the hard truths with alcohol, struggled mightily to acknowledge my need for sex, and overcame my feelings of inadequacy long enough to do something about it. But before I could work it all out, I had to accept the fact that I was behaving badly.

———————

Later that night, I loaded up on corned beef and settled down with *Portnoy's Complaint*. Roth was my go-to guy whenever I needed a dose of reality, but he failed me this time through no fault of his own. With all of our talk of a honeymoon, I was staring at the lie that propped it up; but instead of smothering it, I allowed it to breathe. As I gained confidence with Teresa—believing that I would never have to sleep with her because of my loyalty to Mike—I developed the delusion that I was successful with women, and I attempted to pass myself off that way at every opportunity, despite the fact that I had yet to please a woman sexually.

———————

One night, Morris and I were drinking Cherry Cokes at Mr. Martin's. We had taken out the trash and turned off the lights in the kitchen. Our work was done and we were sitting at the same table that he had "interviewed" me at when I answered Sheldon's ad.

"You was tellin' me 'bout this Karen chick. You slept with her, right?"

"Yeah, I did."

"Den what happened? I know you fucked it up some kinda way."

"Karen moved to California, and she invited me to go with her."

"Damn, man, you didn't go?"

"No, I didn't."

"Dass weak, Mark. Don't bring that weak shit round here."

"It's getting late. Do you want a ride to the subway?"

"Yeah, I'll take a ride. How come you changed the subject?"

When we got to the subway, I tried to explain it to him, shocking myself with my candor. Why Morris, and why then? I have no idea.

"Someday, I'll meet the girl of my dreams and I'll have to confront the fear and risk the possibility that she'll find out the truth. But I've never been able to do that."

"Try bein' a black man. Den you'd have a *real* problem."

"Do you wanna trade places with me?"

"Hell, no!"

"I didn't think so."

———————

Instead of accompanying Karen to Los Angeles—or attempting to sleep with Jane or Teresa—I threw my energy into a hopeless attachment to Sarah Sloane. Of course, I didn't want to admit that it was hopeless until I absolutely had to.

One day, Sarah was sitting in our living room with Sue Abrams, and they didn't realize that I was home.

"What about Mark?" Sue asked, while I descended the steps from the second floor.

"I'd have to wait for him to grow up. I don't think I can do that."

I froze when I heard it, but if I had gone back to my room, they would have been aware of my presence anyway. By the time I joined them, they had no way of knowing what I had heard.

"Mark!" Sarah said. "You're here!"

"Yeah. I got back a little while ago."

I said it as cheerfully as I could, but neither one of them was fooled. They knew from my tone that I had overheard their conversation, and no one said anything until I walked out the door.

———————

Although it is accurate to report that I pined away for Sarah, I was enough of a survivor to throw myself into my social life as well. During that period, I was stupefyingly active, and that made the house on 22nd Street a desirable place to be. This was particularly true on the memorable evening in which Sarah and I had a dinner party and seven different women called me on the phone. The profligacy of my relationships holds a certain interest even now, and provides additional insight into my laughable self-image as a womanizer.

One of the callers was Jennifer Feinman, although we spoke only briefly. Like Martina Blair, Jennifer had no intention of sleeping with me, but she liked to meet me at bars so that she didn't have to sit there alone while making herself available to be picked up by someone else. Initially, of course, I was somewhat offended by this, but once I got over the hurt feelings, I realized that I could willingly accept the tradeoff with the same thing in mind, so that we could arrive at a win-win situation in which neither one of us looked like a loser. I have a vague sense that I can trace the origins of this arrangement, beginning with my one and only attempt to kiss Jennifer at her front door. By refusing to close her eyes—or move her lips even slightly—she had made it perfectly clear that I was the only one who was kissing.

Before I could return to the dinner table, I received a call from Stephanie Pachter, a successful real estate agent who had also remained chaste in my presence. Stephanie had a habit of calling me at all hours of the night to discuss her unrequited feelings for Todd Millstein. Because Todd had made it clear that he wasn't interested in Stephanie, her telephone calls forced me to wrack my brain to find new ways to let her down easily. This state of affairs continued until I phoned her from Chaucer's one night and invited myself over to her apartment. The minute I did, however, Stephanie exhibited a strong preference for initiating the phone calls herself, agreeing to a visit but stating unequivocally that it wouldn't result in our sleeping together. Looking back on it, she probably wasn't surprised that I reversed myself and asked for a rain check.

After the second phone call, Sarah informed me that my food was getting cold, and though I had every intention of behaving like a civilized human being, I had barely sampled the main course when we were interrupted again. This time, Mary McGill was on the line, inviting me to a concert. Ever since Mary introduced herself to me at a party the year before, we shared an appreciation for rock and roll. But for some reason, I wasn't as attracted to Mary as I might have been, and the sexual element went out of it early on. On our second date, she dragged me to a screening of the *Rocky Horror Picture Show*, something that I never would have consented to if Mary hadn't been a lovely human being. But despite my altruistic intentions, I couldn't survive the mental image of her dressed entirely in black, wearing sinister lipstick, and wobbling on spiked heels. Nor could I preserve the original attraction when she took the one physical attribute that I responded to with real enthusiasm (the manner in which her long brown hair descended the front of her blouse) and did something horrible with it, frizzing it out into a disagreeable configuration. At that moment, of course, the horror shifted from the movie title to me. Even when I reminded myself that this was simply a way for Mary to blow off a little steam, I was too much of a snob to want any part of the *Rocky Horror Picture Show*, particularly when Mary and her friend Allison Stein waited for a wedding scene to occur in the script, produced bags of rice from their pocketbooks, and tossed the rice into the air. It wasn't until Mary attempted to press a few grains of rice into my hand that I found it necessary to draw the line, although my repressive behavior didn't prevent her from singing along with Allison to all of the musical numbers, dancing in the aisles when a song called "The Time Warp" appeared on the soundtrack and jostling me repeatedly to get me to show some life.

Now that Mary and I had settled into a "friendship"—the

preferred euphemism for relationships that could not or would not become sexual—Allison Stein had taken to pursuing me behind Mary's back, a development that I might have welcomed if it hadn't evoked so many of the feelings that I was experiencing with Mike. Nor did it help that I was somewhat indifferent to Allison's physical appearance as well, having placed her in the same general category as Mary until her postcard arrived in the mail, a piece of correspondence that featured an obviously phallic image of a woman raising a bright red lipstick to her mouth and parting her lips suggestively. And now, on the night of our dinner party, Allison called to see if I had gotten it. I had "gotten" it all right, but I had no intention of hurting Mary.

While Sarah served dessert—an ice cream cake from Carvel's that she had directed me to pick up that afternoon—I received a call from Colleen Hanratty. Despite the fact that Colleen towered over me by several inches, she had not ruled out the possibility of our sleeping together, provided that we could accomplish it on a night when her six-foot-five brother wasn't sleeping on her couch after a night of barhopping with Fred Carter. Before they had joined the coaching staff at Mount Saint Mary's College, Tom Hanratty had established himself as a basketball legend in Philadelphia's Catholic League while Fred Carter had become a star player on the worst team ever assembled in the National Basketball Association, a Philadelphia 76ers squad that was improperly coached by a nobody named Roy Rubin. As every Philadelphia sports fan of a certain age will tell you, an act of convoluted nepotism on the part of the 76ers' clueless owner Irv Kosloff had lifted Rubin from the junior college ranks and placed him on a stage on which he could do nothing but fail; and the pudgy, underwhelming little man had lasted only a year in the NBA and finished with a 9-73 record, but not before he lent a certain fascination to the evening in which Colleen invited me back to her apartment on Spruce Street and we encountered her brother and his oversized friend. At that moment, of course, I experienced the profound confusion of whether I should have sex with a man's sister or ask him for his autograph; but Colleen solved the moral dilemma by ushering me out of her apartment as politely as she could and promising that she would call, which is precisely what she did on the night of our dinner party.

Within minutes of my hanging up with Colleen, I heard from Migdalia Rodriguez, whom I had boldly kissed in Sarah's presence at O'Neal's Tavern while Sarah conversed with Todd Millstein, Todd's eyes glossing over with sadness at the depths to which I had sunk after introducing myself to Migdalia less than a minute before. Todd had no way of knowing that Migdalia would reward my impertinence by allowing me to drive her to the Chestnut Cabaret and lift her breast out of a sun-dress while her girlfriends waited for her to arrive, Migdalia looking down at her breast as I held it, blinking her dark brown eyes, looking up at me, and saying "Oh, my goo'ness" in her exotic Panamanian accent. Despite her promising response, however, Migdalia rejected my suggestion that she abandon her girlfriends and return with me to 22nd Street, where I hoped to reinstate the sexual confidence that I gained with Karen and misplaced with Jane. Ultimately, this change in direction caused my housemates to awaken the next morning to the violation of our breakfast table, which held a copy of *Deviance*, a balled-up wrapper from a McDonald's quarter pounder, the crumbled remains of a "congo bar" from Koffmeyer's Bakery, and the first six digits of Migdalia's phone number, the seventh digit having disappeared into the drunkenness of her handwriting.

By the time the evening ended, I spoke with Rebecca Savitz as well, a young woman who had been dating Peter Sullivan. Peter had been a friend of Sarah's for years; and Sarah had asked me to provide him with a list of nightclubs. In its original configuration, the plan was for Peter to escort Sarah and Rebecca to one of the nightclubs on the list; but because I outdid myself in completing my assignment, the handsome but socially backward graduate student made the mistake of inviting me along to even out the gender balance. Needless to say, he couldn't have known that I would accompany them to "Oldies Night" at Grendel's Lair, consume six or seven screwdrivers, and make a pass at his girlfriend. By waiting patiently for Peter to ask Sarah to dance—and for the two long-time friends to disappear onto the dance floor—I was able to gaze into Rebecca's eyes in a suggestive manner, a cynical calculation that enabled me to neck with her for the entire duration of "Tears on My Pillow" by Little Anthony and the Imperials. When the song came to an end, Rebecca terminated the necking session abruptly, complaining that she felt as though she were back in high school. Although she was visibly annoyed that I had sat there kissing her for as long as I had, she was unaware that my own high school experience had left a lot to be desired, and that my paralyzing fear had caused me to miss the necking, groping, and fumbling with bra straps entirely. If I had offended her, however, the resentment wore off in plenty of time for her to slip me her phone number before Peter returned to the table. Later, after Rebecca and I had absolutely no additional contact, she shocked me by inviting me to stay with her while she settled into her job at Citibank in New York, and compounded the stupefying improbability of the invitation by telling one of her girlfriends about me. As it turned out, I would have had no way of knowing about the girlfriend if a young woman hadn't approached me out of the blue two or three weeks later, introduced herself as a friend of Rebecca's, and asked me to dance, the absolute absurdity of my dancing with my hands behind my back causing her to lean forward, shout in my ear, and make herself heard over the music. And then, as if that weren't enough, Rebecca's friend shocked me again, saying "She told me you had an incredible body and now I can see why." In the end, the entire heady experience added oxygen to the preposterous belief that I was a philanderer, and I continued to ignore the fact that I had been largely unsuccessful as a lover.

When the barrage of phone calls ended, I had to decide which of the women to meet at a bar for drink, a decision that was surprisingly difficult when seven different women were involved. On the surface, of course, I had to determine which of the relationships was likely to become sexual, and how quickly that would occur; but there was also the possibility that my cowardice would return. Eventually, I realized that the decision had to be based on their various psychological profiles, and that I couldn't decide immediately. As I came to that conclusion, though, Sue Abrams interrupted my deliberations, breaking the silence with her familiar New York accent. "Jeez Louise," she said, "it's like Grand Central Station in here!"

Sarah reacted enthusiastically to this, throwing her head back and laughing, and a feeling of pride came over me. But in the end, her enthusiasm had a dispiriting effect. More than anything else, it proved that she wasn't interested in me romantically. Although I had injected a certain liveliness into her life, and can look back at the house as the command center of my bachelorhood—a sentiment that offers a certain nostalgic pleasure—I realize just how troubled my bachelorhood actually was. In the final analysis, however, none of it distracted me from Teresa for very long, not even Sarah once Teresa staked her claim.

———

In still another manifestation of the glory days of my youth (so gruesome to me in retrospect), I developed the laughable habit of inviting women over for dinner and preparing the same meal every time. On each of these occasions, I offered a highly derivative menu that I had gleaned from the veal marsala at Ralph's, the fettucini alfredo at Villa di Roma, and a frozen package of green beans with almonds, a side dish that I had picked up from my mother. But if I had any chance at all of impressing these women and getting them into bed, I carelessly gave it away by consuming screwdrivers throughout the cooking process, one or two of them while doing my best to soften the cheapest veal I could find, another while immersing a box of Ronzoni pasta in boiling water, and still another while poking at the block of frozen vegetables in order to pry them apart, my drunkenness linked not only to the screwdrivers but to the sickeningly sweet marsala wine that

I swigged directly from the bottle. By then, I was cooking each of the three major components of the meal too quickly, and the burners of our gas range were being pressed to their limits as I hurried to complete the preparations. It is likely that each of my dates was charmed by the fact that I had taken it upon myself to cook for her until the moment that I opened the front door, at which point it became all too obvious that I was plastered, so that in stepping aside to let her in I irrevocably altered her evening and made it impossible to complete the seduction that I had planned.

I realize now that I would have been a lot better off taking the young women to Ralph's or Villa di Roma in the first place, which would have given me a chance to limit my alcoholic intake and suavely drive them home. On nearly every occasion, my dinner guests recognized all of this at once, took whatever pleasure they could in the ill-prepared meal, and refused to see me again. The lone exception was a nurse named Margaret McAlister, who took pity on me when I pleaded in the pathetic manner of Billy McDe-vitt. When my pleading finally got to her, she followed me up the stairs, past Sarah's door, and onto the shag carpet in my room, where I undressed her and failed to become erect. This failure provided me with very little choice but to perform oral sex instead, a joyless exercise that left me with a hangover, a painful recol-lection, and an anecdote to share with Teresa, Mike's girlfriend recounting it to a co-worker at the Western Union switchboard in Moorestown. To hear her tell it, the two women twittered like schoolgirls when they discussed the witticism in question: "As it happened, I found another way to please her, though it gave me something of a stiff neck." But the real payoff occurred in a dusty little comedy club years later, when a hopelessly obese comedian nailed it with a painful precision, referring to that particular form of oral sex as "too many u-turns in bed." As I drowned out all of the others with my laughter, the woman who eventually became my wife caught another glimpse of who I really was.

———

"I love your house," Teresa said, on one of several occasions that she showed up unannounced. This was in stark contrast to Martina, who regarded my dwelling with a mixture of curiosity and disdain, as though she were unaccustomed to visiting neighborhoods like that and socializing with the kind of people who lived there.

After drinking shots of tequila in my kitchen, Teresa and I got stoned on the way to South Street, parked the car, and walked toward Lickety Split. Before we arrived, I looked up at a sign that was stretched across a storefront. The sign said "Zipperhead."

"I haven't seen that movie. Have you?"

"What movie?" Teresa asked.

"Zipperhead."

Teresa burst out laughing, leaning into me so that I was forced to hold her up.

"Mark, that's a sin!"

"What is?"

"It's a clothing store!"

"Are you sure? I thought I read about it."

"That's *Eraserhead!* The movie theater's a block away."

This was still more proof that Teresa held her liquor more successfully than I did. I had seen *The Last Picture Show* at the Theatre of the Living Arts, and now they were screening the David Lynch cult film. But TLA was a hundred yards from where we were standing.

"You're flagged, Mark. No more alcohol for you."

"Not tonight anyway."

"Come on," Teresa said, "let's buy somethin'." And she pulled me into Zipperhead.

Moments later, I was sitting on a stool outside the fitting room, staring at the parts of Teresa that were visible—her feet, her ankles, and a few tantalizing inches of leg. One article of clothing after another fell to the floor at Teresa's feet.

"God help me," I said.

"Is that you, Mark?"

"Yeah, it is."

"Don't go anywhere. I want your honest opinion."

Then she opened the door, modeling the sexiest bra she could find.

"Whadda yuh think?"

"I think you're incredible," I whispered.

When she ducked back into the fitting room, I closed my eyes and banged my head on the wall behind me. The alcohol had numbed me, and I didn't feel the bruise until the next morning.

———————

During that period, Teresa started dropping hints about her birthday, until I offered to take her to Dante and Luigi's, where an overweight waitress did her best to survive Teresa's good looks. When I placed my order, I deliberated over a cup of escarole soup.

"Our portions are pretty big, hun. You may not need the soup."

"OK, thanks for telling me."

"If you're still hungry, you can have a bite o' her lin-gween."

"I'd love to have a bite o' her lin-gween."

"Oh, yeah?" Teresa said. "What's stoppin' yuh?"

That wiped the smirk off my face, and I handed the menu back to the waitress.

"Can I change my mind?"

"You don't want the cacciatore?"

"No, I'll have the capon marsala."

"You got it. What about the escarole?"

"Eighty-six the escarole."

"Gotcha. I'll be back with your drinks in a minute."

———————

Teresa was turning up the heat, and I responded by buying a gift for Sarah. It was a cry for help, which Sarah promptly ignored. She was leafing through a fashion magazine when I walked into the house with a small table lamp with a yellow base and a white lampshade.

"Do you like it?" I asked.

"Mark, it's beautiful!"

"I got it at Woolworth's. It's cheap, but it has a certain quality."

"Where are you gonna put it—in your room?"

"No, I want you to have it."

"Keep it for yourself!"

"Please—let me do this for you. You need more light up there."

We stared at each other awkwardly.

"Mike called while you were out. I'll give you some privacy."

"No—stay!"

"That's OK. If you don't mind, I'll figure out where to put the lamp."

"I don't mind at all."

Although my days as a drunk were lively, Teresa was never far from my mind, and my attempts to do without her for Mike's sake could not be characterized as successful. In my defense, I should offer the fact that Teresa pursued me with some vigor, looking up the phone numbers for the bars I frequented, tracking me down at those places, and making suggestions that I nearly always found irresistible. Few things were better for the ego than to be called to the telephone at a bar—until the bartenders got tired of their work being interrupted.

A few days later, Teresa and I met Frank Tattaglia at Dobbs. He had a drink waiting for her when we arrived.

"Is that for me?" Teresa asked.

"You drink Old Grand-Dad, right?"

"Yeah—on the rocks."

"I thought so."

"Where are the rocks?"

"They melted." He rose from his seat. "Hold on—I'll get yuh

a new one."

"You don't have to do that."

"I want to!"

"Frank—sit!" Frank sat back in his seat. "Mark'll get it."

I winked at him and walked over to the bar.

"Take some of mine," Frank said, scooping ice from his drink.

"I don't want it!" Teresa cried. She moved her glass, and the ice skidded across the table. Frank stared at it with a morbid fascination. Teresa turned in my direction, until she was sure that Frank was looking. "I could really go for that guy. It's a sin."

"Here," Frank said, reaching into his shirt pocket. "I bought you a gift."

"Thanks," Teresa said evenly. She took it from him and slipped it into her purse. Frank's mouth fell open.

"Aren't you gonna open it?"

"Sure—what's the big deal?"

"You're still mad about the other night."

"You're fuckin' right I am! How dare you pick me up in a trash truck?"

"I wanted to show you my life," he said sadly.

"From a trash truck? What do you take me for?"

"But it was brand new. It didn't smell or nothin'."

"What was going through your mind? Did you think I would like it?"

"That was state of the art equipment, Teresa. That was beautiful equipment."

"What if someone had seen me?"

Frank shook his head vacantly. "He knew right away, as soon as he saw it on the lot."

"What are you talking about?"

"My old man! He said, 'Frank, this is the one.' That's his pride an' joy, and it's like you're pissin' on it. It's like you're pissin' on me!"

"I'm not pissin' on yuh, Frank. We're just different, that's all."

She reached for the drink. It had been resting on a cocktail napkin, and the napkin fell to the floor.

"You dropped somethin'," he said.

"So?"

"If it drops, yuh gotta pick it up. That's the name of the game."

"Knock yourself out."

Frank picked up the cocktail napkin and placed it on the table.

"I'm gonna play somethin'," I said, delivering Teresa's drink. "Any requests?"

"Alice Cooper" she replied, and I looked at Frank expectantly.

"Frank Sinatra."

He said it cheerfully, as though he were completely unaware of the impossible gulf between them.

"I'll see what I can do."

"Who does their trash—do you know?"

I stared at him in disbelief.

"I have no idea."

"I oughta talk to 'em. They're beatin' the hell outa their dumpster."

"Why don't you give 'em your card?" I asked.

"I will give 'em my card. Do you think it's funny?"

Teresa placed her hand on Frank's arm, obscuring one of the needle marks.

"Take it easy, Frank. He's just fuckin' with yuh."

"Of course! He's the type that puts the trash out and forgets about it!"

"You're wrong," I said. "I catalog it religiously."

"Don't get him started on religion," Teresa frowned.

"No, I don't think I will."

"Do you think you're better than me?" Frank continued. "There's not a damn thing wrong with bein' a garbage man!"

"I didn't say there was."

Frank took on a vacant expression. "It's a pride thing between me and my family."

———

Betraying Mike was completely unacceptable, but I wasn't firm enough in my resolve, and I made a few shameful attempts to compensate.

"You never ask about Mike," I said to Teresa one night.

"What about him?"

"He's digging ditches in ninety degree heat. Doesn't that mean anything to you?"

Somehow I had managed to combine hypocrisy and projection in the same failed attempt to obscure my disloyalty.

"Why? That was a choice that he made, not me."

"What if he's workin' for your future?"

"I never told him to do that."

Apparently, that was enough to assuage my guilt, and I dove right back in to partying with Teresa. Later, when I was dropping her off, we were parked outside of the Devlins' house.

"Can I use your bathroom? I'll be quiet—I promise."

"What are you worried about—my parents?"

"Yeah—I don't wanna wake 'em up."

"Don't worry—they can sleep through anything."

"Are you leering?"

"I didn't think I was."

"I got news for you—you were."

"OK—I'm sorry!"

"Don't let it happen again."

The phone in the Devlin's living room rang when I was flushing the toilet. Teresa's father emerged from his bedroom to answer it.

"It's three in the morning, Teresa."

"So?"

"You've got a phone call!"

"Who is it?"

"I think it's Mark."

"What are you talking about? Mark's in the bathroom!"

Ralph stared at the bathroom door. Although he had seen just about everything with Teresa, he was shocked just the same.

"How the hell do I know? Maybe's it's Ed."

"Are you out of your mind? Ed's in Korea!"

"Just pick up the goddamn phone, all right?"

"Jeez, you don't have to be so touchy about it."

Teresa picked up the phone. Mike was on the other end of the line, but for a split second she didn't recognize his voice.

"Hello?"

"Teresa? It's me. Did I wake you up?"

"Mike?"

"Well, yeah, who else would it be?"

"I don't know—I was half asleep."

"Never mind—don't answer that. Did you go out tonight?"

Teresa gestured to me, offering me the phone. I shook my head "no" and waved my arms frantically, causing Teresa to stifle a laugh.

"I went out with Mark. We went to Dobbs."

"It sounds like you're seein' a lot of each other."

"Yeah, we are. He's a great guy."

"I'm happy for yuh. When's the wedding?"

"We're not sure."

"Can I at least be the best man?"

"I don't know. That's between you and him."

After she hung up the phone, she walked me to the door.

"That was weird," I said.

"How come?"

"Do you really want me to answer that? I would be stating the obvious."

Teresa shrugged. "It didn't seem weird to me. We were kidding around."

"Right."

"I've been meanin' to ask yuh. What's goin' on with your housemate?"

"Who—Sarah?"

"Yeah—Mike told me about her."

"We shop together, we eat together, but we go our separate ways at the end of the night. I'm her husband until bedtime."

"Mark, that's awful. Why don't you ask her out?"

"Does that sound like a healthy relationship to you?"

"I don't know. I've never had one."

"Come on—of course you have!"

"Don't be so sure."

———————

It wasn't loyalty that caused me to call Mike in New Orleans, but still another attempt to back off from my full-blown love for Teresa.

In order to prepare for the call, I thought back to the last time that Teresa and I had discussed her relationship with Mike, and to the strange experience of hearing about it from each of their points of view. Mike had spent an entire evening trying to reach her, but I hadn't gotten her home until three in the morning on the night that I used the Devlins' bathroom. By then, Mike was drunk and had lost sight of how late it was, forcing Teresa's father to respond to the ringing of the telephone, the mild-mannered man finally exhibiting some gumption by bawling out my friend. Unable to ignore the soft spot that he had for Teresa, however, he handed her the phone.

When Mike kidded around about the possibility of Teresa marrying me, it all seemed a wonderful joke, a happy instance of everyone getting along so well. But the most characteristic response for Mike would have been for him to step aside if I told him that I had fallen in love with Teresa. I also realized that he had a thing about telephones, and that he only used them in a spirit of levity. The fact that he hadn't called for a week indicated that he had something important to say, but I knew that he would deflect any attempt to discuss it over the phone. At the same time, though—given his isolation and my own conflicted feelings about falling in love with his girlfriend—I needed to make the attempt. His usual method was to discuss it in a letter, or wait until we saw one another in person; but somehow, I sensed that he was in pain.

"Mike, how are yuh?"

"I'm doin' great."

"Are you sure?"

He paused, then made the admission. "I wrote you a letter."

"About Teresa?"

"Yeah, it's in there."

"You don't want to talk about it now?"

"No—not over the phone."

"Can you give me some idea?"

"I mailed it the other day. You'll probably get it tomorrow."

"Are you still all right with me and Teresa? I didn't want to spend time with her, but you said it was OK."

"It is OK."

"Is she gonna visit you any time soon?"

"I doubt it. I haven't talked to her for a while."

"Why not?"

"The last conversation was really weird."

"How was it weird?"

"We were supposed to split her plane fare, but she isn't saving any money. Are you there?"

She may not have been saving for New Orleans, but she was sure spending money with me. "Yeah, I'm here."

"How are you doing?"

"I'm fine."

"How's Sarah?"

"The same. I'm hopelessly in love with her, but Teresa's taking my mind off it."

"Yeah, she'll do that."

"When are you coming up here?"

"The Fourth of July probably."

"Were you drunk when you wrote the letter?"

"Yeah, pretty much."

"That's good. Those are the best kind."

"Take it easy, kid. I'll call you in a couple days."

"I'll call you after I get your letter."

"That would be great," he replied.
"But I won't talk to you about it, I promise."

———————

Mike's letter arrived the next day.

Dear Mark –

I've been going back and forth on Teresa since right before the New Orleans trip. There is so much in her character that I still find attractive; I guess that's why certain other impressions are harder to swallow. (If that sounds ominous, it is.)

I see a lot of myself in Teresa, with most of the differences coming from the things we've been exposed to. This is meant to explain and give perspective to subsequent criticisms.

Mark, one of the reasons for my confusion is the great warmth Teresa has for people and the way it is expressed verbally and physically. Associated with this is a certain old-fashioned openness that I love. That makes it easy for me to speculate on throwing myself into a long-term relationship.

However, certain things have changed my mind. I hope you understand there is no good or bad here, only frustration.

I guess it can be summed up in one idea. I don't think Teresa is ready for a commitment (despite what she may think in weaker moments). Mark, it became noticeable to me in several ways through anecdotes about the past and certain reactions. But what I really waited for was to see how she dealt with a trip to New Orleans for Memorial Day. Mark, she has been home for a month and has saved no money for the trip—if she was dedicated enough, she would have. As critical or judgmental as it may seem, that's a real important indication to me.

I'm not here to pass judgment because I love Teresa too much. It's like your letter comparing her to Rosie in "Cakes and Ale"— not on a sexual basis but as a free spirit. It's not right or wrong, only fact. Mark, believe me, this is not the only basis for my decision, only the most dramatic. Teresa expressed a desire to be with me on a more continual basis, and if she can't apply herself to such a short-range goal or feels depressed this past Sunday for being at home alone after going out every night from Wednesday to Saturday, what hope is there of wading through an involved or live-in relationship? (A live-in relationship would be the next step for me since I couldn't continue the lifestyle physically or financially maintained before New Orleans.)

Mark, I want you to understand that I don't think less of Teresa or even myself, it's just life. Teresa deals with it spontaneously—that doesn't leave much room or energy for the future. It's something that makes Teresa special but at the same time impossible to commit to for both our sakes. Mark, I'm terribly lacking in that kind of discipline to begin with and a relationship whose other partner was equally undisciplined would not be very stable. I sometimes doubt if I will ever find an involved relationship but if I do I'm sure it will be with someone like Teresa only older, or what I think Teresa will come around to with age.

Another thing that concerns me is her overuse of crank. Doing it night and day for a week is a painful indication that things aren't right. It's fucked up in a way, but at times I think over-dramatically about Teresa and worry about her future as much as mine—and envision a portrait of her life as giving so much of herself on the spur of the moment that she is unable to see the destructiveness, as though only in the giving is she able to escape from other things.

I hope I don't sound overly harsh but as callous as it may seem Teresa either won't or hasn't settled down enough to look at the painful reality. Mark, all this might change after I sober up tomorrow but I believe it is lucid. I certainly am not rushed for time to decide.

Love,
Mike

*P.S. My family gives their best to you. You can imagine what
that leaves for me.*

After I got past the obscurities and the occasionally fuzzy
logic, I realized that a living, breathing human being was present
here; that he was suffering over a woman; and that I was going
out with her. The guilt was painful; I was filled with love for him;
and all of our great times together danced in front of me. But
what had I really done? I had never kissed Teresa in an overtly
sexual manner; I had never made a pass at her or done anything
tangible to betray him; but I felt connected to her in my heart.
It was up to me, I felt, to step aside as Mike would have done if
I had told him how I felt about Teresa; but I had never enjoyed
anyone as much as I was enjoying her.

Again and again, I read the section about Teresa being
"depressed this past Sunday," consulting a calendar and deter-
mining that I hadn't been with her that night. Instead, I had
taken Sarah to see the John Sayles film, *Baby, It's You.* This was
the first time that I had done anything with Sarah in weeks, so
monopolized had I been by Teresa.

But that was the least of it. There was also the horrible thought
that Teresa had spent most of her money with me, and the possibility that I might have eclipsed Mike in Teresa's affections,
not because I was more attractive but because I was there and
Mike wasn't. In spending time with her, I was only looking for
medicine, a balm for my ego; I wasn't looking for a girlfriend at
all. But as it turned out, the medicine blew me away.

Reading the letter for the fourth time, I still hadn't exhausted
its truth or the light it shed on my behavior. When had I ever
worried about Teresa's future? The truth is, the next time would
have been the first. And what was I doing comparing Teresa to a
character in a book? Like my friend, she was a living, breathing
human being. Arriving at that realization, I was stung by my
recollection of the letter I had written to Mike, and by the fact
that I had deliberated over the allusion to *Cakes and Ale.* I had

come remarkably close to quoting John Updike and likening her to a stewardess instead, Updike having referred to flight attendants as "the horny sailors of our time." (Elsewhere, Updike had referred to sex as "the hell of having to perform," and I could relate to that as well.)

By indulging in my relationship with Teresa, I had caused Mike to suffer. But while I was still reeling from that, I became aware of something else: the fact that I had always thought of Mike as the Dean Moriarty of my youth, the prototypical best friend. It had always given me pleasure to idealize him in that way—and to borrow him from *On the Road*—but I couldn't do it anymore.

As soon as I put the letter aside, I called Mike in New Orleans. He answered on the second ring.

Prior to dialing the phone, I had no idea of what I was going to say or how much would come spilling out of me; but I had a number of choices. I could apologize, ask for his forgiveness, or assert my right to take my relationship with Teresa to its natural conclusion. That last thing, of course, was the least likely possibility of all, but I simply didn't know how the conversation would progress.

In the end, Mike did most of the talking, breaking his own rule about discussing serious matters on the phone, and I found that I could concur with most of the points that he made in his letter. At the same time, I reported the similar feelings that I experienced when Teresa flirted with other men; when she failed to show up for something; or when she forgot what she had said.

"It's the drugs," I managed, but Mike was having none of it.

"That's only part of it, Mark."

I spent the next several minutes urging him to call Teresa, but he repeated her behavior of the night before, each of them insisting that they had been the last one to initiate contact.

"What does it matter if you love each other?" I asked, seizing the opportunity to argue against myself.

Instead of waiting for Teresa to visit him in New Orleans, Mike decided to spend the weekend up north, and to have it out with her in person. Although I shouldn't have been surprised that he would handle it that way, I was startled when he told me. A day or two later, however, he shocked me even more by asking me to pick him up at the airport.

"I thought Teresa was picking you up."

"She is."

"I don't understand. You want me to go with her?"

"Yeah, I do."

"That's crazy. You should be alone with her."

"Please, Mark. I'm asking you as a friend."

"But why?"

"I can't explain it. Our last phone call was really weird."

Like Teresa's father, I was a step slow on the ramifications of her behavior. "Whose last phone call—yours and mine?"

"No! Mine and Teresa's!"

"OK, but still. What the hell would I be doing there?" I was alarmed now, and there is a good chance I sounded guilty.

"I need you there. I'll explain it when I see you."

"It doesn't make any sense, Mike. And what would Teresa think?"

"I don't think she cares one way or the other."

"Don't say that. She's mixed up, that's all."

"Yeah, I guess we all are," he said.

If that sounded ominous, it was.

After tossing and turning, I realized that Mike had a specific reason for asking me to accompany Teresa to the airport: he wanted to see us together, and he intended to play it close to the vest until he could evaluate my feelings for her. According to my reasoning at the time, he wouldn't attempt a reconciliation with Teresa if it would hurt me—or if it was likely to fail. It was ingenious really, and tinged with sadness.

The next morning, I was staring into space at the breakfast

table when Sarah descended the steps from the second floor.

"How's Mike?" she asked.

"He wants me to go to the airport with Teresa."

"How come?"

"I'm not sure. I think he wants to see us together."

Sarah looked at me with genuine concern, and I explained my theory to her.

"That's bad, Mark. I'm sorry."

Teresa seemed apathetic about Mike's return, as though he were already history, or as though he would have to impress her all over again, although nothing in her behavior gave the slightest indication that their relationship would be different. I believe that Mike knew this; that he was prepared for it; and that he had one foot out the door. But at the same time, if he had evaluated things accurately, he was determined to tell Teresa in person that they had to break up, whether she cared about the breakup or not.

Listening to them talk about one another, I was touched by how gentle they were, taking great pains to soften any criticisms they might otherwise have leveled. Even Teresa restrained herself, and there was none of the poison that she exhibited with Frank Tattaglia.

By meeting Teresa at Dobbs, I made the mistake of allowing her to drive, thereby shifting the power to her when it came to getting to the airport on time. She wasn't the least bit preoccupied with Mike's arrival, and I believe that she might have left him waiting at the concourse if Robert Hazard had been playing, if she had met someone new, or if I hadn't been there to urge her along. Now that I think about it, I made the additional mistake of allowing Teresa to take down Mike's flight information.

"What time is his plane?" I asked.

"I don't know," she said, "lemme check."

She emptied her pocketbook to reveal a ticket for a car wash, an offer from a health club, and a bottle of perfume that I failed to recognize. These had to be gifts from an unidentified male admirer, or from several of them, judging by the facts that I had already uncovered.

"My God, Teresa! How many men do you know?"

She assumed the pouting expression that I knew so well, extending her lower lip in the genetically encoded way that I had discovered on Easter Sunday. "Mark, that's mean!"

This was the second time that she had said that about me—or something similar.

"No, it isn't. I think it's great!"

For a second or two, she stared at me in a chilling fashion, until I averted my eyes. "Are you sure about that?" she asked.

"Yeah, I'm sure. Keep looking."

At that point, if you had asked me then if I wanted to be her boyfriend, I wouldn't have been able to answer.

"Here it is!" she cried, waving the slip of paper, completely oblivious to my discomfort. "He gets in at nine o'clock."

"It's eight-thirty, let's go."

"Why? It only takes twenty minutes!"

"We have to park, don't we?"

"We'll park at the curb."

"No, we won't, we'll meet him at the gate." Teresa stared at me again, finally feeling attacked, and a pang of conscience ran through me. The discomfort was approaching from her direction this time, and not Mike's. "Come on," I said, as lightly as I was able. "Where's your sense of style?"

"If you say so," she frowned, gathering up the items and returning them to her pocketbook.

Teresa made good time on our way to the airport, flying along the expressway in a car that Lorraine had recently provided—a jet black Volkswagen Jetta that went from zero to sixty almost as fast as she did. She didn't even have to trade in the shitty little Renault that she had been driving for several years, and was able to offer it at a charitable rate to one of her discarded boyfriends.

"Are you serious? Your mother bought you the car?"

"Yeah. Do you believe it?"

"I guess anything's possible in a love-hate relationship like yours."

"What are you talking about? She's sweet!"

I stared at her in disbelief—until she told me that she had something to tell me.

"What's that?" I asked.

"I love you, Mark."

Just as I had hesitated when she offered to lie down on my sofa, and when she stated that we were "involved," I couldn't respond immediately.

"You love me?" I managed.

"Yeah, and not like a friend. I really love you."

If the declaration had occurred a week earlier, when Mike was safely in New Orleans, I might have indulged in a certain optimism. But her timing was depraved.

"Did you hear me?" she asked. I couldn't tell if she regretted offering herself a second time, if she was afraid that I would reject her, or if there were some other reason entirely.

"Why now, Teresa? Why on the way to the airport?"

"I don't know, Mark. I just felt like tellin' yuh." Her anger hung in the air between us, and I found that I couldn't speak. "I told you I loved you. Is that all you're gonna say?"

"I love you, too. But he's my best friend."

She formed a reply but gathered herself instead. I feel reasonably certain that she was going to dismiss Mike with some finality, as though he had his chance and it was over. In keeping with the remarkably gentle way that the two of them had been treating me, however, she repeated what I already knew: "He's in New Orleans and I'm here."

"I realize that. Try to patch it up with him—please."

"All right, if that's the way you feel about it."

Caving in to the fear of abandonment (or whatever it actually was), I began to backpedal, although I checked myself before retracting my request of a moment before. "I don't know what to feel." This response was so weak that we each looked away.

We were walking across the parking lot now, heading toward the baggage claim area.

"That's not good enough!" I blurted. "You just felt like tellin' me!"

"OK! I'm sorry!"

Teresa had come alive. She was fully engaged in the intrigue of being loved by best friends. I believed that she cared for me, just as she had cared for Mike weeks before, but I could also see that she was excited by the naughtiness of the timing, turned on by the fact that she had declared her love only seconds before Mike arrived. For the first time, I felt as though she had introduced something sinister into our relationship, something corrupt and unseemly. Now, even a smile would be suspicious.

"Are you mad at me?" she asked, breaking into my thoughts as Mike's plane taxied up to the gate.

"How can I be mad at you? You've given me so much."

As it turned out, though, the love that I felt for her had already begun to evolve. It had lost something—enchantment perhaps, or some other elusive quality—and things would never be the same.

"I'm glad," she said softly, lowering her eyes, the shyness existing side by side with the willingness to inflict pain.

Back in the moment, Teresa shocked us with her response to Mike's arrival. Within minutes of declaring her love for me—and while other travelers were greeted with genuine emotion—she hurried over to Mike and kissed him hard on the mouth, as though this was an eagerly anticipated reunion in a committed, long-distance relationship. If we didn't know better, it would have seemed as if she had been counting the days until Mike returned; and I couldn't help wondering if he was melting all over again, while a shock of jealousy ran through me.

As it turned out, though, that wasn't the case. Although we had come to expect erratic behavior from her, we hadn't anticipated that she would act like that, particularly when she continued the vulgar display for the next several minutes, positioning herself behind Mike, climbing onto his back, and forcing him to give her a piggyback ride without his consent as the three of us made our way to the exit. While that was happening, I thought back to the time that Teresa had come up behind me at Dobbs, placed her hands over my eyes, and said "Guess who?" when I had been expecting her to arrive from another direction entirely. Now she was playacting outrageously and Mike was having none of it. Too private to confront her in public and unwilling to make a scene, he suffered in silence, wearing a displeased expression as she nuzzled his ear. It wasn't until we were outside that Mike and I looked at each other closely, not quite knowing where we stood. You had to laugh, you really did.

———————

Every so often, I try to figure Teresa out. It usually happens when I feel sorry for myself, or when I think about the past. Unfortunately, Teresa has always been elusive. But after all of my fumbling, something came to me the other day—long after she had ceased to matter. I finally realized that my anger was out of control, and that Teresa got her kicks by provoking me.

Even now, I have a tendency to look for her when I find myself in a crowd. Although it is largely an involuntary response—and the emotional equivalent of pain in a phantom limb—I realize that I'm partly responsible. After all, I've been known to pick at a scab until it bleeds.

From time to time, I have encountered women who bore a certain resemblance to her. It might have been the woman's physical appearance, her mannerisms, or the way that she sneered at her boyfriend; but somehow, it was Teresa all over again.

Although he felt Teresa's power when she hurried over to him at the airport, Mike was able to sufficiently recover to see her behavior for what it was. By her words and her actions, she made it clear that she intended to pick up exactly where they left off, so that they could have as much fun as they could without committing to the future, and without regard for the fact that Mike and I had known each other for more than a decade. But those terms were unacceptable to him.

With it all, however, I am not so down on Teresa that I forget that her willfulness was a matter of degree. If you had questioned her directly, I have no doubt that she would have preferred for my friendship with Mike to remain intact, but it really wasn't a priority for her and she had no intention of altering her behavior. I believe that Mike and I both realized that when she greeted him as though nothing were wrong, and as though there weren't any complicating factors to consider.

As I suspected, Mike was too much of a romantic to accept a casual relationship with Teresa or think of her as a "friend." He had invested too much feeling to "see other people" as Teresa preferred, and it would have been impossible for him to try. Once he realized that those were the only options, he knew that he had to end their relationship. His decision to do that was also grounded in the loyalty that he felt for me. Although I had never stated it directly, he realized that I was emotionally involved with Teresa, despite my attempt to turn away from them when they embraced at the airport. I had wanted to keep it from him, but he had sensed that I was in pain, just as I had sensed his discomfort when I had called him in New Orleans.

A day or two later, when Mike informed Teresa that they had to break up, she insisted that he meant more to her than his predecessors had. He expected her to say that, but he could never have predicted the tear that ran down her cheek. So much of her emotion at the airport seemed manufactured, but even Teresa couldn't have produced a tear on command. That tear might have haunted him—and caused him to question his decision to move on—but it was a clear indication of how confused she was, and how far she had to go in readying herself for a committed relationship. Still it must have been difficult for Mike to walk away from Teresa when he did.

As it happened, I had a reckoning as well. I had to face the fact that there was nothing to be proud of in my behavior. Clearly, if I hadn't been terrified of Teresa sexually, I would have betrayed Mike, and I wouldn't have kept Teresa at arm's length until Mike's relationship with her ran its course. Now it was time for us to talk about it.

Fittingly enough, the discussion took place in his parents' kitchen. If there was any danger of our behaving badly toward one another, it was avoided by all of the reminders we had of the hilarity we had experienced in that room. Together with the loyalty we felt for one another, the surroundings inspired us to avoid the sort of recriminations that we might otherwise have found irresistible, including the pointless argument of who had gone out with Teresa first and who had spent more time with her overall. Not only would Teresa have been the one to settle the argument by deciding where she wanted to go with her various relationships, but it would have been regrettable for us to revert to the logic of childhood. And so at substantial cost to himself, Mike gave me permission to pursue Teresa and bestowed the blessing I needed to carry the relationship with her to its conclusion. Once I saw where he was going, though, I found that I respected him too much to mislead him any more than I had.

"I can't lie to you, Mike. I fell in love with her while you were away."

"Yeah, I figured you would."

I stared at him. "You what?"

"How could you help it?" he shrugged. "I know what she's like."

"Then why did you encourage me to see her?"

"I love you both. I wanted you to have a good time."

"At your own expense?"

"I didn't look at it that way."

"Maybe you should have!" I cried, regretting it immediately. "I'm sorry. I didn't mean that as an excuse."

"She wanted to get together with you. How could I stand in her way?"

"By telling her you felt funny about it."

"You can't tell her what to do, Mark. She won't put up with it."

Was he giving advice or explaining his behavior? It was impossible to tell.

"Did you feel funny about it?"

"No. I trusted you."

"And I betrayed your trust."

"I didn't say that. You experienced Teresa, that's all."

He smiled now. Despite everything, he could still look back on Teresa with pleasure; and I had the feeling that the same thing would happen with me once the relationship with her played itself out.

"I could never forgive myself if I hurt you," I said, "but it's like an abduction."

"What is?"

"Falling in love with her. First she blindfolds you and then she takes you for a ride."

Mike considered this. By then, he had grown accustomed to my pronouncements, and to the hit-or-miss nature of my remarks; but he had no quarrel with them as long as they were amusing. This time, however, I had actually come up with something. "Yeah," he said, "but look at all the fun we're havin'."

I paused, and looked at him sadly. "What are we gonna do about us?"

"We're fine. We don't have to do anything."

"Are you sure?"

"What do you want me to say? I don't want to think about that part of it."

I fell silent. He was doing as much as he could for me, draping his hand over my shoulder and comforting me the way that Sheldon had comforted Andy at Mr. Martin's. "I'm a big boy," he said. "I'll get over it." But the issue of my culpability hadn't been put to rest.

"If it wasn't you," Mike continued, "it would have been someone else."

"But it *was* me."

"Don't flatter yourself. She's pretty accessible that way."

"I'm not gonna see her any more. I wouldn't feel right about it."

"That's up to you," he said. "Leave me out of it."

"How can I?" I asked softly.

"You should base your decision on other things, as if Teresa and I are history. Because we are."

"It's too soon, Mike. I couldn't do that to you."

This might have been a noble sentiment if it weren't such a glaring example of an excuse.

"Mark, don't let me stand in your way. I'm finished with Teresa."

"Are you sure?"

"I'm positive. I can't put it any plainer than that."

"What was the last straw? Not me, I hope."

"Of course not. I decided way before that."

"You wrote about it in your letter. Did she ever apologize for not saving any money?"

"No—not a word."

"Not even last night? After the airport?"

He looked at me sadly. "You have a lot to learn about her, don't you?"

"I guess so."

"In case you're wondering, that's why I flew up here this time. It wasn't to win her back. It was to confirm my decision."

"What about *my* decision? You said I should base it on other things. What were you referring to?"

"The fact that you need it," he said, frowning at the thought of my sex life.

I smiled as bravely as I could. "I see what you mean."

"It'll do you good," Mike followed, "even if it's a total disaster."

This should have been a punchline, but neither one of us was laughing.

———————

Later that day, we were sitting in a booth at Sal's, experiencing the subtleties of strip mall cuisine.

"It's probably appropriate that she worked the graveyard shift," I said.

"Why is that?"

"Because—she has a graveyard full of men."

By that time, I had thought that we were finished discussing Teresa, but apparently I couldn't let it go. Mike was glaring at me, and steam was rising from his calzone. "I'm not dead yet. Are you?"

"OK, OK!"

"Are you through with that oregano?" he asked, and we went on eating in silence.

The next day, he returned to New Orleans.

———————

Morris was re-stocking the potato chip rack when he complained to me about Teresa.

"I can't keep takin' messages for you. She callin' every night."

"I told you—she declared her love at the airport!"

"So?"

"Her timing was depraved!"

It had taken me a week, but I had finally seized an opportunity to impress someone with the insight. Unfortunately, I picked the wrong person.

"Thass jus' a fancy word for bein' scared. You the scaredest person I know."

I started mopping the floor, and Morris paused at the potato chip rack to observe me.

"You finally doin' it right," he said.

"I had a good teacher."

"Took you long enough. What's it been—a mumph since you been here?"

"It's gotta be more than that. You were still in bible school at the time."

"You think you funny, Mark? I can still slide you upside the head."

———————

A few days later, Teresa reached me at the restaurant.

"I thought you were gonna call me," she said.

"I did, too. It's a little weird for me, that's all."

"Don't make me wait *too* long."

"What are you doing this weekend?"

"You're helpin' me move, remember?"

"I'll call you when I get home from work."

After the 3 a.m. phone call from Mike in New Orleans, the Devlins installed a separate line in Teresa's bedroom; but I got her answering machine when I tried to call her back. Her taped message captured her essence: "If I'm out, it's none o' your business who I'm with. If it's Frank, stop callin'. If it's Mark, I'll call yuh back."

I recorded my message after the beep, doing my best to control the panic. "What if it's Mike? Can you please change your message? I'll talk to you later."

———————

Largely on my recommendation, Teresa moved out of her parents' house and sublet an apartment on Pemberton Street a few blocks from J.C. Dobbs. It never entered my mind that her departure would change their family dynamic, or that it would get the poison out of her system; but I felt certain that it would be healthier for her if she saw her mother less frequently.

Something unexpected happened when I helped her move. After I wrenched my back on a chest of drawers, Teresa punished me for a period of several days after I declined her offer of a backrub. The punishment came in the form of her remaining out of contact long enough for me to recognize the correlation between my turning down the offer and her continued absence. Despite the fact that I had immediately regretted the decision and spent the rest of the day arching my back and grimacing in the hope that she would make the offer a second time, she did nothing of the sort.

It would have been one thing if Teresa had ignored my transparent attempt to turn back the clock, but instead she addressed it directly, saying, "You can forget it, Mark. I'm not gonna offer again." In the end, she refused to make allowances for my fear and remained out of contact until her anger died down. Ultimately, I grasped the full extent of my failure. There it was: the brass ring, the Holy Grail, the pot of gold at the end of the rainbow; but I couldn't reach out and grab it. That backrub would have meant everything to me if it had led to a sexual encounter, but I had allowed the moment to pass. Not only was it hard to look at her after that, but the incident took on a pathetic footnote when I used the backrub as a masturbatory fantasy for more than a year, savoring the mental image of Teresa unbuttoning her blouse without my knowledge, running her breasts over the bare skin of my back, and bidding me to face her, at which point we copulated for a respectable amount of time before enjoying a simultaneous orgasm.

———

Within a week of her move to Pemberton Street, Teresa reported that Frank Tattaglia had gone on an unprecedented binge with crank. As it turned out, she conveyed this to me over the telephone while I worked the grill at Mr. Martin's.

"Thanks, Bun. Can you watch those for me?"

Bunny glanced in the general direction of the kitchen, where I was frying onions, flipping burgers, and concocting a mushroom cheesesteak. The onions were a legitimate part of the job, and so were the burgers; but as Bunny suspected, I had every intention of consuming the cheesesteak myself.

"Hurry up," she said.

"Sure thing."

I handed her the spatula, and made my way to the phone.

"Mark, it's me," Teresa began. "You're not gonna believe this."

"What happened?"

"He robbed a bank."

"Who did?"

"Frank! He tried anyway."

"When did he do that?"

"The other day. He was drivin' the trash truck."

"No. He wasn't!"

"I'm serious! His car wouldn't start."

"What a putz."

"He had a note and everything. He read it to me this afternoon."

"He read it to you? How romantic."

"It was—in a way."

"I was kidding."

"You were?"

"Wait a minute. How could he read it to you?"

"What do you mean?"

"Didn't he give it to the teller?"

"No. He got paranoid and drove away."

"Paranoid? Was he doin' lines?"

"Yeah. One thing led to another."

"Of course. It makes perfect sense."

"Then he got in an accident and totaled his father's truck."

"I feel sorry for him. I really do."

"Do you know what he said to the cop? 'I'm bein' followed.'"

"And what did the cop say?"

"'Yeah. By us!'"

"Where is he now—in jail?"

"No, Ancora. I'm gonna visit him. Will you come with me?"

"Sure. I have a question, though."

"What's that?"

"I've never been arrested, but supposedly you get one phone

call. Who did he call—you or a lawyer?"

"Me. But he called me at my parents—not my apartment."

"You changed your message when I asked you to, right?"

"I haven't gotten around to it, but if you're worried about Mike, I don't think he'll be callin' anymore."

"If you haven't been back to your parents', how do you know about Frank?"

"My mom checks my machine."

Poor Ralph. He paid for a separate phone line and Teresa moved out a week later.

———————

After he was arraigned before a magistrate, Frank was transported to the state-run psychiatric institution at Ancora, where he cooled his heels for a period of two weeks, came down from the crank, and received a thorough evaluation. Instead of calling a lawyer from the police station, however, he had spent his one and only phone call on Teresa, with the message on her machine adding insult to injury. Not only had she failed to pick up the phone, but her recorded message insisted that he stop calling, a withering directive that must have depressed him even more.

From that point on, everything Teresa did seemed to be a reflection on me. After all, she was going through her paces in a vacuum that I created.

Because my response to her declaration of love was unsatisfactory, Teresa took up with still another young man after I refused the backrub, a piece of intelligence that I gathered after bribing Harold McTeer with a shot of Courvoisier at Dobbs.

"I seen your lady the other night. She was lookin' fine as usual," he said.

"Who—Teresa?'

"Yeah, you got more than one lady?"

"What about her?"

"She was with Joe Rinaldi."

"What can you tell me about him?"

"What's in it for me?"

I signaled the bartender, a hard-looking woman in a low-cut leather top. "Can I have a Courvoisier? It's for him."

"You already know the dude. You mistook him for a chick one night."

"Who? The guy with the ponytail?"

"Yeah, and them bright red glasses. You come up on him from behind. You tapped him on the shoulder, 'member? I almost fell out my chair."

"You coulda warned me."

"It happened too fast, man. I hadda let it play out."

When the bartender delivered Harold's drink, he took the opportunity to kiss her hand, a gesture that she promptly ignored. "Thank you, darlin'. You look delicious tonight." She ignored that, too.

"Now I remember," I said. "He was kinda belligerent when he turned around."

"Wouldn't you be? You turn around at a bar and some dude's tryin' to buy you a drink?"

"What are you talking about? I just bought *you* a drink!"

"This a *transaction*, man. That's different." He took a swig of the Courvoisier and waited for it to burn his throat. "Anyway, I been knowin' Rinaldi for the longes'. He's bad news. You best watch out for him."

"It's not me I'm worried about."

"Whoever. I wouldn't go near the motherfucker."

"Coming from someone who's survived several knife fights, I'm sure the advice is sound."

"What—that? That was when I was a *young* man. I was *crazy* back then."

Not only did Harold provide me with the pertinent facts about Joe Rinaldi, but he issued the sternest possible warning, informing me that Rinaldi was a thief, a gambler, and possibly a bigamist, as he was currently involved in a dispute over the legality of his divorce. This information represented a significant break-through, since Teresa had been uncharacteristically silent about Joe—possibly as another form of punishment, or because she anticipated an even stronger aversion than the one I had exhibited with Frank—and had left me with only my own recollection to go on until the conversation with Harold. Because I had been particularly outspoken about Frank since his hospitalization had begun—and had claimed that Frank represented a clear sign of Teresa's "self-destructiveness" (not quite realizing that the word was one of Teresa's pet peeves after Lorraine had used it a thousand times since Teresa had reached puberty)—Teresa kept her thoughts about Rinaldi to herself.

If it hadn't been for Harold, I would have had nothing to add to the impression I had formed on the basis of a single event. On that humiliating occasion, I had seen Joe from behind as Harold described, gotten the wrong impression of the blond ponytail that extended to his waist, and tapped him on the shoulder to strike up a conversation, only to learn that I had been sadly mistaken about his gender. The minute he turned around with an impudent expression and glared in a hostile way, I felt the entire weight of my error and realized that he was much tougher than his long hair, red glasses, and slightness of build had originally indicated.

In addition to wrenching my back, I happened upon a contraceptive gel at Teresa's apartment, and for all intents and purposes, that particular discovery decided the issue of whether or not I would attempt to sleep with her. The fact that Teresa used the same form of contraception that Karen Marcus had employed on Pine Street, and that Teresa had purchased the same product (three ounces of an anti-spermicidal substance manufactured by Johnson and Johnson) should have had a calming effect on my nerves; but the truth is that it unsettled me instead. By reminding myself of my subconscious tendency to divide women into two basic categories—those that I had the courage to sleep with and those that I didn't—I can immediately dispense with any form of surprise and take an honest look at the factors that were actually present. When I force myself to do that, my reaction seems particularly instructive and a clear sign that my suspicions were correct about at least one of my defense mechanisms. Unlike Karen, Teresa was too heedless of other people's feelings for me to risk a disastrous sexual experience, and I didn't even have to consider the other main factor that affected my sex life in those days—the question of whether or not I would miss the woman if my humiliation prevented me from seeing her again.

Now that my cowardice had proved decisive, Teresa went about the task of insinuating herself into Joe's life, successfully completing the preliminary steps of inflating his ego, introducing him to the touch of her hand, and making herself necessary for his very existence, while I held up my end of the bargain by retreating into the safety of my relationship with Sarah, until I arrived at the neat psychological ploy of playing the two women off of one another, persuading myself that I was in love with Sarah whenever my gross failure with Teresa began to oppress me for any appreciable amount of time, and professing my love for Teresa whenever I was reminded of the coldness of Sarah's heart. Needless to say, this strategy was even more transparent than the notion of my being a womanizer (although the two were certainly linked), and it proved to be far more insupportable by collapsing under its own weight within a week or two of my attempting it. I realize now that any number of incidents might have caused it to collapse, but it made a perfect kind of sense that my overconcern for Sarah's well-being was at the center of it, as was Teresa's fierce determination to push her way to Joe's limits, not resting until she identified anger management as the overriding issue of his life. Just as I had felt a sharp pang of protectiveness when Sarah injured her hand on my door, I suffered noticeably when each of my love interests sustained an injury to the same part of her body, Sarah wearing a patch after being diagnosed with conjunctivitis and Teresa provoking Joe into giving her a black eye.

———————

Teresa called me shortly thereafter.

"Mark, I look like a raccoon!" she said, and instead of comforting her—instead of putting all of the resentment aside and reaching out to her in friendship, which is nothing less than she deserved—I did the opposite. "If you're doing this to infuriate me, it's working."

"I'm not!" she protested.

"No, you're just living your life."

It wasn't a proud day for either of us.

———————

As if Joe weren't enough, Teresa added another complication by growing jealous of her mother's presence at Camden County College and matching the real estate course with a literature class of her own. Teresa attended the class for a period of several weeks until her professor asked her out. Prior to this occurrence, she and Lorraine ignored each other on at least three occasions, treating the tiny campus as though it were no different than the house they had previously shared, just as they had refused to meet for coffee when they worked within a mile of each other in Moorestown.

As a sign of the self-interest to come, her professor waited until right before the add-drop period expired before making up his mind to approach Teresa, insisting that she withdraw from the course if they were going to see one another socially. Despite the fact that this suggestion was only advantageous to him—and that it was actually counter-productive to Teresa's continuing education—he made it with little or no remorse before showing himself to be surprisingly cheap on their first date, escorting Teresa to the drive-through window of a Taco Bell before taking her back to his apartment. By the time Teresa realized that he was a woman-hating sicko, he had already intimidated her intellectually, assigned a reading list, and taken off all of her clothes.

Although Teresa tried to be a good sport about it, his behavior soon became certifiably bizarre, and she finally called it quits when he directed her to leave the bathroom door open when she sat on the toilet, insisting that she "reject the conventional." This directive came a day or two after he deliberately hit her with a racquetball when they were playing mixed doubles with two of the professor's colleagues, and after she had shown up at Dobbs with a welt on her shoulder.

Once she confided her professor's misdeeds, I advised her in the strongest possible terms that she should refuse to see him again, although I never expected her to follow my advice until her latest romantic entanglement ran its course. But Teresa surprised me with the fact that she had already cursed the professor out and sent him on his way.

The realization that we would never sleep together came to Teresa gradually, but her ambivalence toward sex made it tolerable for a period of time. At first, she had been charmed by the fact that I was reluctant to return her embraces, characterizing it as shyness, chivalry, and loyalty to my friend. Within a week or two of my seeing Teresa socially, however, I was touching her nearly as often as she was touching me, squeezing her arm, hugging her, and guiding her into the bars we frequented by placing my hand on the small of her back. But all of that stopped when she declared her love at the airport, and after an initial period in which she seemed to be genuinely saddened, a certain resentment found its way into her demeanor.

After laughing at my joke about oral sex—and sharing it with her co-worker at Western Union—Teresa took a different approach after we visited Frank at Ancora, questioning my attitudes at length. As she did that, it became obvious to both of us that

I had obscured my true self, and that she had peeled away multiple layers of artifice to reveal the uptight prude within. When that happened, it was only a matter of time before she detected a rather obvious double standard, as though I had no misgivings about oral sex when a man performed it on a woman but considered it an act of subservience when a woman performed it on a man. "What if they perform it on each other?" she asked aggressively, glancing over at me as she maneuvered her car onto the Benjamin Franklin Bridge. To this day, I can't cross that structure without thinking of my conversation with Teresa.

"I guess it's OK then," I followed, my pose as a ladies' man utterly laid to waste, and Teresa allowed herself the luxury of a sneer.

"Did you know that I went down on Joe?"

"How could I possibly know?"

"What's the matter? You disapprove?"

"Of course not!"

"That's not what you said a minute ago."

"A lot has happened since then."

"It's a part of life, Mark. That's all it is."

After the unpleasantness with Margaret McAlister, I attempted only one more dinner date on 22d Street, and the results were less demoralizing. This slight improvement, however, had nothing to do with sobriety. Once again, I was plastered by the time I admitted my guest into the house—in this case Megan Malone— but Teresa saw to it that Megan never made it to my bedroom, calling me on the phone at the precise instant that I slipped my hand under Megan's blouse.

"Do you mind if I get that?" I asked.

"No—as long as you remove your hand."

"I believe I'll have to," I laughed, removing my hand from Megan's blouse, answering the phone, and carrying it across the room with its long cord stretching to the kitchen.

"Teresa?"

"What are yuh doin'?"

"I'm talking to someone."

"Is it a guy or a girl?"

"It was a girl the last I checked."

Although I recognized the fact that the timing was more innocent—and that the consequences could not compare—I thought back to the night that Teresa had declared her love at the airport, feeling strongly that she should have backed off the moment I informed her that I had company. Just as she ignored the gross impropriety of her actions when Mike's plane taxied up to the gate, she insisted that I invite her over with Megan sprawled on my living room sofa; but it never occurred to me to hang up on her. I realize now that there was a certain arrogance in her behavior, and the kind of presumption that Vince exhibited with Lorraine. Like her brother, she was convinced of the hold she had over me, and the fact that I had fallen short on the issue of our sleeping together gave her even more of an advantage.

Teresa had run out of pot, and I allowed her to knock on my door before Megan's visit concluded, succumbing to Teresa's argument that my dinner guest would have no reason to object since Teresa and I were "just friends." As it turned out, the deciding factor was my realization that Megan would never be as important to me as Teresa was; and once I came to that conclusion, I was more than willing to discard the relationship. Whether or not I believed that my paralyzing fear of Teresa might still be surmountable—or I was making one more attempt to pretend that the fear didn't exist—I can't really say; but in the false euphoria of eleven screwdrivers, a wrongheaded optimism was born, one in which all things were possible. This even applied to the wild hope that I could somehow encourage Megan to leave and invite Teresa to stay, a neat trick that even I would have a hard time accomplishing. But when I saw the look on Megan's face, I finally realized what I had done and stammered an apology, and

Megan began to question me in a conflicted way. Apparently, she feared the worst but wasn't quite ready to give up on me as a romantic possibility.

"Is she the one with the Volkswagen?"

"Yeah, that's her."

"I've seen you with her at Dobbs."

"Megan, you probably don't care, but I've never slept with Teresa."

"That's none of my business," she replied.

"Yes, it is. I invited you here."

Even that was presumptuous, but Megan was still working through the issue of whether or not I had slept with Teresa. She paused in order to do this, and studied me as though our future depended on it. I believe that she regarded me as something of a heel, but not the outright liar that I seemed to be a moment before. This came as a great relief to her apparently, as it meant that we could go on necking until Teresa arrived, and that the evening would not end with her right back where she started, an attractive woman with no real prospects romantically. She drew the line, however, at my returning my hand to her breast.

"Let's take it slow," she said evenly.

"You're right. I'm sorry."

"Don't worry about it," she said, leaning away from me on the sofa.

Just recently, Sarah and I had added another housemate, an engineering student by the name of Dennis Parker. Dennis rode all over town on his bicycle, wearing a helmet that was too big for his head. Now he was opening our front door.

"Don't tell me she has a key!" Megan cried, rising to her feet.

"Of course not! It's one of my housemates!" And I opened the door to the vestibule, yanking Dennis into the room.

"Dennis! Howya doin'?"

This greeting was nearly as effusive as the one that Lorraine had offered to Vince, and far more puzzling to Dennis, given the fact that I paid very little attention to him until it was time to collect the rent.

"Jeez, Mark, it's good to see you, too!"

There was just the slightest trace of calculation in Megan as I made the introductions, as though she were contemplating an adjustment of her own. Maybe there really was a chance of her changing places with Teresa, provided that I changed places with Dennis.

"Come here a minute," Dennis said abruptly, drawing me into the kitchen. And I called out to Megan over my shoulder.

"Will you excuse me for a second?" But Dennis drowned out her reply.

"What the hell are you doing?" he demanded.

"What are you talking about?"

"The other one's parking her car!"

Apparently, Dennis was more frightened than I was. This was where a womanizer really earned his reputation, and I loved every minute of it.

"What other one?" I asked coolly, as though the possibilities only began with Teresa.

"The Italian girl!"

"Actually, she's half Irish."

"Whatever she is, she's walking up the sidewalk."

"So?"

"Don't tell me you invited two girls over on the same night."

"Sure. Why not?" Dennis's mouth fell open. "I was kidding. Teresa invited herself."

"What are you gonna do?"

"Take it easy. She's just picking something up."

"What's she picking up?" he asked, obviously suspecting contraband.

"A couple of joints, Dennis. Some of us smoke the stuff."

"You little pipsqueak. How do you do it?"

"Your guess is as good as mine."

"Two girls in one night, and I'm studying quantum mechanics."

"You made a choice," I said solemnly, "and so did I."

"Yeah, I can see that." He shook his head at the wrong turn

he had taken in life, hitting the books when he could have been unsavory like me. "If Teresa comes in, can I join you?"

"No."

"Why not?"

"It would be awkward, don't you think?"

"For who?"

"For Megan. It was supposed to be the two of us."

Dennis waved his hand in disgust. "You selfish little jerk."

So that was how he felt about me. Until then, I'd had no idea.

When Teresa knocked on the door, Dennis followed me into the living room, initiating a mild flirtation with Megan.

"How long have you known Mark?"

"A couple weeks, I guess."

"How well do you know him?"

Megan's voice rose with alarm. "Why do you ask?"

"I just wondered. He's a great guy, isn't he?"

"I'm not sure yet."

"Take your time," he said. "Get to know him."

From the vestibule, it was impossible to determine if he was playing her or offering advice. Aside from the few occasions on which he had held forth on the subject of engineering, I had rarely spoken with him.

"Teresa, how are you doing?"

"Aren't you gonna invite me in?"

"I told you, I have company!"

"You invited someone else in—I can hear him."

"He lives here. I had no choice."

"Fine," she sneered. "Whadja give me?"

"That should hold you for a while," I declared, wearing my best poker face as I handed her a nickel bag of sensimilla, a much-desired form of the drug.

"Mark, you didn't have to do that! I'm gettin' some t'morrah!"

"I wanted to."

"That's so sweet!" she cried, kissing me on the lips.

By doing that, Teresa reinforced my belief that she had a

kiss for every occasion—including the ambiguous way that she greeted Mikey Wild, a developmentally disabled man who was often invited onstage at Dobbs. Whenever that happened, Mikey would sing his own composition, "Die, Die, Die," which was his idea of a punk song, despite the fact that those were its only lyrics. Although the musicians were nice to him, there was something condescending about their attitude, just as Teresa patronized Mikey by designing a kiss on the basis of his I.Q. Despite the attention that she had given the matter, however—and the success with which she had arrived at a kind of half-kiss in the general vicinity of his mouth—she often missed his cheek when she had a few drinks and kissed him directly on the mouth instead. Before anything could be done, the innocuous greeting that she had intended became something else entirely, carrying with it the ability to confuse him. All of the other women kept their distance from Mikey as a precautionary measure, and it was easy to see why whenever that particular miscalculation occurred, the entire situation degenerating into an awkward charade in which Mikey followed Teresa around for the rest of the night, attempting to kiss her repeatedly until Teresa cried out, "Mikey, stop!" In considering the way that Teresa kissed me after I gave her the pot, I feel certain that she was expressing something other than gratitude. A serious kiss would have been silent, but this one made that exaggerated smacking sound that you never like to hear, as though it were designed to get Megan's attention. Sure enough, Megan and Dennis fell silent.

"Oops," Teresa said. "Sorry about that."

"Teresa, really, I need to get back inside."

"Go ahead. Who's stoppin' yuh?"

Her voice was full of contempt, and it was painful to hear it; but at least I knew what I was dealing with. I finally realized that Teresa was the woman that a lot of us looked for at a certain time in our lives—whether it was good for us or not—and that we each found it out in our turn.

"You could have asked her in," Megan said finally, when Teresa returned to her car.

"Really?"

I was staring at her, and Dennis was staring at me.

"Yeah, I'm gonna get going."

"Why? It's early!"

"It's two o'clock in the morning!"

"Are you all right to drive home?"

"I haven't been drinking—you have."

In the past, nothing had given me more pleasure than chasing women at a party, setting aside for the moment the question of what I would do with the women if I caught them. Coincidentally, however—as things fell apart with Teresa—the parties came to a halt. That was the case even though Phillip Cox and I had continued our tradition of letting each other know if we had been invited to one, and if we had the host's permission to invite other people. Despite the distaste that Phillip and I had for each other, it seemed a reasonable enough thing to do, a simple courtesy in the brotherhood of unhappy men.

The only solution, it seemed, was to host a party myself, a determination that forced me to overcome Sarah's initial reluctance.

"I was thinking about having a party," I said.

"Why?" Sarah asked.

"Because—you've been kinda down lately and I have, too."

"A party would depress me even more."

"No, it wouldn't."

"What's the difference? If I refuse, you'll have one anyway."

Sarah was right. Whether I needed a party to cheer myself up or I subconsciously opted for it to obliterate an overwhelming sense of failure, I can't really say. But it became increasingly important to me as Teresa went on with her life.

Although it was difficult to persuade her to exert herself, it became apparent early on that Sarah would be swept away by my enthusiasm for the party, and that she would be required to expend an even greater effort if she resisted for very long. Sarah was also aware that I was unlikely to take no for an answer, and that I always had the option of ignoring her wishes entirely, particularly since we weren't sleeping together and I had no real obligation to go on entertaining her. The truth is, it would have been easy for me to circumvent the stated desires of all four of my housemates simply by picking up the telephone and calling fifteen or twenty people, so that the entire guest list would be mine. In the end, though, it never came to that, and I was able to impose my will on Sarah by pointing out how desperately Claire and Lois needed to meet a man. Although this reminder was obviously manipulative, it had the virtue of preventing open hostility, and Sarah was forced to surrender.

By that time, my female housemates had convened in the living room, chain-smoked a pack of Sarah's cigarettes, and discussed the bleakness of the romantic landscape, turning the entire first floor of our house into a no-man's land that Dennis and I scrupulously avoided. They could not have known, however, that Sarah would meet a young man named Jimmie McGuane at the laundromat, and that she would begin to date him a few days later. This sudden reversal of fortune placed Sarah in the uncomfortable position of leaving the other two women behind, while she was left with a case of survivor guilt that made it impossible to pull the plug on the party. McGuane was the kind of strong, silent type that Sarah preferred, with just enough incorrigibility to make things interesting, although it would have been difficult to associate him with the sort of low-level criminal that Teresa occasionally explored.

I believe that Sarah and I had a certain cowardice in common. Without a doubt, we had raised non-relationships to an art form, which was another reason that things would never work out between us. Sarah had been badly hurt in her last relationship, and enjoying my devotion gave her what she needed while she worked up the courage to try again. Given my immaturity, however, I wasn't the one she would select. As for me, I suspect that

I would have avoided a physical intimacy with Sarah even if she had offered it to me, which she never did. Despite all of my talk, I would have made some excuse at the last minute.

Although she had protected herself by getting the lowdown on Jimmie (just as I had gotten the lowdown on Karen Marcus from Todd Millstein)—and she had succeeded in obtaining certain assurances from a neighbor who knew him—Sarah was unable to predict Jimmie's behavior in the way that she preferred, but she took a chance on him just the same; and instead of chasing him futilely—which would have provided even more justification for her prolonged depression, her pronounced inability to complete her master's thesis, and her growing reluctance to leave the house—Jimmie surprised her by accepting her invitation to attend the party as her date.

As it turned out, I had my own miscalculations to deal with, beginning with the fact that I had misplaced the dance tape that I had compiled the year before. Sarah watched from the sofa while I searched for it in vain, pulling out all of my cassettes and tossing them aside one by one.

"Have you seen my dance tape?"

"No, it could be anywhere."

"That's not helpful. Can you narrow it down for me?"

"I'm afraid I can't."

"Can you specify a hemisphere at least?"

"If I knew where it was, I would tell you."

"You're enjoying this, aren't you?"

"Not at all," she laughed.

I walked over to the sofa. "Can you get up for a second?"

After Sarah rose to her feet, I inserted my hand into the farthest reaches of the sofa. Although I never found the dance tape—and inadvertently dislodged another cubic foot of foam—I emerged with a pint bottle of Kasser's vodka instead. This was the cheapest vodka on the market and the smallest possible quantity—an alcoholic's choice if ever there was one.

"Look at that. There's some left!"

Sarah's laughter disappeared when I chugged the rest of the vodka, and I knew it was over between us.

––––––––

Instead of compiling another dance tape, I decided to play it by ear at the party and select whichever record seemed most advantageous at the time, feeling confident that my instincts for partying would serve me well. But this unfortunate decision required me to interrupt my debauchery every ten or fifteen minutes once the evening got under way. This was an absolute necessity if I was going to select another one of the records that I had badly scratched over the ten-year period in which I had abused not only my body but all of my personal belongings; but despite my ongoing attempt to tend to the record player, I heard more than a few complaints about the quality of the entertainment. (Although that kind of carelessness represents the least of a person's worries when he has flirted with vehicular homicide, it seemed important at the time.)

Nor had I expected that Stephanie Pachter would lock me out of my bedroom and fuck Ronnie Abrams after rejecting me several weeks before, not only implying that she was saving herself for Todd Millstein (a patent falsehood that she hoped I would report to Todd) but intimating that she was repulsed by my sophomoric behavior. It must be said, of course, that this last thing would have been a reasonable response if she hadn't taken up with a twenty-year-old a month later, and if she hadn't consumed consecutive shots of tequila prior to Ronnie's arrival, until the dignity that she maintained on a daily basis all but disappeared and she established herself as one of the more wanton women at the party. That particular set of circumstances proved to be a real nuisance by requiring me to climb the steps repeatedly in order to check on Stephanie's progress, not because I needed the bed myself but because I had run out of pot; and Stephanie was able to add insult to injury by giving new meaning to the word "screamer," crying out in an unrestrained fashion when Ronnie brought her to a climax. In the end, the only aspect of the situation that was even remotely advantageous was the fact that I could hear Stephanie from the second floor landing, which meant that I didn't have to climb all the way to the third floor and wear myself out, although the overriding factor remained that Stephanie's lascivious behavior forced me to rely on the inferior marijuana of others. Sadly, however, none of this prevented her from returning to the kind of supercilious attitude that made her so objectionable in the first place.

Once the party was in full swing, I was surprised by the fact that Mike Magnelli had reversed his decision to stay home. Although he was back in town, he had initially intended to avoid Teresa, but now that he had taken the risk of seeing her, he threw himself into the experience with very little restraint, starting in on a case of Heineken shortly after his arrival, commandeering the record player, and subjecting us to the first ninety seconds of "Blank Generation" by Richard Hell and the Voidoids over loud protests from the rest of the guests. This group was just as dreadful as its name, and despite the fact that our friendship meant everything to me, I tore across the room and put an end to the disturbance, scratching Mike's record in the process. Although Teresa had yet to arrive, she was affecting us in her absence, and it was obvious that Mike and I were partying in a desperate way.

Somewhere around midnight, Mary McGill walked in the front door holding a small object. "Remember this?" she asked, holding it up so I could see.

"My dance tape!" I cried.

I had completely forgotten that I had lent it to Mary, and though my reunion with this object shouldn't have been as joyful as it was, I rushed over to her, grabbed the tape, and lurched over to the record player, scratching still another record as I removed it from the turntable. Once I inserted the dance tape, the party shifted into a higher gear.

When Carol Luckman entered the living room, I remembered

that she had invited me over to her apartment the week before. Until then, we had expressed very little interest in each other, but the sight of her stretched out on the floor proved to be a challenge. Sure enough, when she arched her back suggestively, I jumped off the couch and kissed her; but a moment later we both regretted what we had done, and I scrambled to my feet like Ralph Devlin had when Lorraine turned off the horror movie.

Seeing Carol was embarrassing enough, but the most disastrous development of all occurred when I uttered the phrase "white nigger." By then, Walter Devereaux had already established himself as the recipient of a "genius grant," a talented film maker, and a strong proponent of civil rights; but that didn't prevent me from offending him in the five or ten minutes that immediately preceded my blacking out. This wouldn't have been possible, of course, if my racist tendencies hadn't been incited by an Elvis Costello song that contained that very phrase, and if the song hadn't planted in my mind the pathological desire to attempt the phrase with the least likely person to appreciate it. In my enthusiasm, I was perfectly willing to pretend that this wasn't a sign of racism at all, but a form of sophistication that was loosely connected to the books I had read, my fondness for the Allen Ginsberg phrase "negro streets," and my admiration for "The White Negro," the title of a Norman Mailer essay that otherwise left me cold. With that one horrible utterance, I lost Walter's friendship forever, but not until he rose from our sofa and informed me that the word "nigger" was unacceptable, using language that was remarkably similar to my brother's when Teresa referred to me as "jewface." Although Walter accepted my apology as I walked him to his car, he made it clear by ignoring the letter I wrote that he had no desire to continue the friendship. To this day, the incident with Walter Devereaux remains one of my deepest sources of shame.

After Walter drove away, Teresa made her much-awaited appearance, pulling up to the house with a strange man sitting next to her. This forced me into the hapless role of guessing his identity, and before I could review the names of the last few men she had mentioned, Teresa informed me that she wouldn't attend the party. About the only thing I did correctly that night was delay our screaming argument. Looking back on it, I believe that she had frustrated my attempt to pass her off as my girl-friend, and that I was enraged by my inability to sleep with her. In the end, those two factors combined to make the argument inevitable. (It goes without saying, I suppose, that the argument was pointless, and that the trifling details are hardly worth mentioning here.)

Later, when I went upstairs, I noticed that Sarah had neglected to close her door, and that the lamp from Woolworth's was sitting on her desk. At that moment, there was just enough light for me to see that she and Jimmie had fallen asleep, and that they had removed all of their clothing. In the tenderness that followed, I resisted the urge to cover her with a blanket and gave in to my fascination instead, staring at her for longer than I cared to admit. But how could I look away? Their lovemaking had chipped the polish on her toenails. Leaning forward, I closed her door, made my way up the steps, and collapsed onto my bed.

The next day—when my room finally stopped spinning—I dealt with some of the fallout: a used condom, Stephanie Pachter's brassiere, and the sex smells of someone else's conquest. It was time to clean up my act.

———

A scratched record was revolving on the turntable when I went downstairs in the morning. My speakers were sending static into the room. I had been too wasted to notice it the night before, but when I saw the record that I had selected, it was no wonder that I had cleared the place out. I had picked "Just Like a Man" by Graham Parker. It was one of his best songs, but it was too depressing to dance to. Under the circumstances, it made me think of my failure with Teresa.

Do you know what got me when I searched in vain for the record cover? The fact that I was still afraid of her, but fear has a logic of its own. All of my logic told me that she would have belittled me in bed. I'm not proud of it, but I just couldn't risk that. It would have set me back another two years.

Then there was Sarah. Although I saw the value of moving on, I had no one to replace her with, and it was hard to follow through. Rather than stick around—and continue to live with her—I opted to change my locale as I had in the past. Before I left, however, there was something I had to do.

"Stephanie? I have your bra."

"Who is this?"

"Mark Glassman."

"Oh, right."

"Would you like to pick it up or should I bring it over?"

"Can you mail it to me?"

"I suppose I could, but it seems like a lot of trouble to go to for a bra."

"Can you bring it to Chaucer's?"

"Sure. I'll wrap it discretely."

"I would appreciate that. Maybe Todd would like to join you."

"That ship has sailed, but don't worry, you've already made it clear that you don't want to sleep with me."

"I just felt it was something I should say."

"Since I was inviting myself over at three in the morning, it *was* something you should say."

"So you're not upset?"

"Not really. It's a numbers game, kinda like sales."

"I suppose that's one way of looking at it. I'm in real estate so I know what you mean."

"Although it was a little painful for me when you ended up with Ronnie Abrams."

"He's a nice man. I like him."

"Yeah. That was pretty obvious."

Stephanie laughed, then continued in the same parrying tone

as before. "We locked you out of your bedroom, didn't we?"

"That's OK. I wasn't doing anything with it."

"I'm sorry. I was out of my mind."

"It's all right, but tell me something. Why aren't you attracted to me? Is it physical, emotional, or intellectual?"

"Actually, it's a combination of all three."

"But if you had to narrow it down, what would it be?"

"Let me see. I guess it's because you're repressed."

"Of course I'm repressed. All of my *real* thoughts are inappropriate."

"Whose fault is that, Mark?"

"Certainly not mine. But let me get this straight. If I could bring the inner and outer man into a greater harmony, I might have a chance with you?"

"I can't answer that. It's purely hypothetical."

"Try."

"I didn't say you would have a chance with me. You asked me to narrow it down."

"It sounds like there are a multitude of reasons, and not just the three we've mentioned."

"Why is it so important to you?"

"That was unresponsive, but I'll tell you anyway. I'm trying to sort things out."

"You could start by cutting back on the alcohol."

"I already have. I haven't had a single drop since the party."

"Unless my watched stopped, the party ended twelve hours ago."

"Yuh gotta start somewhere."

"That is so true."

"Anyway, about the bra. Why don't I drop it off?"

Stephanie relented, but she was none too happy about it. "All right, fine."

"Should I bring a bottle of wine? I have a nice Merlot here somewhere. Stephanie?"

"I didn't hear that."

"I was kidding."

"I'm glad. If you're gonna come over, it has to be soon. I'm showing a house at five."

"It will be. I've got the bra right here."

"Thank you. That was more than I needed to know."

Stephanie was supercilious, but I never said you couldn't have fun with her.

———————

As a result of the psychic pounding I had taken—most of it self-inflicted—I packed my bags for Long Beach Island, where I accepted a job as a dishwasher and spent the winter feeling sorry for myself, walking the deserted beach, and writing long letters to my brother. This was the same narrow strip of land where the Millsteins had a beach house, but at the other end of the island there was a little cottage that Teresa's mother had mentioned. I could rent it cheaply after Labor Day, as long as I vacated it by the spring when the seasonal renters would price me out of the market.

When I quit drinking and moved to Long Beach Island, I confronted the fact that my behavior had been a humiliation to me and that I had to do something about it. Granted, I'd had an enormous amount of fun—and it would have been disingenuous of me to regret it—but I couldn't continue in the same way. Part of my motivation lay in the fact that I had driven home from Dobbs countless times without remembering that I had done it, and my inability to find my parking spot the next morning should have been the least of my worries. I could have easily plowed into a pedestrian, and only dumb luck prevented me from killing someone and spending a decade in jail.

Throughout my time at Mr. Martin's, the Vega was registered at my father's address in Hershey, after he and my stepmother moved there. This mild form of insurance fraud enabled me to pay a lower rate than I would have if I had reported my actual address in Philadelphia. As a result, when I racked up a series of parking tickets while delivering pizzas, a constable showed up at my father's door. Because he was a nonconfrontational person—a trait that I had inherited from him except for the sarcasm that often brought me to the brink of a confrontation before I talked my way out of it—my father never addressed the issue with me directly. Instead, he griped about it to my brother.

Once Carl mentioned their conversation to me, I couldn't consult with my dad's mechanic the next time a car of mine died, which is why I was perilously close to completing a trifecta of the worst vehicles ever produced by the American auto industry now that I had replaced the Chevrolet Vega with an AMC Matador that I purchased for $600 from a seller in Upper Darby. This conniving individual placed an ad in the *Auto Trader*, limited my test drive to a brief spin around his neighborhood, and denied my request to drive the car on a highway, which almost certainly would have revealed the fact that its transmission was slipping.

When I forked over the money in front of the guy's house, he counted the bills slowly as though he distrusted *me*, while his teenage daughter watched with an inscrutable expression. I couldn't tell if she realized how much of a creep her father was or if it would take her another few years to find out. In any case, I ended up acquiring a car that was in the same general condition that the Vega was in a month before it died. All that separated me from completing the trifecta of automotive misfortune was the fact that I had yet to acquire a Ford Pinto, a shameful model that had the disturbing habit of bursting into flames when rammed from behind. I hadn't bought one of them yet, but knowing my mechanical ineptitude I wouldn't have put it past me, just as I would have been perfectly capable of springing for an Edsel, a Pacer, or a Gremlin if any of them remained on the market.

In the Scorsese film *Mean Streets*, a fat young Mafioso referred to his rival as a "mook," and though the man he was speaking with was unfamiliar with the term, he recognized it as the insult that it was. Lunging at his tormenter, the man landed several punches before all hell broke loose in a brawl involving Robert DeNiro, Harvey Keitel, and five or six obligatory character actors to simulate Italian-American culture. This scene was so fully realized that it remained in my consciousness for years. From that point on, I took to uttering the word "mook" at every opportunity, until Dan Hiller had the divine inspiration of nicknaming the Matador "the mookmobile," conveying my vehicular track record with an admirable economy of expression.

Even though I had already ensured my place on the ignominious list of car owners, I still tempted fate by weighing down the Matador with all of the books, records, and clothing that it could accommodate, no doubt decreasing its life expectancy by at least a few days, until the only question that remained was which would give out first, the transmission or the ball joints, the same part of the suspension system that had plagued Joe McBride's truck in Fairmount.

Lacking the funds to pay for a moving company, I was limited in what I could bring and forced to say a sad farewell to the shag carpet that I had lugged around to every living arrangement that followed 2601 in my checkered past. The carpet had begun its existence as a high-ticket item when my mother and Harry had selected it at a showroom on the Main Line but had descended into an odoriferous form of decrepitude that brought to mind the Paul Simon lyric in which a boxer carries the reminders of every glove that's laid him down or cut him 'til he cries out in his anger and his shame, only this time the reminder didn't come in the form of a blow to the head but the redolent odors of onions, peppers, stale pizza sauce, and canned tuna that had been transferred from my sweaty feet to the shag carpet between the time that I removed my clothing and the moment I made it into the shower in the house I shared with Sarah. But now, instead of feeling anger or shame, I took a bloated pride in the fact that I had made a ballsy move to Long Beach Island, once again romanticizing my marginally bohemian existence out of all proportion. (Apparently, whoever replaced me in Sarah's house had no such misgivings about parting with the carpet and promptly carried it to the sidewalk.)

When I drove down to the shore with all of my belongings in

September 1983, my record collection obscured the rear window of the Matador; and whenever I glanced in that direction, I was rewarded with the comforting sight of Bob Dylan holding a cat on his lap on the cover of *Bringing It All Back Home*. The cottage was all mine until May, and my first order of business was to make sure that Dylan made it safely to the sofa, a disconcerting piece of furniture that consisted of an enormous beanbag that threw my back out the only time I sat on it. Once I secured the Dylan album, I opted for one of the wicker chairs to compile a list of the things I needed to get started. As it turned out, it wasn't a long list since the cottage was completely furnished, and I found myself at Hand's department store a few minutes later. This establishment was across the street from a miniature golf course that was days away from shutting down for the winter, but I was in too good a mood to worry about the implications of its closure. I would go on to become a regular customer of Hand's during my time on Long Beach Island, but my initial purchase consisted of a pack of rolling papers, a quart of milk, and an Entenmann's chocolate cake.

Although her business slowed down after Labor Day, Fran Bostick offered me a job at the Village Tavern. The plan was for me to cook for her on the weekends, but when I showed up for my first day, she led me to a cramped office off the kitchen, where the shelves were filled with cheesy-looking restaurant supply catalogs, owner's manuals, and family photographs. After I sat down, Fran told me that her volume at the restaurant had decreased to a greater degree than she had anticipated, and that she couldn't being me on as a cook.

"Don't look so upset," she said, "I know you moved here to work for me. I'm gonna make you a dishwasher and pay you a cook's wages. But you can't tell anybody, especially the other dishwasher."

"Fran, that's really good of you."

"Don't worry about it. Believe it or not, I was young once. I woulda shit a brick if my boss went back on her word."

"I'm ready to work. You'll see."

"OK, but I got one rule for you to follow. Leave my waitresses alone. They're easily distracted."

———————

Although I worked exceedingly hard for Fran—making sure that she got her money's worth—the waitresses were a highlight, particularly Dana Hansen. Most of the other women were in their early twenties and attending Ocean County College or Stockton State University; but Dana was older and a divorced mother of two. I had experienced some good fortune with Karen Marcus, the last divorcee I had met, so maybe history would repeat itself. At any rate, Dana and I took to each other quickly, shortly after I set up my boombox on a little metal shelf above the dishwashing machine and played "A Case of You" by Joni Mitchell. This shameless selection was an obvious ploy to attract a female; and though I was hoping for one of the younger waitresses to make her way over to me, Dana was the first to respond.

I should have known that the younger servers were unlikely to recognize Joni Mitchell's voice, but it no longer mattered once Dana and I got talking and I told her about my freshman year at Pitt, where I defiantly played the album *Blue* in my dormitory room, despite the fact that a pair of football players roomed with each other next door. Ray Olsen was an offensive lineman and Mike Bullino a safety on a football team that was in the middle of a miserable 1-10 season, so when they returned to their room every Saturday afternoon after another humiliating defeat they were in no mood to listen to Joni Mitchell. There is no doubt in my mind that they wrote me off as gay as soon as they discovered that component of my record collection (while using a harsher epithet to express the sexual orientation that they incorrectly assumed), but I got a perverse kick out of provoking them when they drowned out Joni Mitchell by playing *Aqualung* at the highest possible volume.

Dana was plain-looking with a slender figure, long brown hair, and an uneven complexion, but her craggy, cigarette voice held an attraction all its own, as did the fact that the same jokes that fell flat with the younger waitresses made a hit with her, and she took to leaning into me and grabbing my arm just as Heather Freeman had done when I made her laugh at the bookstore a decade before. The same attempted witticisms that caused the other waitresses to roll their eyes compelled Dana to make physical contact, and I loved every minute of it, even when we sat at the bar after my first shift and Dana informed me that she had been sleeping off and on with the dishwasher who worked at the Village Tavern in the daytime, the same individual from whom I was withholding my salary at Fran Bostick's insistence.

"You don't have a thing for dishwashers, do you?"

"No, I'm afraid not," Dana said.

"OK. I was just checking."

———

Dana took to hanging out at the dishwashing station whenever she waited for Fran to place her orders on the counter near the grill. This meant that our conversations proceeded in fits and starts that were interrupted by the need to balance the plates on her arm, walk at a brisk pace toward the swinging doors at the mouth of the kitchen, and stay to her right to avoid colliding with the servers who were entering the kitchen from the other side. Those servers were staying to their right also in abiding by one of the first rules of waitressing, knowing that a catastrophe involving a crock of steaming hot French Onion soup or some other menu item was only a misstep away.

Due to the constant interruptions, it wasn't until Dana and I sat down at the bar together at the end of my second night that we had a more leisurely conversation and she mentioned her widowed father, two school-aged children, and the fact that they were living with her dad in a palatial house on 84th Street in Harvey Cedars while he made the daily commute to his job as a bank executive in North Jersey. I reciprocated by mentioning that I had quit drinking but remained extremely enthusiastic about smoking pot. Judging by Dana's reaction, this was something else that we had in common in addition to Joni Mitchell. As we talked further, Dana shared a little more about her on-again, off-again relationship with the daytime dishwasher.

"Have you met him? His name's Michael."

"Yeah, I met him when I was clocking in. He seems like a nice guy."

"I like him, but he's leaving town next week. He's going back to Colorado."

"Is that where he's from?"

"Yeah, he's going back there to write. At least that's what he says."

"Really? I'd be interested in reading his stuff."

"Good luck with that. He hasn't written a word all summer."

"Maybe he's blocked. I understand that happens sometime."

"I don't know. He smokes huge quantities of pot, but it hasn't seemed to unblock him."

"If it were me, it would have the opposite effect. Pot removes any ambition I might have."

"Do you have any on you?"

"I don't have any here. I have some back at the cottage."

Dana hesitated slightly, as though she were considering it. "That's OK, maybe another time."

"That's fine. I'll bring some tomorrow. We'll just have to find a place to smoke it."

"We'll go behind the dumpster," Dana shrugged.

"Are you sure? I wouldn't want Fran to see."

"Are you kidding? Her brother smokes all the time."

"Is Fran aware of that?"

"Yeah, but she turns the other cheek. It actually helps his cooking."

"I know food tastes better when you're stoned, but whether

you actually cook better is an open question."

Dana smiled, then she got serious. "So how come you don't drink?"

"I drank way too much. I wasn't dealing with my issues."

"But you still get high?"

"Of course. Giving up both would be cruel and unusual punishment."

Dana was drinking a vodka gimlet, and she caught me staring at it.

"Should I not drink in front of you?"

"No, it doesn't bother me at all."

"Let me know if it does, OK?"

"Thanks, I will."

I took a sip of my orange juice, pretending it was a screwdriver.

———————

The system that Fran set up often required the waitresses to bus their own tables with rubber tubs and serve the food with large, round trays, the two activities sometimes taking place within minutes of each other. On the surface of it, it didn't seem the most sanitary division of labor, but on Saturday nights when the busboys were overwhelmed it was the only way for Fran to run her business. Although some of the younger waitresses griped about the need to supplement the busboys' efforts, Dana took it in stride and even made points with the customers in the way she served the food. The serving trays were silver in color, and she was the only waitress who was savvy enough to polish hers before each shift.

Before any of the customers arrived—including the white-haired septuagenarians who lined up at 4:30 to take advantage of Fran's "Early Bird Special"—Dana would punch the time clock, grab her tray, and clean it with Windex at an empty table in the dining room. As a result, her gleaming tray would send a subliminal message of pristine competence to her customers.

These same "early birds" were known locally as "Q-tips" for

the way their white hair appeared when you got stuck behind them on Route 72, a stretch of road where a series of retirement communities with soporific names like Pleasant Manor, Restful Pines, and Sleepy Hollow sent an endless stream of elderly drivers onto the highway for their one errand of the day, driving twenty-year-old cars at thirty miles an hour in a forty-mile-an-hour zone to pick up a single item like prunes, Polident, or Phillips Milk of Magnesia, not really needing those items since they had stockpiled them at discounted prices but opting to venture out anyway to give them a purpose in life and a little fresh air. More often than not, they paid no mind to the younger people they were obstructing and whose daily commerce required them to make full use of the speed limit or exceed it, stubbornly ignoring the younger drivers until they attempted to communicate with the old folks with the only means at their disposal, which was to tailgate, flash their high beams, beep their horns furiously, or utilize all of those measures at once provided they had the manual dexterity to do so, at which point their elderly adversaries not only refused to speed up or pull over to the side of the road to let the more purposeful drivers pass but obstinately decreased their speed to an even greater degree than before, completely monopolizing their portion of the two-lane highway. Shaking a liver-spotted fist at the young people behind them, they invariably forced the other drivers to choose between losing even more time now that they'd had the audacity to pressure the driver in front of them or making the potentially deadly decision to enter the lane of oncoming traffic and pass the old fogey before an innocent person who had absolutely nothing to do with the confrontation found to his or her horror that the last person they would ever see on earth was about to collide with them head-on. If there wasn't a blameless driver in a passenger car approaching, there was a good chance that a tractor-trailer was barreling down the road in the opposite direction instead. Frequently then, you were forced to stare at the back of the Q-tip's head for ten or fifteen miles until he reached his own senior living community and turned into its driveway. For those and other reasons, a fatal accident or two occurred every year on that aromatic, pine-shaded expanse of highway; but the fatalities almost never included any of the old folks who stayed in their lanes, minded their own business, and met the impatience of youth with intransigence and passive aggression. In fact, one of the only things you could do to pass the time and combat the stomach-churning outrage you experienced was to count the dental offices that had also proliferated along Route 72, no doubt owing to the gnashing of teeth that occurred while playing that particular game of chicken.

Although her liberal use of Windex enabled her to distinguish herself from the younger and more thoughtless servers, Dana had the same problem they did with the actual weight of the tray, particularly when it was covered with plates, bowls, and glasses. If you listened closely enough, Dana could often be heard emitting the slightest little grunt when she lifted the tray from the counter or when she lugged a tub full of dirty dishes across the dining room. By the time she reached my station, she invariably needed a rest and often lingered there while I started the process of rinsing the items off with a high-powered jet sprayer, placing them in their designated areas in the dishwashing machine, and sliding them along a metal platform that was equipped with rollers to ease some of the strain on the dishwasher's back. It wasn't until I grabbed the handle on the machine, lowered the metal door, and pushed the button that caused the washing to commence that Dana started to catch her breath. The smoking didn't help, but even if she swore off nicotine, there was no way to know how many more years her body would be able to withstand the physical demands of her profession.

One night when we were getting high behind the dumpster, the pot loosened Dana's tongue and she told me more about her relationship with the dishwasher who worked in the daytime.

"Today was his last day," she said. "He's leaving for Colorado in the morning."

"Will you miss him?"

"Not really. I wasn't that comfortable with it. I had to choose between setting a good example for my teenage daughter or sneaking around to get laid. And the sex wasn't all that good for either of us."

I must have winced, because Dana was studying me. "Did I say something wrong?" she asked.

"No, I wasn't ready for it, that's all."

She continued to read my expression. "It wasn't anything he did," she added. "I don't think he was that into me. In case you haven't noticed, I'm kinda light in the boob department."

"Really? Show me the evidence."

Dana was in mid-toke when I said it, and she immediately fell into a long coughing fit, doubling over and squeezing my arm the whole time.

"I can't take credit for that one. Michael Caine said it in *Educating Rita*. It cracked me up, too."

"I can see why," she gasped.

"Don't talk for a minute. Catch your breath."

"I'll be all right. You're seriously telling me that you never noticed I'm flat-chested?"

"Not really. If you must know, I like your figure. I find it intriguing."

For two people who had known each other for less than a week, we were certainly talking frankly.

"Well, Michael wasn't intrigued. If he was, I doubt he'd be going back to Colorado."

"Maybe he's ashamed of himself for not writing all summer."

"Possibly," she conceded. "But the first time I slept with him, he kept staring at my tits. I told him, 'You can keep staring at 'em if you want to, but they're not gonna get any bigger.'"

"Thatta girl—you tell 'im."

Whether she was being honest with me or not, Karen Marcus had told me that having an orgasm wasn't all that important to her, and that particular declaration had made all the difference in the world as to whether or not I could proceed. But Dana had gone even further by professing an indifference to sex, and I wasn't sure where that left me.

Although Dana made this plain, that didn't stop me from letting her know the attraction I felt when she came to the cottage to borrow some pot. Three of her girlfriends were waiting in her car with the motor running when I handed her a nickel bag just inside the front door. Our eyes met for a second and I placed my finger inside one of the loops on her belt and exerted the slightest pressure to pull her toward me. Again, she clearly considered it—just as she had considered coming over to the cottage on my first night on the job—but finally she gave a slight shake of the head and said, "I'd better not." There was no immediate disdain as there often was in some of my earlier attempts with women, and no telltale look of horror to underscore the rejection. If anything, this was the sweetest rejection I'd ever experienced, and once I realized that Dana had other reasons for saying no, it actually encouraged me to feel more attractive.

"Come to the party," she said.

"I will. I'll be there soon."

The younger servers were an impossibility for me. They never lingered at the dishwashing station or laughed at any of my jokes. Nor did they appreciate my taste in music. Whereas I could entice Dana to stay a moment if I played an oldie like "Suspicious Minds," "The Wanderer," or "Hit the Road, Jack," the younger women would cover their ears, roll their eyes, or beg me to turn the music off if they deigned to speak with me at all. The only common ground I ever found with the waitresses younger than Dana was when I played the David Bowie song "Modern Love" and one of them asked me what I was listening to with an actual spark of interest.

Not willing to compromise on the music I played on my beat-up boombox from Radio Shack—a smaller, cheaper version than the one that Mike Magnelli lugged around in the early days of his relationship with Teresa—I refused to purchase any of the cassettes that might have caused the younger waitresses to linger if not flirt, because that would have required me to waste ten or fifteen dollars on Pat Benatar, Jon Bon Jovi, and a group called Quiet Riot whose dreadful 1983 song "Come On Feel the Noise" contained the lyric "girls, rock your boys" which even enthralled Fran's thirteen-year-old daughter Kelly, who waltzed around the kitchen, got in everyone's way without doing a lick of work, and sang the song so incessantly that it replaced "Mandy" on my musical shit list.

On the other hand, Dana was more guarded when discussing her kids. It took a couple of weeks before she felt comfortable telling me about them, but once she did, she didn't waste any time inviting me over to meet them.

"I want to tell you why I didn't sleep with you that night."

"You don't have to, Dana."

"No, it's OK."

"Honestly? I'm not sure I want to hear it."

"That's exactly what I'm saying. It wasn't you—you're great. If I had met you instead of my asshole ex-husband, we would've had a great time together."

I just looked at her, probably with a stupid look of gratitude. "No one has ever said anything like *that* to me before."

"Well, that's their problem. Maybe they weren't paying attention. But the reason I didn't sleep with you is that I have enough trouble keeping my shit together. I'm not the best mother in the world. My instincts are lacking and I forget things. It's awful."

"What kind of things do you forget?"

"I'll give you an example. Trust me, it's one of many. I went to Shoprite the other day, and I came home all excited. I had bought taco shells and all the ingredients. Billy's eleven—he got this big smile on his face when I told him what we were having for dinner. And than I looked over at Marnie. She's my fourteen-year-old going on forty. She's way more mature than I was at her age."

Dana paused as though she had come to the end of her story.

I had to remind her to continue. "What did Marnie say?"

"See what I mean? I forgot the punchline. She said, 'Mom, I can't eat tacos. I have braces!' How can a mother forget her own kid has braces?"

"Dana, it was a momentary lapse. You can't beat yourself up over it."

"I seem to have momentary lapses ten or fifteen times a day. You have to understand—Michael was a distraction to me. He made demands on my time. And besides, I wasn't all that into having a man in my life. Like I said, it wasn't you."

"OK. Thanks for explaining it to me."

"I don't want to sleep with you, Mark. Try not to tempt me."

"That shouldn't be a problem. Women have rarely been tempted in the past."

Dana shrugged. "Maybe things are changing for you. Do you wanna meet 'em?"

"Your kids? Sure. Do you think they'll like me?"

"I do. You're good with Kelly—even though she's a brat."

"I just ask about her interests and off she goes. I don't have to say anything for another half-hour."

"That's a good trick. Where did you learn that?"

I hadn't thought about it until then, but suddenly it came into focus. "From my brother. I have two nephews. I asked him, 'Carl, what do you say to a three-year-old? What the hell do yuh talk about?'"

Dana laughed. "What did he say?"

"You have to understand. My brother came of age in the '60s. He said, 'You just climb onto their trip. The rest'll take care of itself.'"

"It sounds like wisdom might run in your family."

———

I settled into life at the Village Tavern comfortably—just as I had at Mr. Martin's. Apparently, I could thoroughly enjoy being underemployed as long as the cast of characters was colorful enough and I clicked with some of them on a personal level.

When Dana and I distracted each other from our work—and Dana's break at the dishwashing machine lasted a little longer than Fran would have liked—Fran would bark an order and give me the evil eye. "Mark, I need salad bowls!" she would shout, or "Mark, where are my plates?"

"They're in the dishwasher, Fran. Where do you think they are?"

Because they doubted the wisdom of my saying this, the waitresses held their breath until Fran burst out laughing, ending the silence that had come over them and terminating the brief period in which they stared at me in amazement, having never encountered a dishwasher (or anyone else for that matter) who had successfully penetrated Fran's gruff exterior to uncover the big-hearted matriarch within.

When a little blue-haired lady left three quarters of a New York strip steak on her plate before it was transported to the kitchen one night, I turned to Dana and said, "Do you see what I see?"

"Yeah, what about it?"

"I'm gonna eat that sucker."

"You are not!"

"Watch me."

"Don't let Fran see you. I know you amuse her, but she has her limits."

"It's medium rare, Dana. It's out of my control."

"What?" Fran shouted, removing broccoli from a steamer, putting it on a plate, and dabbing at her forehead with her shirtsleeve. "What's he doin' now?"

Dana looked at me. "You tell her. I'm not."

"What's there to tell?" I said, grabbing the steak, tilting my head back, and taking an enormous bite in plain view of Fran.

"Come on!" Fran yelled. "You were brought up better than that!"

"That's exactly the point."

"Wash your hands at least. They're filthy!"

"I can't help it," I said, "you're too good a cook."

"Save it for later at least!"

Ruthie, one of the shapelier waitresses, entered at this point, enabling me to catch her eye and leer. "I can't! I want it now!"

"What was that?" Fran asked, while Ruthie looked away.

"He said he wants it now," Dana shrugged.

Fran paused to shake her head, losing a good fifteen seconds in the mayhem that cooking at the Village Tavern had become. "I don't wanna see," she said, covering her eyes at the precise instant that her tomato-faced, leafy-eared husband pushed through the swinging doors into the kitchen.

"What's goin' on here?" he cried, staring with a dumbfounded expression at the unprecedented sight of Fran goofing off. "We got a restaurant to run!"

"Joe, get outa my kitchen!" Fran barked, causing Joe to ignore her in his usual fashion for the purpose of asking an inane question that could easily have waited until things quieted down. It had only taken me a few days to realize that all of Joe's questions could wait since they were rarely about the restaurant itself.

"When will my golf shirts be ready?"

"How the hell do I know? Didja stop at the dry cleaner?"

"Heh?"

"Didja stop at the dry cleaner, I said!"

"I thought you were stoppin'!"

"Leave me alone, awright? We'll talk about it later."

"What time's my tee time tomorra? I forget."

"Joe? I'll smack yuh!"

"Oh, fer Chrissakes!" he grumbled, making a hasty retreat, executing an immediate right turn that was visible through the little circular window in the swinging doors, and sitting down on the barstool that was reserved for him, a seat that permanently bore an indentation from his lazy ass while he went on annoying the bartender Carmen, glad-handing the customers, and thinking up another meritless, ill-timed question to bother Fran with as she did 99% of the work that the two of them performed in the operation of their restaurant.

"Can I bring yuh a Coke?" Dana asked, turning away from the

spectacle of the Bosticks' marriage and preparing to reenter the dining room, where she was serving a total of eight tables that ceaselessly required her attention. The other waitresses were limited to five or six, but Dana was enough of a pro to handle it.

"No, but you can bring me a nice Shiraz to go with that steak. Ask Carmen. He knows which one I like."

"I thought you quit drinking."

"Is that what I told you? I must have been drunk at the time."

"Dana!" Fran yelled. "Pick up!"

"To be continued," Dana smiled.

After their shifts, the waitresses typically sat in groups of four to count their tips at the dining room tables, telling war stories and creating huge stacks of bills. Then they would make their way to the bar and ask Carmen to exchange the one-dollar bills for larger denominations. A few of the waitresses would sit at the bar for a drink or two, flirting with the customers or ignoring them as they saw fit, while Joe made his way through an unimaginable number of boilermakers until Fran closed up shop and joined him for a single drink before driving him home.

On my fourth or fifth night, Dana rose from her barstool and found me out by the dumpster, where she gave me a playful little "hip check" that was vaguely reminiscent of ice hockey. There was an industrial-sized garbage bag in my hand and another one at my feet, each of them weighed down by four or five gallons of foul restaurant liquid. The garbage bags often overflowed from the dumpster at the Village Tavern, and though Frank Tattaglia would have been appalled, this was a sign of prosperity. Invariably, several of the bags split open when they were tossed over the side of the dumpster, while others were descended upon by seagulls whose beaks and talons tore into them, successfully reaching the chicken bones, discarded fish heads, rotting fruits and vegetables, leftover sections of steaks and chops, congealed animal fat, and all of the other refuse that kitchen workers deal with on a daily basis. Dana must have really liked me because she reached for the garbage bag that sat at my feet, but I got to it before she did.

"Dana, you don't have to do that!"

"Why? Me strong," she said, pulling back her sleeve and making a muscle.

"I'm sure you are, but you already freshened up in the ladies' room."

"Are you kidding? I stink!"

"I wouldn't say that."

I tossed the last of the garbage bags into the dumpster, where it promptly burst at the seams and became someone else's problem.

"I told yuh it was nasty," I said, "but you wouldn't believe me."

"You're right. I'll see you tomorrow."

I grabbed the metal cart that transported the garbage bags from the kitchen. It had taken several hits recently and had developed a tendency to drift to the right. I had to compensate for that at the end of my shift, while the wobbly wheels of the cart squeaked in protest the entire time.

———

After Michael returned to Colorado, I picked up some daytime hours on the weekend, a development that enabled me to procrastinate a little longer on finding a second job. It was only a matter of time before I would have to do that, and I wasn't looking forward to it given the number of businesses that had closed for the winter.

Between the $400 a month I was paying for the cottage and the vast quantities of pot I was buying as an unseemly substitute for the alcohol I'd been consuming back home, I was barely getting by financially. But at the same time, I was thinking far less frequently of the two women that I had been infatuated with. Instead of wallowing in self-pity as I had anticipated, I was actually enjoying myself.

Picking up the extra shifts at the restaurant gave me another two meals a week that I didn't have to pay for. It also gave me something else to talk about with Fran. By now, our kidding around had become a regular thing. Fran's maternal tendencies expressed themselves in the way that she treated all of her workers, but she seemed to particularly enjoy feeding me. Unlike my own mother, Fran seemed to be amused by the fact that I had the eating habits of an eight-year-old boy.

"I could heat yuh some Cioppino in the mike," she said at one point, when I made my way to the dishwashing station.

"Does it have vegetables in it?"

"A few," Fran scowled. "Why?"

"I hate vegetables."

"You may like it. It's got jumbo shrimp."

"I'm sure it's superbly prepared, but vegetables are a deal-breaker."

"I'm not sayin' I'd do this, but what if I made a batch without vegetables, would yuh eat it then?"

"Only if you removed all of the seafood. I won't eat that either."

"It wouldn't be Cioppino then."

"That's not my problem. You'd have to call it something else."

"You live a block from the ocean, but you won't eat fish. How do you explain that?"

"Fran, did you see how I tore into that steak?"

"Yeah. So?"

"By that logic, I would live near a cattle ranch. One thing has nothing to do with the other."

"You have an answer for everything, don't you?"

"Pretty much, with the exception of my sex life."

"I told yuh—I don't wanna hear it. How 'bout a cheeseburger? I got some nice ground chuck."

"Sounds good—I like 'em medium rare. Do we have any seeded rolls?"

"No—Joe ate the last one."

"What else did he do? I'm afraid to look."

This was a reference to Joe's habit of leaving his breakfast dishes near the dishwashing machine for me to wash. More often than not, there was a nasty surprise whenever I handled one of his plates. There was a pair of oversized rubber gloves hanging on a hook nearby, but I had made it a point of pride to do the work with my bare hands—until I discovered the gob of phlegm that Joe had deposited into a crumpled-up napkin. Not only did the discovery cause me to reverse my decision about the rubber gloves—at least when I was doing Joe's dishes—but it gave me a new-found respect for Michael who was now two thousand miles away pretending to be a writer.

Even when there was no mucus to be found in Joe's leftovers, the experience of washing his dishes was gross enough owing to his gentile tastes in food, which often consisted of creamed chipped beef on toast (a breakfast entrée that had earned its original nickname of "shit-on-a-shingle" and had preserved it on merit ever since); the kind of greasy link sausages that no self-respecting Jew would eat whether he was observing dietary restrictions or not; and a Philadelphia area favorite called scrapple that consisted of the parts of a pig that were judged to be "scraps" for a reason. Even if it would make my case stronger, I can't possibly contend that Joe was the only person on Long Beach Island who consumed that monstrosity, but he may have been the only one who expected another human being to clean up after him once he added seven or eight cigarette butts to his early morning output, the cigarettes, of course, being the main cause of the hacking cough that had produced the vile-looking sputum in the first place. The only equal of this repulsive substance might have been the secretion produced by Linda Blair in *The Exorcist*, a film that would have scared the shit out of me even if I hadn't ingested mescaline beforehand.

While Fran prepared an early lunch for me at 10:30 in the morning, my first task of the day was to clean the dishes that Joe had used and abused three hours before. Sweating, engulfed in steam, my glasses fogged up by the 160 degree heat, I contemplated the thought of Joe's bright red face, broken blood vessels, oversized ears, arthritic back, and sour facial expression, shuddering to think what was going on in the man's ulcerous stomach.

Until Fran told me that my lunch was ready, I was able to behold the fascinating arrangement that existed in their marriage, a give-and-take in which Joe's only real responsibilities were to stay out of the way, line up a summer's worth of entertainment once a year, and make the occasional trip to the liquor store, a labor of love that almost exclusively involved his own booze since Carmen had a pretty good handle on the inventory that was required for the customers.

Every spring, Joe would contact the same tired old performers that the Village Tavern had featured previously, calling a motley collection of Elvis impersonators, Frank Sinatra wannabes, and second rate Al Martino's, not to negotiate with them (since they were so desperate they would have taken nearly anything, even a plate of Fran's man-a-got) but to determine if nature had taken its course and caused any of them to expire, thereby reducing Joe's roster of entertainers. But just when Joe thought that death would overtake Arnold Zeller and he would finally have to replace him, he learned that the tough, grizzled, pot-bellied man had survived another winter and could offer his King of Rock and Roll shtick at least one more time.

None of the front men that Joe hired would ever be mistaken for Mick Jagger—existing as they did at the opposite end of the spectrum and saddled as they were with toupees, false teeth, and dubious taste in music—but that did nothing to curb Joe's enthusiasm or prevent him from embarrassing himself on the dance floor at one of their performances.

As it turned out, a little Arnold Zeller went a long way, and when he sang the Willie Nelson song "On the Road Again" for the umpteenth time and reached its last gasp declaration—"I can't wait to be on the road again"—I couldn't help myself and shouted "What's stoppin' yuh?" from the depths of the kitchen, much to the delight of the waitresses. Needless to say, Fran heard the remark also, so her amusement was tempered by the knowledge that Joe would come barging into the kitchen at any moment if he heard my comment from where he was sitting, or if Carmen had repeated it to him perversely. Knowing that Joe would be forced to determine the source of the impertinence, Fran directed the servers to steer clear of the swinging doors and observe a sixty second moratorium on the serving of food, until Joe barged into the kitchen on cue, sent his boozy gaze around the room, and fixed his bloodshot eyes on the only person who could have been responsible for such incivility.

"Was that you?" he demanded.

"It sure was," I said, but before Joe's jugular vein could become any more engorged, Fran ordered him to leave. As usual, Joe capitulated with his wife's demand, but not until he pointed at me with a crooked finger and told me to watch my step. Unfortunately, he would have been better off watching his own step because the act of raising his hand and speaking at the same time caused him to lose his equilibrium, extend his other hand to steady himself, and yelp in pain when his hand made contact with the coffee pot that rested on a nearby table. Joe did his best to bear up manfully until Fran read his expression after a lifetime of practice. "Dana, bring me the first aid kit, would yuh?"

As it turned out, the only saving grace in Joe's hideous taste in music was his fondness for the female breast. Once a year he would bring in a Dolly Parton look-alike who couldn't sing a lick but was obviously well-endowed, her chest straining the buttons of her faded Western shirt as she pranced around the Village Tavern's rinky-dink bandstand. Although it was amazing what a little comeliness could do for a bad voice, nothing could have redeemed the woman's version of "Here You Come Again" or prevented me from protesting her ruination of a genuinely good song that had been originated by an artist who deserved better. Country music had never been my thing until I discovered Hank Williams in *The Last Picture Show*, but this particular rendition seemed a perversion of it, and when combined with the shoddy acoustics in the Village Tavern dining room and the incessant clattering of dishes, it was no wonder that my commentary walked a fine line between sarcasm and insubordination.

"The only real entertainment is looking at these people," I said, "since listening to them is so intolerable."

"Keep your mouth shut," Fran replied, stifling a laugh. "The last thing I need is Joe comin' into the kitchen."

"I won't keep my mouth shut, but I'll lower my voice."

"Will that satisfy your urge to show off for my waitresses?"

"No, but as long as I can hear myself, it has a certain value."

"Do you see the tits on her?" Dana asked, jerking her head toward the bandstand. "Even Michael wouldn't have liked *that* chest."

"How 'bout her tone-deaf backup band? Between *her* tits and *their* toupees, I don't know where to look first."

"Why don't you keep your eyes on the dishes?" Fran retorted, knowing full well that I would ignore this directive until all of my wisecracks were exhausted, whether or not there was a drop-off in quality.

"Some of them have breasts *and* toupees, and that's what's really scary."

"Oh, Jesus Christ!" Fran screamed. "Stop awready, you're killin' me."

"Dana," I said, "go borrow some nitroglycerin from Joe. We may need it for Fran."

"No, I better not," Dana replied, employing the same diction that she had used when I propositioned her at the cottage. But before I could mention it to her, she returned to the dining room.

"I'm starting a list of the most nauseating songs that have ever been performed here, Fran, and it may take a while. Do you have enough salad bowls to tide you over?"

"Why don't you work and run your mouth at the same time?" she asked, despite the fact that I was doing exactly that.

"Can you give me a minute? I'm busy. How 'bout 'Tie a Yellow Ribbon Round the Ole Oak Tree'? That would qualify, wouldn't it?"

"Christ, I hate that friggin' song," Fran followed. Bending down, she opened her oven and poked at a line of potatoes.

"You don't know how much *I* hate it," I answered, sounding as murderous as I could. "And I don't blame the musicians, I blame your husband. You may want to increase his life insurance."

"It's already maxed out," Fran said. It was almost blasphemous how she was busting on Joe with the slightest encouragement from me.

Dana returned with a tub full of dirty dishes, walked over to me, and hoisted the dishes onto the counter with the little grunt that I had come to know and love. "What are we doin'?"

"We're makin' a list," Fran said. Now it was official: she had increased the number of slackers in her own kitchen by one, having too much fun to restrain herself.

"Of what?" Dana asked.

After I filled Dana in on what the list was all about, she stared at Fran and shook her head. "I've never seen her like this." That was my opening, of course.

"She hasn't had this much fun since Joe was hospitalized with diverticulitis."

"Have you no shame?" Dana asked, shaking her head again.

"If I do, it has yet to make an appearance."

"I've got one," she said. "How 'bout 'Rocky Top, Tennessee'? I hear that one in my sleep."

"Fran, should we accept that one?"

"Marrone, I hate that song, too!"

"Dana, I think that's a yes."

"Yeah? What do I win?" she followed, with trace amounts of flirtation.

"What do you *want* to win?"

"I don't know," she said, still holding my gaze. "Can I think about it?"

By now, she had aroused the early stages of an erection, but the fog of the dishwasher was helping to obscure it. Just to be sure, I threw in another song.

"How 'bout 'Rockin' Robin.' Is that brutal or what?"

"I'm tellin' yuh," Fran agreed.

"If he sings that again, I'm gonna deck the bastard."

"Yeah? You and whose army?"

"I'm just sayin', Fran."

"I think she got you on that one," Dana smiled, and down went the erection. "That asshole last week?" she continued, returning to "Rockin' Robin" as the butt of our joke. "He couldn't even whistle."

"You can't whistle with false teeth," I said.

"Is that true?" Wendy put in. She was too young to have thought much about false teeth—so she came by the question honestly.

"Sure, it's a known fact," I insisted. Being full of shit had never stopped me before. "The next time you go out there, ask Arnold if he knows any Buddy Holly."

"Who's Arnold?"

"The King of Rock and Roll. Our entertainment for the night."

"Oh, him."

"Singing is only one of his skills. He sells auto parts in Forked River."

"You're making that up," Wendy said, growing impatient with me again.

"He actually does," Fran added. "How did you know that?"

"I asked him when he was on a break. Wendy, do you even know who Buddy Holly is?"

"I've never heard of him," she said, carrying a tray of food to the dining room.

"That's still more proof that youth is wasted on the young. I should know—I'm an expert on the subject."

"To hear *you* tell it, you're an expert on *every* subject," Fran said, "Now can you please get back to work?"

A few minutes later, Arnold Zeller came out with an announcement. "The next one goes out to the dishwasher—bless his heart." With that, he launched into a God-awful version of "Peggy Sue." This rendition was so faulty that I might not have recognized it if I hadn't requested Buddy Holly myself.

"Clear the doorway!" I yelled, as Joe came storming into the kitchen, his tomato face appearing in the little round window and enabling me to warn the others. Before he came to a halt at the midpoint between Fran's workstation and mine, he slipped on a wet spot and wrenched his back, his bloodshot eyes bulging out a split second before the pain made its way through the boilermakers pickling his nervous system. When Joe's stomach was acting up—as it apparently was now—his bloodhound face was the saddest thing you could imagine. How a man could be ambulatory looking like that I will never know.

"What the fuck did I tell yuh?" he demanded, grimacing, grabbing his back, and fixing me with his gaze. "Franny, you gotta fire this guy!"

"I'm not firin' him, Joe, and that's final."

Before Joe could answer, Cindy entered the kitchen. She was an elementary school teacher, and if her demeanor at the Village Tavern was any indication, she had the most well-behaved classroom in the state. Not only was she all business, but she made it perfectly clear that she didn't suffer fools gladly, which meant that Joe and I fell silent and waited for her to speak. "Fran, can I substitute rice pilaf for a baked potato?"

"Sure, what the hell?" Fran answered, still a little giddy from the list we'd been compiling.

Cindy raised her eyebrows at this apparent breach of protocol, but decided against delaying her return to the dining room any longer than she had to, now that she had discerned the chaos I had caused in the kitchen. "Should I charge anything extra?"

"Nah," Fran said, "let it go."

Still smarting over my continued presence in the kitchen—and Fran's refusal to fire me—Joe picked a fight with one of the customers, taking a poke at a Q-tip who was even more incapacitated than he was. The two of them faced off in the bar area and swung at each other wildly, their punches missing by more than a foot until Carmen bear-hugged the customer and I wrapped my arms around Joe, a step slow in realizing that Joe had already collapsed into a protracted smoker's cough that prevented him from doing damage to anyone but himself.

As soon as the fight began—if you can actually call it that when no punches were landed—the music came to a halt in the middle of a stirring rendition of "I Write the Songs," another cringe-worthy effort by Barry Manilow, a recording artist that I couldn't seem to avoid.

"I just thought of another song for our list," I said, turning to Dana while Joe went on hacking in my arms.

"Can it wait, Mark? Joe's in bad shape."

At that point, I grabbed a glass of water from a nearby table and turned back to Joe, saying "Here, drink some of this." Joe's eyes bulged even more now that he saw who was ministering to him, and his cough deteriorated into an even more propulsive hack. "Dana," I said, "you might want to take over."

Dana led Joe to a neutral corner while Carmen did the same with Joe's opponent, finally drawing Fran from the kitchen. "Joe, are you OK?"

"Hell, yes, I'm OK! I was about to kill the old bastard."

"What old bastard? Mr. Sweeney? He doesn't even know who he is!"

"He called me a drunk!"

As addled as Mr. Sweeney was, his hearing had apparently survived, because he interjected a comment. "I don't know what else you would call it. Every time I see you, you're throwin' down a whiskey."

"What business is that of yours?" Joe followed, slightly distracted by an examination of his handkerchief, which currently housed another alarming substance.

"I'll show you whose business it is!" Sweeney cried, lurching to his feet while Carmen re-applied the bear-hug.

"What did he say?" Joe asked.

"Forget it," Carmen said, "It's over."

Just then—as Arnold Zeller belted out the first few notes of "It's Not Unusual" by Tom Jones—I caught the eye of a saucy little waitress named Francine, hoping to glean some residual benefit from helping Carmen break up a fight, only to have Francine ignore the overture and walk away while Dana smirked at me from across the room. "My hero," she said.

Back in the kitchen, I launched into a boozy rendition of "Spanish Eyes" by Engelbert Humperdink, but before I could reach the chorus, Fran tossed a wet washrag at me from the sauté area. The rag missed me by a foot and a half but draped itself over my boombox.

"That's enough, Mark. I really mean it this time."

"OK," I said, removing the washrag and wringing it out in the sink.

Fran stared at me. "Don't tell me. I found a way to shut you up?"

———————

By mid-September, Dana and I were spending time together away from the restaurant, getting stoned at one point and making our way to the Shoprite in the Manahawkin Plaza. The time was drawing near for me to find another job, and this particular strip mall had eight or ten businesses that would eventually come into play. I made a mental note of it as I followed Dana into the store. By then, she had lowered her head, raised a finger to her lips, and said, "What's fast?" Being habitually late for nearly everything, this was often a concern, but now the need was particularly acute since there was less than an hour to go before her kids would get home from school and her father would complete his commute from North Jersey. Her dad was a tall, white-haired widower who had been in the field of information technology from its inception. Now he headed the IT department of Provident Bank and divided his time between his winter and summer homes, ignoring the fact that Dana was something of a fuck-up, forgiving her for her past sins, and easing her financial burden. This enabled Dana to live in a good school district year-round for the betterment of his grandchildren.

Dana paused in front of the deli counter, concentrating with all her might to keep the preferences of her children straight.

"I could pick up something from here," she said, "or would

GLASSMAN

that be a bad idea?"

"Are you asking *me*?"

"Yeah, what do you think?"

"For the side dishes maybe. You might want to cook something."

"You're right, but it would take too long."

"How 'bout a rotisserie chicken? Can Marnie eat that?"

"Your guess is as good as mine."

"Dana!"

"I was kidding. Yeah, she can eat chicken."

"I'll pick one out. Where will you be after the deli counter, in case I wander off?"

"I know where I *won't* be—the taco aisle."

While Dana conversed with a deli clerk—a teenage girl who had been forced to wear a hairnet—I rescued a chicken from the heat lamp, returning in time for my co-worker to take possession of her order. Whenever Fran made more than one entrée available to the servers for their free meal, Dana had a habit of changing her mind. Judging by the clerk's expression, she did the same thing at the Shoprite, finally settling on a pasta salad, rice pudding, and Muenster cheese, which her father adored. The fact that she remembered her dad made the selection process all the more endearing, and I realized how challenging her life had become as she lugged the heavy trays at the restaurant, raised her voice to communicate with the hard of hearing, and fended off the male customers who'd had too much to drink.

Dana survived the irresponsibility of her ex-husband by virtue of her work ethic, her father's generosity, and the relative maturity of her children. But despite the fact that she loved her children dearly, she wasn't entirely wrong about her parenting skills. Her kids practically raised themselves in her father's spectacular home near the ocean, putting themselves to bed at night while Dana counted her tips and her dad stayed with a lady friend in North Jersey. Although Dana was home every morning, Marnie often had to make breakfast and pack a lunch for herself and her brother while Dana slept off her exhaustion from the night before. Still, with it all, these were happy children who loved their mother for the effort she expended on their behalf.

When we got back to their house, Marnie was playing piano in the living room, and Dana glanced nervously at her watch.

"Hey, babe, you're home early."

Marnie gave a brave little smile. "Band practice was canceled."

"How come?"

"We're not sure. Mr. Connelly left after second period."

"He probably had a migraine," I said. "They're extremely common among high school music teachers."

Dana glanced at Marnie again, unsure how she would react. But Marnie was smiling.

"This must be Mark."

"It's Mark, all right. Is your brother home?"

"Yeah, he's doing his homework."

"Wow, how'd you manage that?"

"No, he's been doing it on his own. Honest."

"Thanks, Marn. How does rotisserie chicken sound?"

Marnie stared at Dana. Did her mother come up with this idea on her own, or did the new guy she was talking about have the good sense to suggest it?

"It sounds great," she smiled.

"Don't look so surprised. It was *his* idea."

"I thought so, but I didn't want to say anything."

"Marnie, what were you playing on the piano?" I asked. "I feel like I recognized it."

"'Morning Has Broken' by Cat Stevens."

"Wow, Dana, your daughter has exquisite taste."

"I know. She doesn't get it from me."

"Don't say that, Mom. You're always putting yourself down." She turned back to me. "Maybe you can help with that. My dad's a jerk—the divorce wasn't her fault."

"I'm trying, Marnie. I think your mom's fantastic."

Before I drove home that night, Dana borrowed ten dollars from Marnie to tide herself over until the next day.

More than anything else, I believe that I took Dana's mind off of her failures and that she did the same for me. Before long, we reached the point that Teresa and I had in creating a series of inside jokes that left everyone else out. For instance, I would wait for just the right time to ask her to hand me the cleanser, referring to it in the old-fashioned way that her father did, saying "Dana, hand me the Bab-o." While the younger waitresses stared at us with impatience, bewilderment, or undisguised disdain, Dana and I huddled in a corner and laughed.

Eventually, she began to visit me at the cottage without any sexual tension at all, and we confined our discussions to the Village Tavern, Dana's home life, and the lives of her children. These conversations often included the problems she was having extracting money from her ex-husband, a deadbeat who rarely made an alimony payment; but whenever things got heavy, we were able to shift into a lighter mode.

By then, I had already incorporated Joe Bostick into the cast of characters in my mimicry, and Dana particularly appreciated my impression of Joe sitting at the bar on a Sunday morning, his bloodhound eyes inflamed, his ashtray full, and his bandstand empty, waiting for Fran to stop brushing her frosted hair in the reflection of the walk-in refrigerator so that she could finally make him breakfast.

A day or two before, I had watched Joe push the wrong button on the soda gun, filling his beer mug with seltzer instead of the Coke that he desired, one of the few non-alcoholic beverages that he ever chose to drink, and only when he was more hung over than usual. Carmen was watching also, just as amused as I was. He could have interceded at any time, but the spectacle of Joe getting hot and bothered was too priceless to pass up, and Carmen allowed Joe to struggle for a good thirty seconds.

"What's the problem, Joe?"

"We're outa Coke, that's the problem!"

Carmen made the long walk from the other end of the bar, took on a triumphant expression, and sized Joe up for the spiritless drunk that he was. "Get with the program, Joe. You're tappin' the wrong one."

"What are you talkin' about? I am not!"

"Did you read the label? C is for Coke and S is for seltzer. It's not that complicated." He took the soda gun from Joe and filled his glass with Coke. "Do you see how easy it is?"

Carmen couldn't ask for a raise since Fran had been eminently fair to him, but he could make the most out of teasing Joe unmercifully.

"Who switched 'em?" Joe sputtered.

"No one switched 'em, Joe. Sit down."

"Goddamn you, Carmen, I know you switched those fuckin' things."

"Sure, Joe, whatever you say."

Once I relayed the incident to Dana, we reenacted it as best we could.

"I'll be Joe," I said. "You be Carmen."

"*I* wanna be Joe!" Dana followed, assuming a pouty expression.

"Sorry, kid, you're not ready for that." I launched into the reenactment, getting the gravel in Joe's voice just right. "Goddamn you, Carmen, I know you switched 'em!"

"Nobody switched 'em," Dana replied, forgetting her line but ad-libbing skillfully. "You're seein' things!"

"Fug it," I said, sliding an imaginary beer mug across the bar. "Fill 'er up."

"Poor Fran," Dana said, out of character now and shaking her head. "You sound just like him."

There were specific instances in which it was difficult for me to distinguish between the real Joe and the one I concocted for Dana, like the time I came in on a Monday morning for some extra cleaning and found him moping around the kitchen. I usually had the kitchen to myself on Monday mornings, particularly when I arrived a half hour early to beat everyone else to the leftover sticky buns from the bakery next door, knowing that the baker would give us whatever he didn't sell. If anyone caught me biting into a bun or licking my fingers, I could always claim that I was checking the weekly schedule that Fran posted before she left on Sunday evening. By passing this off as a sign of dedication, I could withhold the fact that—other than the sticky buns—I was only there to find out which of the waitresses I would be working with in the days ahead, the entire wait staff forming a banquet of its own, a roster that included a buxom, pig-tailed Scandinavian girl who had a tendency to spill drinks; the maddeningly sexy schoolteacher who I have already mentioned; the reputedly promiscuous Paula, a Cherry Hill East grad who had described one of her boyfriends in the sort of precise anatomical detail that would have caused her to become dead to me even if I hadn't been intimidated by her already; and Fran's older daughter Gail, who had some of her mother's drill sergeant qualities but tempered them with a hot-rodding mentality that would have fit in perfectly in *American Graffiti*. One of the family photographs in Fran's office captured Gail in a majorette outfit from high school, and I had to ban myself from ever looking at it again lest it inspire impure thoughts.

"Joe, what's the matter?" I asked, swallowing my amusement when I noticed his forlorn expression.

Despite his Herculean attempt to give me the cold shoulder, his circumstances demanded that he reply. "Fran got held up at the podiatrist."

"So?"

"So who's gonna fix my breakfast?"

"Can't you fix it?"

"Hell no, I can't even fry an egg."

"I'll see what I can do," I said. "But I'm planning the menu."

"What the hell does that mean?"

"That means you're not having scrapple, link sausages, or shit on a shingle. You're having scrambled eggs."

"Oh, yeah? Why don't we take this outside?"

"Are you sure? Your last fist fight didn't work out so well."

"Fuck you, Mike."

"My name's Mark. Mike was the other guy."

"Fuck you both. I'll be at the bar."

Dana walked in the kitchen a few minutes later. "What's up?"

"We have an emergency. Joe's whining about his breakfast."

"Why don't you make him something? You're supposed to be a cook, aren't you?"

"I'll make him something all right. Hand me the Bab-o."

"You'd never get away with it, Mark. It would show up in the toxicology report."

––––––––––

When Fran first offered me the job, I indulged myself for the rest of the day, borrowing the men's room key at a gas station, changing into my bathing suit, and falling asleep on the beach. Eventually, I found a spot to watch the sun go down at the southern end of the island. The coast was rocky there, and it curved in such a way that you could park your car with the sun shining down through the windshield. By exploring the area, I also found a marina, an outdoor shower, and the South End Deli, which contributed a cheeseburger, a Hawaiian Punch, and a carton of Rocky Road ice cream to my overriding feeling of bliss.

Before I started back to Philadelphia, I rummaged through my glove compartment for the Big Band tape that my barber had compiled for me years before. His own son had shown no interest in the music of the barber's youth, and every time I came in for a haircut there was another cassette waiting for me. When I smoked a joint that day and listened to the Rosemary Clooney version of "I'm Beginning To See the Light," all of the elements came together to heighten my anticipation of the Long Beach Island experience: the boats gently rocking, the water changing color gradually as the sun set in the west, salt air in my lungs down deep, pelicans perched on the pilings, seagulls signaling to one another in their language, and the water flipping over itself with the hulls of the boats making a squeaking sound in the distance.

———————

Once Fran eliminated lunches from our hours of operation, I couldn't procrastinate any longer on finding another job, and starting with the South End Deli, I confirmed what I had already suspected: nearly all of the businesses that remained open were operating on the same reduced schedule that Fran was. Between the southern-most point of the island—where a depressingly cheerful sign thanked the South End Deli's loyal customers and looked forward to seeing them in the spring—and the handful of businesses in the immediate vicinity of my cottage, I found nothing of any promise, having been forced to eliminate a bike rental shop, an amusement park, and two or three arcades, none of which were open. The only headway I made was an application I filled out at a small, family-owned supermarket across the street from the Village Tavern, but the manager cautioned me against getting my hopes up until the following year.

My only recourse was to climb into the Matador, head down Long Beach Boulevard, and force myself to walk into nearly any place of business that could be expected to stay open for the winter, a strategy that forced me to lower my standards to an inch or two above the ground if I wanted to survive.

Even the traffic lights were a reminder of how dubious this venture was. From Memorial Day to Labor Day, when traffic was heaviest, the lights were fully operational and drivers were forced to pause every few blocks and wait in heavy traffic. But after Labor Day there were no red lights at all and the traffic signals flashed orange instead. When I first noticed this, I anticipated a potential free-for-all and a series of road rage incidents that never materialized, because traffic was so light after Labor Day that you could drive the entire length of the island and encounter only ten or fifteen drivers for a stretch of eighteen miles.

As I made my way northward, I was determined to be as flexible as possible in finding work to do on the weekdays, granting myself immunity only when it came to a beauty parlor, a retail store that specialized in women's apparel, and a Christian Science Reading Room whose religious pamphlets were so objectionable that I refused to even consider it. I did force myself out of the car to explore the possibility of office work at three or four insurance agencies, but none of them were hiring.

Driving the entire length of Long Beach Island with the South End Deli as my starting point, I passed through all of the communities that I ignored previously, reading the road signs with an escalating sense of desperation. Flirting with the waitresses was all well and good, but it didn't pay the bills, and I had the sinking feeling that I was looking at a rather pronounced comeuppance if my luck didn't change by the end of the day. The first few road signs included Holgate, Beach Haven, Brant Beach, and Ship Bottom, the business owners exhibiting a breathtaking array of responses, including regret, compassion, apathy, amusement, and the perverse satisfaction of denying a person a livelihood and sending him back into the world, although I may possibly have been imagining that last one. It wasn't until I came upon the headquarters of Sunset Realty that I was able to preserve my dream of fucking off in an exotic setting.

By then, I had been in my car for the better part of an hour and had been perspiring for nearly as long, so I couldn't have looked very presentable when I introduced myself to Joe Giammona, the thirty-five-year-old son of a real estate tycoon who owned multiple properties on the island. Despite that, something in my story must have touched Joe—or in my pathetic appearance—because he offered me a job very quickly, as long as I was willing to serve as a "gofer" on his construction crew. I had already been honest with him when he asked if I had any construction experience, and because I had refrained from laughing in his face at that preposterous suggestion, his good nature took over and he made the unilateral decision to treat me charitably without consulting his father, a decision that he would come to regret in the days ahead.

Once I got to know Joe, I suspected that he had responded to my presence with a romantic yearning of his own, as though he had never done what he wanted to in life because the family business had always been there for him. He still couldn't do what he wanted because business was booming, but he was in a position to encourage the romanticism in me. At the time, I had no idea that Joe had five workers that he was running ragged in a futile attempt to keep up with the demand for beach houses, and that I would be run ragged also with the tasks that the more skilled workers had no desire to perform. It didn't matter, of course, once Joe offered me seven dollars an hour and forty hours a week. I thanked him and accepted the job.

Once I did that, the next logistical consideration was for Joe to introduce me to his foreman, Shawn, knowing all the while that Shawn already thought that Joe was a horse's ass and that he would regard my hiring as still another sign of Joe's utter inability to measure up to Joe's father, a man who had the sagacity to recognize Shawn's carpentry skills and hire Shawn when he was still in high school ten years before. While Joe waited for Shawn to arrive in the light brown pickup truck with "Sunset Realty" painted on either side, he had me cool my heels by filling out an employment application that revealed my unfitness for the position that he had just offered. Did I have carpentry experience? No. Drywall? Of course not. HVAC? Are you fucking kidding me?

Joe never suspected that I would lack the ability to perform a single one of the tasks that he envisioned, or that I would clash so violently with the members of his construction crew, whose redneck tendencies I would resent almost immediately. It followed that none of us could have known that my resentment would be accompanied in short order by the perverse, self-destructive need to screw up the one thing that I could have done with a degree of competence: driving to the Wawa convenience store for their coffee every morning so that the most expendable person on the crew could execute the task that required the least skill. It made perfect sense for me to be dispatched on the errand so that the others could spend their time more productively, doing whatever men do with two-by-fours, cement, dry wall, sheet metal, plumbing fixtures, Tyvek, Andersen windows, and all of the other items that are so indispensable to the construction industry.

If Shawn failed to realize that it wasn't his day when he pulled into the parking lot next to the Matador, it didn't take him long to catch up the minute he laid eyes on me, although he refrained from squeezing my biceps as Morris had at Mr. Martin's. But if I had any illusions about my latest employment experience working out, they were dispelled by the way Shawn looked me up and down, glanced disgustedly at Joe, and practically ignored Joe when he attempted to justify my presence. It had already begun to feel as though I would have been better off if I were still seeking employment, but rather than take the unprecedented step of quitting a job before I had actually begun to work, I attempted to answer Shawn's questions as reassuringly as I was able, although nothing I could have said would have caused him to reconsider.

Although my initial answer should have sufficed, Shawn asked me a second time if I owned a set of tools, making it clear that he was either more absent-minded than he appeared or he simply couldn't imagine a male of the species being bereft of a carpenter's apron, hammer, back brace, and generous supply of nails. Shawn possessed every one of these items as he grilled me in Joe's air-conditioned office.

In addition to the absence of a carpenter's apron, I proved to be deficient by owning a sedan and a pathetic one at that, a lifestyle choice that lowered me in Shawn's estimation even further. Each of my new co-workers had a metal box bolted to the bed of his truck, and though this was a universally accepted accessory in their world, I tended to look down on anyone who had one, meaning our disdain for each other was mutual. By the time Shawn dismissed me from our initial meeting and directed me to show up the next day, both of us knew that my employment was a disaster waiting to happen, while Joe sat at his desk with the self-satisfied air of a man who had done another human being a good turn, a feeling that persisted until the door of his office closed and Shawn berated him as though he were the boss and Joe one of the workers. I'm not sure if Shawn would have gone over Joe's head to talk to the old man if I had lasted more than two weeks in the job, but it was a mystery that would never be solved. (To this day, I cringe whenever I see a pickup truck with a Craftsman toolbox, and it isn't until I summon a lascivious image of Connie Stevens from her Ace Hardware days that I am able to banish the unwelcome image from my mind.)

———

My first task as an employee of Sunset Realty was to accompany Frankie Doyle to Ship Bottom Lumber. He was an oversized eighteen-year-old with no intellectual interests whatsoever—at least none that I could discern—but because he wore a sweatshirt of the University of Miami football team, I had a fighting chance of getting along with him.

"Do you like football?" I asked.

Frankie sounded more sullen than suspicious when he answered, but it was probably a combination of both. "Yeah, why?"

"Take it easy. I do, too. I was at Pitt when Tony Dorsett won the Heisman Trophy."

Frankie stared at me blankly, which wasn't entirely surprising given the fact that he was eight years old when Dorsett won the award. Based on his reaction, I'm not sure he had any real concept of the past or the future, but it was my own fault for making another futile attempt at passing myself off as a regular guy.

"How come you follow the University of Miami? Do you have relatives down there?"

"Nope."

"You like their uniform?"

"It's OK."

It's been my experience that fair weather fans like Frankie who have no geographic allegiance tend to fall into one of two categories: either they're stone cold frontrunners or they simply like the team's uniform. Front-running is bad enough but falling in love with a uniform is totally lame, although I have to admit that I had a thing for the San Diego Chargers when I was a kid. My enchantment with the flash of lighting on their helmets lasted until I got tired of the Oakland Raiders kicking their ass every year.

I should have quit when I was ahead with Frankie, but it wouldn't have been any fun.

"Why do you like 'em then?"

"Because they're a good team."

"So, if they fall out of the Top Ten you'd switch your allegiance to someone else?"

"Huh?"

"You'd root for another team?"

"Sure," he shrugged. "What's the point in following a loser?"

"I don't know—to preserve your personal integrity?"

For the next fifteen minutes, I followed Frankie around the lumber yard, carried my share of lumber, and did my best to sound interested in his rundown of the construction projects that the crew was working on. By the time the cashier calculated the charges to Joe's account, Frankie seemed to like me well enough; but the second we rejoined the others at a vacant lot in Harvey Cedars—a block or two from where Dana and her kids were living—Frankie turned on me in a predictable way.

The minute Frankie introduced me to the rest of Shawn's crew, I could tell that he would cave in to peer pressure and withhold the fact that he had judged me to be a decent person—or at least that the jury was still out. Instead, he began almost immediately to replicate the abusive behavior of the others, smirking, rolling his eyes, and seizing every opportunity to talk behind my back, whether I was likely to overhear him or not, the entire crew ostracizing me in record time. In fact, I believe that Frankie made even more points with the others when he insulted me when I was in earshot, as though an important feature of the game they were playing was to rub the victim's nose in the fact that he wasn't going to do anything about it.

The cursory attempt I made to fit in with Frankie and the others was obviously doomed to failure, especially when Shawn caught me reading *The Sorrows of Young Werther* on my lunch break a few days later. Naturally, he griped about it to Joe, and Joe defended me as best he could. I was taking a piss when they had it out in Joe's office.

"He was on a break, for God's sakes!"

"*When* he was reading isn't the point! It's *what* he was reading!"

"What was he reading?"

Joe sounded curious, as though he might take a cue from me in pursuing his own intellectual development.

"How do *I* know?" Shawn asked. "It had a fancy title, OK?"

"So if he was reading *Hustler* you wouldn't have a problem with it?"

"No, why should I? I'm tellin' yuh right now, if I have to fire the guy, it's on you."

"What's the difference as long as he does the job?"

But of course I couldn't do the job—not a single aspect of it—and that was immediately apparent. When Garth, the undisputed ringleader of Shawn's crew, took one look at me, my fate was sealed. He was a bearded hillbilly with a mean streak and a front tooth missing on the left side of his mouth, and he identified me at the outset as just the kind of patsy he was looking for. Because he behaved like a schoolyard bully, Garth and I were a match made in heaven from Garth's point of view; and nearly all of the other crewmembers encouraged him to tease me unmercifully, with the exception of Garth's older brother Garrett, the only member of the crew who exhibited a shred of decency in the two weeks that I worked there.

Naturally, I knew that the Darwinian nature of the situation didn't favor me, but it was impossible to predict how bad things were going to get. It was entirely a function of how sadistic the crewmembers were prepared to be—something that I had no control over. But as long as their taunts were predictable—and governed by the limitations of their intellect—I knew that I could withstand the taunts, as I did when Garth questioned my sexual orientation when he saw me sweeping sawdust at one of the construction sites. Turning to the others, he said, "Mark'll make a good wife some day." I could understand Garth's saying that, but all of the evidence suggested that he would never make a good husband; and he got red in the face when I pointed it out.

Other than our place of employment, the only thing that Garth and I had in common was that we listened to the same radio station—WMMR, which came in loud and clear from Philadelphia—but that's where the like-mindedness ended. As an example, Garth favored ZZ Top while I preferred Huey Lewis and the News, whose 1983 song "Heart and Soul" always lifted my spirits no matter how miserable Garth and his cohorts made me. It was no surprise that Garth favored ZZ Top since two of the band members looked like hillbillies themselves, and Garth never failed to turn up the volume on his boombox whenever "Legs" was played on the radio. I never let the others see my boombox—since Garth's was bigger than mine—but that didn't stop me from purchasing the 45 rpm version of "Heart and Soul" from Hand's department store so that I could play it whenever I wanted.

The drive-time disc jockey on MMR was a middle-aged broadcaster named John DiBella who made the big bucks by achieving unprecedented ratings in his time slot. DiBella favored Hawaiian shirts, and like John Tyler, the bartender at J.C. Dobbs, he was exceedingly proud of his handlebar moustache. For some unaccountable reason, DiBella's favorite expression was "It is what it is," and Garth took to mocking me with it to little or no effect in a failed attempt to keep up the pressure at every turn. Whenever I embarrassed myself at one of their construction sites, Garth could be counted on to employ the phrase, grinning in a way that drew even more attention to the tooth he was missing, and that was about as much wit as Garth could muster. But that didn't prevent three of the other four crew members from nodding their heads encouragingly as though they were an ideal audience.

The final member of Shawn's crew—after Garth, Garrett, and Frankie—was a fifty-year-old named Bill whose pickup truck featured the obligatory Craftsman toolbox, a bumper sticker from the American Rifle Association, and another one with the phrase "America—Love it or Leave it." Whenever Garth turned to Bill for encouragement, Bill never failed to oblige, snickering at Garth's witticisms before crushing out his cigarette in the gravel at his feet.

The other pastime that the crew enjoyed was watching closely whenever I was forced to hammer a nail. Their experience told them that I was about to raise a series of blood blisters on my fingers. With Sunset Realty, the few nails that I did succeed in attaching to a piece of lumber had to be removed by a more skilled carpenter a few minutes later, the improper angle at which I had driven the nail into the wood rendering it objectionable.

When I finally questioned them on why they were making such a big deal of the way I pounded nails, Garrett took me aside.

"I don't get it," I said. "You guys act like the house is gonna collapse because a few of my nails are crooked. What's up with that?"

"It's not that, Mark. The homeowners show up sometime."

"So?"

"So they're lookin' for skilled carpentry. No offense, but you're kinda weak in that department."

"Yeah, I guess I am."

From that point on, I could only agree that it would have been unfortunate if the homeowners had seen me injuring myself, crying out in pain, or causing dissension in the ranks. Similarly, it would have been just as unwise for us to let them inspect my handiwork up close. Most of the nails I pounded disappeared into the wood, broke off at the head, or came to rest at a useless angle. None of this provided sufficient grounds, however, for me to refrain from retaliatory behavior, and I was determined to get my licks in for however many days I had left in their presence.

Between the insults and the blood blisters, my ego was so badly bruised that a shocking lack of character manifested itself again, showing up in an eagerness to nap at every one of their construction sites and undermine their coffee orders, adding cream and sugar to Shawn's when I knew that he liked it black, and returning with an exotic foreign blend for the obsessively patriotic Bill. I typically selected Mocha Royale, Hawaiian Splendor, or Tropical Paradise, marketing ploys by the Wawa corporation that were popular among young women and raised the ire of confirmed Sanka drinkers like Bill. But I reserved the most insidious form of sabotage for Garth. Because he abhorred artificial sweeteners of any kind, I made sure to spike his coffee with Sweet'N Low, relishing the look on his face when he took his first sip and spat the coffee onto the ground, splattering his steel-toed boots in the process.

After bringing them the wrong kind of coffee on a staggered schedule—knowing that if I did it every day they would take away my small-minded pleasure—I took to transposing their snack items, presenting each of them with Krispy Kreme donuts, Hostess Twinkies, and TastyKake Tandy Takes that one of the others ordered, but not until they climbed into their vehicles and went their separate ways. Because they didn't discover my "error" until after they reached their destination, they were forced to choose between eating a snack item they disliked or waiting for me to track the proper item down at the other location, neither of which was particularly desirable. The only person I spared in my intentional malfeasance was Garrett, but no one gave him any shit about it because he could have kicked the crap out of them if they did.

By the third or fourth day, Shawn and the others were resigned to the fact that I was the millstone that Joe had hung around their necks, and that the only things they could safely assign me were to sweep out the sawdust from a house in progress and walk around the grounds to retrieve the plastic wrappers from the Andersen windows that had already been installed, not quite realizing that my groundskeeping duties would result in a severe case of poison ivy and that Joe would have to pay me for the morning I spent waiting for a steroid injection at a clinic in Tuckerton.

Having never been at risk for poison ivy before—after avoiding the outdoors like the plague—I was shocked to discover how furious the itching could be, particularly when it woke me from a sound sleep and caused me to claw at my legs with both hands, draw blood, and seek medical attention after keeping me up for three nights in a row. And so, once again, I had foiled their attempt to identify a task in which I would not endanger myself or others, and about the only calamity I avoided when I worked for them was a deep enough laceration for stitches, although I did manage to smite myself in the forehead with a ball-peen hammer one day while formulating a response to Garth. As usual, however, I failed to make solid contact with the hammer and produced only a glancing blow that the others were too busy to notice.

I won my share of skirmishes with Shawn's crew and so did they, but the biggest loser may have been Frankie when they removed me from coffee duty and forced him to make the trip to the Wawa instead. It must have felt like a demotion because he hadn't been asked to serve as a "gofer" since my first day on the job.

Because Joe had a number of projects going at once—and the projects were in various stages that caused the men to be deployed individually depending on their specialties—I was often left alone at a construction site to perform my custodial duties. Needless to say, this was perfectly fine with me. When I wasn't napping in the cool shadows of a half-constructed beach house, I was reading *Rolling Stone* magazine or devouring chocolate chip cookies from the General Store, choosing to grow proficient not in the pounding of nails but in listening for one of their pickup trucks to pull onto the gravel outside. Invariably, the crunching sound served as a dead give-away for their presence and alerted me to the necessity of scrambling to my feet, locating the broom that I had propped against a wall for safekeeping, and sweeping away the sawdust that the men who actually *were* working had left behind. Curiously enough, their pickup trucks were nearly identical and could only be distinguished from one another by the bumper stickers they displayed, Shawn with a Confederate flag, Garrett with a skull and crossbones commemorating the Grateful Dead, Bill with the Vietnam era relic that I previously mentioned, and the sadistic Garth with the most revealing one of all, "My Kid Beat Up Your Honor Student" adorning his rear bumper. Frankie was the only one who didn't have a legible bumper sticker, but he had the remnants of one from a year or two before, no doubt paying tribute to whichever national champion the University of Miami Hurricanes had replaced in the rankings. Although Frankie had kept up with the times by owning a Hurricanes sweatshirt, he had yet to acquire the kind of memorabilia that could be displayed on the bumper of a truck. Compared with the other members of the crew, Garrett struck me as the only one who had probably not livened up his childhood by pulling the wings off flies, incinerating some other kind of insect with a magnifying glass, or drowning a kitten for fun.

Despite the indisputable fact that John DiBella's signature phrase had fallen flat whenever Garth attempted to mock me with it, he removed it from mothballs one more time when I made the near-fatal mistake of using the word "harrowing" to describe the poison ivy ordeal to Joe. Had I known that Garth was within earshot at the Sunset Realty water fountain, I might have had the presence of mind to alter the diction that came naturally to me after reading hundreds of books, but sadly I didn't and Joe and I were startled to hear Garth announce his presence from a few feet away by muttering a comment to himself, "Harrowing? It is what it is."

In antagonizing me this way, Garth correctly assumed that I wouldn't haul off and punch him since I flatly rejected the notion of taking on the schoolyard bully and living to tell about it, let alone the preposterous fairy tale of pulling off a stunning upset in the fist fight and revealing the bully as the sniveling coward he was. The farthest I had ever gone in contemplating fisticuffs was wrapping my arms around Joe Bostick when he had taken on the Q-tip at the Village Tavern, but I had even chastised myself for that and sworn that I would never do it again because Joe could have just as easily broken out of my grasp and injured me. If I had learned anything from the realization that Hollywood was mythologizing when it portrayed sex as being easy for everyone, it was that you couldn't believe everything you saw in the movies. So, if that was the case, it was probably wise to reject any script that called for a pipsqueak to exact revenge on a bully with his bare hands, especially one that called for me to attempt it.

In addition to relishing the carpentry work that I abhorred, Garth was able to exercise all of his sadistic tendencies by saying whatever he wanted to me, provided that he employed the same method I did in listening for the sound of Garrett's truck, because ever since Garrett had pinned Garth to a wall and told him to leave me alone Garth had only tormented me when Garrett was elsewhere. Other than Garrett, Shawn was the only other one who treated me humanely, although I recognized this as a function of his being the foreman as opposed to any innate decency that he might possess. In fact, I got the distinct impression that he would have welcomed an opportunity to fall back into the pack temporarily in order to release some of the frustration that had been building in him since Joe had hired me. There was no telling what kind of abuse Shawn might have unleashed if he wasn't constrained by being my boss. Later, however, I had to give credit where credit was due and genuinely appreciate the fact that Shawn gave me a heads up on what he was thinking, the freckled, red-haired man taking me aside one Friday afternoon, handing me my meager paycheck, and saying "Mark, I'm not firin' yuh, but yuh might want to look for another job. I don't see you makin' it through the winter."

This warning occurred after Shawn made a last-ditch effort to salvage whatever he could from the fact that Joe had insisted on my presence in the first place, but his decision to have me tag along with Garrett ended disastrously when I added too much water to the drywall powder and ruined a batch when Garrett was otherwise occupied. Garrett returned fifteen minutes later to find me staring at the "stomper," a device that resembled an oversized version of the potato masher that Fran used at the Village Tavern.

"The stomper isn't the problem," he said. "There's way too much water in there. It'll never firm up."

"I'm sorry, Garrett."

"It's OK. Don't sweat the small stuff."

"What do I do with this?" I asked, gesturing toward the drywall that I had ruined.

Garrett held a cup of Wawa coffee at the time—having politely declined my offer of picking up the coffee for him—and he bent over to inspect the bucket. "You can do whatever you want with it," he said. "It's ruined." Even he had to concede that I wasn't cut out for construction work, and while I offered a mild protest to preserve my employment a little longer, Garrett correctly pointed out that the number of blood blisters on my hand exceeded the number of nails I had pounded correctly in the ten days that I worked for them.

Once Garrett reported my mishap with the drywall, Shawn had no choice but to issue the warning and terminate me a few days later, mercifully ending a period in which my evenings were seriously damaged by the compulsion of watching the clock for the arrival of another day. Because I dreaded Garth's bullying, I refrained from making any kind of case for myself when Shawn lowered the boom and returned to the cottage instead, finding the atmosphere a good deal more cheerful than it had been when there was no end in sight to my misery.

Although I still had two shifts a week at the Village Tavern, my situation was precarious again, but it didn't prevent me from celebrating my departure from Sunset Realty by indulging in the regressive behavior of grilling myself a steak, boiling Uncle Ben's rice, and digging into a jar of Musselman's applesauce, successfully recreating a meal that my mother had served me at 2601.

Instead of making a marijuana run to Joe McBride's corner

in Fairmount—which I would have preferred to do—I kept my nose to the grindstone by resuming my search for employment, picking up exactly where I left off two weeks before. Minutes later, however—after exhausting every possibility in Harvey Cedars, Loveladies, and Barnegat Light, a trio of towns that were far less commercial than their southern neighbors even at the height of the season—I got that old sinking feeling again as I headed inland with the seagulls flying above me on the causeway bridge. This was my own fault, of course. Dropping out of school is rarely a good idea, but I dropped out anyway, mostly to punish my mother. Once again, I was paying for it.

In addition to the Shoprite, the Manahawkin Plaza featured a dry cleaning business, an office supply store, and a photo processing kiosk. All of these were objectionable in their own way, but sitting in an eight-by-twelve booth in the middle of a parking lot was hardly my idea of a good time even if it meant developing the occasional photograph of a scantily clad woman. There was also the possibility that the attendant would be required to develop a more explicit photograph of an actual sex act, and though the idea held some prurient interest for me, I'm not sure I would have been able to refrain from blushing when the customer returned to the kiosk to complete the transaction. Besides, from the looks of things, there was already someone working at the Fotomat and there didn't seem to be enough room for a second person even if they needed one. Eventually, I entered Office Plus, where a forty-year-old man with a strangely boyish haircut, a slight cowlick, and horn-rimmed glasses greeted me.

"Can I help you?" he asked.

"I hope so. Are you doing any hiring?"

I realized later that this was a positive development for him and even better than my being there to buy something.

"What can you do?" he asked.

"Whatever you need."

His three female employees were watching from a few feet away. One of them was young and attractive, the second was merely young, and the third was the kindly grandmother type.

"I'm Chip," he said, extending his hand. "Who are you?"

I shook Chip's hand and told him my name.

"Can you sell?" he asked.

The ideas of selling was objectionable to me, and I could only hope that the revulsion wasn't written on my face.

"Sure," I said. "Why not?"

"With that beard?" he followed.

Ever since I was old enough to shave, I had attempted to replicate the kind of stubble that Bob Dylan exhibited on the cover of *New Morning*. But even though this represented a failed attempt on my part, I had realized a savings on the razor blades that I hadn't had to buy.

"What does my beard have to do with it?"

"Do you really want to know?"

"Yeah, I do."

We were butting heads already, but at the time we had no way of knowing how much we needed each other.

"If I give you a job, will you shave the beard?"

"Probably not, but I'd consider it."

I had already concluded that I wasn't going to work there, and had made the decision to have as much fun with the "interview" as possible before heading to the Shoprite.

"I already have a job," he said. "You don't."

"I have a job, but it's part-time."

Needing a salesman in the worst way—since his unbearable personality had cost him my predecessor—Chip decided to table the issue of my facial hair.

"Do you have a car?"

"If you can call it that. I have an AMC Matador."

"Ouch. Why'dja buy one o' those?"

"It was in my price range."

"What kinda shape is it in?'

"The transmission's been slipping since the day I bought it. Other than that, it's hangin' in there."

I didn't have the heart to tell him that the Matador had suffered the indignity of a broken glove compartment on the way over.

"D'yuh think it'll hold up? There's a lotta driving with this job."

"I'm willing to take that chance."

"Yeah, but am I?"

"Honestly? The car's on borrowed time, but at least I'd be money-motivated."

"If you do well, you can buy a Cadillac."

"Are you saying I have the job?"

"Do you want it?"

"I don't know. How much driving are we talking about?"

There was no truth to the rumor that I was trying to mimic the job interview scene in *Trainspotting*, a movie that came out a decade later. But either way, my interview with Chip had certain similarities.

"Roughly?" Chip said. "A hundred miles a day."

I assumed that Chip was referring to a round trip of a hundred miles, and I started my calculations there. Realistically, the car had no chance of surviving more than a few weeks of what he proposed, but on the other hand, being fifty miles from your employer at any one time had certain advantages. If I chose to goof off in the middle of the day, there wasn't much he could do about it, as long as I made the occasional sale.

"I'm game if you are. Do I have the job?"

"Not yet, but you're pretty close."

I remembered something my father had said on a sales call for his restaurant supply business. I was a kid at the time, and he had taken me with him to Shamokin, Pennsylvania. I had nothing to lose by trying it out on Chip.

"What would you need to hear to make a decision right now?"

Apparently, this was exactly what he was looking for, as though my transformation into a salesman was complete—or at least far enough along for him to be inclined in my favor.

"I'll pay for your gas," Chip shrugged, shifting into a cagier mode now that I had accepted the position without any discussion of salary. "Just keep the receipts."

"What about tolls?" I parried, since the Garden State Parkway was notorious for them. Chip must have been thrilled that I was thinking so small, and that it was beginning to look as though he could low-ball me on my take home pay.

"I'll pay them, too."

"Great. And now the million-dollar question. What's my base salary?"

"It's not a million dollars, I'll tell you that."

"I wouldn't think so. But Cadillacs aren't cheap."

"I'll pay yuh two-fifty a week plus gas and tolls."

"Is that over the table or under?"

"Under. Do you have a problem with that?"

"Not at all," I said, happy to cheat the government and pocket a little extra. "When do you want me to start?"

"You can start on Monday—wear a tie."

"That's not a problem. I still have one from my bar mitzvah."

"Forget it," Chip sneered. "I'll give yuh one."

When I showed up for work on Monday, Chip handed me a tie. It seemed generous at the time, but he had a box of them in the back room, having traded a pallet of copy paper to a tie salesman the year before.

On my first day, he showed me the route in his Ford Taurus, merging onto the Garden State Parkway at the Manahawkin entrance and traveling north until we reached Toms River. He was making an effort to be agreeable, but his nastiness seeped out of him from time to time, just as mine seeped out of me.

"Why are you on Long Beach Island?" he asked, heading East on Route 37, which extended from the Atlantic Ocean to Lakehurst, where the Hindenburg exploded.

"I like the slower pace."

"You're not bored?"

"Not yet."

"What do you do for fun?"

Books, music, and popular culture kept me going in those days; but there was no need to elaborate. "I read and listen to music."

"You can do that anywhere."

"Chip, you asked if I was bored. I'm not."

"Do you like girls?"

I stared at him. "Are you asking if I'm gay?"

"No, why would you think that?"

"If you meet a guy for the first time, wouldn't you assume that he likes girls, unless he gives you a reason not to?"

"I'm just checking. Don't worry about it."

I had no intention of worrying about it, unless he brought it up again, got even more personal, or propositioned *me*. It wasn't until a few days later that I found out where he was going with that particular line of questioning.

For me at least, that stretch of Route 37 came to represent everything that was wrong with our country. It had all of the usual restaurant chains, Big Box retailers, and automotive service centers that made us vulgar in the first place. But my new boss was truly in his element.

"I have a question," I said. "Can I get an employee discount on a legal pad?"

"I'll *give* yuh a legal pad. What do you need it for?"

"I'll take some notes while we're driving."

"Sure. I've got a hundred of 'em in the trunk."

Implying that I would use the legal pad for official business wasn't entirely accurate. Instead, by listing the companies on Route 37, I intended to bear witness to our collective suffering.

"Do you know where they got the name AAMCO?" Chip asked, already anticipating the small victory that my ignorance would provide.

"Not specifically. But the two A's at the beginning of the name gives them the first listing in a phone book."

The poor bastard looked crestfallen, and he didn't say another word until we sat down at Friendly's Ice Cream for lunch, where Chip ordered a French dip and treated me to a Salisbury steak.

"What are you thinking?" he asked, while I paid attention to everything but him. "You look like you're in outer space."

"It's amazing that you would say that. I was thinking, what if a spaceship landed on Route 37? What kind of report would they bring home?"

"What are you talking about?"

"I mean, when they got back to whatever planet they came from, would they even recommend a follow-up visit? You have to admit, our culture might look repulsive to them if Route 37 was all they saw."

Chip took me up on the challenge. "But if they were arriving from another planet, they would have seen the entire earth on their way down, not just Route 37."

"We better hope so, because Route 37 is an embarrassment to all of us."

"Must you be such a snob?"

"I'm not a snob. For instance, I'm enjoying my Salisbury steak immensely."

"I can see that," Chip shrugged, as I dragged a crescent roll through a glob of mushroom gravy. "Maybe you're just glad to be alive. At your age, I was, too."

"That's exactly right. I've been telling my mother that for years."

———————

After lunch, my new boss inserted a Lionel Richie tape into his cassette player, settled back in the driver's seat, and tapped the steering wheel in time to the music. He used his wedding ring to do this, just as my stepfather had while listening to the

Ray Conniff Singers. I was still holding a grudge over Lionel Richie's association with "Brick House," a deplorable recording if ever there was one, and I had no idea that he had become a solo artist and announced his emancipation with "You Are," a song that blew me away.

"Here," Chip said, handing me the tape. "It's yours."

"Come on—you don't have to do that!"

"Don't worry about it. My wife hates Lionel Richie. I'm not allowed to play it in the house."

Counting the necktie, this was the second thing that Chip had given me in my first few hours of working for him; and I would have thanked him if I weren't so determined to express my contempt for his values.

Once I made the decision to keep silent, all I could do was sit back and enjoy the ride, waiting for Chip to break the occasional silence with an aphorism from Dale Carnegie, Fred Pryor, or Zig Ziglar. In fact, after he ejected the Lionel Richie tape, he subjected me to the entire duration of the Fred Pryor classic, "Sales: Attitude Is Everything." Pryor wasn't kidding. Attitude *is* everything, and I was more determined than ever to resist Chip at every turn, even if it meant turning to the Fotomat for employment.

The whole point of sales is to separate people from their money, and when Chip wasn't dazzling me with a pearl of wisdom along those lines, he was pointing out the various accounts he had and giving me a rundown on what I needed to know. In the process, he conveyed the items they bought, how frequently they ordered, and whether or not it was necessary for him to show his face. Not surprisingly, some of the accounts actually preferred that he *not* show his face and were content to order over the phone.

"You said you would take notes," Chip said. "How come you're not writing any of this down?"

"You know what? You're right. I'm so blown away by Fred Pryor that I forgot where I was for a minute."

"You're a good liar. That should serve you well in sales."

Although Chip was in direct competition with Carney's, an

office supply store across from the courthouse in Toms River, both he and his primary competitor obtained their merchandise from United Stationers, a regional distributor in Pennsauken. That enabled Chip to price his products competitively, make prudent decisions on which items to mark down, and hire sales representatives who had better personalities than he did. By doing those things, he was able to carve out a nice little territory for himself that included Barnegat, Toms River, Point Pleasant, Seaside Heights, Manahawkin, and my beloved Long Beach Island. Chip's piece of the pie included large accounts like the pharmaceutical company Ciba-Geigy and a number of doctor's offices, law firms, and insurance agencies, several of which were located along Route 9, the highway immortalized by Bruce Springsteen in "Born to Run."

"Did you notice what I did on our last stop?" Chip asked.

"The doctor's office? You asked the nurse if her son was getting better."

"And do you know why I did that?"

"Sure. It was a sniveling attempt to ingratiate yourself to her."

A true masochist at heart, Chip actually seemed to enjoy my cutting remarks, especially when they were directed at him. The only thing holding me back was the possibility of going too far and getting fired.

"Besides that?" Chip said.

"I have no idea."

"I made a mental note of it the week before."

"Let me get this straight. Her kid's in the hospital with a life-threatening illness, and you told yourself to ask her about it the next time?"

"Sure. That's what sales is all about."

"What—selling office supplies to a grieving mother?"

"What did you think it was? Our Safeguard folders are better than Carney's? The products are all the same. You're selling your personality."

"What if it's not for sale?"

"What are you saying—you have a problem with asking about the kid?"

My employment with Chip had reached its first major test, and as hard as I tried to wriggle out of it, it was obvious that the Fotomat was a distinct possibility. One more flippant remark may cost me the job. It was a gut-check that I failed miserably.

"No, of course not!" I cried.

"Are you sure about that? You look like you're sick to your stomach."

"Actually, I do have a problem with it, but I'll do it if you insist."

"That's right," Chip frowned. "Blame it on me."

The final life lesson of the day occurred in Forked River, where that esteemed lead singer Arnold Zeller sold used cars. Chip had parked in front of what appeared to be an abandoned property.

"What do you see?" he asked.

"Besides a code violation, not much."

"Would you believe he's one of my biggest accounts?"

"Really? I feel sorry for the smaller ones. What does he do in there?"

"He's a dentist. See the sign?"

"The place is filthy, Chip. Who would open their mouth in there?"

"He does all the welfare cases and trailer trash from Bayville."

"Better him than me."

"All I know is, he buys hanging folders by the truckload."

"From the looks of it, he'd be better off hanging himself."

"Talk about inconsistent. For someone who was too sensitive to ask the nurse about her kid, you're recommending suicide."

"How much does he spend with you in the course of a year?" 1 asked, ignoring his last remark after it hit too close to home.

"You're lookin' at a $3,000 account."

"Is that good?"

"Good? It's great! The point is, don't assume anything. And don't talk yourself out of making a cold-call based on how a place looks."

"OK—if you say so."

"I hired you, didn't I? Even though you have that fucking beard."

The Oyster Creek nuclear plant was a mile away, and its presence increased the anxiety I felt with Chip. But if we were incinerated with radiation, I wouldn't have to work for him anymore.

"Will you lay off the beard, please? I told yuh I wasn't gonna shave."

"You said you'd consider it."

"That was before I realized what a soul-killing job this is. The beard represents my last shred of dignity."

"How 'bout we ask my wife? She'll tell you the truth about your beard. If she likes it, it stays. If she doesn't, you'll shave it off."

"What do I care what your wife thinks?"

"I've been meaning to talk to you about that."

My training was supposed to last a day, but Chip did the driving for my entire first week. If I didn't know better, I would have thought that he was lonely, and that he actually enjoyed my company. Maybe he was working up the courage to tell me about his sex life, which is exactly what he did on Day Three.

As it turned out, Chip had lost interest in sex, but his wife hadn't, and he no longer wanted to be bothered. For the first few minutes of this, I wrote it off as still another example of a phenomenon that I had noticed a few years before. Every once in a while, someone would see through my sarcasm, and though they couldn't possibly have known that I had a Jewish Mother in me (despite the fact that I had done my best to reject my own), they would peg me as a good listener. Whenever that happened, I would invariably respond in a nurturing way. But when Chip produced his wallet and handed me a family snapshot, I got the distinct impression that he wasn't showing me his children.

"Is this what I think it is?" I asked. "You're setting me up with your wife?"

"She's pretty, isn't she?"

Although there was little doubt that I had propositioned less attractive women than Chip's wife, the conversation had descended into the unseemly.

"She's attractive, but you didn't answer my question."

"She's thinner than that," Chip continued. "She's on the Pritikin diet."

"Is that why you hired me?"

For all his faults, Chip had a superior intellect, and he had already anticipated the question. "We're all adults here. It could be a win-win for all of us."

"Does she know you're doing this?"

"Of course not. We'd have to be subtle about it."

"I'm not interested, Chip."

"Why not? You don't like sex either?"

"I didn't say that."

"Then what's the problem?"

When I realized that Chip gave things away, I had no idea that he would offer his wife.

"The problem is my sense of decency."

"Do you have plans for the weekend?" he continued.

"Yeah. I'm working at the Village Tavern."

"I thought you were gonna quit that job."

"I never said that."

"I just assumed it once I hired you full-time."

"I can't do it to Fran. She's been great to me."

"I was gonna invite you over to meet the wife and kids."

"Now I'm definitely working at the restaurant."

"Just think about it. I'm gonna need you to quit that job eventually. Once you get rolling, you'll be too busy to work at a restaurant for peanuts."

"That may be true, but there are also the waitresses to consider."

Chip thought about it for a minute, obviously catching my drift. "Once you meet Nancy, you might not need the waitresses."

The notion of a sexual harassment suit came and went very

quickly—before I could work out the details of being fired for refusing to sleep with my employer's wife, consulting an attorney, and having my sexuality splashed across the newspapers.

"Why don't we restrict our discussions to selling?" I said, without regard for the consequences.

"I gave it a shot." Chip shrugged. "You can't blame me for that."

I was as hungry for experience as the next guy, and some of the reluctance was melting away.

"We'd have to do it on a weeknight," I said, "if we do it at all."

———————

Once I accepted the dinner invitation, Nancy prepared a terrific meal for us at their home in Lanoka Harbor, but not until her sister got the children out of the way by taking them to a Walt Disney movie at the multiplex. My main preoccupation that night—once I determined how recent a photograph Chip had shown me—was to gauge Nancy's state of mind as I made my way through her leg of lamb. Because there was absolutely no evidence that Chip had spoken to Nancy about sleeping with me, I was able to treat her with respect and enjoy a conversation that was devoid of sarcasm, which I was sure she'd had her fill of with Chip. Chip and I were on our best behavior in that regard, and we went on to discuss Nancy's teaching career, which she had put on hold to raise their children.

At one point, Chip excused himself to use the bathroom, leaving Nancy and me alone at the dinner table.

"I know what this is about," she said.

"You do?"

I had no idea if I was blushing, but it was likely that I was.

"I can find my own sexual partners, thank you."

"Really? I can't."

So much for the moral high ground I had taken when Chip first suggested that I sleep with his wife. Clearly, I was sending a signal, but I had waited for Nancy to state unequivocally that she had no intention of sleeping with me before I put it out there. If she hadn't done that, I wouldn't have said a word.

"I'd like to help you with that," she said, "but I have my girls to think about."

When Chip returned to the table, Nancy exacted a bit of revenge by keeping him in the dark about what we had decided.

"Everything OK?" Chip asked.

"Everything's great," Nancy said.

This was naughty enough, but winking at me was over the top.

———————

Would I have slept with Nancy if she were willing? I don't know; it was more complicated than it appeared. Not only would it have been morally repugnant—after all, she and Chip had two pre-school children, a pair of innocents whose lives I had no right to disrupt—but it would have been an accurate gauge of where I was at sexually. I had pulled Dana toward me at the front door of the cottage, but I was stoned at the time, and there was no way of knowing if I had overcome my performance anxiety or would be undone by it again. In the back of my mind, I harbored the lingering fear that Karen Marcus might have been a once-in-a-lifetime thing, and that I may never meet anyone else who eased my mind the way she did, simply by downplaying the importance of an orgasm. I hadn't slept with anyone since Karen and I had spent a few nights together two years before, and it was obvious that I had yet to achieve even a semblance of normalcy. The length of the interval said it all.

When I arrived at Office Plus the next day, Chip brought up the beard again.

"Do girls really like that?" he asked.

"You tell me. What did your wife say?"

"She hated it."

"Really? I'm not sure I believe you."

"Actually, she said she liked it, but I know she didn't."

"And you know that how?"

"I'm sure she was just getting back at me—like when she winked at you there at the end."

"I thought the wink was heartfelt, but that's just me."

"If I give you a raise, will you shave that fucking thing?"

"How big a raise are we talkin'?"

"I need a commitment before I tell you."

"That's not gonna happen. I'll be here when you're ready to negotiate in good faith."

"I can get you a good deal on a razor."

"I'm sure you can. You'd probably give me one if I asked you to."

"You bet I would—just say the word."

Although I refused to shave it off, I increased the frequency of my snipping at the stubble with a pair of scissors, but my attempt to placate Chip fell short of the complete capitulation that he desired. There were no further developments in the facial hair dispute until I established myself as one of the best salesmen that Chip ever had, which left him with no other choice but to keep his mouth shut for as long as he could.

Within a day or two of my hitting the road on my own, I discovered an essential truth about pushing office supplies in places like Lakewood, Freehold, and Point Pleasant—the fact that I had the perfect persona for it inside of me all along. By projecting the kind of Nice Jewish Boy demeanor that my mother had longed for, I gained the confidence of my customers, persuaded them that I was trustworthy, and charmed the orders right out of them, until I reached a point where I was routinely opening two or three accounts a week. Before long, I developed the ability to open these accounts by eleven in the morning, which enabled me to strip down to a bathing suit in the Matador, grab a towel from the trunk, and lie on the beach for an hour. As long as I applied sufficient amounts of sun block—and could produce my order pad for Chip's inspection—he was never any wiser, or if he was, he performed a mathematical calculation that demonstrated the fact that my numbers were vastly superior to those of Irv Samuels, a Willy Loman type who worked for Chip part-time. About the only thing that Irv had going for him at that late stage of his career was the fact that he was clean-shaven.

This outrageously cocky behavior persisted for several weeks until Chip became suspicious and started checking on me with the customers. I could only imagine their conversations until Dr. Shulman, an orthodontist in Manalapan, reported back to me.

"Was my guy there today?" Chip asked him.

"Yeah, he was here."

"What time did he leave?"

"I don't know. Eleven?"

"That's what I thought. Didja buy anything?'

"I didn't need anything, but I ordered something anyway."

"Oh, yeah? Whadja order?"

"He told me he could get me a good deal on a plastic floor mat for under my desk. You know, the kind that digs into the carpet?"

"How big a mat?"

"I don't know—he measured. He said I should get a bigger one just to be safe."

A few days later, when I delivered the mat to Dr. Shulman, he promised to fudge the time of my departure whenever Chip called, as long as I knocked a few bucks off of his next order.

"I'm not sure I'm comfortable with that."

"Why not? How much does he pay you?"

"Two-fifty a week."

"That's all? He should be ashamed of himself. I make more than that on an extraction."

"It's apples to oranges, doctor."

"I've known Chip for years. Trust me, it's OK to screw him over."

"If that's the way you feel about it," I said, "it won't be a problem."

"What time should I tell him—two? Three?"

"Three's too late. I'd never get back in time if I actually left at three."

"OK. Two then. What's on sale this week?"

"Anything you want."

After a month of double-dealing with Shulman, I started to

feel guilty about it; but before I could alter my behavior, Chip confronted me.

"Going right to the beach?" he asked.

"What are you talking about?"

"I checked your odometer. There's no way you were in Barnegat yesterday."

"So what if I fudge it a little? We're building an empire together."

"Rome was an empire. We're a pimple on the ass of history."

"I'm surprised at you. You should have more respect for your own company."

"At least I respect it enough to put in an honest day's work."

"You'd rather I work until five o'clock and never make a sale?"

"I knew you'd twist it around. That's what you do."

"Can I go now?"

"Why? We're wasting whatever time you're willing to put in?"

"Something like that."

"So you *are* going to the beach."

"Not until later. The forecast calls for showers."

"Don't get too much sun. It can have serious effects on your health."

"Don't worry. I have plenty of sun block in the car."

"How *is* your car? Still holding up?"

"You tell *me*. You checked the odometer."

By that point, I never had to deny anything. I simply pointed to my results, the way successful salesmen do when their selling skills rise to the level of their laziness. That was my idea of success—getting what you wanted out of a job—whether it was money, a sense of fulfillment, or in my case, the kind of laughs that I lived for. The only concession I forced myself to make once Chip started talking that way was to refrain from smoking pot in the middle of the day, not out of a sense of loyalty but because the latest batch I had obtained from Joe McBride had a tendency to make me paranoid. Once that happened, I began to fear the possibility that Chip would conduct a more sophisticated surveillance operation than he already had. After all, he had access to any number of electronic devices in the ADT catalog that he kept in a drawer of his desk, and he was eminently capable of making a check of my odometer look like child's play.

In order to punish me, Chip threatened to ride with me one day, attempting to pass it off as a quality control measure that was necessary for the good of the company. My own view was that he was determined to cost me an afternoon in the sun. A vindictive pleasure was the only thing available to him now that I had rescued him from the kind of red ink that he had experienced in the past, when his carelessness with money and compulsion to give things away outpaced the healthy sales figures that his sales reps generated before they reached the point where his personality made it impossible to work for him.

"You don't have to ride with me," I said. "The numbers don't lie."

"Come on—it'll be just like old times. Do you remember when we went to Friendly's together and you made the point about outer space?"

"How could I forget? It was only three weeks ago."

Chip could not be dissuaded, and my only task in riding with him that day was to stick it out until he called it quits, knowing full well that he had fallen behind in his paperwork at the store. His decision to accompany me turned out to be more of an inconvenience for him than it was for me, particularly since he took one look at the Matador, noticed a slow leak in its left rear tire, and refused to ride in it. He had intended to sit in my passenger seat and observe my routine, but instead we piled into his Ford Taurus and he fiddled with a citizens band radio that he had recently purchased in still another example of profligate spending. Although he had no use for it and wasn't the CB radio type, Chip found it difficult to resist any gadget that had been substantially discounted, whether he needed it or not. Another area of contention between him and Nancy—besides the issue with Chip's sex drive—was that he would jump at the chance to buy two products for the price of one when he didn't need the product at all. In fact, he was the only person I knew who owned two electric shoe polishers, one for each foot.

"Do you like my radio?" he asked.

"It's kinda loud," I said. "Can you turn it down?"

"Why? This is the recommended volume."

"Really? I haven't heard this much static since I left a broken record on my turntable."

"You'll never guess my handle."

"You're right. What is it?"

"It's 'Spaceman.' You inspired me."

"Do the truck drivers actually respond to that?"

"They respond to everything—they lead a lonely existence."

"Can I say something on it?"

When I reached for the microphone, Chip grabbed my wrist. I had never seen him move so quickly.

"Don't you dare. The last person you wanna make a wise-ass remark to is a truck driver. They're all zonked out on amphetamines—they'll run you off the road."

Chip let go of my wrist, and I examined it for bruises. It hadn't smarted like that since I had swung a hammer for Joe Giammona.

"Did you ever notice that the only people who use the expression 'zonked out' are the ones who've never taken a drug in their life?"

"Sure," he said. "I'm one of 'em."

"I've got news for you. You're in the minority."

As soon as we merged onto the Garden State Parkway—and he zeroed in on a tractor-trailer—Chip's CB radio went on the blink. After emitting a torrent of static that caused us both to wince, it let out a screeching sound that compelled us to cover our ears, although Chip had only one hand available to him.

"Either you turn that fucking radio off or I sue you for a hostile work environment. It's your choice."

"Why should I turn it off? We ran into a little static, that's all."

"The next thing I know, you'll be steering the car with your knee."

"So what? I've done that plenty of times."

"That explains your tendency to drift into the opposite lane."

Chip leaned forward and pulled the plug on the radio. "No wonder I got such a good deal on it. It doesn't work."

"Who'dja buy it from?"

"Irv. He said he didn't need it anymore."

"It's about time he made a sale. Unfortunately, it won't show up in your bottom line."

Chip ignored this. "What's your first stop of the day?"

"Jenkinson's Pier in Point Pleasant. I like their hot dogs."

"I meant a stop that's business-related."

"That would be business-related if we sold ketchup on the side."

Chip made a face. "You put ketchup on your hot dogs? You really *are* a barbarian."

"What do you put on yours—mustard? Just because everyone else does?"

"Mustard and relish. Are there any offices near Jenkinson's Pier?"

"I'm not sure. There's a condemned property close by. From the looks of it, it's just your speed."

Once in a while Chip cracked a smile, and I could tell that he was enjoying himself; but he did his best to maintain a poker face. This time, he seemed truly distracted, and a minute later, a state trooper pulled him over.

"See that?" I said, after Chip was issued a citation. "That whole thing could have been avoided if your CB radio actually worked. You woulda known about the speed trap."

"I'll deal with Irv later."

As it turned out, Chip got the last laugh when I experienced a mechanical failure of my own. The next day, the transmission on the Matador slipped for the final time, giving up the ghost in the middle of a Hassidic community in Lakewood. Instead of making my usual sales call to Kosherama, I suffered the disapproving frowns of the Hassidim as I left a trail of transmission fluid on their otherwise pristine streets. Although I shared the same ethnic background as the people who gathered in front of their synagogue to stare at me, I felt like General Custer, only this time the "Indians" had beards and *payes* and accurately identified me as a lapsed Jew. No one came to my aid, but I didn't really blame them as I scanned the crowd for a kindly face. Finally, I settled on a twelve-year-old whose *tsi-tsis* were emerging from the front of his shirt. I had worn *tsi-tsis* myself during the three years I spent at the Yeshiva Academy in the aftermath of my parents' divorce; but it seemed like a lifetime ago. Did the Matador really have to die at a house of worship?

"Is there a pay phone around here?"

"Come with me," the kid said. "You can use the phone in the office."

He took a few steps toward the temple before he realized that I hadn't moved.

"Are you sure it's OK?" I asked.

The kid shrugged. "The rabbi won't mind. It's a mitzvah."

Not only was the rabbi agreeable, but his nephew owned a tow truck, and I was able to call Chip from a Cottman Transmission. I had made Cottman Transmission an object of scorn in Toms River, but I was glad to see it in Lakewood.

———————

Chip answered on the first ring.

"I have some good news and some bad news," I said.

"I can't wait. What is it?"

"The bad news is my car died. The good news is I found the perfect place to sit shiva."

"Wonderful. What are you gonna do?"

"I have to leave it here. The transmission's completely shot."

"Where are you?"

"Lakewood."

"Did Kosherama order this week? Your sales have been tailing off with 'em."

"I never got there."

"I told yuh that car was a loser. You shoulda listened to me."

"I'd already bought it by then. How 'bout you say something constructive for a change? I'll wait."

"How much for a new transmission?"

"Whatever it is, it's more than I can afford."

"Don't do anything. I'll make a few calls."

"It's five o'clock. They can't work on it 'til tomorrow."

"I can't remember the last time you worked until five o'clock."

"It serves me right for opening an account thirty miles from the beach."

"Are you near the bus station?"

"How should *I* know?"

"Ask them!"

"I *will* ask 'em. Did you think I would walk home?"

"Do you have money for the bus?"

"Yeah. The veterinarians paid me with cash."

"They usually do. I think they're cookin' their books."

"You may be right, but they seemed preoccupied today."

"Why do you say that?"

"They were treating a poodle. He swallowed some kosher soap."

"Is that a shameless attempt at humor or are you telling the truth?"

"Come on—do you really have to ask?'

"Not really. How was the receptionist?"

"Rivka? She's fine. I had lunch with her."

"She's a real looker, isn't she?"

"That's the thing about Hassidic women. Some of them are flat-out gorgeous, but they're married to the homeliest men on the planet."

"If they'd shave their fucking beards, they'd have a fighting chance."

"Enough with the beard already. You're embarrassing yourself."

"Where'dja go with Rivka—the deli across the street?"

"Yeah. Their brisket's to die for."

"You can bring me back a sandwich next time."

"I'd be glad to. I'll come back a little early to make sure it doesn't go bad."

"The hell you will. I'll give you a Styrofoam cooler."

"OK, but Rivka's going to Israel for a month—so it won't be any time soon."

"Do the best you can. That's all I ask."

"Speaking of that, I made one other sale today, besides the veterinarian."

"Oh, yeah? To who?"

"Paul Kimball Hospital."

Chip paused, and I could picture his mouth falling open.

"You got the Paul Kimball account? Irv couldn't do that in his prime!"

"You won't believe it when you see what they ordered."

"Tell me now."

"I can't. The order pad's in my car."

"So?"

"My car's up on a lift."

"Just give me the highlights. I won't hold yuh to it."

"OK, but this is purely from memory. They ordered three calculators, five Rolodexes, seven cartons of double-sided tape, and a standing order for staples, paper clips, and magic markers once a month."

"You did all that from memory?"

"Some of it. The rest I made up."

"You're a sick bastard, you know that?"

"My therapist says I shouldn't be so hard on myself so it'll be a while before I answer."

"Your therapist should have his head examined."

"He already has. It's a requirement, I believe."

"What happened at the hospital? We've been soliciting them for years."

"You and Irv, you mean? You answered your own question."

"They musta built a new wing."

"As a matter of fact, they did."

"I knew it had to be something."

"Chip, no offense, but the new wing had nothing to do with it."

"You're full of yourself today."

"That's every day. I try to stay consistent."

"If your goal is to be obnoxious, you've succeeded admirably."

"Failure wasn't an option."

"What kind of calculators did they buy?"

"Texas Instruments—the expensive kind."

"See what happens when you work the whole day?"

"What are you taking about? You quit at three o'clock when we ride together."

"Yeah, but I'm the boss."

"But look at the example you're setting."

"We'll continue this another time. I gotta go."

In addition to all of his other redeeming qualities, Chip was absent-minded; so his use of "another time" was disconcerting.

"Are you picking me up at the bus station or not?"

"Of course I am. What time?"

"I don't know yet."

"Call me when you find out."

"Where—on your CB?"

"Very funny. I'll see yuh later."

"I bought you a car," Chip said, tossing me a set of keys as I stepped off the bus.

"You what?"

"Come on—I'll show you."

He had told me earlier that he intended to make a few calls, but I had no idea that one of them would be to Richie Crockett at Causeway Ford or that he would pick me up in a brand new Ford Escort with a price sticker attached to the window. Only an ingrate would point out that the car was a bottom-of-the-line model in their standard powder blue, or that it had no radio, air conditioner, or options of any kind. It was a set of wheels, which was more than I could say for myself while I waited for the mechanic in Lakewood to haul the Matador off to a junk yard or chop shop, whichever was more profitable.

"*Now* will you shave off the beard?" Chip asked.

I stared at him. His expression was inscrutable, and there wasn't an ounce of irony in his tone.

"I guess I have to at this point."

"And all I had to do was buy you a car. Why didn't I think of it sooner?"

"I don't know. But if I remember correctly, you promised me a Cadillac."

"Get in," he said.

I sat down behind the wheel while Chip struggled to arrange himself on the passenger side. They didn't call them compact cars for nothing, and those extra pounds he was carrying had never been more of a factor.

"You OK?" I asked.

"It's a little tight," he said. "Whadda *you* care?"

"I'm just showing concern for my fellow man. It was a New Year's resolution."

"What took you so long? It's October."

"I couldn't get to it right away. Hey, what's this?" I cried, staring in horror at the console between us.

"It's a stick shift," he said calmly, still more concerned with the fact that he was exceedingly uncomfortable.

"Will you stop squirming for a minute? I can't drive this thing!"

Finally, he looked up at me. "What are you saying—you don't want the car?"

"I appreciate it, Chip. But I've never driven a stick in my life."

"So you'll learn."

"When—right now?"

"Not with me in the car. I'll get Richie to give you a lesson."

"Who's Richie?"

"He's the salesman—who do yuh think?"

"Do you think he will?"

"He has to. The fuckin' car doesn't even have a radio."

"Does he owe you a favor?"

"I buy cars from him all the time."

"Do any of 'em have automatic transmissions?"

Chip rolled up his sleeve, made a big show of displaying his Rolex watch, and glanced at it. "What did I have—forty-five minutes to put the deal together?"

"It's unbelievable. I'm just nervous about the shifting."

"You went from a useless transmission to a perfectly good stick shift and you fail to see the improvement?"

"At least I knew how to operate the transmission."

"Fine," he said. "Get up."

It took him a few seconds to extricate himself from the passenger seat, but he made up for lost time on his way to the driver's side, where I refused to budge.

"What do you mean get up?"

"Which part didn't you understand?"

"Are you taking it back to the dealer?"

"I have to. That's where my car is."

He was obviously enjoying this now, and who could blame him after all of the shit I had given him? Then there was the fact that I had ruined the surprise of his picking me up in a new car. He could have met me at the bus station in the Taurus, but it wouldn't have been as dramatic.

After letting me suffer for a few more seconds, he said, "I told yuh—Richie'll give you a lesson. You'll be fine."

Somehow, the "lesson" with Richie Crockett turned into a single torturous session in a field behind their body shop, with the sun setting over Manahawkin Bay. We terminated our brief encounter by mutual agreement after I thoroughly humiliated myself with my mechanical ineptitude and Richie was betrayed by a slipped disk in his neck. He was a hulking, middle-aged man—the same size as Frankie Doyle but thirty years older—with a salt-and-pepper moustache that extended to the edges of his upper lip but no further. Richie's face turned purple before he even said anything or lifted a hand to his neck; but with each jerking motion of the car his discomfort increased in severity while my own mortification kept pace, until I finally realized how much business Chip must have thrown his way over the years. Unless Chip was putting Richie's kids through college, there was no other explanation for the abuse Richie took at my hands.

"Why don't we call it quits?" I suggested, after the car stalled for the twentieth time as I attempted to shift from neutral to first gear. Putting us out of our misery was the only thing I was thinking about, but fortunately Richie had the presence of mind to realize that the car was rolling toward the bay. Massaging his neck with one hand and applying the emergency brake with the other, he brought the car to a halt with fifteen feet to spare.

"That was close," I said, staring at the marshy swampland that represented the only thing that stood between us and drowning in a submerged vehicle.

"It sure was," Richie agreed, reaching for a bottle of Tums in his pants pocket. While I breathed a sigh of relief, Richie emptied five or six tablets into the palm of his hand and swallowed them without water. This was the first time that I had seen something like that since my father had an adverse reaction to the chicken cacciatore at Lucy's Café in Hershey, where the proprietor Emilio "Bozo" Tatangelo favored a challenging combination of peppers in his sauce. To his credit, however, Bozo never failed to stop at a customer's table to make sure he was suffering from indigestion and not a heart attack at the first sign of distress.

"Do you want to take over from here?" I asked.

"That's probably a good idea," Richie said. "Don't worry. You'll get the hang of it."

"That may be true, but how am I gonna get home?"

Richie took on a horrified expression, then assumed a poker face to make me feel better. There was only one road in and out of Long Beach Island, and he had no desire to encounter me on the highway at the end of his shift.

"I could drive you," he offered, "but you wouldn't have a car in the morning."

"Don't you have any Escorts with automatic transmissions?"

He hesitated for a moment, unwilling to betray Chip.

"We do, but they're generally more expensive."

The thought occurred to me make up the difference, but I had a hundred dollars to my name.

"Never mind. I may do a little better when I'm alone."

"You were probably worryin' about me."

"I was, Richie. Your neck looks kinda painful."

"Don't worry about it. It's an old bowling injury."

"That's a tough sport," I said. "I stay away from it myself."

As far as punchlines went, it wasn't one of my better ones; but Richie cracked up anyway.

"Oh, Jesus Christ!" he cried, grabbing his neck again.

"Are you sure you're OK to drive?" I asked.

"It's either that or lettin' *you* drive," he said crossly. Chip or no Chip, he had finally reached his limit.

———————

I was worse than a Q-tip on my way home, even though I had stayed behind at Causeway Ford to practice shifting for another twenty minutes in the privacy of their auxiliary parking lot. By then, Richie Crockett had already clutched his rosary beads, said his Hail Mary's, or performed whatever ritual Catholics perform when they have narrowly avoided a watery death, and I was left on my own to suffer the hellish experience that awaited me. I fully expected to have a certain amount of difficulty on the eight-mile journey from the dealership to my cottage in Beach Haven, but it quickly became apparent that the progress would come slowly over the next few weeks, and that I might as well face the music immediately.

Not surprisingly, I stalled the car fifteen or twenty times when no one was watching and then drove in first gear for half a mile until I summoned the courage to shift into second. By that point, I had already calculated the number of stop lights that I was about to encounter, thanking my lucky stars that the traffic signals had been placed on their post-Labor Day schedule. That meant that there was a single stop light between Causeway Ford and the bridge and only one more after that when you prepared to navigate a small traffic circle and make your decision to head north or south. After that second major intersection, all of the other traffic signals exhibited a flashing yellow light, and unless it took me until Memorial Day to get home, I would be able to avoid additional humiliation.

As it turned out, I caught a major break when the first of those lights happened to be green as I approached, and so I was able to shift the car into third gear and cross the bridge without incident, paying absolutely no attention to the finer points of shifting into a higher or lower gear as I climbed the initial incline of the bridge or descended on the other side. But as fortunate as I had been with the first traffic signal, there was hell to pay with the second, and for approximately twelve minutes after the light changed from red to green repeatedly, I struggled to shift the car from neutral into first gear, stalling the car thirty or forty times while my fellow motorists became irate behind me. Once it became apparent that I was either experiencing mechanical problems or was completely inept, they leaned on their horns and glared at me as they passed. I realized, of course, that they would have resorted to these tactics whether the issue was mechanical or not, but they might have gone a little easier on me if the car had broken down like the Matador had in Lakewood instead of holding me personally responsible for not knowing how to drive.

Although I had started to feel sorry for myself, I still had enough empathy left for the unlucky souls who found themselves at my mercy, because those drivers were forced to wait not only for me but for the long line of cars that were directly behind *them.* If you were far enough back and had time to react, you could have given yourself enough wiggle room to clear the rear bumper of the car in front of you, maneuver into the passing lane, and leave the entire fiasco behind; but if you were immediately behind me, your wait wouldn't end until I got my shit together.

There were several near-accidents as other motorists attempted these maneuvers, but even those were superseded by the sight of purple faces, pantomime curses, and veins bulging from people's necks in my rear-view mirror, until I finally covered the mirror with a Kleenex and one of Chip's best-selling rubber bands to block my view of the mayhem. After shrugging my shoulders apologetically, I realized that no apology in the world would make up for the time I was costing them or get me in their good graces, and it became apparent that however many seconds I spent apologizing, I was only delaying my next attempt to shift into first gear, send the car into motion, and end the nightmare that this stoplight had become. Before I actually succeeded in doing that, I lost count of the number of cars I affected in the space of twelve minutes and caused more than a few of them to violate the law by driving on the shoulder of the road, until I finally heard the dreaded sound of a police siren. Even the police officer was put out at that point, conflicted as he must have been by the question of whether to pursue the drivers who entered the shoulder of the road or terrorize the putz who was causing the problem in the first place. Fortunately for me, there is almost always more sport involved for a police officer in giving chase to an unlawful motorist than assisting a hapless one who doesn't appear to be leaving the scene any time soon. In that manner, one of the reckless cowboys driving on the shoulder served as a decoy for me and the police car sped past me without stopping.

As it turned out, this was the only time I was glad that my car didn't have a radio. Otherwise I might have tuned in to the rinky-dink station in Stafford Township just as it interrupted its regular programming to advise motorists to avoid the area. Even though I was finally home free in terms of red lights after sending the car into motion, I was so freaked out by the experience that I left Long Beach Boulevard and drove on the back streets the rest of the way, realizing that if there was ever a time that I'd fall off the wagon and start drinking again, this was it. But if I had stopped at a liquor store, I would have had to shift from neutral to first gear again, and that might have been the only thing that preserved my sobriety.

———————

After dinner, I decided to practice my driving, figuring that even a slight improvement would make things easier for me when I drove to work in the morning. Now that there were no other drivers pressuring me, I was able to think more clearly and isolate the main problem. It wasn't the stick shift itself—that was easy enough to maneuver—it was the clutch that afflicted me.

When you drive an automatic transmission, your left foot has no skin in the game. You can rest it on the floorboard for the entire duration of your journey, or you can tap it in time to the music if you actually have a radio. You can even stick it up your ass if you're double-jointed. But finding your way to the exact amount of pressure required to release a clutch slowly requires trial and error and more agility than I possessed. For an hour, I drove back and forth in the same two or three block area until an elderly woman in a housecoat and curlers convinced herself that I was casing the joint. Ninety percent of the residents of her block had vacated after Labor Day, but it was just my luck that this old lady hung around long enough to mistake my practice session for a criminal enterprise. By then, my neck was nearly as sore as Richie Crockett's from the jerking motion of the car, and I was too busy trying to get the hang of it to notice her. Had I been aware of her on her front porch, I might have been able to explain myself before she called the police, and before she gave the same policeman who had sped past me on the causeway a chance to exact his revenge.

"I know you from somewhere," he said, as I looked up at him with the car idling in neutral, the emergency brake engaged, and my left foot developing a cramp.

"I know this looks suspicious, but I just got this car today and I have no clue how to drive it. I'm just practicing before I have to drive to work in the morning."

"I knew I recognized you," he declared. "You were the guy from the traffic jam!"

"Yeah—that was me. I'm sorry."

"Don't be. A stick shift's a bitch 'til you get the hang of it."

"You're not kiddin'. I can't shift to save my life."

"Do me a favor. Either pack it in for the night or practice somewhere else. The old lady's havin' a conniption."

"Should I go talk to her?"

"No, that's the last thing we need."

He was right about that.

"Who sold you this car?" he continued. "Richie Crockett?"

"Yeah. How'dja know?"

"The decal says Causeway Ford. Richie's on my bowling team. I haven't seen him since he hurt his neck."

———————

Once I refused to become a doctor, lawyer, or accountant—the three professions that seemed to epitomize the Nice Jewish Boy syndrome that I desperately wanted to avoid—I caused myself to live near the poverty level for a period of many years. But until recently I was glad to make the tradeoff. My desire to behave defiantly preceded my reading *Portnoy's Complaint*, but when I encountered the episode in which Ronald Nimkin dutifully pinned a note to his shirt sleeve prior to hanging himself, my point of view hardened into the counter-productive thing that it was. In Roth's novel, Nimkin was so blindly obedient that he posthumously reminded his mother to bring her "mah-jongg rules to the game." Finding that sort of conformity to be toxic, I became someone who abhorred the seeking of wealth. But now, at the same time, I was getting tired of counting pennies, stretching every dollar, and sweating out unforeseen expenses. I asked myself, did it really make me a sellout if I liked having money in my pocket, enjoying the ocean breeze, and looking out the window to see a new car parked outside? It had never been a matter of worrying about where my next meal was coming from—particularly since I had worked in a series of restaurants—or of putting food on the table for anyone but myself, but my financial situation had always been uncomfortable. I could rest a little easier now that my paychecks were bigger, but unlike Duddy Kravitz in his unscrupulous rise to the top, I was conflicted about it for a long time.

Although I wouldn't have been caught dead listening to Lionel Richie in the past, Chip had turned me into a fan. By then, I had bought several of Richie's tapes, and these purchases enabled me to roll down the window in the Escort, draw the salt air into my lungs, and serenade the seagulls with the bombastic ballad "Truly." Although I tried to placate myself with the snide remark that no self-respecting Black man should have sung that song in public, I finally gave in to my happiness, surrendered to Richie's obvious gifts as a vocalist, and sang along with him as I made my sales calls.

Before I knew what was happening, I found myself in a euphoric state that robbed me of all reason, and I actually took it into my head to do something nice for Chip, an idea that proved to be dangerous when it occurred to me to sit down with him to discuss what I might do differently to generate more revenue for the business. But the moment I began to think it through, I was horrified to realize how close I had come to inviting Chip to make a series of suggestions that I would never be willing to execute, now that I had arrived at a perfect balance between work and play in my efforts for Office Plus.

In the end—whether I was deliberately repaying Chip for buying me a car, thanking him, or I had simply had enough of him mentioning my beard—I bought a razor and a can of shaving cream at Hand's department store and removed the stubble that I had cultivated so unsuccessfully for the better part of five years. I did this in my bathroom mirror at the cottage. At first, I was curious about how I would look, but as the seconds passed and the hair fell to the sink, I was actually pleased with the results. I wouldn't go so far as to say that I looked handsome, but it felt like a distinct improvement, and I could only wonder if I would have been more successful with women if I had shaved a lot sooner. I didn't want to think about that, because it would have added to the long list of actions I had taken that were self-sabotaging.

Chip was in his office when I arrived at Office Plus the next day. He was adding up a column of figures on a Texas Instruments calculator, so engrossed that he failed to look up when I reached the doorway.

"I hope that thing works," I said, "since I sold a ton of 'em to Paul Kimball Hospital."

Chip raised his head, took one look at me, and refused to give me the satisfaction of acknowledging that I had shaved. Spiteful to the core, he looked down again without saying a word.

"Come on. You know you're *kvellin'*."

"You and Irv are the only Jews around here. I have no idea what that means."

"It means you're bursting with pride."

Chip looked up again. "Sure," he said glumly, "it's the happiest day of my life."

"It should be. You've been obsessing over my beard since the minute you laid eyes on me."

"You should have shaved a long time ago."

"Maybe I should come over for dinner again. Is Nancy available tomorrow night?"

"We already floated that balloon."

"I know. For the record, I was only kidding."

"I always assume you're kidding. You don't have to announce it."

"What's the matter? You're even more depressed than usual."

"Sit down. I have to tell you something."

"You're firing me for being a wise guy?"

"Of course not. You woulda been gone a long time ago."

"What is it then?"

"I'm taking on a partner."

In addition to mutually benefitting from the money I was

bringing in, Chip and I actually enjoyed each other, since it was so damn liberating to have at least one person that you could be impolite to whenever you felt like it.

"What brought that on?"

"Money," he frowned. "What else?"

"Who's your partner?"

"His name's Ray Carlucci. You'll meet him tomorrow."

"How do you know him?"

"He runs a poker game on Monday nights."

"Don't tell me. You lost your business in a poker game."

"I didn't lose it—he's a partner."

"Where's he from? You never mentioned him before."

"Bayonne."

I shook my head. "Oh, Chip. What have you done?"

"He's not a bad guy. You'll see."

"Does he know anything about office supplies?"

"No, but neither did you."

"This changes everything. You know that, right?"

Chip shrugged. "At least we still have a job."

———

When I showed up clean-shaven at the Village Tavern, one waitress after another did a double-take and smiled at me approvingly. This was even the case with Wendy, the stern-looking young woman who had maintained a strict policy of doing nothing whatsoever to encourage me, but who took it upon herself on this occasion to walk an extra fifteen feet to the dishwashing station to pay me a compliment on my appearance. But of course it was Dana Hansen's reaction that meant the most, and when she arrived a few minutes late as usual, she stopped in her tracks, raised a hand to my cheek, and allowed it to remain there. The other waitresses were watching, convinced that Dana and I were sleeping together when we weren't, since I had done nothing to disabuse them of the notion.

"What's going on?" Fran asked, catching the tail end of it and deciding whether or not to be angry.

"He shaved," Wendy shrugged.

"Haven't you ever seen a shaved face before? Get back to work!"

———————

In the past several weeks, I had gotten a pretty good idea of when I could tease Chip and when I couldn't; and though I may have even delighted him on occasion, I realized that this was no time to be impertinent. With Carlucci on the way, I was feeling nearly as depressed as Chip was, strongly suspecting that the kind of irreverence that we engaged in could only work when it was the two of us. It didn't matter what kind of person Carlucci was—or whether or not he had a sense of humor—it was unlikely that he would approve of his partner being talked to the way I talked to Chip, unless Carlucci was even more sadistic than Chip and I were, which remained to be seen.

Chip had never gone into detail about his profligate spending, and had only allowed me to catch glimpses of it here and there; so it was more than a little surprising that he told me about the poker game. In any case, Carlucci was due to arrive at high noon—from Bayonne, no less—and I would find out one way or the other.

"Things are gonna change around here," Carlucci announced, chomping on a cigar. He had flashy clothes, a fleshy face, and a glaring demeanor.

"You're right," I thought. "I quit."

Instead of giving voice to this sentiment, I glanced quickly at Chip, immediately noticing that he looked like he was sick to his stomach.

"For one thing, I'm gonna ride with yuh and see what you're doin'."

Carlucci was like oil and water with everyone, and I strongly suspected that this would be my last day with the company.

"That's gonna be a problem," I said. "There's no smoking in my car."

"Chip told me you're a wise-ass. That don't fly with me."

"You might as well fire me right now. I have an instinct for these things. There's no way in hell that we're going to get along."

"I could fire yuh, sure. But we both might regret it. Why don't we give it a chance?"

"All right. But I was serious about the cigar."

"No problem. I won't smoke in your car."

On the surface of it, this was a welcome concession, but the guy reeked of cigars whether he was smoking one or not. Then there was the fact that he was even chubbier than Chip. We would probably end up going in his car anyway, once he attempted to lower himself into my front seat. Just by looking at him, I was sure that his vehicle smelled like a humidor that had never housed a decent cigar—only cheap ones—so I was screwed no matter which car we took.

"How come you're ridin' with me? You're unhappy with my numbers?"

"They're good, but they could be better."

"They're the best numbers Chip has ever had. Didn't he tell you that?"

"Yeah, he told me. I'll level with yuh. He wants you here; I don't. Capisce?"

I couldn't tell if Carlucci was a mafia guy, a mafia wannabe, or just a poor slob who sounded like one. After all, my experience of the mob was limited to movies, television, and the occasional Jimmy Breslin novel. All I knew was that Carlucci was dropping hints left and right, as though he were encouraging Chip to imagine the worst.

"We're goin' over the figures now," Carlucci continued.

"I thought you said they were good. That implies that you already went over them."

Carlucci smiled. "I like this guy. He's got balls."

This comment drew me up short. I was hoping to get fired—not fastened to a cement block and lowered into Manahawkin Bay. I had narrowly escaped drowning there once and had no desire to tempt fate again.

Carlucci pulled out a money clip for no apparent reason—other than to impress me with his wad of bills. He was a vulgar bastard—he really was.

"Why are you showing me that?" I asked. "I assumed that you had at least *some* money in your pocket."

"I'm an *earner*. Yuh know what that means? All you have to do is follow my orders and you'll be an earner, too."

"I haven't gotten to where I am in life by following orders."

Chip stifled a laugh. Clearly, the discussion we were having had a certain entertainment value. But Carlucci failed to see the humor. He probably realized that he had his work cut out for him if he was going to whip us into shape.

"I notice that most of your sales come in the morning."

"I'm a morning person."

"I'm not askin' about your biorhythms. In fact, I couldn't give a fuck."

"What *are* you asking about?"

"I'm askin' why you're showin' up with a suntan every day instead o' two or three extra sales. What time do you stop working?"

I glanced at Chip again. It was hard to tell if he was heartsick at the thought of losing me or fascinated with my escalating war with Carlucci.

"I head back around four o'clock. Why?"

"I just *told* you why. You're supposed to work until five."

"Part o' my work day's getting back here by five."

"From now on, you'll work until five. *Then* you'll head back."

"Are you payin' me for the extra hour?"

"Who the fuck are *you*?"

"I'm the best salesman you've got. Say something, Chip."

"No, I think I'll listen."

Since he failed to defend me, all bets were off. "Tell him what time *you* stop working." I turned back to Carlucci. "He heads back at three. I split the difference and work until four."

"Where I come from loyalty's important. You're the *opposite* o' loyal. You just threw your boss under the bus."

"I'm just pointing out the facts."

"He owns the friggin' company. At least he used to. Now we both own it."

"I'm sorry to hear that."

"Is that a resignation?"

"Yeah, I think it is."

It was either that or he would end up whacking me.

Finally, Chip spoke up. "Hold on, you two." He smiled weakly. "I just bought him a car."

Carlucci's mouth fell open. "You *what*?"

"You heard him," I said. "He bought me a car."

Carlucci turned back to Chip. His face was bright red. "What did I tell you about your spending?"

"What choice did I have? His car died in Lakewood."

"Forget it. We'll deal with that later."

"Actually, he leased the car," I pointed out. "According to Richie, it wasn't a straight purchase."

"Fuck the car," Carlucci said.

"I'd like to see you try."

"That's it—you're outa here!" Carlucci declared, returning the money clip to his pocket. Chip was the next one to speak.

"Come on, Ray. It's new to him, that's all."

"What is? The real world? Did you hear how he talked to me?"

"He insults me all the time," Chip said, smiling fondly at the reminiscence. "I enjoy it."

"You enjoy it? I got news for yuh—I'm not a sadist."

I rolled my eyes. There was no way I was letting that one go. "A masochist, you mean. You probably *are* a sadist."

"All right, that's enough!" Chip cried. "Mark, if you want the job, you gotta stay out until five."

"No way," I said. I was fighting like a bulldog to preserve my right to go to the beach—and giving new meaning to the phrase "drawing a line in the sand."

Instead of firing me again, Carlucci went in a different direction.

"And another thing: You'll quit the job at the restaurant."

"The hell I will!"

"The hell you won't! I don't care how much pussy you're gettin' from the waitresses."

This was objectionable on every level, but I was particularly disturbed by the fact that it was patently untrue. I turned back to Chip. "Is that what you told him?"

"He kinda put two and two together," Chip shrugged.

"We're lookin' for a commitment," Carlucci continued. "It's either us or them."

"Not that you care, Ray. But you're being unreasonable."

"How do you figure?"

"I work at the restaurant on the weekends. It doesn't affect what I do here."

"Who knows? You might come in some Monday and work a full day."

"I guess you'll find out."

Carlucci smiled, loving it as much as I was. "And we'd like you to work one Saturday a month."

"Maybe," Chip put in. "We haven't decided."

"You mean *he* hasn't decided. You want me to sell office supplies on a Saturday when all the offices are closed? Hoo boy, that is rich."

My brother had used that phrase in a letter to me years before, when I was stuffing envelopes for a living. I had been waiting all that time to try it on someone, and who better than Ray Carlucci?

"We don't want you to think of them as office supplies. They're stationery products."

"Stationery products? Are you kidding?"

"You think this is a game, don't you? You won't be laughing when you're out of a job."

"What are you talking about? I resigned five minutes ago."

"Whoa! Hold on!" Chip cried. "Ray, let me handle this."

"Be my guest," Carlucci said, firing up a cigar.

"Can you smoke that somewhere else?" I asked.

"No, I can't."

"Chip, can we go outside?"

Chip looked at Carlucci. Apparently it was Carlucci's call.

"Go ahead," Carlucci followed, settling comfortably into Chip's chair. "I said my piece."

Chip and I finished our conversation outside, while I stole a series of glances at the Fotomat. Their little booth in the middle of the parking lot was looking better all the time.

"Do you actually expect me to learn something from that guy?"

"Who knows? You might."

"What—how do use a baseball bat on a customer?"

"I've never known Ray to be violent."

"Of course not. You do everything he says."

"Not everything. You still work here, don't you?"

"My god, look how far we have fallen."

"What are you talking about?"

"We've gone from Fred Pryor to Ray Carlucci in less than a month."

"It's a game of adjustments, just like poker."

"Really, Chip? You might want to find a better comparison."

Chip ignored this. "You'll ride with Ray on Monday," he said. "We'll see how it goes."

"What time?"

"Be here at eight o'clock sharp."

"I'm sorry. I'm not making any promises."

———————

Because Saturdays turned out to be negotiable—and they dropped their demand about quitting my other job—I agreed to take the weekend to think about it, carefully weighing the irresistible desire to quit against the dread of being out of work. As of ten o'clock on Sunday night, however, I still hadn't decided, although I leaned heavily toward offering my resignation. The deciding factor was typically short-sighted: the fact that I had no desire to ride with Carlucci the next day.

When I called Chip, he was already asleep, but Nancy talked

some sense into me, and I found that I could face Carlucci after all—at least for a day while I sorted things out. But I did pass along a message, drawing a laugh from Nancy when I told her that I refused to shave.

The next morning, I arrived before Carlucci did, and noticed that Chip had reclaimed his chair.

"Howya doin'?" I asked.

"What—you're growin' another beard?"

"I was thinkin' about it."

Chip shook his head. "I can't get a break around here."

"Where is he?"

"How do *I* know?"

"What happened to eight o'clock sharp?"

"What are yuh askin' *me* for?"

While I gathered up my order pad, catalog, and promotional items, Carlucci made his way through the door, walked up the aisle, and stuck his head in Chip's office. "I thought I'd take your car. Is that OK?"

"Do whatever you want," Chip said glumly. "What do I care?"

Carlucci ignored him and walked over to me. "You ready?"

"I've *been* ready. I was here at eight o'clock sharp."

"Great. What do you say we call a truce?"

"Fine," I said, heading toward Chip's office. "I'll be right with yuh."

"What?" Carlucci said. "Yuh gotta kiss him goodbye?"

"Did you hear that?" I asked, closing Chip's door behind me.

"I heard it," he said. It was clear that he was thoroughly demoralized.

"Why did you do this to us? We were perfectly happy without him!"

"I told yuh—I had no choice."

"I can't work for the guy. What happens to the car?"

"I don't know. Keep it 'til you get a new one."

"Are you serious?"

"Yeah. What am I gonna do with it?'

"That's good of you, Chip. I mean it."

271

"You—grateful? That might be the most depressing thing of all."

"I doubt that. That's why I'm getting out of here."

"Do me a favor. Buy a car as soon as you can. He'll be all over me when he finds out."

"He's gonna see me drive away."

"No, he won't. I'll get Kim to distract him."

Kim was the pretty one, and Chip's final maneuver worked.

———————

I needed a job and a car, but that didn't prevent me from taking a day off to visit Sheldon Greenblatt at Mr. Martin's. Although it was mostly a social visit, I realized that I might not reach my objective of lasting an entire year on Long Beach Island; and it wouldn't hurt to see if he had a spot for me at the restaurant. After all, I had already driven the entire length of the island looking for work recently, and there might not have been much else in Manahawkin or the depressing little towns that surrounded it. I gave some thought to begging Rivka to run away with me, but even if she had said yes in that preposterous fantasy, I would have had to attend religious services on a regular basis, a prerequisite that was out of the question. Visiting Sheldon seemed like my best option, particularly since I was running low on pot and Joe McBride was just as likely to be loitering across the street as anywhere else.

When I walked into Mr. Martin's, Sheldon was working the counter by himself, obtaining a computerized printout from the newfangled cash register that he had purchased the year before.

"I see you finally know how to use that thing," I smiled, reaching out to shake Sheldon's hand.

"I didn't have any choice. Bunny went back to Middletown."

Although I had no idea that Bunny had come from Middletown—a speck on the map that was less than five miles from the Harrisburg of my youth—the sound of her name brought an immediate mental image of her bending over to scoop ice cream.

When I finally roused myself from the reverie, I found that I was unable to respond. Instead, I did a double-take at the jar of chocolate chip cookies that rested on the ice cream case. Reaching into the jar without asking, I helped myself to a cookie, which was precisely the sort of familiarity that Sheldon's easygoing manner inspired. True to form, Sheldon took it in stride.

"These are a different kind," I said, narrowing my eyes as I recalled the cookies we sold previously. You could sell those to children, but adults were more discriminating.

"What do yuh think?" Sheldon asked. "They're pretty good, aren't they?"

"They're great. Can I have another?"

"Sure. I'll have one, too."

I handed Sheldon a cookie and grabbed another one for myself. The jar said "Stewie's Chewies."

"I hate the name, but I love the cookies. Where do you get 'em?"

"From some guy in the Northeast. He drops 'em off once a week."

"How much are they?"

"Three for a dollar."

"You're kidding!"

I was chewing as quickly as I could to make room for the next cookie. "I'll buy three of 'em right now."

"Why would you buy 'em when I'm giving 'em to you for nothing?"

"Because—I don't want to take advantage of your good nature."

"He bakes 'em at his hoagie shop," Sheldon continued.

"He does? Why can't *you* do that?"

Apparently, my business sense had improved in the ten years since I had discouraged David Rosner from becoming a millionaire.

"I could," Sheldon said, "but I don't have the space."

By way of reply, I reached into my pocket and threw coins onto the counter indiscriminately. "Here, take whatever you want. They're worth it."

Sheldon used two hands to slide the coins off of the ice cream case and take possession of them. "How many cookies will that get me?" I asked, doing my best imitation of a kid in a candy shop.

"What's the difference? You can have as many as you want."

Without counting, he placed the coins into the cash register and closed the drawer.

"I thought you were working at a restaurant," he said.

"I am, but they're only open two nights a week."

"Is that enough to live on?"

"No, I was working a construction job also, but that lasted about a week."

"You? Working construction?"

"I know. It's a long story. And I was selling office supplies until two hours ago."

"You're a man of many talents. Hand me that rag, wouldja?"

Sheldon grabbed a bottle of Windex while I reached for the rag. "Here," I said, "I'll do that."

I started polishing the ice cream counter, where a large smudge obstructed the customer's view of the chocolate marshmallow.

"What? You want your old job back?"

"I don't know. I was thinkin' about it."

"I have a better idea. Do you wanna sell chocolate chip cookies?"

"Sure. Why not?"

"Hold on—I'll call the guy."

Sheldon slipped on his glasses and read from a hand-written note that was taped to the wall near the phone.

"I didn't know Bunny was from Middletown. I grew up in Harrisburg. It's the next town over." At the time, only her physical appearance was important.

"I met her at Penn State. I thought you knew that."

"Where—the Harrisburg campus?"

"Yeah, it's right near the airport."

"How do you know? Did you fly there? It used to be Olmstead Air Force Base."

"I landed there once."

Sheldon found the number he was looking for, and dialed the phone.

"Stuart? It's Shelly. Have you ever thought about hiring a salesman?"

I could hear Stuart on the other end of the line. "Why? Are you closing the restaurant?"

"It's not for me," Sheldon replied. "It's for a guy that used to work here."

"See that?" I frowned. "He sounds like a wise ass."

"That shouldn't bother *you*."

I started to reply, but Sheldon held up his hand.

"I could use a salesman," Stuart said. "But I wouldn't know how much to pay him."

Sheldon gave me the high sign while I waited for my fate to be decided. "I don't think it matters."

"Of course it matters!" I said angrily, forgetting the gratitude of a moment before.

Sheldon held his hand over the phone. "Don't worry about it. Stuart's a reasonable guy."

"He better be if he expects me to work my ass off."

Shaking his head, he took his hand away from the phone and resumed his conversation with Stuart. "He's a nice Jewish boy. He'll make yuh a lot of money."

I winced the second he said it. "Please don't call me that."

Sheldon ignored this, addressing his next question to me. "When do you wanna meet him?"

"As soon as I finish my cookie."

———————

At his wife's urging, Stuart Rosen had named his restaurant the Yellow Submarine. More importantly, he put Marcia's chocolate chip cookie recipe to good use by selling them from the same kind of jar that he had supplied to Sheldon. Coincidentally, Stuart had started out by selling the cookies to elementary school students as well, but unlike the proprietor of Mr. Martin's, Stuart had a Catholic school right across the street. As he explained it to me, the unofficial "taste testing" of the elementary school kids led directly to the initial success of his product, with Stuart and Marcia adjusting the recipe until they hit upon the precise combination that caused the children to cross the street in droves. Within weeks of introducing the cookies as an impulse item, it became obvious that the little hoagie shop was too small, both for baking purposes and turning out the hoagies that Stuart still offered as staples of his menu. By then, however, the strikingly handsome forty-year-old with the spiffy sports car and exceedingly attractive wife was already dreaming in dollars and scouting locations for a commercial bakery in New Jersey, counting the days until he could close up the hoagie shop at the convergence of Harbison, Battersby, and Robbins Avenue and no longer deal with the public.

After satisfying himself that he and Marcia had arrived at the correct recipe, Stuart took to driving his sports car throughout Northeast Philadelphia in search of 7-Elevens, mom and pop grocery stores, and sandwich shops like his that might want to sell freshly-baked, all-natural chocolate chip cookies from a jar. After a few weeks of selling for two or three hours each day, Stuart had developed a route of thirty or forty accounts, bringing himself that much closer to purchasing the property he had targeted on the Pennsauken-Camden border. All that remained was for Stuart to conquer Center City, and the combination of an incredible cookie recipe and his striking good looks opened doors for him once again, until he secured another fifty accounts downtown.

Now that he had close to a hundred accounts, he experienced the pleasant problem of having to buy a Dodge minivan to make all of his deliveries, an acquisition that would pay for itself after approximately 1,150 boxes of cookies at $17.56 per box minus raw materials, transportation costs, and other expenses. By averaging one box of cookies per week for twelve or thirteen weeks, these accounts would not only pay for the Minivan but enable Stuart to buy the mink coat that Marcia had first laid eyes on at Zinman Furs, a discovery she had made while accompanying her husband on his scouting mission to a vacant building a few blocks away.

When Sheldon Greenblatt called him about adding a salesman, Stuart had been stretched thin by the remarkable success of his cookies for the past two months. But in addition to being run ragged, he was in a positively giddy frame of mind in which he would say yes to nearly anything, including the modest expenditure of trying out a salesman for a few weeks.

"I could open up accounts for you down at the shore," I suggested, never suspecting that those were magic words for Stuart, the phrase "down at the shore" conjuring images of drag racing, staying out all night, and copping feels from the loose teenage girls of his youth. When he took all of that into account and added the prospect of accruing wealth, the proposition was irresistible.

"I'm sure you could," he said cautiously, uncertain of my demands when in reality I didn't have any.

"It's the end of April. They'll be getting ready for the season down there. I can develop a route from Point Pleasant to Cape May. There's hundreds of places to sell 'em to!"

I don't know about Stuart, but I was getting excited just thinking about it.

"I have no problem offering you a job, but I've never had a salesman before. I have no idea what to pay you."

"Just be fair with me."

"I will, but what's fair? What were you making at your last job?"

This was the perfect opportunity to lie, but I didn't.

"Two fifty a week plus gas and tolls."

"That's fine to start out, but we have to figure something out about the mileage."

This wouldn't be the last time that Stuart was way ahead of me. I just sat there and listened.

"If you keep driving back and forth to pick up the cookies, you're gonna run your car into the ground. I'll have to compensate you for that. But at the same time, it's not my fault that you live sixty miles away."

"No, it isn't. But if I lived up here, I'd still be driving back and forth. Isn't there a formula for wear and tear on a car?"

Stuart nodded. "It goes by the mileage. Why don't we do this? I'll pay you three hundred a week plus all your gas and tolls. And I'll ask my accountant what the going rate is for mileage."

My head hurt from all the calculations, but it sounded like he was honorable.

"That's fine. When do I start?"

"Whenever you want. You can take some samples with you today."

"How long do the cookies last?"

"They're great for the first two days, then they're good for a couple days after that."

"But by the fourth or fifth day?"

"There's nothing special about them."

"Are they so stale that you couldn't eat 'em?"

"No, you can eat them for up to a week."

"So they have to buy at least a box a week?"

"Right. Who wants to mess around with half a box?"

"Are they good after they're frozen?"

"They're OK, but they're not great."

"So some of these places may need two deliveries a week."

"If they sell enough cookies, sure."

"We should be so lucky, huh? I'll take three hundred bucks a week plus all the cookies I can eat."

Stuart smiled. "You got it. If things go well for us, I may be able to get somebody to drive 'em down to you."

"Who would that be?"

"One of the girls who works here."

"One of the girls, did you say?"

"Yeah, she's married."

"If she's married, the deal is off."

Stuart kidded me right back. "I'm sorry you feel that way."

"I don't really."

Stuart extended his hand. "When do you want to start?"

"As soon as I buy a car."

"What do you mean? What are you driving now?"

"My boss's car. He lent it to me."

"If you say so. You can use the van until you buy one."

───────────

I was usually polite to the customers, but Walt got on my nerves.

"These are good," he said. "How much are they?"

"Seventeen fifty-six for a box of seventy-two."

"What does that come out to?"

"Twenty-four cents a piece."

"What do I sell 'em for?"

"Whatever you want, but we recommend thirty-five cents or three for a dollar."

"Are they wrapped or loose when I sell 'em?"

As far as I was concerned, that was one question too many.

"They're loose. Wrapping them in plastic would destroy the illusion that they're fresh baked."

"They're not fresh baked?" he asked.

"I'm just fucking with you. Of course they are!"

For a moment, he blinked in confusion, giving up on the previous line of questioning. "Howja come up with $17.56? Why not $17.55 or $17.57?"

"You'd have to ask my boss. He's the one with the calculator."

I lived in fear of an anti-Semitic remark—which was often inevitable—and sure enough he came out with one. At least that's the way I interpreted it.

"Is the extra penny gonna kill him?"

"I wish it would. I'm next in line to take over."

"What do I put 'em in?" he asked suddenly.

"We provide a jar."

"OK—let me think about it. Do you have a business card?"

"Yeah, but I don't give it out."

He stared at me as I handed it over. "Stewie's Chewies," he smirked. "Are you Stewie?"

"No. Can we get on with this, please?"

"Do I get to keep it?"

"What—the jar?"

"Yeah."

"Sure, if you sell enough cookies."

"Do you have one with you?"

This was often the turning point. If they asked to see the jar, the rest was history.

"I'll be right back."

I walked out to the parking lot where a cookie-colored minivan was waiting for me—emblazoned of course with the shameful name of our company. Was it my imagination or was a crowd of strangers gawking at the van from across the street?

In any case, I grabbed one of the jars—which was also decorated with our humiliating logo—and stuck the little three-by-five order pad in my pocket. There was no sense in letting the decision maker see the pad prematurely, lest he develop a last-minute case of cold feet.

When I got back inside, Walt was eating another one of my samples. This was an occupational hazard. Some of the owners pretended to deliberate in order to get another cookie out of me before they started to pay for them.

"What if I don't sell 'em all?" he asked.

"Then we take the jar back."

"If you let me keep the jar, I'll try 'em out."

"Not gonna happen," I said. As risky as it was, you had to be firm at a time like that. "The jar goes home with me."

"OK! I was just asking."

"Don't worry about it," I said. "We seem to be getting along pretty well. It's a shame there's no soliciting."

"I have to say that. I'd be dealing with salesmen all day."

"There's a way to get rid of us, you know—and that's to buy something."

"OK, I'll buy a box."

I took out the order pad, which had carbon paper between each of its sheets.

Although I knew the name of his establishment perfectly

well—having scoffed at it when I pulled into the lot—I forced him to say it out loud to balance the scales. "What's the name of your business?"

"The Double Duck Deli."

Now it was my turn to smirk. "Really?" I said, scribbling the name in my pad. "How'd you come up with that?"

"When I first opened –"

I held up my hand. "Never mind. I didn't mean to pry."

Walt had a small cylindrical container near the cash register. It had a slot on top and bore the inscription "Cystic Fibrosis Society." There were a handful of coins scattered along the bottom of the container—not many, but some. I felt a sense of dread as he reached for the container.

"You're not gonna move that, are yuh?" I had a mental image of Cystic Fibrosis never being cured.

"Why not? Where else would I put the jar?"

He brought the container to rest next to a cardboard display of beef jerky. Then he positioned our jar. "It looks good there, doesn't it?"

"No comment."

"What if the cookies don't sell? Do you buy 'em back?"

"Not on your life. They'll sell—trust me."

"TastyKake buys 'em back."

"They're bigger than we are. We're still working on our first million."

"What if they break?"

"Then we'll buy them back. But if we suspect that you're breaking them on purpose, that would conclude our relationship."

"Who else sells 'em around here?"

"In Ventnor? Hoagie Heaven, the Neptune Market, just about everybody."

"Then why should I sell 'em?"

"To keep up with the Joneses. Do you really want to be known as the only local merchant that doesn't carry a quality product like this?"

"I'll tell you what. You take 'em out of the Neptune Market and I'll carry 'em here."

"Now think about what you just said," I replied.

"I'll sell twice as many as they do!" he insisted, completing a journey in which he had gone from a no solicitation policy to begging me to sell him the cookies.

"I'd rather give you the jar than take the cookies out of an existing account, and I won't do that either."

"You know what?" he said. "I don't like your attitude."

I waved the order pad in his face—at a discrete distance, of course, but the point was unmistakable. "This is kinda like a parking ticket. Once I start writing, it's official."

Giving up now, Walt pushed a button on the cash register. A bell rang as the drawer of the register opened.

"There it is," I said, "the sound that I know and love."

"I'm sure you do. Do you have change for a twenty?"

———

My next sales call was to an arcade on the Atlantic City boardwalk—one of seven that a tanned, middle-aged playboy named Roger operated along the Jersey Shore. His manager was a woman named Peggy.

"I want to sell these," Peggy decided, after tasting one of my samples.

"I would like that."

A speck of chocolate had taken up residence on Peggy's cheek—the only flaw I could detect in her beauty. I reached for a napkin dispenser that was resting on the counter nearby.

"Thanks," she said, removing the chocolate.

Once in a while, sales afforded an even greater pleasure than fucking with the head of a business owner, and flirting with a female employee was one of those occasions.

"I want to order twenty boxes for the Memorial Day weekend."

I nearly choked—even though Peggy was the one who was

chewing. "I'm sorry—did you say twenty boxes?"

"Yeah—maybe more. Roger owns seven of these fucking things." She gestured toward the inner sanctum of the arcade, where the sound of pinball machines combined with flashing lights to create a nightmarish effect. I could only hope that there weren't any epileptics among the gaggle of pimply-faced teenagers skillfully dry-humping the pinball machines just short of causing them to tilt. I wasn't in the mood to witness a seizure.

"You wouldn't have any aspirin?" I asked.

Peggy reached under the counter, producing a bottle of Excedrin. "Between the pinball machines and the Skee-Ball, it's hellish in here. I don't know why I put up with it."

"I don't know—you can work on your tan on your day off?"

Peggy opened the bottle of Excedrin and shook a couple of pills into the palm of her hand. Now there was no mistaking the fact that she had me eating out of it.

"Who gets a day off? Do you want some fresh-squeezed lemonade with that?"

"Thanks," I said. "I must have died and gone to heaven."

"If you like it so much, I'll get Roger to hire you."

"Where *is* Roger?"

"On his boat probably. Or back at the condo smoking weed."

"What can I say? Some guys have all the luck."

"You know what? Make it thirty boxes. These are really good."

By now I had lost my head completely, forgetting that the cookies had no preservatives, lasted only a week, and could not be returned unsold—facts that I had preserved in my memory when speaking with Walt moments before. The entire proposition of ordering thirty boxes indicated one of two things—either Peggy was an ice water-in-her-veins gambler or totally out of her depth when it came to operating a business on the boardwalk. Rule number one, of course, was to account for the weather, a variable that could dash the hopes of the uninitiated.

Once I left the arcade, greedily clutching the order for thirty boxes of cookies, I walked a block or two to find a pay phone that was out of earshot. It would have been bad form to allow Peggy to hear me celebrate. Although I had a check for $526.80 in my possession, I had given Walt the last of my change and was forced to buy a soft ice cream cone from a frozen custard stand. Otherwise, I wouldn't have had enough coins to make the call to Stuart. It was either that or another lemonade, but I doubted it would taste as good if Peggy wasn't the one serving it.

Stuart answered on the first ring. "Mupti? What's happenin'?"

Although he was another good-looking man, he wasn't a philanderer like Roger, happily married as Stuart was to the Jewish American Princess of his dreams. He had borrowed the nickname "Mupti" from Irv Homer, a right-wing radio host on WWDB, Stuart piping in the broadcast every afternoon through a thousand dollar stereo system over the objections of his employees, a small band of potheads who would have strongly preferred Led Zeppelin.

"If you call me Mupti one more time, I'll embezzle from you and you'll never see me again."

"You're replaceable, Mupti. Those cookies sell themselves."

"What if I take the minivan? That paint job was expensive."

"I'll take my chances. What didja call me for?"

"Are you ready for this?"

Stuart was exceedingly patient as I did the multiplication, factoring in the number of boxes that Peggy ordered, the number of arcades that Roger operated, and the number of weeks left in the summer, arriving at a dizzying total that left my boss entirely unimpressed.

"Let's not get ahead of ourselves," he said, a reasonable suggestion that dashed my hopes of an early retirement.

"What do you mean? Aren't you excited?"

"I will be if it actually happens."

"It already happened. I'm holding a check for five hundred dollars."

"Aren't you forgetting something?"

"Yeah. I forgot how much of a killjoy you are."

"What if it rains?" he replied, and my end of the line went

dead. "Mupti, are you still there?"

"Yeah, I'm here. It's not *going* to rain."

"If you can predict the weather, I'm not paying you enough."

"You're damn right you're not paying me enough. Peggy's talking about a standing order for three deliveries a week."

"She is? Who's gonna make the deliveries?"

"I am! Who do yuh think?"

"What about your other accounts?"

"Fuck 'em!"

"You're such a child, Mupti—but I love you."

"You better love me. I'm making you rich!"

"I'm not sure your other accounts would appreciate your fucking them like that."

"That's where the selling comes in."

"I think you've done enough selling for one day."

"I'll cut 'em back to one delivery a week, and I'll work on Sundays."

"All because of a vague promise?"

"It's not a vague promise. Peggy's an honorable person."

"Based on what—her measurements?"

"I told yuh—she wrote me a check!"

I never suspected that the biggest sale I ever made would give me such grief, but that was the way it was unfolding.

"Can't you hire another delivery person?"

"Possibly, but what would he drive?"

"If you bought one shamelessly embarrassing minivan, you can buy another."

"With whose money—yours? And that's not all I would have to do. I'd have to move to a bigger location, buy another oven, and bake around the clock."

"Hey, I'm only the salesman. My job is to get the orders and yours is to produce the product."

"I'll produce it all right, if it actually happens."

"I have five hundred dollars that says it already has."

"It happened once. Let's see if it happens again."

"My God, Stuart, I thought you'd be happy."

"I am happy."

"No, you're not. You're pleased but you're not happy."

"And you're not seeing straight."

Just then, a teenaged girl walked past the pay phone in a string bikini.

"I'm sorry. What did you say?"

"I said you're not seeing straight. We can't change our whole operation for one account."

"Why can't we if it's a big enough account?"

"Hold on—the timer's about to go off. I've gotta check on the cookies."

"Isn't that what you pay the potheads for?"

"What are you taking about? You're the biggest pothead of all!"

"Yeah, but I don't smoke on the job."

"The odor in the van tells me otherwise."

"Let's see you drive around with a van full of chocolate chip cookies and refrain from smoking pot."

"What if this Peggy person orders them for three weeks and then changes her mind? What do I do with my new driver then, and my new oven, and my new bakery? No, we wait and see—that's final."

"So what are you saying? I should march back in there and say, 'Peggy, I appreciate the confidence you have in our product but unfortunately we don't share it'?"

"If you say that, make sure you get it on tape."

"How come?"

"Because—I'll want Marcia to hear it. She thinks I'm exaggerating when I tell her you're crazy."

That particular Memorial Day was in 1984. It rained heavily, and Peggy was so beautiful that I bought back the unsold cookies, encouraging Stuart to take it out of my pay. Needless to say, he was only too happy to oblige, thus concluding my first month as a cookie salesman.

———————

Once I knew the cookie job would work out, I went back to Causeway Ford. After all, I had to return Chip's car at some point and replace it with wheels of my own. The other incentive was the abject humiliation I felt at driving the minivan. The name Stewie's Chewies was plastered all over it, and that was reason enough for me to feel the way I did.

When I finally went looking for him, Richie Crockett wasn't in the showroom, so I sent a message to him through the sales manager. "Tell him I'm not here for a driving lesson," I said, and the sales manager went off to find him.

While I waited for Richie to miraculously appear, I inspected an impressive array of Tauruses, Explorers, and LTDs. Not one of them was an Escort, the redheaded stepchild of the Ford Motor Company. The Escorts didn't even merit a spot in the showroom and were parked on the lot outside. I already knew that the powder blue Escort was the generic, bottom-of-the-line choice, having seen the price sticker when Chip picked me up at the bus station. But I didn't care as long as they had one with a radio and an air-conditioner.

Since I was still living hand-to-mouth, I would have to rely almost exclusively on my father. He would have to front me the money and co-sign the loan. After Richie tracked me down, he led me to his cubicle and worked up the numbers, telling me exactly what I would have to come up with in terms of funding and cooperation from my dad.

"How's your neck, Richie? Any better?"

"It's coming along."

"It must be now that I'm in your rear-view mirror."

"I can't complain. How's your driving?"

"Less torturous. As I assured your sales manager, I won't be needing a lesson."

"I wouldn't be sitting here if you did. There's no trade-in, right?"

"Now that would be a neat trick, since I'm driving Chip's car."

"Yeah, right."

"Have you met his new partner? He's a prince among men, I'll tell yuh."

"No, I haven't had the pleasure."

"Keep it that way, for your own good."

I left the dealership with a computerized printout of what Richie had told me, with his business card stapled to the front page. I had the printout in front of me when I called my father from the cottage.

My father and I had an imperfect relationship, due in equal parts to my lack of character and my father's decision to withdraw from the lives of his sons, make surrogate sons out of his drinking buddies in Hershey, and live in a state of denial. In that respect, I was a chip off the old block. But ever since my parents' divorce, a steady current of tenderness had gone back and forth between us; and I knew that my collecting a series of parking tickets in his name wouldn't prevent him from helping me. If a constable showing up at his door didn't prevent it, nothing would.

My father met me at Causeway Ford a day or two later, and Richie Crockett huddled with the finance manager to make the more challenging requirements go away. This might not have been possible if I hadn't gained some residual benefit from having worked for Chip; if the letter that Stuart Rosen had written hadn't been so persuasive; and if the finance manager hadn't been blown away by the quality of the cookies. But all of those factors fell into alignment and my father and I emerged from the dealership with a set of tags, insurance documents, and the keys to a powder blue Ford Escort that was identical to the one that I had been driving during my employment with Office Plus, save for the fact that my father had sprung for a radio and an air-conditioner.

Whatever disappointments we had caused one another, our limited relationship had always had a sweetness to it, and my steady, reliable, and uncomplicated father was too kindhearted to turn his back on me in a time of need, despite the very real possibility that my stepmother objected to some degree. In the end, my father assumed an entirely new set of risks in the name of paternity, co-signing the car loan, obtaining a "binder" on his insurance policy, and springing for the $500 down payment. In return, I promised to pay him back for the down-payment as soon as I was able, assume complete responsibility for the insurance premium, and refrain from collecting any more parking tickets, an easy promise to make now that I was no longer delivering pizzas, cheesesteaks, and hoagies in a neighborhood that was notorious for its dearth of parking spots. When I thanked him for what he had done, he only griped a little, referring to his insurance broker when he said "I made a lotta goddamn phone calls, I know that!"

Prior to driving back to Hershey, my father followed me over to Office Plus so that I could return the other car to Chip, waiting outside while I handed over the keys, my order pad, and the office supply catalog. I had some cookies with me also, in an unmarked box.

"I bought a car," I said, suppressing an impulse to rub Chip's nose in it any more than I had to.

"Oh, yeah? With what?"

"My father helped me."

"What is it? A Pinto?"

"No. I don't think they make those anymore."

"No, but there are probably some used ones out there some-where. If anybody can find one, it's you."

"You won't be able to criticize me this time."

"Why not?"

"Look outside."

Chip peered out the window. The powder blue Escorts were parked side-by-side, looking identical except for the fact that one of them was occupied by a bald, heavy-set Jewish man picking his teeth with a toothpick.

"Is that your father?"

"Yup."

"Are you sure there wasn't any hanky-panky? There's no resemblance whatsoever."

"Actually there was plenty of hanky-panky, but it occurred after

I was conceived. He's my dad, all right. I have a pointed head like he does and we have the same big ears."

"If you got a haircut once in a while, I might believe you."

"You don't have to believe me. I doubt we'll see each other again."

"He's clean-shaven, I see. How come that is?"

"He doesn't like beards any more than you do. Here, try one of these." I opened my box of samples and waited for him to reach in. "What do yuh think?"

Chip bit into a cookie. "They're great. Can I have another?"

"Have as many as you want."

"Can I give one to Ray?"

"Sure. With any luck, he'll choke on it."

"Hey, Ray come out here."

Carlucci had probably been listening, because he appeared a second later.

"Howya doin'?" he said agreeably, as though we had grown up together in Bayonne, reaching a hairy hand into my samples.

I looked him right in the eye, daring him to deny the obvious.

"They're pretty good, aren't they?"

"Is zat your new job?"

"No. I can't stand to see you wasting away."

"I'll bet yuh a hundred bucks you'll be sellin' somethin' else in a week."

Carlucci was sneering now, but that didn't prevent him from reaching for another cookie.

"He hates 'em," Chip smiled.

"Yeah, I can see that. You can have the rest of them. I gotta go."

"How much do yuh get for a box?" Carlucci followed, pulling out the money clip again.

"For you, twenty dollars."

"How much are they usually?"

"Seventeen fifty-six."

"Forget it. I was tryin' to help yuh."

"Thanks anyway. Chip, do you want one for Nancy and the girls? It's on me."

"Sure!"

"Ray, how 'bout you? I was only kidding."

"Don't do me any favors."

Within a year, Office Plus would go bankrupt and Carlucci would be left with an empty money clip and a cancerous lesion on his tongue.

Like Chip, my father had flirted with a CB radio, but he had gotten bored with it very quickly, in part because he had spent so many years on the road that he had a sixth sense when it came to speed traps. He also had another factor in his favor—the "plus four" rule that stated that a driver can exceed the speed limit by as many as four miles per hour without getting a ticket. For instance, in the turnpike travel of that era, my father would habitually accelerate to a cruising speed of 59 in a 55-mile-per-hour zone and never get stopped on the highway. Undoubtedly, he saw more than his share of state troopers in the roadside restaurants he frequented, and he might have even struck up a conversation with one that enabled him to formulate the "plus four" rule in the first place, its exact origins remaining unknown to me after I missed my initial opportunity to question him about it when I was a kid. Not only could my father go years without a speeding ticket, but I can't remember him ever being in a serious accident, although with the amount of driving he did he must have had some near misses. The only time I can remember a near miss was when we returned from a visit to Aunt Shirley and Uncle Sid in Baltimore in the middle of a blizzard in 1965 when I was eleven years old. My father's station wagon spun out of control with my brother in the front seat and me in the back near Yocumtown, Pennsylvania, but we made no contact with other vehicles and came to rest against a guard rail on the shoulder of the road. Our father took on a horrified expression and checked on Carl and me to make sure we were OK, and said, "We'll put money in the *pushkuh* when we get home."

Sure enough, when we got back to the Towne House Apartments, he reached into the cupboard and removed a small tin box with a slot on top that enabled him to deposit a series of coins whenever the need arose. Located directly behind the *Yahrtzeit* candles that he lit for his parents every year—and intended to solicit and contain charitable donations—the pushkuh was adorned with a Star of David against a blue and white background, the colors of the Israeli flag.

My father used the pushkuh to give thanks when he survived the near miss with his kids in the car, but something tells me that he never used it after having a mishap while traveling alone. He loved Carl and me like crazy—there's no doubt about that—which was another reason that his incremental withdrawal from our lives was so sorrowful for the three of us.

Although it would be charitable to say that my stepfather taught me to drive originally—and not my father—I'm not sure it would be accurate after Harry gave me a single driving lesson in which I nearly got us killed in his Cadillac under the El tracks on Kensington Avenue. Immediately after he popped a nitroglycerin tablet when we got home, he ordered my mother to locate a driving school, and it was a series of total strangers who risked their lives until I was finally ready to take the driver's test at the State Police barracks on Belmont Avenue. Not surprisingly, it was the driving instructor who cheered me on from the observation area while I completed the serpentine maneuver and proved that I could parallel park with my mother and Harry waiting safely at home. Not that I blame them for any of this, because Mike Magnelli and Dan Hiller have frequently reminded me of the disturbing habit I had of driving within a few inches of parked cars, which caused them to dive for cover in the front and back seat respectively. They had a running bet going as to when I would knock a side-view-mirror off of a parked car, a bet that ended in a draw when I managed to avoid that particular calamity. (As Dan Hiller well knew, my driving skills were in sharp contrast to his.

Once, when he was retrieving Laurie Rosenberg, he pulled up to the house in his parents' car, gazed into the rear-view mirror, and parallel parked in a flawless manner. Although Laurie might not have noticed, I was impressed once again with Dan's manual dexterity and hand-eye coordination, which showed themselves in every athletic endeavor he attempted on a soccer field, basketball court, or baseball diamond, routinely scoring goals, sinking foul shots, and making sliding catches that might otherwise have injured him.)

After Harry gave me a single driving lesson and paid for the rest, he washed his hands of the matter and turned it over to my biological father entirely, which not only led to my father reiterating the "plus four" rule but to his collaborating with his mechanic "Curly" Gingrich in locating the first three cars I ever owned and eventually receiving the aforementioned parking tickets and visit by a constable.

With all that, I can say with reasonable certainty that my father was still observing his own "plus four" rule when he made the return trip from Causeway Ford in Manahawkin to the apartment he shared with my stepmother in Hershey. Unless I miscalculated—or drew the wrong conclusion from the countless visits I had made to their apartment—he was looking at a three-hour-and fifteen-minute journey that would enable my stepmother to precede him by a quarter of an hour, unless my father took a longer-than-usual bathroom break at a Howard Johnson's on the turnpike. Just thinking about his arrival—and the domestic harmony that he and my stepmother enjoyed—reinforced something that I had known for a long time: the fact that everyone else had sufficiently recovered from my parents' divorce, but I hadn't. Mom had Harry, Dad had Pat, and Carl had Catherine. I was the only one who didn't have my shit together enough to pair off with another human being. Sadly, I wasn't a fit partner for an adult relationship, and my grotesque approximation with Sarah brought the reality into focus.

Life was good for me at Stewie's Chewies. I had moved to Long Beach Island in order to dry out, and eight months later I still hadn't had a drink. Better still, my relationship with Stuart was healthier than the one I had with Chip. That one was per-verse—there was no getting around it. By contrast, Stuart and I teased each other more gently, and there was never an edge to it.

There was no reason for me to resent the guy—he was treating me fairly—and I was making him a pile of money. Throughout my ascension as a cookie salesman, Stuart betrayed very little emotion, concentrating instead on making a series of refinements in the way we were doing business. He even raised my salary without my asking after I opened fifteen accounts in my first three days. Before I even saw my first paycheck at $300 a week, he paid me $350.

While working for Chip, I had been able to avoid most of Route 72 for days at a time, but now I was dealing with the Q-tips again in order to reach a shortcut I had discovered in Chatworth. Not only did that particular back road reduce my driving time but it enabled me to discover a man-made lake whose beauty I greatly exaggerated before it brought me to the intersection of Route 70 near the Red Top Market, which competed improbably enough with the Green Top Market 100 yards away in the selling of Jer-sey corn, tomatoes, and other farm products. Those landmarks signaled the halfway point in my journey to Stuart's hoagie shop in Philadelphia, and despite the shortcut I would still pass the Evergreen Dairy Bar, a soft ice cream joint in Medford whose waitresses walked out to your car and attached a tray to your open window like in the old days; the Indian Chief Inn whose billboard advertised a prime rib special every Saturday night; and a series of Dunkin' Donuts, automobile dealerships, and strip malls once I reached the more commercial stretch of that road. There was nothing I could do to avoid many of the same national chains that defaced Route 37 in Toms River if I wanted to be logical about it, which meant leaving Route 70 to head North on 73 to cross the Tacony-Palmyra Bridge, whose twenty-five cent toll was still cheaper than the more costly bridges a few miles away—the Ben Franklin Bridge that had provided the setting for my discussion of oral sex with Teresa the year before and the Walt Whitman Bridge where Harry Burke's brother Michael got a gun pulled on us by heckling another driver in high school.

In order to make the switch from 70 to 73, however, you had to encounter one of the most perilous traffic circles in a state that was known for them, a hellish intersection in Marlton, New Jersey, where multiple lanes of traffic converged on a single midpoint that would have greatly benefitted from a traffic light, a rather simple solution that had managed to elude a series of well-educated civil engineers for a period of fifty years. If you had told me at the time that tow-truck operators had teamed up with local funeral directors to bribe the engineers, I might have believed you. At any rate, I was almost tempted to buy a pushkuh of my own after my first near-miss with the cookie boxes sliding back and forth in the back of my car.

Route 73 had lowlights of its own, including unsavory looking liquor stores, gas stations, and strip joints with names like Day-dreams, Double Visions, and the Dollhouse. Even Nero's Woodbine Inn had given up its pretensions of being a full-time rock club by bringing in strippers three nights a week. Then, after paying the quarter to cross the Delaware (much less heroically, of course, than George Washington, the father of our country), I could exit at Bridge Street, turn left, and wait for Battersby, Harbison, and Robbins to converge at the Yellow Submarine around eight in the morning, where I had already initiated a hopeless but enjoyable flirtation with one of Stuart's workers, a married woman named Marissa whose police officer husband would have torn me limb from limb if he had suspected the central place his wife occupied in my rich fantasy life at that time. In my defense, however, it was Marissa who got me going by commenting on how long it took me to pull up in front of the hoagie shop, unload the empty boxes, place the money I had collected into Stuart's greedy little hands, and load the car again. Marissa batted her eyelashes, and said, "If you do everything as slowly as you do that, your wife's a lucky girl."

Not only did Marissa's remark force me to confess that I wasn't married, but it put a damper on our budding flirtation, although she initially failed to notice that I had stopped reciprocating and had replaced the flirtation with a less problematic attempt at male bonding with Billy Glaser, a twenty-five-year-old who went on to endure the unspeakable drudgery of baking thousands of cookies a day for Stuart for the next ten years.

Despite Marissa's comment about the pace at which I worked, I was always back on the road by 8:30 in the morning, facing the daily challenge of figuring out my route. I could remain on Route 70 all the way to Point Pleasant, the northern-most town in my territory; turn onto Route 37 to start my day with the three 7-Elevens that had quickly agreed to sell our cookies; or bear right onto Route 72 and begin with the accounts I had opened on Long Beach Island by shamelessly dropping the names of Fran Bostick, Joe Giammona, and Chip Wilson. Selling the cookies turned out to be too easy for my own good when I factored in the presence of the Lebanon State Forest, long stretches of farmland, and a sufficient portion of the Pine Barrens. Although the mythical home of the Jersey Devil sent a pleasant, pine-scented aroma into the interior of my car, where it combined with the scent of warm, freshly-baked chocolate chip cookies, it broke up any possible route I formulated into a tangled, zigzagging mess that could not be easily navigated. Because the farmland that existed in the triangular area formed by Routes 70 and 72 was bereft of potential accounts—and God-forsaken places like Whiting, Breton Woods, and the impossible to pronounce Metedeconk were hardly any better—the best I could do was divide my territory into northern, southern, and central routes and hit each of them twice a week, creating a Saturday schedule that had me delivering cookies in the morning and working as a dishwasher for Fran at night.

My northern route also included a stretch of Route 35, which represented the only way I could reach the shocking number of oceanfront accounts I had opened in Bay Head, Lavallette, Ortley Beach, and Seaside Park. Joe Pesci of *Goodfellas* fame had a beach house in Lavallette, but I never saw him, or if I did he had disguised himself to avoid being hassled by pop culture enthusiasts like myself. This series of establishments included the Crown Market in Mantoloking, which deceived its customers by foregoing the Stewie's Chewies jar in favor of a metal bakery tray and a sheet of wax paper as though our cookies had been baked on the premises. After initially experiencing a milder form of the revulsion I had felt when Chip inquired about the nurse's gravely ill son in order to pump up sales at the doctor's office, I talked myself into being comfortable with the Crown Market maneuver since I would benefit from the deception and it had been the store owner's idea and not mine. Just as food items routinely fell to the floor in restaurant kitchens and were placed back on the customer's plate as long as the "five second rule" had not been violated—the amount of time that a piece of food could spend on the floor without being thrown out, enabling waiters and waitresses to rationalize this filthy habit—my latest profession had dark secrets as well.

Although the weather rained on my parade on Memorial Day— and the arcade owner put the kibosh on selling Stewie's Chewies because they were perishable—I went on to develop a thriving central route that encompassed Atlantic City, Ventnor, Margate, and Longport. But once again my hot streak in sales got me into trouble. Instead of leaving well enough alone, my greed got the better of me and I ventured inland for the hell of it one day and found myself in the town of Pleasantville, where I discovered a Jewish deli called Melnick's. It turned out the owners were a pair of siblings from my hometown of Harrisburg—Andy and Arnie Melnick—and they recognized my last name the minute I introduced myself. Andy, the polite one, asked if I was any relation to

Carl Glassman.

"Yeah," I said, "He's my brother. I thought you looked familiar."

While this exchange took place, Arnie Melnick eyeballed me with undisguised contempt. "You're a cookie salesman?" he asked, paving the way for a sweeping statement about my education, my upbringing, and the other advantages I had squandered. "Boy, did *you* blow it!"

Now Arnie and I were glaring at each other—not the ideal preamble for closing a sale or even proposing one. The reality of being underemployed was already a raw nerve for me. I didn't need a prick like that poking at it. I turned back to Andy.

"Is he always this unpleasant?"

"Yeah, pretty much."

"OK, I'll catch yuh later."

"Hold on!" Arnie said. "Lemme see the cookies."

Thirty seconds later, he was inhaling one.

"As you can see, Arnie, my samples are in pristine condition, except for the one in your mouth."

"They'd be a lot better if they were warm," he replied.

"What are you suggesting? I should keep a Sterno Stove in my trunk?"

Things were going so well that not even my little tiff with his brother prevented Andy Melnick from ordering two boxes a week for the rest of the summer. But instead of making the route more profitable, it ended up costing me money when the rest of Pleasantville turned out to be a dud and I was forced to make a twenty-mile round trip on the Atlantic City Expressway once a week just to service their account. The only saving grace in the situation was the presence of their kid sister behind the counter. She was right up there with Peggy when it came to good-looking cashiers.

No matter which accounts I serviced on any given day—and how much logic I applied to them—they were still scattered enough to cause problems, and I had to resign myself to the zigzagging. This was the case even after Stuart got Marissa to drive the cookies down to me a couple times, making the transfer with her two little boys staring in wonder at the ornate, multi-columned Word War I Memorial near the Knife and Fork restaurant in Atlantic City. As soon as I laid eyes on Melissa's children in the back seat of her car, they served as a reminder that she wouldn't have gotten involved with me in a million years, no matter how much we flirted.

Some of the logistical decisions were complete toss-ups—perfect examples of a "six of one, half dozen of the other" quandary—and I often based my decision on what I would be in the mood for when my stomach began to growl in mid-morning. The fondness I had developed for the hot dogs at Jenkinson's Pier had only intensified, but it was joined by a number of worthy alternatives, including small containers of macaroni and cheese from one of the ubiquitous Wawa's scattered along my route; hand-carved roast beef sandwiches on the boardwalk in Wildwood; and a chicken cutlet sandwich with lettuce, tomato, and sharp provolone sold by a ruffian from the Canarsie section of Brooklyn at his deli in Ortley Beach, where he catered to petty thieves, low-life crim- inals, and vacationing firefighters from Ray Carlucci's neck of the woods in North Jersey. Their idea of a family vacation was to squeeze themselves, their wives, and however many children they had into row after row of horribly cramped little shacks in Seaside Heights.

In addition to the problematic geography, I quickly encountered a second issue that I should have been able to anticipate: the fact that the storeowners in the smaller towns were just as enthusiastic about our product as their big-city counterparts but singularly incapable of selling as much as a half a box per week. That left the final few all-natural cookies rock-hard at the bottom of the jar until Stuart was forced to alter a policy in which he provided a refund for any unsold cookies in favor of a more restrictive one in which he accepted only broken cookies back from the retail- ers. As a result, one owner after another jumped at the chance to smash the unsold cookies to bits, a strategy that caused the multifaceted headache of buying back extra cookies and being unable to determine exactly how many of them the storeowners had demolished. It was too bad that I no longer possessed the little scale I had purchased at a head shop on Sansom Street to weigh ounces of pot a decade before, because if I still had it, I would have been able to weigh the cookie crumbs at the bottom of the jar and offer a more precise reimbursement. But because I had long since developed the ability to eyeball glassine bags of marijuana with remarkable accuracy—and to hold my own with the drug dealers of my youth—I had no idea where the little scale had gotten to. I may have lost it in one of my peripatetic moves from one residence to another, but I also had to consider the possibility that I had gotten rid of it intentionally in order to remove as much drug paraphernalia as possible in the unlikely event that I would ever get raided by the cops.

In the end, though, Stuart altered the return policy a second time and declared that we would discontinue any accounts that couldn't sell at least a box a week, incurring the wrath of small town store owners who already had inferiority complexes and chips on their shoulders. Many of these proprietors had no clue that we were doing them a favor by eliminating them, because the action we took saved them from introducing a product to their customers, creating a demand for it, and having to break it to the customers that the product had been discontinued through no fault of their own. The only way for some of them to deal with the public relations nightmare that ensued (if it can actually be called that when only ten or fifteen customers were affected) was to engage in a venomous discussion in which the storeowners and their customers commiserated over the evils of big-city life and city slickers like Stuart and me who were born with silver spoons in their mouths and didn't know the meaning of hard work. Once I found my way to that possibility, I chose not to go any further because I was sure it would lead to my suspecting them of anti-Semitism.

All of this meant that I had to ignore the advice Chip gave me on my first day at Office Plus. In addition to population, demographics, and other discernible factors, I really did have to take the physical appearance of a place into consideration. Once I took that liberating first step, I never gave it another thought whenever I turned my back on a store for looking shabby, reasoning that it was better to do that than to create an enemy who might badmouth us in the future. The "food chain" being what it was, however, I was the one who had to break it to them when Stuart altered a policy and they were the ones who had to inform their customers. In neither case did Stuart have to face the disappointed party, but instead could remain in the relative safety of his office and count the money that I brought back to him. In the end, I didn't resent Stuart for it; I just came to see him for what he was—a decent, fair-minded person whose values differed greatly from mine.

After I had placed the proceeds from the cookie sales into an otherwise empty Stewie's Chewies box during my first few weeks of employment, Stuart obtained a night deposit bag from a nearby branch of CoreStates Bank. The idea was for me to safeguard the money more securely when I was collecting it and hand it over to him in a more dignified fashion the next morning. The bag was dark brown, made of a coarse material, and had a locking mechanism on its zipper.

"What's the lock for?" I asked.

"Whadda yuh *think* it's for?" Stuart replied.

"The lock isn't gonna do any good if I lose the entire bag."

"Are you planning to do that?"

"No, I'm just saying. The lock seems superfluous."

"Mark? I'm not in the mood. Get outta here."

Stuart was in a better mood the next morning when he separated the bills I dropped off into stacks of ones, fives, tens, and twenties, totaling $1,123. At the time, Marissa and I were sitting across from him, performing the more subservient task of dealing with the coins. Our boss had provided us with coin wrappers in all the denominations, and none of us was saying much. Other than the clinking of the coins and an occasional shuffling of the bills, there was nothing to break the silence until Marissa and I realized that Stuart had begun to hum a tune that somehow seemed familiar. Although I wracked my brain to figure out what it was, it wasn't until I reached the Medford Diner with a car full of cookies that I was able to identify it as "We're in the Money," a song that appeared in an old Bugs Bunny cartoon. Of all the tunes he could have been humming, that one made the most sense in terms of who he was.

Before I knew it, I was working seven days a week, selling cookies from Monday through Saturday in the daytime, washing dishes for Fran on Saturday nights, and doing my paperwork on Sunday mornings, the same day of the week that my old man did his in his restaurant supply business. Although I couldn't give myself a break on the nagging belief that I was selling out, it sure was enjoyable to total my weekly sales on the Texas Instruments calculator that I had permanently "borrowed" from Chip and to egg myself on with exultant phrases like "Do you believe this?" and "I can't deliver 'em fast enough!" and my favorite one of all, "Fuck you, Carlucci! Eat your heart out!" Looking back on it, my theatrics were almost certainly a mingling of vengefulness and amazement at the fact that I could actually make money in this world if I put my mind to it. Till then—after dropping out of college—I had never thought it possible.

There were other connections to my dad as well, in addition to doing my paperwork on Sundays. My aversion to following in his footsteps had softened considerably, and I actually went out of my way to identify similarities that increased my fondness for him. He had spent the better part of his life climbing in and out of cars, showing his wares in a succession of rinky-dink towns, and depending on his powers of persuasion. Ultimately, he was at the mercy of the decision-makers, as salesmen have been since the beginning of time, and it required a marketable product. But without a certain toughness, a thick skin, and a lively personality, it would have been hard to sell anything. Once I realized that I was getting to know him better by following in his footsteps, the act of selling took on a filial importance. Before long, instead of being defensive about it, I gained a sense of pride from my success as a salesman and the connection to my father, and I started to look for additional similarities between us since the first few I identified were so pleasurable to me. I even found my way to the discovery that my left arm had a darker tan than my right after resting it on the open car window while driving. My father's arm had been the same way for as long as I could remember.

———

As Mitch Frankel reminded me in the drug store at 2601, my stepfather had a heart attack at the age of thirty-eight, was grossly overweight, and battled health problems for the rest of his life. For the entire duration of their marriage, my mother battled the health problems with him, including the time when a cardiologist informed them that Harry was "held together with band aids," a remark that hastened his retirement and their subsequent move to Florida. Despite his obesity, however, he had developed a passably effective golf swing, kept a set of clubs in the trunk of his car, and belonged to a country club wherever he lived. Before he and my mother relocated, Harry spent one or two summer nights a month at a driving range near Cooper River Park in Pennsauken.

Prior to their marriage in 1970—when Carl was a freshman at the University of Florida—Harry had taken my mother and me to the swimming pool at the Diplomat Hotel, one of his accounts at Rosenthal and Glickstein. Like the trip to Puerto Rico that ended with me passed out on the shag carpet a few years later, the perks of Harry's job included occasional travel to the Miami area, which made our afternoon at the Diplomat possible. In keeping with the unexpected athleticism of his golf swing, Harry surprised me by climbing onto the diving board that day, executing an astoundingly effective "cannonball," and sending a stream of water billowing into the air. At its best, of course—in that era and with the right people present—a "cannonball" was designed to cause children to squeal and women to pat protectively at their hairdos while dangling their feet over the side of the pool. Harry's plunge into the water had its intended effect, although there was no need to impress my mother, since she had been smitten with him for years. For my part, however, I gained a grudging admiration for Harry after the dive, having never suspected that he had it in him.

As it happened, the "cannonball" caused me to pause in the sipping of a non-alcoholic piña colada that a Cuban teenager not much older than myself had delivered moments before. The bartender had spruced up the beverage with a maraschino cherry and a slice of pineapple on a toothpick with frilly blue cellophane, but I set aside this sophisticated concoction to stare at the pool in slack-jawed amazement. Little did I know that the afternoon we spent at the Diplomat was a preview of the luxurious life that I would luck into once Harry's divorce was finalized and he was able to marry my mother.

At the same time, however, I wanted no part of whatever else was going on between my mother and Harry physically. Given their respective body types, it was difficult to imagine them copulating, but even then my negative imagination urged me in that unwanted direction. Although I had scrupulously avoided the subject in the privacy of my thoughts—especially since I had already been traumatized by interrupting Carl and Catherine's lovemaking at the apartment on Biarritz Drive a few weeks before—I couldn't escape the reality of the situation when Miami Beach High School let us out early one day so that the teachers could attend an in-service training.

Unfortunately, my classmate Robert Zuckerman and I had different ideas of how to spend the half day we had been granted. Zuckerman wanted to grab a cheeseburger from the Lemon Tree restaurant near Eddie's newsstand while I wanted to invite myself over to his apartment to compete in an elaborate board game that I had ordered from the annual baseball yearbook published by Street and Smith's. By rolling a pair of dice and consulting a series of pitching, batting, and fielding charts, it was possible to simulate Major League Baseball with such remarkable accuracy that if you played enough games the statistics of each of the players would wind up within a few percentage points of their real-life performance. These charts were governed by the actual statistics of the players the year before, each player being assigned a set of statistical probabilities of his own. Because it was possible to purchase the playing cards of any team you desired, Zuckerman and I could pit my Phillies against his hometown Cleveland Indians and play remarkably close games due to the fact that both of the teams we followed were equally inept, last-place ballclubs in their respective divisions.

When Zuckerman wouldn't budge on his desire for a cheeseburger and I refused to capitulate, I contented myself with a visit to our upstairs neighbors the Feingolds, a married couple with a strung-out amphetamine addict of a son and a gorgeous fawn and white boxer named Lady. Lady had a tendency to rest her head on the concrete landing outside of their apartment with her jowls hanging over the edge and to send a steam of drool onto the sidewalk below, where the scorching hot Florida sun evaporated the drool before a puddle could form. This was my first exposure to a breed that would become my favorite, and I absolutely adored petting that gentle dog and having her lick my hand. Occasionally, when he wasn't hopped up on speed, Bobby Feingold would take me with him to a park a few blocks away where Lady would tear across the lush green lawn majestically before Bobby summoned her back to her leash.

Because the parents had not been informed, my mother had no idea that Beach High would let us out early, and I was completely unaware that she would play hooky for half a day from her job as a secretary at Burdine's department store in order to hook up with Harry at our apartment. When I entered the apartment unexpectedly at one-thirty in the afternoon, her bedroom door was ajar, she had turned back the sheets on her bed, and she had stripped down to a bra and panties. I'm not sure which was worse in the second or two before my mother stared at me with a look of absolute horror, reached past my future stepfather, and closed the bedroom door—seeing my mother that way or catching a glimpse of Harry wearing a pair of knee-length socks and triple X boxer shorts. Those were the two articles of clothing on a body that only my mother could love, and she was forced to postpone their pre-marital tryst in favor of a clumsy, blushing explanation to a fifteen-year-old boy who was shockingly ignorant of what sex was all about.

By the time he was in his fifties, Harry had survived a horrendous marriage, a bitter divorce, and constant trips to the cardiologist, not to mention more failed diets than he cared to remember and the instances in which his employers uprooted him to start or restructure accounting departments in Atlanta, Miami, and Puerto Rico. Despite the fact that at least two of these would have been considered plum assignments, the truth is that he was working too many hours to enjoy them. Furthermore, the constant movement from town to town made it difficult for him to get together with my mother.

By the time Elaine finally granted Harry a divorce, I had already begun to emotionally blackmail my mother every chance I got and make her pay for the divorce that had torn *our* family apart, so that her guilty conscience manifested itself in a variety of ways from the relatively inconsequential tendency to allow me to avoid green vegetables to more significant ones like permitting me to steal from their liquor cabinet, smoke pot at every turn, and throw loud parties whenever she and Harry stayed overnight at his sister's apartment in Queens.

Throughout the eight years of haggling with Elaine, Harry and my mother conducted an on-again, off-again romance, not because they didn't have their eyes on each other the whole time but because the vicissitudes of Elaine's mental state, the waxing and waning of her vindictiveness, and the overall uncertainty of whether or not they would end up together precluded a sense of security. During that entire time, my mother was forced to wait powerlessly with her love life hanging in the balance, while all the while I was talking back to her, bridling against any attempt to exert her authority, and making absolutely no effort to hide the fact that I was ashamed to be seen with her in public. It was no surprise then—after years of unhappiness with my father—that she came to regard her existence as something that came alive only on the infrequent occasions on which she and Harry were together, and that she came to place all of her hopes in his obtaining a divorce and asking her to marry him. When it finally happened, however, she was shocked to discover that a number of formidable obstacles remained. Instead of living happily ever after, they still had to deal with Harry's health, his disapproval of me as a young person, and his anger at my mother for indulging me at every turn. Based on my obvious desire to make her suffer for the divorce, there really would be no peace for them until I went away to college, which meant that my junior and senior years in high school became a problem that they had underestimated. My mother was firmly in the middle between her husband and son at that point, so much so that she glanced nervously at the clock whenever I sat down in Harry's easy chair, a seemingly innocent act that clashed violently with my mother's desire to treat Harry's home as his castle, which in turn forced her into the no-win situation of deciding whether to wait for him to open the front door before asking me to vacate the chair or take the absurd step of requesting that I do so before he even came home so that the living room wouldn't give even the slightest appearance of impropriety. My mother compounded the foolishness by smoothing out the cushion on the chair so that it no longer bore an indentation, meaning that Harry would be none the wiser when he actually entered the apartment and sat in the chair himself. When that finally happened, my mother could move on to the domestic battleground of the kitchen where she was forced to come up with a meal that I would actually agree to eat or cook something entirely different for me whenever she served the pieces of fish that she and Harry favored.

Just when it seemed that the psychic tension was positively unbearable, my grandmother would arrive from Florida for the summer, introducing another obstacle into my mother's marriage. Before her own health problems had begun to accumulate, my grandmother had been positively delightful, marrying my grandfather when she was eighteen and he was thirty-two; learning all of his curse words; and reciting them at parties. After my grandfather retired from the postal service and the two of them relocated from Harrisburg to Miami Beach in the late fifties, my grandmother developed the habit of befriending bus drivers to and from the cut-rate bargains on Lincoln Road, learning the drivers' names, and sending them Christmas cards for the next thirty years.

My grandmother gave her husband rubdowns with wintergreen alcohol after his shower every day, running her gnarly fingers through the gray hair on his chest and kissing the top of his head afterwards. On the rare occasion when she wasn't home to serve him lunch herself, she constructed elaborate sandwiches for him and covered them with Saran wrap. She discharged those and other wifely duties with such complete contentment that even when she was more difficult to get along with in her later years, you couldn't help reminding yourself of what widowhood must have felt like for her.

Two or three times a week, she would remove odorous packages of raw shrimp from the freezer, thaw them out for precisely three hours, and present them to her husband so that he could fish for mullets from the little dock beyond the swimming pool at the Twin Towers Apartments. When he wasn't fishing or getting a rubdown, my grandfather was often emulating his elderly brother-in-law by creating a series of paintings that were often based on scenes he had encountered in magazines, particularly after he had exhausted the limited possibilities that were presented to him by his view of the intracoastal waterway from the dock. Uncle Jim had taken up painting as an escape from Aunt Sadie, my grandmother's older sister, whose arteries had hardened to such an extent that she often flew into a rage for no reason at all; and Pop's painterly efforts ultimately included a depiction of what appeared to be a

Mexican village given the presence of sombreros on several of the male figures and a pair of donkeys in the background. For some reason, my grandfather had seen fit to label two of the doorways that appeared in the foreground in a specific way, spelling out my name and Carl's in crude black lettering. Neither Carl nor I could find the painting years later, but I have another one of Pop's efforts hanging on a wall in my basement.

While my grandfather was painting or fishing, my grandmother was often swimming laps in the pool; lying on the floor of their spotless efficiency apartment and working her legs as though she were riding a bicycle upside down; or brushing her short red hair with fifty strokes in each direction. On Passover—at the fancy Seder that Jack Feldman hosted for family members at the Fontainebleau Hotel—my grandmother would join Aunt Dora in dancing on the tables, much to my mother's embarrassment. In addition to being married to my grandmother's older brother Saul, Dora was a green-eyed firebrand from somewhere in the vastness of Russia who rocked Saul's world sexually, helped him operate their chicken farm in Dover, Delaware, and wore the pants in the family, creating an environment in which their only son became a highly effeminate interior designer in New York.

Prior to any trip to Publix, my grandmother would make the rounds to Aunt Sadie's apartment and to six or seven others to see if her neighbors needed anything, including the Weingrads, a sweet-natured old couple who had their hands full with Barney's recent diagnosis of Parkinson's Disease. These preliminary excursions often resulted in my grandmother purchasing four or five items for herself and my grandfather and another twenty or thirty for other people, until the little metal cart that she wheeled back and forth on the thirty-block round trip began to squeak and grow wobbly over time. Eventually, Jack Feldman had to drive my grandmother to a hardware store for a new one.

When my grandfather's diabetes increased in severity, it was my grandmother who injected him with insulin, and when he was wracked with pain during his horrific bout with cancer, she ministered to him tenderly, never letting him see her cry as she mopped his brow with a damp washcloth, gave him his pain pills with a glass of water, or provided my mother with an update over the phone; but I have no doubt that she bawled her eyes out in private. By the time Pop died, I had already granted her immunity in the inquisition I conducted after my parents' divorce, declared my relationship with her to be free of emotional baggage, and bestowed upon her the same exalted status as my brother.

My grandmother continued to swim laps until her eighty-second birthday, but eventually her emphysema caught up with her and the massive doses of Prednisone had a diminished effect. Even when the father-and-son tag team of Stanley and Ivan Jonas provided medical care simultaneously, there was nothing the well-meaning physicians could do to prevent arthritis from crippling my grandmother's hands, circulation problems from swelling her feet, and chest pains from occurring regularly. Now, by necessity, she kept a bottle of nitroglycerine tablets in her oversized pocketbook at all times. (Bless her heart, the pocketbook had to be oversized in case a younger relative took her to Pumpernik's for lunch, so that she could empty a basket of sweet rolls into it when no one was looking.)

Despite being a fun-loving woman in her prime—and the most sweet-natured grandmother anyone could have asked for—her mounting health problems and the cumulative effect of losing all twelve of her siblings one at a time led her down a path toward becoming progressively more difficult to get along with. Finally, she developed a persona in which she refused to admit to experiencing any pleasure in life, pinched every penny, became belligerent after half a glass of bourbon, and focused most of her fury on my mother, until nothing my mother did was ever good enough for her.

This persona placed her in direct opposition to Harry, who very nearly squirmed in my grandmother's presence, with even her most innocent remarks causing a spike in *his* blood pressure. This was the case even when she wasn't deliberately baiting him or misbehaving in a manner that reflected poorly on my mother, like the family gatherings in which she made her remarks just loudly enough for Harry's sister to hear from the other room, a typical example being her declaration that "I have nothing in common with these people," which often caused me to hurry over in a desperate attempt to shush her before any more damage could be done. Whenever she issued one of these zingers not just within earshot of Harry but in plain sight of him, he would often blurt out the kind of direct challenge that a self-pitying old woman lives for, a common utterance being "Oh, Maxine, don't be ridiculous," which enabled my grandmother to respond in front of a group of people with some variation of "Did you hear that? He called me ridiculous" or "He's so abrupt!" or the even more damning, "My husband was right. Without love and respect, there's nothing." Whenever I took my grandmother aside after one of these episodes, it was even money as to whether or not she would apologize; but she never failed to conclude our discussion with the same piece of advice: "Don't get old, kid—it stinks."

More and more frequently, my mother would overindulge while joining my grandmother for a mid-afternoon drink, and Harry would be the first person to discover her face-down on their bed, responding to her unseemly condition by putting down his briefcase, shaking her by the shoulders, and demanding that she rouse herself, addressing her with his harsh New York accent. "Mir, wake up—it's four in the afternoon!"

Once I went away to college—and my grandmother was safely in Florida for the winter—the two of them had the apartment to themselves and could concentrate on the few differences that remained, paving the way for them to find a diet that worked for both of them, take long drives together on the weekends, and settle into a routine that was relatively free of tension. Finally, after all the upheaval of their respective divorces—and the long wait for Harry's ex-wife to throw in the towel—my mother could bask in the glow of a man who seemed so much more sophisticated than my father, when it may only have been her own lack of sophistication that made him seem so exotic.

Eventually, their happiness spilled over into my relationship with Harry, and though I never would have thought it in high school, there were specific instances in which my stepfather and I were actually affectionate with each other by the time that he and my mother relocated to Florida. Although this eased my mother's burden quite a bit, the relocation itself was a mixed blessing, since it combined her ability to be with the man she loved every hour of the day with an increased proximity to her mother every month of the year. Sure enough, when she and Harry settled into their condo overlooking a golf course in Hollywood, my mother found herself in far greater peril than she had been up north and directly in the crosshairs of my grandmother, who resided less than ten miles away in the comfortable Jewish ghetto of Miami Beach.

For approximately three years after their move to Florida, my mother successfully juggled Harry's health issues with the demands that my grandmother made on her, devising a reasonably effective compromise in which they had my grandmother over for dinner once a week and my mother drove down I-95 alone for two or three afternoon outings in the same stretch of days, shopping for bargains at Publix, Walgreen's, and Gulf Liquors while my grandmother clutched a fistful of coupons. These outings provided Harry with some peace and quiet for a few hours without any incoming phone calls from my grandmother or the countless relatives that contacted my mother incessantly now that they were alerted that she was back in the area.

By 1984, however, Harry's one functioning kidney began to fail and he was forced to undergo dialysis twice a week, thereby reducing the number of opportunities that my mother had to appease my grandmother. At first, my grandmother rose to the occasion, but it was against her nature to keep her mouth shut indefinitely and the pressure inevitably increased on my mother to serve two masters at the same time. By then, the Florida experience left a lot to be desired, but Harry's health made it impossible for them to do anything but ride things out as well as they could. In the end, although the last few months before he died of a heart attack in the middle of the night were painful for my mother, Harry's death brought to a close the only period in her life in which she had been truly happy.

After burying her husband, the emotional horror show that she had been dreading all along began, and my mother's life gave every sign of winding down in precisely the way that she had hoped to avoid, with my grandmother forcing a confrontation over her desire to spend more time with my mother, talk to her on the telephone more frequently, and have more of her emotional needs met. As my mother knew, these desires carried with them the thinly veiled threat that always existed, the lingering sense that although my grandmother could not be accused of wanting Harry to die, she would have liked nothing more than to move in with my mother now that he was gone. A more toxic combination could not have been imagined, however, than these two people sharing an apartment; and no one had to tell my mother that an arrangement of that kind would rob her of any peace of mind that she would be able to achieve in her own widowhood.

While my grandmother's whereabouts were being decided, a strong ally emerged for my mother in the person of Lena Feldman, Aunt Sadie's formidable daughter and my mother's first cousin. Lena and my grandmother were fairly close in age, and they actually lived together when Aunt Sadie and Uncle Jim took my grandmother in prior to her marriage. As a result, Lena had a way of shaming my grandmother into behaving more respectably whenever it became necessary. At the very least, I believe this to be a factor in my mother's ability to stand up to my grandmother and deny her the kind of unlimited access that she desired, particularly when the unspoken issue of their living together broke out into the open. This left them with a relationship that wavered back and forth between my grandmother's unreasonable demands, her tearful apologies, and the sweet, enduring love that existed beneath everything else whenever my grandmother's behavior enabled them to experience it. As my grandmother's disposition continued to sour, however, occasions like that became increasingly rare.

———————

Harry had worked hard for thirty years, and by the time he retired—and was replaced by Rosenthal's son—he had set aside enough money to provide for my mother after his death. This enabled her to move into a high-rise condominium on Brickle Avenue in Miami, in part to escape the ghosts of their marriage in Hollywood, but also to be closer to my grandmother in Miami Beach.

My mother's selection of an apartment was revealing. The Brickle Bay Club was as exclusive as its name suggested, and provided a prestigious address for anyone who could afford it. Its tenants included other wealthy retirees from "up North" and younger people as well, including bankers, lawyers, stockbrokers, and a relatively high percentage of businesspersons who had emigrated from Cuba and South America. It was a bilingual building with a great deal of Spanish spoken by the tenants and staff, which provided my mother with an opportunity to embarrass me with a series of mispronunciations.

Among its other amenities, the Brickle Bay Club had a commissary, a fitness center, tennis courts, indoor and outdoor swimming pools, and a dry cleaning business that charged an arm and a leg to starch a shirt. Overlooking Biscayne Bay—and situated near the local landmark Vizcaya—it also included an eighteen-hole golf course. In terms of luxury, it made 2601 look like the poorhouse. Missing Harry greatly, my mother consoled herself by living that way and making several purchases that may not have been necessary. Deciding, for instance, that Harry's car had always been too big for her, she visited an automobile dealership with Cousin Lena in an advisory role and quickly consummated a deal for a four-door Volvo sedan. In separate phone calls to Carl and me, she proudly announced that she had purchased a "Vulva," with the same pronunciation as the female reproductive organ, and Carl and I were forced to compare notes as to whether or not our mother was making a joke or actually believed that she had pronounced the car correctly.

Within a month of Harry's death, I had the disastrous idea of inviting my mother to visit me on Long Beach Island. By then, I was confident that I could behave like a dutiful son for the entire duration of her visit, reasoning that it couldn't possibly kill me. Although I was self-aware enough to know that I would never entirely forgive her for the divorce, I felt certain that I could control myself, show her a nice time, and take a step toward improving our relationship.

The first few days of the visit went smoothly. At her urging, I picked up a brisket at the Shoprite, acquired the ingredients for a spice cake, and allowed her to buy me a shirt at Hand's department store. For my part, I bought her the kind of bagels she liked, a stack of magazines to read, and some music to listen to, including Frank Sinatra, Tony Bennett, and Mel Torme. I even showed her how to operate my tape deck, which wasn't complicated but required more than one lesson for my mother to master the process of inserting or ejecting a tape. Although I had offered to take a few days off from work, my mother was so thrilled that I had a job I actually liked that she urged me not to bother, insisting that she would be fine sleeping late, going for walks, and stocking my freezer with enough food for a month.

By the morning of her scheduled departure, I was shocked to realize that we had gotten along well the entire week, and that we had refrained from getting on each other's nerves. And then I blew it on the way to the airport.

"You should have been doing this all along," she said.

"What?"

"Selling. You're good at it!"

My nostrils flared, a trait I had evidently inherited from her, although this was the first time I had noticed it.

"What?" she said innocently, sounding like *her* mother now. "I meant it as a compliment!"

"That's some compliment—thanks."

"You hate me, don't you?"

"Of course not!"

"You've always hated me. I can see it on your face."

I hesitated—but only slightly. "Not always. Since 1962, maybe."

That was the year of the divorce, as she well knew. Tears rolled down her face, and I suddenly felt sick to my stomach.

"You can't let it go, can you?"

"Apparently not," I said.

"You need to meet someone. It's my only chance."

"Mom!" I screamed, before lowering my voice. "This isn't helping."

In addition to *The Universal Baseball Association* by Robert Coover, my brother had turned me on to Thomas Wolfe in the reading list he gave me in 1972. At one point in Wolfe's follow-up novel to *Look Homeward, Angel*, he described Eugene Gant's sense of failure as being "crushing and complete." I believe that the guilt that my mother and I felt could be characterized in the same way.

We drove on in silence until we reached the departure terminal. She had paid top dollar for her suitcase at the Aventura Mall, but now there were cookie crumbs all over it and smudges of chocolate on the handle. I did my best to remove them with my shirt sleeve before lowering the suitcase to the sidewalk, realizing too late that I was wearing the shirt she had gotten me.

"Mom, I'm sorry."

"I'm sorry, too."

A skycap approached from a few feet away, effectively ending the visit.

"Where to?" he asked.

We answered simultaneously, blurting out her destination. "Miami."

"It's hot down in Florida," he replied.

My mother answered for herself this time. "I love the heat," she said. Her eyes were still puffy from crying. She glanced at me while the skycap attached the luggage tag, trying to determine if I would embrace her. Once again, I took a second to think about it.

"You don't have to," she said.

"I want to!"

She could tell that I was faking, but we embraced anyway.

"Are you ready, ma'am?"

"Almost."

She turned away from the skycap and whispered to me. "How much should I tip him?"

Harry had always handled this, of course, and that made the loneliness of her widowhood more palpable, which in turn ratcheted up my guilt. Unfortunately, the worldlier of her two sons was fifteen hundred miles away; but I did the best I could.

"I don't know? Ten dollars?"

She dug through her pocketbook for a ten-dollar bill, and told the skycap she was ready.

"Call me when you get home," I said. It was a lame attempt at a peace offering, and she knew it.

"I will."

She faked a smile and followed the skycap into the terminal.

———————

After my mother's remark about meeting someone, I started thinking about Sarah Sloane and decided to write her a letter. It had been eight months since I had moved out of her house and I'd had no contact with her at all. I had never told her how I felt—not with anything I said directly—and it seemed like the worst kind of loose end to never speak with her again. Of course, I can tell myself that I had no expectations in writing to her, and that I wasn't hoping that she would have a change of heart; but a part of me was hoping for just that. Knowing Sarah, however—and reminding myself that I'd had alcohol on my breath when we'd said goodbye—I would be lucky if she responded to my letter at all. Hoping for the best but expecting the worst, I sent the letter off to her, but not before hedging my bet by writing to Karen

Marcus also. Whatever rough treatment was in store for me with Sarah, I was confident that Karen would soften the blow.

Sarah called me at the cottage. I don't know which she objected to more—my sappy love language or the fact that the letter was totally pointless since the matter had already been settled.

"I'm sorry, but I don't feel that way," she said.

"I know you don't."

"Then why did you write the letter?"

"It was an exercise in futility, but I had to express myself."

"And now I have to live with it."

"Throw it away, Sarah, or burn it, whichever you prefer."

"Goodbye, Mark."

Karen Marcus wrote me back asking for my phone number. She had returned from California a month before, and the post office had forwarded my letter to her new address. Apparently, she had no hard feelings about the way I had broken things off, and she proposed that we meet for a drink. We fell into bed later that night, and I got it right on my second try.

"How was that?"

"Better."

"I'm glad."

I reached over and hit "play" on Karen's cassette player.

Thirty seconds in, she asked what we were listening to.

"It's 'Samba Pa Ti' by Santana. I used to fantasize about it as a teenager."

"What do you mean?"

"I've always believed that it would be the perfect thing to listen to at a time like this. But I've never had a chance to play it for anyone."

"It's beautiful," Karen whispered.

Her head was resting on my chest. It was the greatest feeling in the world.

"Thank you, Karen."

"For what?"

"Asking for my phone number."

"I had to. Your letter blew me away."

When we made love in the days that followed, I was shocked to realize that nearly all of my anxiety had disappeared.

"Karen, your body is…"

"Is what?"

"Is…"

"Stop blubbering and maul me already!"

And I did exactly that.

———————

Karen met me at Chaucer's the next day. She was drinking a seltzer with lime when I got there. A wrapped package was sitting on the bar in front of her. Jack was holding court with a hand puppet, but Karen was ignoring him, as many unattended women did when they failed to find him attractive. As soon as he saw me, Jack reached for a bottle of vodka.

"Thanks," I said, "but I'm not drinking."

"Whoa! That's not *like* you!"

Karen glared at him. "Just pour him an orange juice, OK?"

It took a minute for that to sink in.

"Do you still have 'Up on Cripple Creek' on the jukebox?" I asked.

"I think so," Jack said. "Why?"

"I'm just asking."

But I wasn't just asking, not with lyrics like this:

> *Up on Cripple Creek, she sends me*
> *If I spring a leak, she mends me*
> *I don't have to speak, she defends me*
> *A drunkard's dream if I ever did see one*

Karen slid the package along the bar to make sure that I saw it.

"What's that?" I asked.

"It's a present," she said. I went to take it from her, but she held on to it. My mother had done something similar when I reached for her twenty-dollar bill in high school.

"I'm giving you this on one condition."

"Uh oh."

"You don't have to be a Nice Jewish Boy—I know you have a thing about that—but you have to tone down the sarcasm."

"Tone it down how?"

"As in, I don't wanna hear it. If you have a sarcastic thought, write it down somewhere. Keep a scrapbook for all I care. But hide it from me. Do we have a deal?"

"Yes, Karen, we have a deal."

She let go of the package. "Open it."

It was a key to her apartment.

———————

I was back in touch with Mike Magnelli by then. He called me from New Orleans one night to tell me about a woman he was seeing. She was teaching French to Cajun kids to keep the culture alive.

"Are you happy?" I asked him.

"Yeah, are you?"

"I never would have believed it, but I am."

Karen was listening to this, and she smiled at me from across the room.

Mike paused for a moment. "Do you remember what you said about the glory days of our youth? That they were gruesome to you in retrospect? Maybe we've finally put those days behind us."

"I do remember. We've got a lot to be embarrassed about."

I could hear him laughing on the other end of the line. "It looks like we made it," he said. "At least I hope so."

Karen walked over to me after I hung up the phone. "Who was that?" she asked.

"That was Mike Magnelli. My sarcasm is all his fault."

"I find that hard to believe."

"I know what you're thinking. Please—leave my mother out of it."

———————

I had a question for Karen, but I wasn't sure if I wanted to know the answer.

"Do you remember the first time we slept together? You said that having an orgasm wasn't all that important to you."

"I remember."

"Were you just saying that to make me feel better?"

"I may have been exaggerating a little."

"What do you mean 'a little'?"

"I enjoy an orgasm as much as the next person, but it's not gonna rule my life."

"I see."

"Don't look so upset. It worked out for us, didn't it?"

"I guess so."

"That was then, Mark, this is now. I'm not faking it if that's what you're worried about."

"Promise me you'll never lie to me again."

"It wasn't really a lie. I put a certain spin on it, that's all."

I burst out laughing—from nervous energy, I guess—and it was a few seconds before I could speak.

"Promise me anyway."

"Does a little white lie count?"

"No. I'm talking big lies."

"Then I promise."

———————

Claes Oldenburg has a clothespin sculpture across from City Hall in Philadelphia. Street vendors sell incense there, dashikis, and other African fashions. The clothespin draws its fair share of self-proclaimed preachers also. One day, I saw Morris Braxton preaching from a bible with a cigar box resting at his feet. The box had a few coins in it, just like the cystic fibrosis jar had at the Double Duck Deli the year before. Morris's set-up included a cardboard sign that had been rained on a few times without being replaced, and now the letters were smudged. It was still possible, however, to determine that the word "ministry" was misspelled. Five or six ragged-looking people were half-listening to Morris as I approached. Morris fell silent when he saw me, as though he were concerned that I would blow his cover.

"Morris! What are you doing?"

"Spreadin' duh word, Mark. I'll be frew in a minute."

"Are you still workin' for Sheldon?"

"Hell, no. I got work to do here!"

"What about your wife and kids?"

"I ain't worryin' about that. Duh Lord will provide."

Morris turned back to his congregation. "You got to believe in duh Lord, people, and rejoice in duh pavs o' righteousness!"

I reached into my pocket and tossed a few coins into the cigar box. "I guess I can spare these if you're that hard up for money."

"See? I told yuh he would provide."

———————

The phone rang at our apartment one night. Karen was out with her friends.

"Mark? It's me."

"Teresa?"

"Well, yeah, who did yuh think it was?"

"I haven't spoken to you in over a year! How did you get my number?'

"Your housemate gave it to me."

"Who—Sarah?"

"Yeah."

"She's my *ex*-housemate."

"Whatever. She tracked you down for me."

"How did she sound?"

"She was talkin' in a whisper. I could hardly hear her."

"She gets like that when she's depressed."

"What's she depressed about?"

"She had two wonderful weeks with Jimmy, and then he stopped calling. Teresa, are you crying?"

"Mark, my dad died."

"My God, I'm sorry to hear that."

"It was lung disease. We talked about that, remember?"

"Yeah, I do. Are you all right?'

"Everybody's mad at me. I don't have anyone to sit with at the funeral."

Two days later—with Karen's blessing—I accompanied Teresa to her father's gravesite. Her family was huddled together as the priest conducted the ceremony. Teresa and I were standing apart from the others. Every few seconds, one of her family members glared at her. I put my arm around her shoulder, and we fell silent to listen to the priest.

"Oh, Lord, support us in this troublous life, until shadows lengthen, and evening comes, and the busy world is hushed, and the fever of life is over, and our work is done. Then, Lord, in thy mercy, grant us a safe lodging, a holy rest, and peace at last. Amen."

As a religious leader, I almost preferred Morris, although I had to admit, I admired some of the priest's phrasing.

———

Karen thought I was napping when her mother called. I was in the bedroom, but I could hear what they were saying.

"How's Mark?" Adele asked.

"He's doin' great."

"Is he still selling cookies?"

"No, he's tending bar now."

Adele paused about as long as my mother would have before indulging in an offensive remark—meaning, a second or two at most. "Are you sure that's the best environment for him?"

"Mom!"

"What? I'm just asking!"

"No, you're not. You're butting in."

"I'm sorry you feel that way."

"It makes him happy. Besides, he was never an alcoholic. He had some issues, that's all."

"What kind of issues?"

"That's between me and him, Mother."

"Be careful, Karen."

"He's mentoring a little boy!"

"So?"

"If he was a danger to anyone, do you think he would have been accepted into the program?"

"No, probably not. What kind of program is it?"

"It's for underprivileged children."

"What's the boy's name?"

"Why don't you come right out with it, Mother?"

"Come right out with what?"

"Whether or not he's Black. I'm sure you're dying to know."

"Is he?"

"Just worry about you and Daddy, OK?"

Karen was washing dishes when I emerged from the bedroom. I walked over to her and put my arms around her waist from behind.

"How's your mother?"

"You heard that? I thought you were asleep."

"I was, but I have an extra frequency when it comes to mothers."

"Unlike you, I've never let it bother me."

"I'm better than I used to be."

"Really? How would I know?"

"You could take my word for it."

"Don't flatter yourself. I have a question for you."

"What's that?"

"What were you like as a teenager?"

I thought about it for a second. "My only ambition was to

triple the size of my record collection."

"And now it's in my living room. Help me dry, would yuh?"

"Sure." I grabbed a towel and removed a dish from the drain-board. "I was wondering. Can I borrow your car tomorrow? There's something I need to do."

———————

The next day, I was parked outside the rundown home of Corey Weeks, an eight-year-old boy assigned to me by the Big Brothers Association. Corey lived with his mother, Carolyn. There were abandoned homes on either side of their property.

I beeped the horn twice. That was our signal, and Carolyn opened the front door, kissed Corey goodbye, and waved to me from the step. I waved back as Corey climbed onto the front seat.

"Have you ever seen the ocean?" I asked.

"No."

"Come on—I'll show it to you."

Ninety minutes later, Corey was staring at the ocean on Long Beach Island, while I sat on a rock a few feet away.

"It's big, isn't it?"

"Iss *real* big," Corey said.

"Zip up your jacket."

Corey zipped up his jacket, keeping his eyes on the ocean the whole time. I walked over to him. He looked up at me with a concerned expression.

"I can't swim," he said.

"Don't worry about it. I'll teach yuh."

Corey stared at the ocean for a few more seconds, then turned back to me.

"When?"

"In the summertime. It's too cold right now."

"Where duh fish at?"

"Under the surface."

"I ain't swimmin' in dat."

"That's entirely up to you."

Corey was satisfied with my answer. He picked up a clamshell, reared back, and threw it into the ocean with all his might.

———————

Karen was waiting for me when I got home.

"How did it go today?"

"It went well. Corey had a good time."

"I'm sure he did. The kid worships you."

"I can relate to Corey. He's the same age I was when my parents got divorced."

"Speaking of which, I got you something."

It looked like a magazine when she reached for it, but it was wrapped in plastic.

"A college catalog?"

"Hahnemann has a dual degree program in counseling and child psychology. I want you to think about it."

"Did my mother put you up to this?"

"No. Why?"

"Because it has her fingerprints all over it."

"She didn't put me up to it. I thought of it myself."

"I know she handed me off to you, Karen, but this is ridiculous."

"It's my job, Mark. She said, 'I don't have to worry about him anymore. He has *you* now.'"

"So now you're doing her dirty work."

"I object to that. It's not dirty work."

"The heavy lifting then."

"It's not heavy lifting either. It's a little encouragement here and there."

"OK, I'll think about it."

"You *better* think about it. You have an appointment with the admissions office on Thursday."

"Why are you smiling?" I asked.

"If your mother had made that appointment, you would have

been enraged."

"Don't rub it in, Karen. You're better than that."

"That's right, I am."

———————

Although I wasn't fully committed to going back to school for some of the same reasons that clouded my judgment in the past, my objections were less powerful in the present. By then, my mother was no longer an issue, and I was only mildly bothered by the thought of her getting her way. There was also the fact that I couldn't embarrass Paula McCormick, my high school guidance counselor. Paula had provided me with a letter of recommendation.

But, of course, Karen was the biggest factor of all. She was my miracle, and I couldn't look her in the eye if I didn't agree to matriculate.

"How did I do?" I asked when the interview was winding down, and only the smallest part of me hoped that the admissions rep would dash our hopes.

"Everything seems to be in order, Mr. Glassman. It looks like we'll be seeing you in the fall."

"That's great. Do you need anything else from me?"

"Not at the moment. We typically have an orientation for nontraditional students prior to the semester. You'll be notified by mail."

The term "nontraditional" was gratifying to hear, but I suppressed the urge to comment. Instead, I kept my mouth shut and went home to Karen. She was cooking a brisket when I arrived.

———————

Chaucer's was my home-away-from-home for years, but now I work there to pay for my tuition. I'm on the other side of the bar at this point, getting paid to babysit a bunch of drunks who remember little or nothing the next day. As distressing as their blackouts are, however, they afford me a certain freedom when it comes to revealing myself. I can talk my fool head off—and moralize all I want—but it doesn't matter. The one exception was a guy named Tom Reilly. He disappeared for a while, but when he came in again, he looked better than I had ever seen him. As it turned out, there was a simple explanation. During his absence, Reilly dried out like I did.

Acknowledgments

SEVERAL OF MY FRIENDS came through for me on this project.

Dave Pistilli gave me the freedom to write what I wanted, an act of selflessness that few others would have undertaken.

Steve Gamburg read an earlier draft of *Glassman* when it was 200 pages too long. His encouragement—and sometimes extravagant praise—enabled me to keep the faith through one rejection after another.

Barbara Crawford combined her tremendous skill as a copy editor with the patience of a saint while I ran hundreds of opening sentences past her. And then—after helping me to restructure the manuscript—she outdid herself by giving me an idea for the last paragraph of the book. Barbara's website is https://bcediting.com/

An additional acknowledgment goes out to Chris Fluck, an old friend, gifted actor, and proud father who provided feedback on the second half of *Glassman.*

Thanks also to Anthony Noel, who took a sharp-eyed look toward the end of the editing process, saving me from myself on a number of occasions.

The rejection of *Glassman* ended when I found my way to David Ross and Kelly Huddleston of Open Books. Authors in their own right, they enabled me to end my fifty-year quest on a positive note. I'm eternally grateful for that.